THE RACING HEART

Ava Roosevelt

Springwood SA

Published by Springwood SA

c/o Platinum Administration SA
Via Pioda 12, CP 6275
6900 Lugano
Switzerland

www.springwood.ch

Available for purchase through the following outlets:

Amazon.com
Kindle.com
Nook.com

Cover Design by Lori Ende-Skidell

ISBN-10: 1466319763
EAN-13: 9781466319769
Library of Congress Control Number: 2011916566

EDITED by LES STANDIFORD,

and dedicated to all of you, my friends and family, who didn't let me lose faith; both Warrens, Sunny, Gilberte, Tom, Rick, Paul, Debbie and Curt, Helene, Stephania, Bridget, Janna and Marc, Liz, Lisa, Ilyse, Renata, Inger, Frances, Audrey, Vanessa, Bea, Maureen and Ortie, Chandler, my sister Manuela and above all, to Christopher, for his love and support.

THE RACING HEART

Author's note

Ever since the day in 1978 when I first traveled to France to witness the death-defying madness of the fearless, multi-lingual men risking their lives in sleek, aerodynamic mechanical bullets to win the most prestigious, oldest and greatest endurance sports car race in the world, I knew that I wanted to weave that experience into a novel.

For those not familiar with Le Mans, the race is set against a backdrop of the countryside of northern France that looks like a Cezanne painting. Every June since 1923, from one Saturday at 3 pm to the following Sunday at 3 pm, the public roads combine temporarily with the permanent race track, the Circuit de la Sarthe, to become the 13.63 km site of the 24 Hours of Le Mans, commonly known as the Grand Prix of Endurance.

Organized by the prominent Automobile Club de L'Ouest and by invitation only, the 24 Hours of Le Mans is the culminating point of nine races in the United States (called the American Le Mans Series) and various affiliated races in Europe. There is no prize money, and the cost of participating, including transportation, spare parts, drivers, fuel, tires, and the like, is the highest in the racing world, running well over a million dollars for a two-car entry.

There are four competing classes–custom built LMP1 and LMP2 prototypes and production based GTE-Pro and GTE-Am cars—totaling 55 cars in all. No other motorsport event is as thrilling, and legendary, as Le Mans, where speeds have been clocked in excess of 214 mph down the Mulsanne Straight.

The battle between diesel and petrol powered, factory-sponsored prototypes is fiercely fought, and even the most highly developed and technically enhanced equipment is put to the supreme test at Le Mans, where accidents and mechanical breakdowns are commonplace.

The rules stipulate that the car that crosses the finish line after 24 hours having completed the greatest number of laps is the winner. No more than three drivers can have participated in the driving of each car. Thus, the physical endurance and skill of 165 hand-picked drivers are measured every second, as they strive to achieve the fastest lap speeds and complete the race.

Simply put, Le Mans is not for the faint of heart, as Lady Luck shines only upon zero-mistake performances under such nerve-wracking conditions. It all makes for the most exciting road race in the world. What better setting for a novel of intrigue and romance?

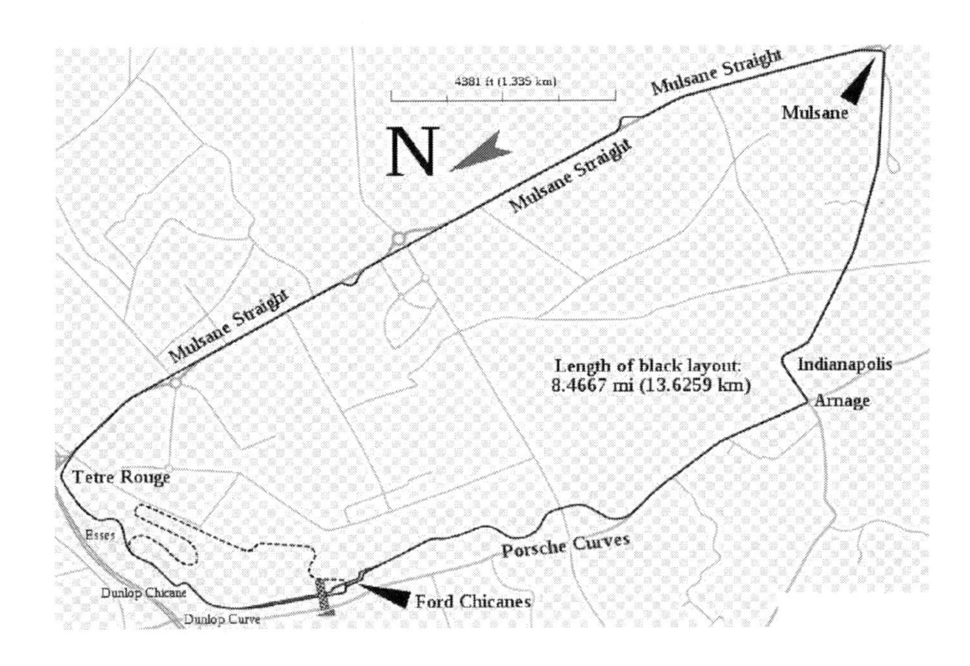

Chapter I

Le Mans
Sarthe, France
1:05 p.m. Saturday

Cameras clicked and flashes popped like strobe lights as the supermodel struck a pose in the arms of a debonair racecar driver. In the background, engines revved and crowds thronged. It was the perfect image to evoke the electric anticipation and the glamour of Le Mans, the most fabled road race of them all, and tomorrow morning, Tygre's picture would be displayed in papers throughout Europe and North America. Voyeuristic men and curious women across both continents would search the Web for pictures of her in that ash-gray Nomex jumpsuit with the front zipper lowered to barely cover her firm breasts.

The flame-resistant coveralls were regulation wear at the Le Mans pit lane and, to the delight of Tygre's admirers, they hugged her every curve. The high-heeled leather boots, wide crocodile belt and dark La Dolce Vita sunglasses resting atop her head were the perfect punctuation. Not many could pull off such a fashion feat, but Tygre had managed to turn her mandatory pit crew gear into a European Vogue cover look. Still, no one could have guessed what lay beneath the surface of that cover girl image. Her body was warm and vibrant, but a closer look would show her smile was strained, her gaze distant, her heart drained.

"Tygre! Over here! Please!" one of the paparazzi shouted. She turned away from the exploding flashbulbs, hoping to catch a glimpse of the man of her dreams, even as another man, the man who now inspired her nightmares, held her in a tight embrace. Once the scent of Khalil Karim had washed over Tygre pleasingly, but now it was the odor of nausea and dread.

She stole a glance at the famous Le Mans Rolex clock. As the official timekeeper for more than half a century of Le Mans races, the iconic clock had overseen many spectacular wins and ego-breaking defeats. But Tygre's job, her involuntary mission at this year's race, was even more critical than that of the Rolex. She couldn't help notice the irony of her connection to the old timepiece. Her every move was to be timed with precision. Her very life, and the lives of others, depended on it.

Tygre felt all eyes focused in her direction. That was nothing new. For as long as she could recall, she had drawn gazes, gawks and stares from men and women in all walks of life. Her appearance destined her for supermodel status, which came calling at a young age. But, while her beauty blessed her with financial freedom, it cursed her with maddening constraints. The balancing act between the perils of fame and sustaining a modicum of anonymity started early on. But that was nothing compared to the pain she was experiencing now. A few short weeks ago, her life had been her own. And now, impossibly, it no longer was.

———

Special Agent Doug Martin, of the Miami Division of the FBI, had made it abundantly clear. Without her participation, he warned, the potential loss of life and devastation would be severe.

"We have an urgent matter to discuss with you," Martin said as he presented his FBI credentials at that first meeting with Tygre in Miami less than a month before.

"What is this all about?" Tygre asked, shaking his hand.

"We understand you know Khalil Karim intimately," Agent Martin said.

Martin had caught Tygre coming from a photo shoot in South Beach. She was holding a chilled bottle of Perrier water. Her manicured toes were lightly dusted with sand and her sun-tinted shoulders glistened with scented oil. By contrast, Agent Martin was pale-skinned and stiff, dressed in plain-vanilla attire. His khaki Dockers barely reached the tips of his shoes.

His lanky body shadowed Tygre, blocking the looming noon sun as they walked into an ocean-side café.

"You don't spend much time in the sun, do you, Agent Martin?" Tygre smiled nervously as the middle-aged FBI Agent pulled out a chair for her.

"I've been temporarily re-assigned to FBI HQ. It's been pretty chilly in Washington these past few weeks, ma'am," he said, as he set a file folder on the table and took the seat opposite Tygre. "You know a little bit about D.C., don't you, Ms. Topolska?" He opened the folder to reveal a black-and-white photo of an attractive Arab man.

"Tell me about your relationship with Abdul Khalil Muhammad Abu Karim." Agent Martin said without taking his eyes off of Tygre.

Tygre glanced at the picture, then back at Agent Martin. "I'm not sure what you're interested in knowing."

"Are you aware that he's a suspected terrorist?" Agent Martin asked in a low monotone.

"I had no idea." Tygre said, "I honestly don't know him that well. But I'm not sure I believe you."

Tygre forced a smile as Agent Martin watched her carefully. She noticed his gaze following the movement of her hands as she placed the starched white napkin on her lap. Trying to read her, she supposed.

"Weren't you aware of the Khalil Karim Islamic Foundation and Academy outside of Washington, D.C.?"

Agent Martin pushed the photo closer to Tygre. He watched her eyes as they scanned Khalil's image once again. The black-and-white headshot didn't do justice to Khalil's dark olive complexion and espresso hair. His piercing brown eyes had once charmed her into an evening of passion. Tygre's eyelids lowered involuntarily as she recalled his scent.

"I know he has a foundation," Tygre said, quickly shaking off the memory of her intimate moments with Khalil. "Everything seemed perfectly legitimate to me. Khalil is a very religious man. He isn't a terrorist."

"Are you sure about that?" Agent Martin asked. He followed Tygre's fingers as she brushed her hair back behind her ear.

"Yes, of course. He told me so."

"He told you he's not a terrorist?"

"I mean...he told me because I asked him...if he was."

"So you had your suspicions about him?"

"No!" Tygre blurted out louder than she meant to. "Look, you're taking all my words the wrong way. I don't know anything about him being a terrorist. And I don't have anything to do with his foundation."

"So you weren't aware that the foundation is a cover for terrorist activities?" Agent Martin asked.

"Absolutely not!" She took a sip of her mineral water.

"And you aren't conspiring in a suspected terrorist plot against President Harrington and his family?"

"His family?" Tygre was sure Agent Martin could see her face flush.

"Isn't that why you're dating the President's son?"

"No!" Tygre protested. She set her glass back with shaking hands. A few droplets of water splattered onto the photo of Khalil. "I wasn't...infiltrating..." Tygre's voice shook. "I'm in love with him." She lowered her voice to a near whisper. "What makes this any of your business?"

"The Bureau finds it...intriguing...that you jumped from the bed of a suspected terrorist into the bed of the only son of the President of the United States." Agent Martin stated calmly. "We'd like to know how that came to happen."

"It wasn't like that!" Tygre explained. "Khalil means absolutely nothing to me. He was a fling...a stupid mistake. It is different with Brad."

"Different?"

"I love Brad...," Tygre broke off, surprised at her own words. She'd never said such a thing to a stranger. "I care about him very much."

"You seem a bit unsure," Agent Martin said.

"I simply don't appreciate being grilled on my personal life," Tygre said, trying to gather herself. She flashed back quickly to the first time she'd seen Brad Harrington at a White House gala dinner. He stood out distinctly from the rest of the young politicos in the room. His dark blond hair was wavy and sun-streaked, the perfect frame for his tanned face. His high cheekbones and strong jaw were impressive, but his pale blue-green eyes, soothing and yet exciting, were what had initially lured her to him. The gentle strength and conviction behind those eyes made Tygre come undone.

"I won't listen to any more of this! This is ridiculous!" She stood quickly and took one step away from the table but Martin put up a hand to stop her.

"If you care about Brad Harrington, you should probably sit down, Ms. Topolska," he said flatly. He indicated the folder in front of him. "There's a lot more to this story."

Tygre paused. Something about the agent's manner chilled her. She returned to her seat and took another sip of water.

"You should know that the FBI is investigating you as a possible co-conspirator in Khalil Karim's suspected terrorist activities."

Tygre felt her mouth open in shock. "Co-conspirator?" her voice quivered. "That's preposterous! Look, I really don't know what Khalil Karim is all about. I spent one night with him. I don't have any contact with him anymore."

Martin studied her closely, "There is another matter, Miss Topolska. You are facing possible charges by the SEC for alleged insider trading in connection with information you obtained from Sir Ari Beafetter, the owner of La Dolce Vita. Does that name ring a bell with you?"

Tygre could only imagine the look of dismay on her own face. Yes, she vividly recalled the day her boss and mentor, Sir Ari, gave her a stock tip that doubled her original million dollar contract. And she had willingly taken it. The fear that lingered in her expression was clearly not lost on Martin.

"Are you still under contract to Beafetter? Do you own shares in CRG?" Martin continued.

"What are you getting at?" Tygre's halting voice was barely audible as she began to consider her limited course of action, "Just what are you asking me to do?"

"First, you'll have to end your relationship with Brad Harrington. You've become a liability to the President's son…and to the entire Harrington family."

"You can't be serious," she said. "Brad and I love each other! We are going to Le Mans together!"

"Your plans have changed, Miss Topolska. You are going to get yourself invited to Le Mans by Khalil Karim."

"You must be out of your mind."

Martin smiled and tapped the folder in front of him. "Perhaps you'd rather go to prison?"

Tygre stared. Something told her that the FBI agent was not bluffing. No one else could possibly have known about that stock tip.

"Well then…we need you in Le Mans, France," Agent Martin continued. "Both Khalil Karim and Brad Harrington are competing in the race, and your attendance is critical. You can agree to cooperate with us now, or I'll bring you in front of a grand jury, Miss Topolska. I would suggest you make it easy on yourself."

"Le Mans?" Tygre's eyes widened.

Agent Martin reached across the table and slipped Tygre his card. "You'll need to come to the local office tomorrow morning. Here's the address. Your flight to Le Mans has already been booked. I'll go over the details then."

"But I've got a shoot scheduled…" Tygre protested.

"Tomorrow morning 9:00 a.m., Ms. Topolska." Agent Martin stood and leaned in close. "And please do not speak to anyone about this conversation."

Tygre stared back at Martin evenly. "Who would believe me if I did?" she said.

Agent Martin moved away from the table. "I'll see you at 9 a.m."

Chapter 2

Le Mans
1:30 p.m. Saturday

As the cameras continued to flash and the paparazzi jostled for position, Tygre let her gaze wander over the animated scene struggling to calm herself, trying to put herself in the place of all those other people, there just to watch a race, just to enjoy the magnificence of the scene. Glistening in the bright afternoon sun, 55 cars of different classes, including prototypes, sat jewel-like in their pits as crew technicians buzzed eagerly around them. Preparations were well underway for the beginning of the 24 Hours of Le Mans, commonly known as the Grand Prix of Endurance.

The throng of spectators was as thick and bustling as a Fifth Avenue lunch hour crowd—more than 250,000 of them scurrying to find the best spots for a glimpse of the forever-changing landscape of the race along the 13.63 kilometer track.

Access to pit lane where she stood was strictly limited to members of the racing teams and the press. Tygre was neither of those, but she had an all-access pass on the arm of Abdul Khalil Muhammad Abu Karim. Not by choice, certainly, but because she was Tygre.

She had been born Theresa Topolska in Warsaw, Poland, twenty-four years ago, but it was not long before her father, Adam, coined the nickname that reflected her true nature: Everything she did was marked by an added tempo—she ate quickly, walked rapidly, zipped through chores with relentless energy, and coupled her actions with an insatiable curiosity almost impossible to satisfy.

Her father found all this charming, but then he had always been endeared by actions her mother rarely found so pleasing. He often referred to Tygre's premature birth as her "backstage debut," as it occurred during an intermission of *Hamlet.* Tygre's mother, Helena, was not so amused. It had been a notable occasion for the Warsaw socialite, but the early arrival of her child dampened an otherwise delightful evening at the theater.

Because the delivery happened at such a high-profile event, it was carried by all the papers of note the following morning. But, Helena soon realized she would not receive this kind of attention for very long. As the years passed, her daughter's beauty surpassed her own. The moment a person caught a glimpse of Tygre's crystal blue eyes, they were immediately captivated.

Had anyone bothered to look deeper through those windows of Tygre's soul, they would have discovered a profoundly thoughtful and sharp-witted young woman. But most people couldn't get past those extraordinary eyes.

Just pray that Khalil Karim, the man to whose arm she now clung could not read the truth behind her eyes, Tygre thought, as the roar of powerful engines grew about her. If he had any idea of the agony she had endured to bring herself to this moment, it would surely mean catastrophe.

"Khalil, it's Tygre. I've broken up with Brad Harrington." Tygre choked back tears as she spoke from Miami under the watchful glare of Agent Martin.

"Why am I not surprised?" Khalil snorted, reeling in delight. "What happened?"

"Brad is just not what I had thought," she said. "I need someone more sophisticated...and worldly...like you." Tygre's heart ached as she lied to Khalil on the order of the FBI. "If your invitation still stands, I would like to join you at Le Mans." Tygre's voice quivered but Khalil seemed not to notice.

"By all means, Tygre. I'm thrilled you came to your senses. Never say never to me again."

Tygre cringed as she vividly recalled that conversation. Her words had been agonizing to utter, each a betrayal to her beloved Brad. But she had had no choice but to comply.

Today at Le Mans, she watched with detachment as Khalil Karim met the cameras with a look of smooth confidence. Of course, he had plenty to be boastful about. Not only was he an immensely wealthy Saudi and the owner of Karim Racing, a company that prepared, maintained and raced high-performance LMP1 diesel prototype cars, he was escorting the most stunning woman at Le Mans. No one could deny that the handsome dark-featured Arab and his magnificent blue-eyed blond made a striking couple.

As for the race itself, The 24 Hours of Le Mans had been dominated by Europeans until recent years, when Brad Harrington, the son of the American President, had developed into a serious competitor. And now, the very first presence of a Muslim owned and financed team stirred a new interest and curiosity. It was an opportunity for the Muslim world to shine in a new arena, a fact not lost on Malik Youssaf, Khalil's co-driver, friend and general factotum. He was nervous and disheveled in sharp contrast to Khalil's suave appearance, and he was clearly disinterested in the spectacle surrounding the fashionable couple in the pit area.

"Khalil, get rid of her. It's time to get ready," Malik snapped. He handed Khalil a balaclava and a pair of fireproof gloves.

Khalil ignored his cohort's warning, keeping his focus on Tygre. "If you try, you can be quite charming my dear," Khalil whispered in her ear. His clipped British inflection was cultivated by years of affluence and an Oxford University education.

Tygre forced a smile for the cameras.

"Your smile becomes you. You should wear it more often." Khalil's tan face broke into a grin. He leaned in to kiss Tygre goodbye, and the cameras flashed wildly. He barely managed to brush her cheek with his eager lips, as Tygre turned her face quickly and untangled herself from his arms, signaling to all that the paparazzi session was over.

"I must run, so until later..." Khalil called after Tygre as she darted off and quickly disappeared in the immense crowds forming outside pit lane.

—

Malik scoffed at the sight of his disappointed friend. "What does he expect?" he muttered, watching Khalil nod nervously to the relentless paparazzi.

"Now…I am ready, my friend." Khalil turned to Malik and gently tapped his shoulder. "I can take care of myself, so don't worry about me."

Malik Youssaf had grown up alongside Khalil, spending many years enjoying the spoils of his employer's vast fortune. And he had earned every bit of it. Nobody had been more loyal to Khalil. Malik had spent years in the Saudi desert attending to Khalil's every whim, fulfilling his countless commands. He was not about to be derailed by a woman, a blue-eyed Christian at that. Malik could barely tolerate seeing Khalil be made a fool of by this tart. How could he allow such a frivolous distraction in the middle of what should be their most important and – please Allah – glorious day?

"You must be mad to bring her here. If something goes wrong…" Malik muttered.

"Relax, nothing will go wrong. It is a lucky break for us that she severed her ties with Harrington and came here to be with me." Khalil stated unfazed. "Her beauty is an ideal distraction."

"I don't trust her. The reward had better be worth the risk," Malik warned.

The race announcer's voice interrupted their exchange, resounding through the artfully deployed speaker system: *"Last year's winners, the New Deal two-car team, are back to defend their title! The New Deal's No. 1 car set the fastest qualifying time and a new Le Mans record at 3m 22.888s, a full 1.2 seconds faster than the second qualifier and 1.5 seconds faster than last year's pole time!"*

Tygre stopped short amid the bustling crowds. Those two little words – "New Deal" – broke her gait and left her standing frozen in place. She looked up at the loud speaker as the crowds bumped into her motionless body.

"Watch it, gorgeous!" someone warned, barely capturing her attention.

"Sorry," she whispered back, keeping her focus on the announcer's silky voice.

"... That's correct ... three-time Le Mans winner, Brad Harrington, is the favorite to win this year's race! His team just won the American Le Mans Series team championship. Harrington's two brand-new, highly anticipated diesel prototypes were built entirely in the U.S. He has been quoted as saying that 'America's auto industry, with its low sulfur diesel fuel, has fallen behind the European diesel car markets and is losing its competitive edge.' That explains Harrington's personal racing quest to develop new diesel car technology."

"*The* William Bradford Harrington, II?" a girl in the tiniest mini dress cooed to her girlfriend as they passed by Tygre.

"Oooh," her friend chimed in, "Mr. Le Mans! I hear he's even better looking in person..."

Tygre watched the girls saunter past. *If they only knew how wonderful Brad really is,* she thought. *Two sluts like that could never turn his head.* She closed her eyes and pictured his body and his hypnotic gaze, hoping desperately to find him standing in front of her when she opened her eyes again. But her hope was in vain.

During her last phone conversation with Brad from New York, she had wanted to tell him the truth about her mission, but of course she couldn't. The reality of the situation was maddening. She had dreaded making the call, but she had no choice.

Tygre's hands trembled as she picked up the phone and dialed the international exchange. Brad was already in Le Mans preparing for the race and awaiting her arrival.

"Brad, can you hear me? It's Tygre. I need to talk to you."

"Sweetheart, I've missed you," Brad answered. "It's great to hear your voice. What time are you arriving?"

"Brad, I have something to tell you. Please listen to what I have to say. This is not easy." Tygre's voice cracked.

"What's the matter, darling? Are you okay?"

"Brad...I can't see you again."

There was silence on the line.

"Brad?"

"I'm here."

"I'm sorry to hurt you, but...I have to move on. I can't see you any more."

"I don't understand. Did something happen, Tygre?" he finally asked in a near whisper. "Was it something I did?"

"No, Brad. It's nothing like that."

Brad was quiet for a moment before letting out a long sigh. "Darling, please come to France so we can talk about this."

Tygre inhaled deeply hoping to find courage. "I will be there at Le Mans, Brad, but I'll be with someone else." Tygre was surprised by how quickly she had said it.

"Tygre, what the hell is going on? What are you talking about? What has happened since I last saw you?"

Tygre couldn't find the right words. She sat silently, pressing the phone against her ear as her head began to throb.

"What do you mean you're coming to Le Mans with someone else? Who? Tell me...who is it? What's gotten into you?"

"I'm sorry, Brad. I am so sorry. But there's no other way. Please accept it," Tygre shot back desperately trying not to break down.

"Who is it, Tygre?" Brad persisted. "You owe me that much."

"It's Khalil Karim." Tygre felt her stomach turn as she uttered the name.

"Khalil Karim? I can't believe it – you and Khalil?"

"It's just that..."

"What are you doing with him? Why are you doing this to me...to us?"

Brad waited for an answer but was met with silence on the line. Tygre was holding the phone outstretched to keep him from hearing her muffled sobs. Finally, he conceded.

"Good-bye, Tygre."

She wished she could answer.

"Good-bye, Tygre." His last words echoed in her head now as she stood amid the excited crowd at Le Mans. Eyes closed, she tormented herself replaying that final moment, Brad's final good-bye ringing through her thoughts. When she could no longer stand it, Tygre opened her eyes.

She thought at first they were playing a cruel trick on her, but she looked again, and the image before her became clear. It was one of New Deal's prototype cars slowly moving forward as the crowd parted. And Brad was behind the wheel. Tygre inched forward.

As Brad's car passed, he and Tygre locked gazes for only a second. Tygre trembled as his pale eyes met hers with pain and confusion. She wanted to reach out to him, but she couldn't. If only she could explain to Brad what she had to do. His life was in danger, and the only way Tygre could protect him was to hurt him. Her heart ached as she watched Brad drive away. *I love you, Brad. I wish I could tell you the truth, and one day I will.*

From his vantage point a few paces away, Malik pulled the visor of his cap down over his eyes and scoffed at what he had just witnessed. *Severed ties with Brad Harrington?* Malik muttered to himself. *It doesn't look that way to me.* He watched intently as Tygre gazed after car No. 1 with the longing eyes of a love-struck schoolgirl. *If only Khalil could see this!* He flipped opened his cell phone, dialed a number and began cursing loudly in Arabic. "*Inta majood?*"

Chapter 3

Le Mans
1:59 p.m. Saturday

From the outside, the trailer looked like any one of the hundreds of racing teams' support vehicles, which mushroomed in the back of pit lane. Filled with tires and every imaginable spare part, these mini factories on wheels were the bloodlines of the 24-hour race. But this one was different on the inside. It was filled with surveillance equipment, hi-tech computers, state-of-the-art electronic devices, secret files, FBI agents and a few French Special Forces officers. She had not even knocked before the door opened and Agent Martin pulled Tygre inside.

"Get in! Hurry up!"

Tygre, breathless, could only nod.

"Where is Malik? Are you sure he didn't follow you?" Martin pressed her.

"I'm positive. He was in the pit lane."

"Did you actually see him there?"

"That's where he was when I left." She shrugged. "I saw Brad just now."

"This is not acceptable, Tygre. You need to forget about Brad and focus." Agent Martin's voice was angry. "We cannot afford any slip-ups. Is this clear to you? This mission is of critical importance."

Tygre nodded silently, recalling her last few meetings with Martin in Miami. He had conducted them with a demeanor that was all business but he had never been overbearing. His voice was always steady and calm. With little choice, Tygre had relied on Agent Martin as her trusted teacher of this crash course in surveillance, counterterrorism and undercover work.

"At the special request of the International Joint Terrorist Task Force," Agent Martin had told her, *"my colleagues and I will be providing additional security for the upcoming U.S. presidential visit to Le Mans. Given the FBI's information about Youssaf and Karim, their presence there poses a very serious threat. The FBI is counting on your full cooperation. It is very important that you remain focused on their activities. Stay composed, Tygre, and do not display any signs of nervousness. It will be difficult, but I have complete confidence in you."*

All well and good, back then, she thought, but today, Agent Martin seemed less protective, more officious, and his tone was frightening. Before she could say anything else, Martin turned and introduced a fellow agent, a muscular tall man who'd been lingering nearby. "Agent Weber will place a microphone concealed in a pendant around your neck. This is your transmitter. Try not to move unnecessarily or the reception will be muddled on our end."

Easier said than done, thought Tygre. But she nodded. "Yes, I understand."

"This is your receiver, Tygre," Agent Weber explained. He showed Tygre a flesh-colored object the size of a pea. "Place it in your left ear and pull your hair down over it. You'll be able to hear me at all times."

Tygre took the receiver and watched it wobble slightly in her trembling palm.

"You'll be all right, Tygre." Martin said, as if he'd read her mind. "Also, there's one last thing we have to address. You need to place this additional listening device in Karim's trailer. Then we will have you, Karim and Youssaf completely covered." He handed her a small, white envelope. "This is a remote microphone. Until we advise you to act, just keep it in a safe place."

Tygre slipped the envelope in her pocket.

"Should you ever feel your life is in danger, we have established a distress code that you should use as a last resort. The word is UNIQUE."

"Unique?" Tygre repeated. "So I can say something like 'I am unique.'"

"You've got it, but only in a life-threatening emergency, Tygre." Martin handed her an additional earpiece.

"This is a non-functioning Bluetooth, Tygre. Wear it exposed in your other ear. This is your cover. In case you are ever overheard talking to us, you will be able to justify the conversation." Agent Martin's voice took on a stern note, "Never refer to me as Agent Martin. Use my first name only—just Doug, remember that!" Martin reiterated.

Tygre's throat tightened. She shook her head in disbelief and glanced around the trailer at the surveillance equipment and electronic consoles. *This is not a game,* Tygre told herself. *This is not a scene from a movie. This is real life! And I am in it! Dear God, help me!*

"Tygre..." Martin broke into her thoughts. "If you can't handle this ..."

"No!" Tygre protested. "I can do this."

"Keep in mind how important this is, Tygre," Martin continued. "The 24 Hours of Le Mans coincides with the opening of NATO meetings in Paris. President Harrington, British Prime Minister Anthony Sprake and the French President Jean-Jacques Pellier are all planning to attend the end of the race."

"And they're all at risk," Tygre said, lowering her head.

"You're exactly right. I can't stress to you enough how high the stakes are," Martin said.

"I get it!" Tygre cut him off. "Look, I've done everything you've asked. I don't know how much more clearly I can express my commitment!"

She placed the pendant around her neck and felt it fall against her chest.

"I know it hasn't been easy for you," Agent Martin said, switching to a gentler tone. "You played that very well with Harrington's son. We know you're capable of seeing this thing through."

Tygre felt the tears welling up inside her. She simply nodded to Martin.

"Now, as you know, the President's son..."

"Brad," Tygre interrupted. "His name is Brad." She pulled gently on the pendant.

"Brad…could be a prime target for Karim and his men. He's highly visible…which makes him…highly vulnerable."

Tygre looked away. She feared for her own safety but Brad's well being was even more important to her, a realization that took Tygre by surprise. Was this what true love felt like? She shook her head and breathed deeply to keep the tears from coming. *I need to do this! For Brad, and for the sake of many innocent lives!*

"I understand," Tygre said. "I'm committed."

"That's what I want to hear," Martin said.

With a trembling hand, Tygre re-checked the placement of the earpiece. Her long blond hair fell forward, concealing the device from view. *For the first time in my life,* she thought deeply anguished, *I love someone…and now I have to let him go in order to save him. How does that make any sense?*

"Okay, let's test this thing," Weber said. "Can you hear me?"

Tygre nodded when she heard his voice come clearly through her earpiece. "I *am* unique. I can do this," she muttered softly, patting her hair down over her ear and adjusting her pendant.

"Did you pick her up?" Martin asked.

Weber tapped his headset and nodded, "Loud and clear. But don't say you are UNIQUE again unless you mean it! Do you understand?"

"Yes…my mistake."

"All right then," Martin said, giving Tygre a nod of reassurance. "You're good to go."

Tygre stood and walked toward the door, stopping for a moment to adjust her coveralls and straighten the pendant one more time. She felt for her earpiece, along with the fake Bluetooth, sighed deeply and reached for the trailer door.

"Okay Doug, I'm ready."

Chapter 4

Le Mans
2:31 p.m. Saturday

Less than half an hour remained until 3:00 p.m., the official start of the race. To all who were intimately involved, it was an eternity. As it had for more than 78 years, Le Mans promised to deliver a superb show, an ongoing duel between diesel and petrol-fueled engines, supreme sportsmanship, reliability, stamina and death-defying excitement – 24 hours of it.

But the thrill of Le Mans was lost on Tygre. She moved mechanically through the manic scene without absorbing any of it. She heard the noises and smelled the smells but none of it had an effect on her. She felt strangely removed from it all.

As she glanced nervously at the legendary Rolex clock perched high above pit lane, Tygre felt her pulse race. *I am running out of time! I have to make it back before Malik starts looking for me.* She turned back and started to run.

She didn't get far before bumping into a local TV crewman filming a segment about Le Mans. Tygre gasped and reached for her FBI-issued pendant to ensure she hadn't lost it. "Watch it, young lady. We're taping a live show here," the crewman warned.

As Tygre anxiously repositioned her earpiece and adjusted her pendant, she caught sight of a tall reporter looking into a camera lens and speaking cheerily into his microphone.

"The crowds, some of whom traveled thousands of miles to attend, will stay awake for the entire race," the reporter announced. "They are well-informed enthusiasts of all ages, spoiled by the spectacular past performances at Le Mans. These crowds expect more excitement each year as the factory-sponsored and hand-picked drivers continue to break their lap records using state-of-the-art technology for these mechanical bullets."

Tygre began to walk away when she felt a hand clasp her upper arm. She turned quickly to see a second TV crewman holding onto her and guiding her toward the reporter.

"Among the many high-profile celebrities at this year's Le Mans is La Dolce Vita spokesperson, Tygre, who has graced us with her stunning presence!"

Before Tygre could absorb what was happening, the cameraman pushed the lens in front of her face, and the reporter moved in for the attack. "And she's here with us today. Hello, Mademoiselle Tygre. Can you tell us how you're enjoying Le Mans?"

"I … it's a … well, it's very nice, indeed." Tygre did her best to force a smile.

"You and Brad Harrington are certainly the hot couple of the year, Tygre. Are you here to cheer on your man?"

Tygre paused and fought back a lump in her throat. "I hope Brad does well," she said, smiling gracefully. "And now if you'll excuse me, I must run." She blew a kiss toward the camera and dashed off quickly.

"Well, mesdames et messieurs," the reporter told the camera, "There you have it – the glamorous and fast-paced life of an international supermodel! We'll have more coverage of Le Mans coming up later in the broadcast. Until then, I'm Herve du Bois reporting live for Tele-Mondial."

Du Bois handed his microphone to a technician and called after Tygre, "Mademoiselle Tygre! Can we get an in-depth interview for our evening broadcast?"

Tygre didn't respond. She was already making her way into the crowds, away from du Bois and his camera crew. "Doug, I'm still here," she spoke anxiously into her pendant. "I nearly lost the transmitter. Can you hear me?"

"Yes, loud and clear. Now hurry back to pit lane. The race is about to start. Stay cool and avoid making a scene."

"I'm on my way," Tygre said as she quickened her pace. "I'll be there as soon as I can."

"What's going on with you?" New Deal co-driver, Sonny Hicks waved a hand across Brad Harrington's line of vision. "Are you with us today?"

Brad shook his head and gave a quick kick to the back tire of car No. 1. "I'm sorry," he said snapping to. "I have a lot on my mind."

"The only thing that should be on your mind for the next 24 hours is the 13.63 kilometers of track outside your front windshield."

"You're right. I know..." Brad replied.

Sonny interrupted. "I've never seen you like this. Whatever's bothering you, you're going to have to put it aside for the next 24 hours."

"Consider it done," Brad said. "I'm ready to win this thing... whatever it takes. Let's do it!"

"That's the Brad I know and love." Sonny slapped Brad on the back of his shoulder and walked away.

The Rolex clock read 2:46 p.m. With only 14 minutes left before the start of the pre-race reconnaissance lap, the cars were placed one by one on the grid.

Tygre pushed through the crowds, desperate to get back to Karim Racing's double pit before the start of the race. "Excusez moi...pardon..." she pleaded as she struggled to break through the excited mob. Tygre's beauty worked against her as a number of onlookers tried to delay her for a closer look.

"Pardon!" she shouted, continuing to press forward.

As Tygre approached pit lane, she caught sight of Malik watching her, focusing carefully on her every move while wiping his hands with an oil-stained rag. Tygre had the sinking feeling he had been watching her for a while. She met his stare then quickly looked away, trying not to let her panic show.

By the time she entered the pit, she was soaked in sweat. She stepped behind a tall cabinet where she took a moment to catch her breath. She inhaled deeply and let out a sigh. When she stepped out from behind the cabinet, Malik was standing directly in front of her, grinning evilly.

"Why are you running around like this? Where have you been?" His broad torso inched closer to her body, backing her into a corner.

"Where's Khalil?" Tygre asked.

"Do you think I am stupid?" Malik glanced at the Rolex clock. "I know you are up to something! Who are you meeting with?" Malik's fingers dug deeply into Tygre's shoulder as he pulled her close to him. His fake smile broke into a scowl, then. "If you know what's good for you, you'll stay out of our business!"

Tygre took a step back. Before she could speak, Malik turned and walked away. She followed him discreetly with her eyes until he stopped at the passenger door of Khalil Karim's car No. 7. She watched him lean into the passenger window. He gently touched Khalil's shoulder while whispering into his ear.

Tygre reached for the small silver pendant hanging from the chain around her neck. It was supposed to give her a feeling of security, but it felt like a noose. She wondered if the FBI could hear her pounding heart.

"Doug, did you get all that? It was Malik!" She turned away and lowered her voice. "He's on to me! He's watching every move I make."

"Stay the course and remain calm. He knows nothing. He's just fishing," Martin reassured her. "You're doing fine."

The revving engine of Khalil's car No. 7 pulled Tygre's attention, and she bravely walked toward it. Malik watched her intensely as she approached.

"My dear Tygre, come here and wish me luck!" Khalil called to her from behind the wheel.

She smiled and leaned in to give Khalil a quick kiss before backing away again. Her eyes darted quickly around, hoping to catch a glimpse of Brad.

Khalil frowned and revved his engine until Tygre turned her attention back to him. "I'm off!" he said, attempting to redirect her focus.

"Good luck. Stay safe and win!" Tygre forced a smile and stepped away from the car, waving sweetly to Khalil as he drove off to complete the pre-race lap.

Tygre watched the other drivers follow behind him. As soon as Khalil was out of sight, Tygre's tight smile vanished. In that same moment she caught Malik's stare. He scowled at her deliberately as he walked past her. His face broke into a malevolent smile. Tygre grasped at the pendant around her neck and swallowed hard.

Game on.

Chapter 5

Le Mans
2:58 p.m. Saturday

"Drivers, start your engines!"

The deafening roar of 55 engines ramped up the energy and excitement level of the already-ecstatic crowd. Thousands of arms flew into the air, waving the French tricolor flag. The 24 Hours of Le Mans was about to get officially underway. The cars, in a two-by-two start formation, lined up on the grid and began their first lap to the starting line with a thunderous, guttural growl.

Brad Harrington tightly gripped the wheel of his LMP1 prototype. He could not erase the image of Tygre standing in Karim Racing's pit. *What is she doing there? Why is she with Khalil?* These nagging questions and others reverberated in Brad's head, as he guided his car along the track. *I must put her out of my mind. I have a job to do!*

"Brad, watch the Ferrari on your left! What the hell is the matter with you? Get your head straight!" The New Deal's technical manager radioed in. "You'll be out of the race in the first lap, for God's sake."

Excitement peaked and filled the air with an intensity only seen and heard at Le Mans. Tygre stood in pit lane, watching French military jets fly overhead, trailing red, white and blue smoke in a display of national pride. For one brief moment, she allowed herself to get caught up in the thrill and sensation of Le Mans.

The voice of Agent Martin resonated through her earpiece, startling her back to reality. “Tygre, are you in Karim Racing’s pit? Is Youssaf there?”

“Yes, I’m here, Doug, but I don’t see him.” Tygre answered.

“You need to engage him, but be careful. Watch him closely,” Martin warned. “We have new information. This is serious.”

Tygre sighed deeply. She quickly surveyed the scene. “What have you found out?”

“We’ll brief you as soon as the intelligence is confirmed. For now, be sure that you don’t let your guard down for even a second.”

“I won’t.” Tygre said, and meant it.

Until now, Tygre’s own national loyalties were diffuse, to say the least. She often felt homeless despite the carte blanche privileges her supermodel status and contract with La Dolce Vita cosmetics afforded her in any nation. The multiple, part-time international residences provided for her were the finest, but still it was a nomadic existence. She was the face of La Dolce Vita, the face that was recognized in nearly every home in every country in the free world, yet she had no home of her own.

She had never experienced the feeling of home until she met Brad Harrington. With the exception of her own father, Brad had been the only man Tygre had truly trusted and loved. With Brad, she had finally felt that calm sensation of being truly cared for, of feeling warm and safe. Tygre had fallen in love with him on the first night they spent together at the Harrington Ranch. She had traveled so many miles from everything she knew, and yet Tygre felt home at last. She grew to love the serene setting of the Harrington Ranch, Brad’s family and everything about his life. She felt content to be a part of it all.

And despite her Polish heritage and her international entrée, she had come to feel an undeniable allegiance to the United States. And now, the safety of its First Family was in imminent danger.

Tygre’s fear suddenly intensified as Malik, escorted by another Middle-Eastern man in Karim Racing’s overalls, appeared a few feet away. Tygre’s voice trembled as she spoke into the pendant. “Doug, I can see Malik lurking around New Deal’s second car. He’s at the end of pit lane. He's talking to another man. I'm not sure who it is, but he looks familiar."

"Describe him. Try to focus, Tygre. Where have you seen him? This is very important."

"Let me think." Tygre hissed back. "He's an Arab. I've seen him before. I can bet my life on it."

Tygre advanced slowly toward the man, but her line of vision was suddenly interrupted by a fast-moving racer coming into pit lane. By the time the car passed, the man was gone.

"He disappeared. I lost him! Malik is alone again."

"Tygre, it's very important that you find out who he is."

"I'll try. Malik is watching me! He's on his way!"

"Be cool and stay calm! You'll be all right, Tygre. We're right here!"

Tygre looked up at the Rolex clock just as it registered 3:00 p.m. With the precision of the famed Swiss timepiece, the pack of roaring racers, tamed by a pace car during the pre-race lap, crossed the start line and was let loose.

Tygre felt an involuntary rush of exhilaration move through her amid the thunderous noise and high-speed fury. And then, without warning, a hand crawled up her spine and onto her arm. She turned to find Malik standing close beside her.

"Come with me, Miss Supermodel," he said, gripping her arm firmly. "It's time for a little chat, at last."

Tygre gasped. Her arm tensed beneath Malik's unyielding grip. She reached for the pendant with shaky fingers to discover it had slid back to the side of her neck and stuck there. *No!* Tygre tried not to panic, even though she suspected the worst. She would survive, she told herself, as she stumbled along, caught in Malik's vise-like grip. She would. She had always been a survivor. Always.

Chapter 6

Ten Years Earlier
Warsaw, Poland
The Convent of the Sisters of St. Joseph

On a gray and rainy afternoon, fourteen-year-old Theresa Topolska and her father apprehensively approached St. Joseph's Church. The imposing Gothic structure and its adjacent convent and school buildings were covered in ivy. In Poland, having survived wars and communism by collaborating skillfully with government officials, the Catholic Church remained a powerful and well-financed force despite the physical destruction and closure of almost all other private schools.

Sister Maria, the headmistress at St. Joseph's, was a stern looking woman with a blotchy complexion. The customary habit did little to disguise her heavy-set figure. She greeted them formally, wearing a forced smile, as she led them into the lobby.

"Hello, Mr. Topolski. I am Sister Maria, and you must be Theresa. Now both of you, if you will, please follow me."

Adam Topolski nodded as he struggled with his daughter's suitcase. Crying softly, Tygre clung to her father's side.

"Go ahead and set the luggage down, Mr. Topolski. I'll arrange to have it taken to the dormitory immediately."

"Thank you, Sister Maria," Topolski acknowledged, "Please look after my daughter. She is so young."

"Mr. Topolski, with a little time, Theresa will adjust to her life here," Sister Maria assured him even as she appeared irritated by Tygre's muffled sobs. "Don't worry, young Theresa, you'll be fine. We'll take good care of you."

Tygre grasped her father's hand as the reality of her predicament set in.

"Daddy, I don't want to stay here. Please let me go home with you…please!"

"It's time to say your farewells." Sister Maria folded her hands as if preparing herself for the inevitable drama that ensued each time a new student was brought to the convent. "It is my experience that the sooner the parent leaves, the more quickly things get settled and the easier it is on the child."

"Very well then," Topolski leaned toward his daughter. "It's okay, darling Tygre. Be a good girl. Don't make this any harder than it already is."

"But, Daddy, you can't leave me here!"

"Your mother and I cannot be together any longer. This is best for you. Study hard. I know you can do it, my darling." Her father said in a halting voice.

"Daddy," Tygre pleaded with him clinging onto his hand with both of hers.

"I'll see you soon. I promise."

Topolski kissed his daughter's hand before prying it from his wrist. "Be strong, my darling Tygre, be strong."

Tygre's heart ached as she watched her father walk away with quick measured steps, his head pitched downward. He did not look back to see his daughter's pained expression as tears streamed down his own face.

"Please don't leave me, Daddy," Tygre screamed, her shoulders heaving between sobs.

"Come along with me, Theresa. Quickly now, calm down. I'll show you around," Sister Maria said impatiently as she led Tygre down the hall. The enormity of the dreary old buildings and overgrown gardens was like nothing Tygre had ever experienced. The dormitories and classrooms were occupied by subdued teenage girls studying in silence.

As Sister Maria arrived upstairs with Tygre in tow, the silence between the two was periodically interrupted by the ticking of a large antique clock or the rustling of the sisters' rosaries as they passed in the hallways.

"All students are required to take showers before changing into their uniforms," Sister Maria instructed Tygre as they reached a large bathroom located in the gray Gothic Hall, "You need to do it now. I'll meet with you later."

Tygre tentatively entered the tiled bathroom. The hall felt chilly and damp. In a distant corner, a young sister on her knees scrubbed the floor near the toilets. A heavy smell of ammonia permeated the air. The communal shower contained dozens of stalls, which were separated by flimsy cotton sheets.

Tygre stepped into a stall and hung her drab uniform on a hook. She shivered nervously as she stripped off her clothes and began to cry, alone under the lukewarm stream of water.

Without warning, a teenage girl parted the sheet and scrutinized Tygre closely. "Hey, I'm Magda. Who are you?"

Tygre jumped and instinctively hugged her thin arms over her breasts. "You startled me," she said. "I didn't know anyone was in here."

"It's okay. I was about to take a shower," Magda said with a sly smile. She ran a chubby hand through her short, scarlet hair and watched Tygre intently.

"I'm Tygre Topolska."

"May I join you?" Without waiting for Tygre's answer, Magda quickly slipped out of her uniform. Her ample body jiggled and shook as she stepped into Tygre's stall. Ignoring Tygre's perplexed look, Magda continued chatting, "What kind of a name is that? It sounds strange."

"It's not so strange," Tygre said as she took a step backward. "Just say it TEE-gray."

"Tee-gray. Like a tiger?"

"No. It's just Tee-gray."

"Whatever you say, Tee-gray or Tiger. It's okay with me." Magda rubbed soap along one of her arms. "That was some performance you put on when you first got here! Everyone knew that a new girl arrived." She casually brushed her own breasts until her nipples grew hard. "It's exciting for us."

"It wasn't a performance," said Tygre. "I don't want to be here."

Magda studied Tygre from head to toe. “I’d like to be your friend,” she murmured in a slow, raspy whisper. “Everyone is sad when they first arrive, but you’ll get used to it here.”

“I hope so. This is all so different from how I imagined,” Tygre said quietly.

Magda inched forward and asked, “Would you like me to wash your back?”

Cornered by Magda’s large looming body, Tygre shook her head frantically. “No, please, no, no…just leave me alone. I’m fine.”

“You certainly don’t look it,” Magda snorted in Tygre’s ear.

“You should leave,” Tygre said nervously, visibly shaken by Magda’s presence.

“Have it your way, then.” Magda backed off. “You’ll come around, though. Wait and see.”

In the weeks that followed, Tygre spent the majority of her time alone at prayer, in classes and at meals. She tried at first to fit in, reaching out to her fellow classmates, hoping to find a friend. But most were orphans who were profoundly alone, unhappy and burdened with serious personal issues. None were interested in befriending the pretty blond girl. And, as Tygre excelled in her studies, they came to further resent her talent for mathematics and her superior grades.

To her own surprise, Tygre found solace in her studies, developing a special fondness for literature. Novels by Victor Hugo and Jane Austen and poems by Emily Dickinson took her to places she hoped to visit one day. Her favorite book, *Gone with the Wind,* brightened her painfully dull existence, for Scarlett O’Hara’s extraordinary life inspired Tygre. She found a special strength in Scarlett’s conviction. *When I meet my Rhett Butler,* she told herself, *I won’t make Scarlett’s mistakes.*

One night, a few weeks after she had arrived at the convent, Tygre lay awake after her classmates had long since retired. A full moon shone through an open window, illuminating a large and austere dormitory. Several iron beds made up with starched sheets stood on a wooden floor. All of them, a fair distance apart from each other, were occupied by sleeping children, except for Tygre's. With the exception of a flashlight beam moving around under her covers, Tygre's bed was still.

The floor squeaked as Magda entered, her full breasts pressing through a dowdy flannel nightgown.

"Who's there?" Tygre's voice whispered. The flashlight shut off.

"Tygre, it's me, Magda. What are you doing? You'll get in trouble if Sister Maria catches you with a light on."

"I am studying math," Tygre answered defensively, puzzled by this late-night visit. "Why aren't you sleeping?"

Magda climbed into Tygre's bed and sighed. "I am freezing. Come closer and warm me up." Magda grabbed Tygre's arm and pulled it to her body as she slipped under the covers.

"What are you doing? You should be in your own bed." Tygre pushed Magda away.

"It's so dark in my dorm, I was scared. I could use some company." Magda dismissed Tygre's objections. "Besides, you don't need to study that hard. You're so pretty. You'll find a husband to take care of you."

"I don't want a husband." Tygre protested.

Magda beamed with excitement. "Be quiet, Tygre, someone will hear us." She carefully scanned the dorm. Once satisfied all the children were asleep, Magda kissed Tygre tenderly on her neck.

Had Tygre been older and more experienced, she would have better understood what Magda was about to do. But being naïve, lonely and afraid, she was ill equipped to defend herself against Magda's advances.

Magda worked her way slowly up to Tygre's face, her breathing heavy. She was oblivious to Tygre's baffled look and tense body.

"What on earth are you doing? Why are you kissing me like this?" Tygre recoiled from Magda's touch, bewildered.

"I like you, Tygre, a lot. Don't you like me?"

"I think so, but..." Tygre hesitated.

"Well then..." Magda lowered her voice to a faint murmur. "Do you know how beautiful you are?"

"I'm not!" Tygre said. And it was true. From the moment her father had walked away from her in the convent offices, she had felt like the ugliest creature in the world.

Despite Tygre's protests, Magda slowly opened the small round buttons of Tygre's nightgown. "Let me show you! Just look how perfect your body is." Magda leaned closer to kiss Tygre's tiny breasts.

Tygre pulled back. "I don't think you should be doing this to me. It feels wrong."

"Shh, Tygre...it's okay... but be quiet. If Sister catches us, we'll both be in big trouble," Magda warned as she continued caressing Tygre. "Aren't you lonely here?"

"Yes, but..."

"Relax Tygre, I'm just trying to be your friend."

"But not like this." Tygre fought back tears, trying to comprehend what was happening to her. "Why are you touching me this way?"

"Because I want to be your best friend. Wouldn't you like that?" Magda asked, sensing Tygre's breaking resolve.

"I guess..." Tygre hesitated, tempted by the chance to break away from her loneliness and isolation, no matter how strange and confusing it felt.

"Do you know how wonderful you are?" Magda lifted the covers to stare at Tygre's body.

"No," said Tygre. "If that were true, I wouldn't even be here."

Magda briefly removed her hand from Tygre's flat belly. "What do you mean?"

"Who gives away their daughter if she's so wonderful?"

Magda was intrigued now. "Your parents gave you away?"

"My mother and father abandoned me here. They don't want me anymore."

"You mean you're not an orphan? I am, and so is almost everybody else in this place. Why would your parents put you here?"

"They're getting a divorce. My father said I would have a good education here."

"Here? For an education?" Magda stroked Tygre's hair. "My poor Tygre, no wonder you are so upset!"

"My mother doesn't want me around anyway. She hates me."

"That's impossible." Magda stole the opportunity to kiss Tygre's shoulder.

"No, it's true. She's hardly ever home. And when she is, she's usually with her…lover."

"Her lover?" Magda said, feigning compassion. "Tell me more about her lover."

"His name is Jash," said Tygre. "And I think he's part of the reason my mother wants me gone. I didn't do anything wrong!" Tygre began to weep.

Magda looked at Tygre tenderly and, sensing a ripe moment, reached out to her with pale arms. "Oh, Tygre, I'll take care of you." Magda pulled her closer, then placed her hand between her own legs and started to caress herself. Her nightgown had fallen open exposing her full breasts and thick white thighs. She parted her legs. A moist sheen of perspiration appeared on her plain, round face. Her deep-set eyes focused intently on Tygre as her breath came in gasps.

"What's happening? You're scaring me!" Tygre cried out, well aware now that her hope for companionship had taken an unexpected turn.

Magda continued to masturbate and, with her other hand, gently touched Tygre's breasts. Magda moaned with delight as her hand slid between Tygre's long, firm legs.

"Magda, stop!" Tygre protested and forcefully pushed away Magda's hand. "What are you doing?"

"Be quiet. You'll wake up the girls." Magda's pale face became flushed red. Her voice grew deep and hoarse with excitement. "Let me kiss you, Tygre," she pleaded. "I'll make you feel so good, I promise. Just let me, please. I'm your only friend here. You need me."

Tygre recoiled. "No, I don't," she said. "This isn't right. Whatever it is, I don't want this kind of friendship!"

As if the words were a trigger, Magda gave in to her pleasure, climaxing powerfully as she clutched Tygre's hand. She buried her face in Tygre's pillow to muffle her excited moans.

Repulsed by the sight of Magda's sweat-soaked body, Tygre turned away. But Magda continued to beg in her soft, low voice. "Kiss me, Tygre. Kiss me just once."

"Get away from me." Tygre wanted to push Magda off of the bed, but she loathed the thought of touching her perspiring skin.

"Touch me, Tygre. No one ever touches me. Oh, it feels so good. Let me show you."

"No. Stop talking!" Tygre insisted.

"Okay..." Magda's voice trailed off to a soft sigh.

Tygre stared at Magda's naked body feeling the same sense of betrayal that had washed over her the day her father walked away. For a moment, she had weakened before Magda's blandishments, and the experience had left her feeling devastated, more abandoned than ever before.

Tygre stood up from the bed. "Get out, Magda." Her small feet felt frozen on the bare wooden floor. "I don't want to feel good. Not in that way! It's a sin! I don't need you. Leave right now or I'll report you to Sister Maria!" she said firmly.

Magda opened her eyes lazily. Her voice came in a raspy murmur. "So what? I'll deny it." She smiled. "I'm the dorm captain. Sister Maria will believe me! You're new here. Trust me, nobody will pay the slightest attention to what you're saying." Magda pointed at the beds, "And don't expect anyone else to speak up. These girls are so medicated they wouldn't know a dream from reality!"

"Get out." Tygre persisted, "Leave me alone, and don't ever try this again."

Magda shrugged and lifted herself off the bed, picking up her clothing. She pulled her nightgown over her head and gave Tygre another smile. "Wait and see, beautiful girl. With each passing day, it gets harder and harder to go it alone here."

"I don't need you," Tygre said, firmly. "I don't need anyone."

For a moment Magda stood watching her. Finally, she spoke. "Perhaps you are right, beautiful girl. Perhaps." And with that, she was gone.

Chapter 7

Le Mans
3:15 p.m. Saturday

Indeed, it was true, Tygre told herself as she was pulled through the crowd. She had learned to trust no one but herself. To depend on no one but herself. Until she'd met Brad Harrington. At the very thought of him, she dug in her heels, forcing Malik to turn back toward her.

"Let go of me, Malik. I have nothing to say to you." Tygre tried to free herself from Malik's grip but he yanked her even closer.

"Not until we get inside Khalil's trailer. From now on, I decide when you talk and what you talk about. Smile and keep moving or I'll break your fucking arm, bitch."

"Don't you dare threaten me! I am here with Khalil. Leave me alone, or I'll tell him about your behavior," Tygre said bravely.

Malik grinned. "Oh, will you now? And what if I tell him about you and Harrington? Khalil is very proud and very jealous. He won't like it one bit."

"There is nothing to tell. I broke up with Brad. That's all there is to it," Tygre stated calmly, but her heart pounded with fear.

"You can fool Khalil, but not me, bitch! You are still in love with Harrington. It's so obvious. If you want to be with him, go, get lost. Khalil does not need to be distracted by your foolishness, by your lack of loyalty." Malik strengthened his grip on Tygre's arm. In the dense crowd, they were just another couple, lost in a jostling sea of humanity.

"This is none of your business." Tygre said, trying to pull away. Her eyes darted around the crowd, but no one paid any attention.

She could already see the team logo on Khalil Karim's trailer directly ahead. Within walking distance from pit lane, it was one of many support vehicles provided for Khalil's comfort.

"None of my business?" Malik growled. "I am making it my business for the next 23 and half hours. You had better believe it, Miss Supermodel." Malik pushed her forcefully inside the trailer. He slammed the door shut and locked it behind them.

The room was dark. Despite the soft hum of the sophisticated air conditioning system, the air was heavy. Tygre's eyes adjusted to the dim lights. She gently rubbed her forearm, sore from Malik's unrelenting grip. Without warning Malik flip-released a palm-sized tactical knife and held it to Tygre's neck. He backed her against the wall and grabbed her by her hair.

"What the hell are you doing?" Tygre screamed.

"Shut up and get on your knees. You're up to no good!"

Tygre was terrified of what Malik might do if he spotted her earpiece or receiver. She searched his face for a sign that he might be bluffing, but the fire behind his eyes revealed a man who was manic and unpredictable. She gasped for air. The blade of Malik's knife felt razor sharp.

"Tell me what's going on with you and Harrington!" Malik demanded. He stared at Tygre with such fury it took her breath away. "I see you looking at him with lust in your eyes, you infidel trash!"

"I already told you, Brad and I are through." Tygre struggled for breath. "You are hurting me, you bastard!" Small droplets of perspiration formed on her forehead.

Malik's body inched closer to her. "Perhaps a little truth serum will help refresh your memory." Malik produced a small white pill. He forcefully parted Tygre's mouth, squeezing her jaws with his free hand. She pulled back and clenched her teeth firmly together.

Malik yanked on her hair. "Take this or I'll break your fucking jaw, you whore." He forced the pill between Tygre's tightly clenched lips. Tygre rolled the pill under her tongue and pretended to swallow. "Your drugs won't help you. I have nothing to hide. I'll scream, you son of a bitch. Let go of me."

"Those will be the last words you'll ever say." Malik's knife pressed into the skin on Tygre's neck. As the blade bit into her, several drops of blood began trickle down her chest.

"I… I am …" Tygre attempted to utter her distress code. Malik quieted her with a hard slap to her face.

"Shut up, shut up, or I'll kill you right here," Malik warned. "I *will* get to the bottom of this. I'll find out what you're up to! One thing I know for sure is that you are a two-bit whore, a gold digger, and you will do anything for Khalil's billions."

Tygre shook her head in protest as Malik pushed down on her shoulders. He forced her onto her knees in front of him. Malik put the knife in his teeth and unzipped his fly. Tygre tried to inch away from the repulsive spectacle, but the glistening blade was back in his hand, keeping her frozen in place.

"You like money so much, put this in your mouth. I'll give you 50 euros? Isn't that why you're with Khalil? It's just that when you pleasure him, you hope it will be for 50 million?"

Tygre shuddered. Malik reeked of garlic and motor oil. Tygre felt nauseated by his small, limp penis brushing against her face. "I would rather die than touch you."

"Take it in your mouth," he ordered. "Show me what you do best." Malik's weak erection turned Tygre's stomach. He laughed and waved it proudly in front of her face. "I'll teach you who is in charge."

Tygre kept her jaw tightly shut and her lips closed, barely able to breathe. The passing seconds seemed endless.

"Make it hard! Suck on it." Malik had pushed his penis against Tygre's cheek, when a sudden knock sounded on the trailer door.

"Are you in there, Malik? We need you in the pit to take over for Khalil." Tygre recognized the voice as that of Karim Racing's team manager. She breathed a sigh of relief as Malik quickly put away the knife and zipped up his overalls.

"Give me a moment," Malik shouted. "I'll be right there." He yanked Tygre up off her knees, snorted as he glared into her face, and then shoved her away. "I'll deal with you later!"

Tygre stared back evenly. "I'll never forget this."

"If you say a word to anyone I'll cut your pretty face, and you'll never work again," he warned. "Be on your guard!" He grabbed a towel from the counter and threw it at her. "Get yourself cleaned up."

With one last scowl, he stormed through the door on his way to pit lane.

—

Brad Harrington was a troubled man, and the race had little to do with it. He had just entered the *Mulsanne Strait,* the fastest section of the circuit interrupted only by two *chicanes.* It was here that he needed his most intense focus. But something broke his concentration and sent a chill through him.

A glimpse of Tygre's face flashed in Brad's mind. She had looked frightened and distant. *Something's wrong,* Brad thought again. The idea nagged at him. The New Deal prototype swerved and sent the back wheels spinning, kicking up loose gravel on the edge of the track and eliciting a collective gasp from the crowd, audible even above the roar of the engines. Within moments, Brad righted the car and got back on track. His heart thumped quickly against his chest. *Focus, Harrington!* He muttered. But he couldn't shake the feeling that Tygre was in trouble. *Something's wrong, I know it!*

Brad forced his focus back to the track. *I'm no good to her dead,* he reasoned. *I've got to get through this thing.*

And getting through the race would be no easy feat, even though the 13.63 km track had been extensively modified since the first race in 1923. Safety had become the top priority of the French Racing Federation, especially after the 1955 accident that killed driver Pierre Levegh and 80 spectators. Despite sweeping safety regulations, the danger of a collision and death at extremely high speeds always loomed. The knife edge of life and death would always be an extraordinary draw of Le Mans, one of the few tracks in Europe capable of producing recorded speeds of 214 mph down the *Mulsanne Strait.*

Les Hunaudieres, Tertre Rouge corner, the *Esses, Maison Blanche, Virage Porsche* and the super-fast stretch before *Indianapolis,* the circuit's names were haunting with daring turns and their promise of danger. Drivers traveled at speeds that made steering and passing an exercise in ballistics, the likes of which made child's play of even the most aggressive highway maneuver.

The race controlled Brad and the rest of the drivers. The endurance and the stamina it required were mind-boggling. Today's cars were faster and more aerodynamically efficient than ever before, the danger more palpable. Brad could feel it. The balance of competing pressures both invigorated and terrified him, and that's exactly how he liked it.

Focus! He continued chiding himself at every death-defying turn. *You can do this! And then you will go to Tygre.*

Struggling to keep herself steady, Tygre pulled herself to a wash basin. She barely could recognize her own reflection in the mirror. She splashed cold water onto her face but it barely helped to revive her. The simple tasks of brushing her hair and touching up her lipstick seemed insurmountable. Finally, after taking several deep breaths, she walked unsteadily out of the trailer.

The bright sunshine fell across Tygre's body, but it provided little comfort. She donned her sunglasses to disguise her shaken face. Her heart pounded as she walked quickly through the crowds, tears of anger and frustration beginning to sting at her eyes.

The instant Malik was out of the trailer, she'd spat out the pill and whispered into the blood-spotted pendant microphone. Her voice cracked as she spoke, "Did you hear what happened, Doug? Did you hear what I just went through?"

"Yes, we heard it all and we were ready to intercept. But the manager got there just before us. The good thing is that it saved us from showing our hand."

"The good thing?" she said in disbelief. "I was terrified. I thought Malik was going to kill me. He cut me! I thought I could count on you!"

"I'm sorry you had to endure that," Martin said. "You handled it extremely well, Tygre. I knew you could. Let them think this is all about your relationship with Brad. It's good cover for you."

"It's not a cover. It's the truth. But I don't know if I can keep up with this." Tygre tried to clean the blood from her fingernails as she spoke.

"Yes, you can. You must!" Martin spoke firmly. "Tygre, calm down and listen to me. You don't have a choice, not if you care about Brad Harrington and his family."

"I don't know what to think right now," she said. "I'm no secret agent. Malik is threatening to disfigure me! I'm bleeding, Agent Martin…I mean Doug!" Tygre added with sarcasm.

Martin sighed deeply. "So all of that was just talk about you loving Brad, is that it, Tygre?"

Tygre wiped the last of the dried blood from her fingers and readjusted the pendant that lay against her breast. "I love Brad more than life itself." Tygre began to regain her composure.

"Prove it then. The FBI needs you to find out if Youssaf and Karim are involved in a terrorist plot. You're the only one who can infiltrate their pit without causing suspicion. Nobody else is better suited to help us with this mission. Just remember, Tygre, we are only seconds away from you. You have to trust that we have your back."

Tygre looked around to make sure Malik wasn't anywhere nearby. She took a deep breath. She felt a faint touch of color returning to her pale, drawn face. She straightened her back, and, standing tall, uttered with a certainty that surprised her, "I will do it … for Brad."

"That's my girl!" Martin said with relief. "Hurry back to the pit. Karim is coming in for an unscheduled stop. That must be why they're looking for Youssaf…to take over his stint."

"I'm on my way!" Tygre patted down her hair, adjusted her sunglasses and walked briskly toward pit lane.

She hadn't taken a dozen steps before she felt a hand on her wrist, pulling her roughly into the crowd. *Malik!* She thought. But when she turned to confront the aggressor, she found herself face to face with a giant Tele-Mondial camera lens. Before she could react, the TV crewman that had latched onto her wrist pulled her close to Herve du Bois who thrust a microphone under her chin.

"Here once again is our favorite supermodel, Tygre, of La Dolce Vita fame! Exciting start of the race, isn't it?" Herve asked.

"More exciting than I ever expected!" Tygre flashed a radiant smile and rushed away before Herve could press her for more.

Sitting alone in the pit, she pondered her horrific circumstances. The race was in its third hour. Tygre faced her deadliest enemy to date… time.

"Where are you, Tygre? I haven't heard from you since your interview." Martin's voice brought her back. Tygre stood up and casually walked to the adjacent team's pit where she could hide from Malik.

"I'm near Khalil's pit waiting for the change of drivers. Malik is busy studying charts and talking on his cell phone. I'm worried about Brad. How is he doing? Do we know?"

"Keep an eye on Youssaf. He is our main concern. Focus on your mission. Don't worry about Brad. He's fine for now," Martin responded in an irritated voice.

"I can't. Thinking about him keeps me going. Isn't that what you want?"

There was no way Tygre could stop thinking of Brad. She thought about the way he held her. She remembered all of their magical times together. She especially recalled the way he described his feelings about racing:

"To me, racing is the only way to express my freedom away from my last name, my parents, and the White House. I know the possible price. Every fraction of a second, I am aware of death, but still I love the speed and excitement. Racing is in my blood along with the tears of those who love me if I find misfortune. I am truly living, alive with the passion of it coursing through my veins every hour of the race, day and night. This is my choice,

Tygre. If I had to make the choice, I would rather die in my New Deal prototype than in my bed... alone."

"Tygre are you paying attention?" Agent Martin's heightened tone snapped her back to the present.

"I'm here," she whispered.

"Yes, but the question is *why* are you here." Malik's voice sent shock waves through Tygre. She turned quickly as he approached. "Why are you here and not in our pit?" He asked again.

"I ... I was just taking a break," Tygre answered.

"And who were you talking to, blond woman?"

"Your paranoia is getting the better of you. I was talking to a friend," Tygre pointed at her fake Bluetooth. "Mind your own business! Isn't it your turn on the track soon?"

"What's it to you? Just remember what I said in the trailer. I won't think twice about doing Khalil a favor and cutting your face if you talk!"

Tygre sighed as he walked away. She had begun to grow weary. She glanced at her wristwatch. Only 6:20 p.m. Time had become a slow-motion torture.

In the distance, the setting sun shed a reddish glow over the race circuit. Oblivious to nature's beauty, brightly colored cars, high-speed advertising bullets, screamed past Karim Racing's pit, jockeying for position.

The noise was deafening and ferocious within the canyon of the pit straight, walled by looming stands filled to capacity by enthusiastic spectators. The smell of burned oil and rubber hovered in the air of a clear cool evening. Tygre shivered, from the chill she told herself. Nothing more than that.

Khalil Karim pulled into pit lane for the change of drivers, clearly agitated. His LMP1 prototype's engine sputtered. The team mechanics swarmed all over the racer. Malik, composed and ready to take over, approached the car as Khalil jumped out.

"Don't say I didn't warn you," Malik whispered to Khalil as he slid into the driver's seat.

"What are you talking about?" Khalil was not in the mood for guessing games.

"Don't trust that blond woman. She is still involved with Harrington," Malik sneered.

Frustrated by his car's engine trouble and angered by the accusation, Khalil glowered back. "Where is Tygre? She should be here to greet me."

Tygre witnessed their exchange from a distance and now moved quickly toward the car. She pasted her best smile across a drained face.

"Glad you could find the time to join me," Khalil greeted her sarcastically. "I am tired and hungry. Perhaps you would care to walk with me to my trailer." Before Tygre could answer, Malik climbed into the car and roared away.

Khalil took hold of Tygre's arm. "Malik tells me you're still holding a torch for Harrington. Is that true?"

Tygre threw her arms around Khalil's neck and gave him a passionate kiss. "I have no idea why he would say such a foolish thing," she said, when she finally pulled back. "He must be jealous of us."

Khalil dismissed her kiss and glared at her angrily. "If it is true, I don't want you around!"

"I am here for you, Khalil, and only you. I can't wait to be alone with you to prove it." Tygre linked her arm through his and pressed herself against his body, beaming with a radiant smile. Cameras flashed as the ever-present international paparazzi rejoiced in the double opportunity. As the billionaire Arab and the European supermodel patiently posed, Khalil regained his composure and pulled Tygre closer to him. This was Khalil's world and he reveled in it.

It took all Tygre had to suppress the nauseating sense of dread that overcame her as she kissed Khalil again. She repeated a mantra in her head: *I am unique. I am strong. I will not fail. Brad…my Brad… I love you so much!*

Chapter 8

Eight Years Earlier
Warsaw, Poland

"Don't ever forget where you came from, Tygre," her father reminded her during one of her rare visits home from the convent. "We were wealthy and powerful once."

"That was in the past, Father...before I was born," Tygre responded.

"Our family has a rich history here," Adam persisted.

"But it's *your* story, not mine." Tygre sat behind an ironing board in the living room of the Topolski apartment.

The windows in the apartment were covered by heavy, dark burgundy curtains, tightly drawn together. Tygre sat slumped at the ironing board wearing a smudged pocketed apron. Her golden hair was pulled back from her face, which was drawn and pale.

Tygre was about to pick up the iron when her mother breezed into the room. "Hello, Mommy," Tygre said quietly.

Her father instinctively lowered his head and quickly left the room.

"What, no goodbye kiss?" Helena taunted him.

Her father responded by closing his bedroom door and noisily clicking the lock on the doorknob.

"Mommy," Tygre whispered. "You don't have to be so rude to him."

"Please, Theresa," Helena scoffed. "How many men do you know who cannot afford their own rent and refuse to leave their ex-wife's apartment after a divorce?" She rolled her eyes. "Pathetic. Really pathetic."

"This apartment has been in the Topolski family for generations," Tygre said. "I can understand why Daddy doesn't want to leave it. Maybe *you* should be the one to leave."

"Insolence does not become you, my dear," Helena snapped. "And, besides, you shouldn't comment on topics that don't concern you." Her mother strutted down the hall to close her bedroom door and then left the apartment.

Enough work, Tygre thought, as her mother stomped out. She put away the iron and in one smooth movement, untied her apron, released her ponytail and headed to the bathroom, eager to slip into a warm shower. The ringing of the telephone stopped her on her way.

Anxious that her father not be disturbed, Tygre answered on the first ring.

"Well, if it isn't the most beautiful girl in Warsaw." The gentleman's voice was sexy and smooth.

"Who are you calling for?" Tygre asked, suspicious.

"I'm calling for Miss Tygre Topolska."

"Speaking," Tygre answered timidly.

"Then I'm in luck. I *have* reached the most beautiful girl in Warsaw," the mysterious voice said." This is Roman Zajda."

A smile spread across Tygre's face at the mention of his name.

Roman Zajda, one of Warsaw's leading bachelors, was a successful architect. At the age of 33, he had already established an impressive career dossier along with a world-class reputation for womanizing. The first time Helena saw him leer at her young daughter at a small café in Warsaw, she issued a stern warning.

"Don't allow his charm to fool you, Theresa. He will eat you alive and spit you out."

"I don't know what you're talking about, Mommy," Tygre answered innocently. "I was only waving back at him." Tygre coyly slid a wisp of hair behind her ear and smiled in Roman's direction. "He looks like a nice person."

"Well, he's not!" Helena argued.

"Good afternoon, ladies," Roman purred, passing their table on his way out of the café. He came close enough for Tygre to feel his body brush softly against the back of her hair.

Tygre stole one last look at Roman's handsome figure as he straddled his blue Vespa and drove off. She wondered what it would feel like to sit on the back seat with her arms wrapped around him as they rode through town. She imagined leaning her head against his strong back.

As if she could read her daughter's thoughts, Helena chided her, "Get any thoughts of him out of your head immediately, young lady!"

"Mommy," Tygre said, "I was just saying hello."

"Make sure that that's where it ends." Helena warned.

Tygre had promised her mother that her interaction with the Warsaw playboy would end right then and there. But now, in the late-evening quiet of the apartment, she felt a strange excitement brewing inside her.

"How did you get my number?" she asked, feeling at once curious and elated.

"I can be very resourceful when I see something I want."

A nervous laugh erupted involuntarily from Tygre. "What is it you want?"

"I want to see you…tonight. I'd like to take you to a very special movie. *La Belle de Jour* is playing at nine o'clock at the Polonez."

"I'm flattered…but I'm not sure my mother would approve," Tygre said apologetically.

"Don't tell me you allow other people to control your heart," Roman said, "especially not your mother!"

"Well..." Tygre hesitated, pondering the idea of making an adult decision about her life for the first time.

"You don't strike me as the obedient type. You look like more of a free spirit," Roman added.

"Where shall I meet you?" Tygre asked, breaking into a smile.

"That's my girl!" Roman said. "I'll meet you at the Polonez in one hour."

Tygre showered quickly then took her time applying her makeup. She carefully pulled her hair into a twist and framed her face with a pair of small pearl earrings. Finally, she slid into a clean satin slip and crept into her mother's bedroom to steal a few sprays of Shalimar and a beautiful pale organza dress from her closet. She gently stepped inside the dress and zipped it up, examining herself from all angles in Helena's full-length mirror.

Satisfied, Tygre slowly tiptoed out of Helena's bedroom, high heels in hand. Exuberant, she quietly closed the door behind her, leaving the apartment on her first official date.

Within 20 minutes, Tygre found herself absorbed into a large crowd queuing in front of the Polonez Architect Club. Located in a three-story townhouse with a large garden, this former private residence was the "it" meeting place of the moment.

When she stepped through the door, Tygre was immediately approached, not by a bouncer as she had feared, but by a relentless photographer. To Tygre's surprised, he pointed his lens directly at her and followed her every move.

"Hey, pretty girl. Look at me. Smile, smile at the camera! One more time please. Again, beautiful, that's perfect! Now, look at me one more time. Here, come here!

Finally Roman approached. He *smiled courteously at the paparazzo and whisked Tygre safely away.*

"Is this what it's like for girls who date the legendary Roman Zajda?" Tygre asked.

"No, my dear," Roman answered her. "It's only when they are as beautiful as you."

Tygre smiled, pleased with herself. Roman looked exceptionally handsome tonight, she thought, sporting a brown suede jacket, pale blue polo shirt and a pair of gray flannel slacks. And tonight, he's with me.

From the first time Roman held her hand until the tender kiss he pressed on her moist lips as he put her carefully into a cab at the end of the evening, Tygre's first rendezvous was perfect in every way.

That night, as she settled into her bed, Tygre replayed the evening over and over in her mind. Dancing in Roman's arms had undoubtedly been the romantic highlight of her life. She smiled and buried her cheek in her pillow. She knew she would have wonderful dreams that night, and she couldn't wait until the next time she would see Roman Zajda.

—

For the remainder of her vacation, Tygre played and re-played the evening with Roman in her mind. Even her return to the dreaded convent was softened by the exhilaration she felt each time she conjured up the feeling of Roman's arms about her.

One day at lunch, as she poked a fork into a transparent cucumber, calculating how soon she might persuade her parents to allow her another visit home, she heard her name called: "Topolska, to the principal's office, immediately!"

What have I done this time? Tygre wondered, knowing that visits to Sister Maria's office meant nothing but trouble. She kept her gaze lowered as she passed by a table of girls provoking her with mocking chants. "Trouble ...trouble! Uh oh, Topolska, you're in trouble now!"

Tygre timidly tapped on the principal's massive oak door. "Come in." Sister Maria's stern voice pierced the thick walls.

Tygre entered Sister Maria's office. A former library, it was dimly lit and adorned with hand-carved, dark wood paneling. Leather-bound books lined the walls of mahogany shelves. The smoldering logs in the fireplace emitted a musty smell of damp pine.

Sister Maria sat behind a massive partners-style desk, her hands resting atop a tan file folder. Beside her, in a large leather chair, sat a weary looking Adam Topolski. Tygre instantly knew she was in serious trouble.

"Father," she said, trying to calm the quiver in her voice. "Is everything all right?"

"Sit down!" Sister Maria rose quickly to her feet and glared at Tygre. Adam leaned forward and looked directly at his daughter as she slipped slowly into a chair next to him. His face was twisted with shame and disappointment.

"What is it, Father?" Tygre asked, afraid to know the answer.

"You just turned 16!" Sister Maria's voice boomed in an unfamiliar high pitch, taking Tygre's breath away. "You have top grades. You were my favorite pupil!" Sister Maria, exasperated, lifted the folder and slammed it on her desk. "You have a real talent for mathematics. I had such high hopes for you becoming a teacher," Sister Maria said through clenched teeth.

"Thank you, Sister," Tygre said, perplexed.

Sister Maria's high-pitched tone intensified. "And now those dreams have been dashed! Because of your stupidity!"

"I don't understand," Tygre said, her eyes darting from her father to Sister Maria and back again. As terrified as she was, she wished one of them would explain.

"Just look at what you have done!" Sister Maria seethed, hardly able to contain her anger. She pulled a magazine from inside the folder and held it up for Tygre to see.

The magazine was MODA, a popular tabloid with the largest circulation in Poland. On the cover was a photo of a stunning young woman posing in front of the Polonez Architect Club. A broad smile graced her face.

Tygre gazed at the photograph, hardly able to believe it was her. A tiny smile formed on her lips and, for a moment, she allowed herself to feel flattered.

"Theresa!" her father spoke up.

Tygre looked up from the cover. "I don't understand how this happened," she blurted.

"The picture does not lie!" Sister Maria said, "It is you Theresa, isn't it?"

Tygre sank in her chair, barely able to look at her father. Shame and dread swelled within her and broke like a crashing wave.

"I'm sorry, Father," she said, "I know I shouldn't have gone there. I'm so sorry."

Visits to clubs such as the Polonez, synonymous with late nights of drinking, explicit dancing and all that came with it, were strictly off limits to all students of the convent. The club represented everything the Catholic Church stood firmly against. Tygre knew she would never be forgiven for daring to go there. Still, somewhere inside, Tygre felt a sense of relief. She knew her dreaded days at the Convent of the Sisters of St. Joseph were coming to an early end.

"Tygre, you have disgraced yourself. But, more importantly, by association with this den of sins, you have dishonored the Church, our school and the convent. Shame on you!" Sister Maria's words cut through Tygre like a knife, but didn't inflict nearly as much pain as the silent look of despair on Adam's face.

"I am so sorry, Father. Please forgive me." Tygre reached out to Adam and kissed him on his hand, deliberately avoiding Sister Maria's glare.

Sister Maria growled unsympathetically. "Your days at the convent are over, and so is your future education. Pack your things and leave at once. I pray to never see you again!"

As Sister Maria stormed noisily out of her office, Tygre kept her gaze firmly fixed on her father. "I'm very sorry, Father," she said again. "I should've known better. It was a mistake. I didn't mean to embarrass you."

—

Back at home, it was scarcely better. The moment Tygre entered the apartment, her mother advanced in a fury, waving the copy of MODA angrily in front of her. "Is that my blue organza dress you're parading around in like a little trollop?" she asked.

Tygre looked away.

"How could you, Theresa?"

"I'm sorry, Mommy." Tygre's eyes were glassy and full.

"Save those tears for someone who cares!" Helena growled. "You are a disgrace to this family!"

Helena paced in circles around Tygre as Adam sat by, helpless, silent and sad.

"Your father would let you get away with murder!" Helena taunted. "He looked the other way when you were sneaking out at night in my clothing."

"It wasn't Father's fault," Tygre said.

"Of course it's his fault!" Helena snapped. "This is just another one of his many faults!"

Tygre glanced quickly at her father. She couldn't stand seeing him humiliated.

"Stop!" she said firmly to Helena. "Don't blame Daddy for this!"

Helena advanced at Tygre, moving boldly into her personal space. She stared angrily at Tygre. Time stood still. Tygre held her breath and prepared for the worst. She had never spoken back to her mother this way before.

When Helena raised her hand, Tygre shut her eyes tightly and shuddered. After a few seconds, she felt Helena's warm breath up against her cheek as she spoke in short measured beats, "You're ... not ... even ... worth it."

"That's enough, Helena," Adam said quietly. Watching the tears run down his daughter's pained face was more than he could stand.

Helena turned quickly and shot a look of contempt at Adam before storming out of the apartment with a parting shot. "Congratulations! You are a complete failure as I knew you would be! All the doors to your future are now slammed shut! I hope you're proud of yourself!"

Chapter 9

Le Mans
8:15 p.m. Saturday

Tygre glanced at her watch and took a deep breath. *Nineteen hours to go before this nightmare is over!* She quickly scanned the interior of Khalil Karim's trailer, one which offered all the modern luxuries his vast fortune could afford, including a bank of high-tech computers.

Nor had any expense been spared on his favorite dishes. They had been prepared and displayed on the small countertop. Some were chilled to perfection while others were preheated. The interior banquettes were wide and covered with silk pillow cases. Several prayer rugs were rolled and neatly stored.

Khalil began to stir from a deep sleep.

"Did you have a good rest?" Tygre asked when she saw him beginning to wake. "You've been sleeping for almost two hours. I'll bet you're hungry." Tygre got up from her seat. She gently ran her fingers over the earpiece to assure it was in place. "Can I fix you a plate?"

"I am always hungry for you, Tygre." Khalil reached out and grabbed Tygre's arm, pulling her down onto the bed next to him. "Come here and let me ravish you."

"Don't you have to save your energy for driving?" Tygre said sweetly.

"You are such a tease, but unfortunately, you are right, my dear. When this race is over, we will make up for the lost time!" Khalil gave her a look that was both desirous and intimidating. "Then you can show me how much you care for me. For now, let me have a little peek."

He slowly unzipped Tygre's jumpsuit and brushed his lips against her nipple, grazing the silver pendant that dangled between her breasts. Tygre slowly pulled it to the side and moaned softly, faking pleasure.

"Malik is convinced you are talking to Harrington," Khalil said keeping his lips close to Tygre's breast.

"No, Khalil, I am not talking to anyone but you," Tygre whispered, hoping he couldn't sense her fear. "Malik is paranoid. If I didn't want to be here, I wouldn't have called you in the first place. I'm here with you now, am I not?"

Tygre put her hands gently on each side of Khalil's face and drew him up away from her breast. She placed a soft, reassuring kiss on his lips and ran her fingers through his dark hair, smiling coyly. "You must be tense after all that driving. Would you like me to rub your shoulders?"

"That's not what I had in mind, but it would be a good start."

Tygre laughed nervously and began to rub the back of Khalil's neck. To her relief, a radio call on the crew channel from Karim Racing's pit pulled Khalil's attention quickly back to the race.

"We are still having issues with the engine," the pit crew manager's voice crackled over the radio. "Malik has pulled in again. You have less than an hour to eat and be ready for your next stint. Pierre is up next."

As the radio snapped into silence, Tygre looked at Khalil inquisitively.

"Pierre Auter is our third driver, a great Le Mans veteran," he explained. "You may have seen him in pit lane earlier. You'll meet him soon enough."

Khalil stood and stretched. "I don't have a lot of time. Let's take a walk to the Village for some fresh air." He grabbed a Red Bull from the refrigerator and reached for Tygre's hand. "This is all I need for now."

"That sounds great," Tygre said, happy to be anywhere but inside the trailer. She donned her Karim Racing logo cap, took Khalil's hand and followed him outside.

In the twilight, Le Mans Village resembled Manhattan's Union Square in the evening, she thought. With the Hermès boutique, the ultra-sophisticated car manufacturers' suites and exclusive restaurants available only to the factory reps, sponsors, drivers and the media, the Village looked like a motor-racing bazaar.

"Mmm, doesn't that smell good?" Tygre said as the aroma of freshly roasted peanuts and burnt sugar lingered pleasantly in the air.

"Would you like to try a crêpe?" Khalil invited.

Tygre looked longingly at the strawberry-filled crêpes topped with crème fraiche. "They look irresistible," Tygre said, "but they're definitely not on a model's diet."

Khalil stopped in front of one of the many massive video monitors strategically placed along the 13.63 km track. "Let's check on Harrington's lap time. I'm sure you're curious to know how he is doing."

"Why do you say such things? I'm only interested in Karim Racing," Tygre lied as she took a peek at the video monitor. She smiled discreetly when she saw the New Deal's No.1 car was in first place.

"He is in the lead," Khalil grudgingly announced, "but he won't be for long. I'll take care of him soon enough, you'll see."

Tygre stayed silent. But as they walked toward pit lane, a sinking feeling came over her. She hardly dared to think what Khalil might have meant by his last comment.

Amid the sounds of animated conversations and roaring engines, it took Khalil's cell phone several rings before it caught his attention. He answered curtly, then turned to her. "It's time for me to drive," he told her as he pocketed the phone.

Within minutes Khalil was standing in the Karim Racing's pit dressed again in his fireproof Nomex jumpsuit, ready to go at a moment's notice. Seconds later, Malik pulled in and jumped out of the racer as the team went to work on the car. The precision of the crew made a 10-second tire change appear effortless, Tygre thought.

Malik pointed at the manager and shouted, "Get in touch with Pierre. Have him ready to drive in two and a half hours max. After this I want Khalil to rest." As soon as Malik finished laying down the orders, the five-man crew stepped back to let Khalil slip into the car.

Without acknowledging Tygre, Khalil jumped in and immediately gunned the engine under the watchful eye of the noticeably frustrated Karim Racing manager. Khalil then flawlessly roared back onto the track as Malik observed.

Amidst increasing tension in the pit, Tygre watched Khalil until the car disappeared out of sight. As she turned to walk away, she collided with Malik who was looming directly behind her.

"Stop creeping up on me like that." Tygre exclaimed.

"Get used to it, blond woman." Malik replied with disdain.

"You are a gutless barbarian!" she spat. But Tygre's anger was Malik's cue to move in even closer.

"You'll get yours! And that's a promise." Malik said as he placed a well-worn hat bearing Karim Racing's logo on his head. Finally, he turned away to answer his ringing cell phone.

She took the opportunity to walk away and, once out of Malik's sight, made contact with Agent Martin. "Aside from the obvious, something's just not right about this man," Tygre whispered into her pendant. "Malik is a psycho. He's everything a race-car driver should not be."

"Stick with it, Tygre," Martin quickly answered back. "You're doing just fine. Don't let him get under your skin. I know that might be difficult, but hang in there."

Tygre walked back toward Malik just as he was ending his phone call. He adjusted his ill-fitting metal-framed glasses and glared angrily at Tygre, ready to spit more venom at her. But Tygre was quicker on the draw. "How can you see through those glasses? They don't even fit." Tygre commented, feigning interest.

"It's nothing you need to be concerned about," Malik shot back.

"I'm not concerned. I'm just curious."

"Anything else I can answer for you, Mademoiselle?" Malik scoffed.

"As a matter of fact there is." Tygre focused on the unusually luxurious-looking, fabric covered car seat inserts she noticed earlier, "I was actually wondering what those are for?"

Malik tensed, perhaps surprised that she had taken his invitation for questions seriously. But his intrinsic need to demonstrate his intellect overtook him, and he answered evenly. "These inserts are used to form fit the driver comfortably in the car."

"I see."

"For a dumb blond bitch, you ask a lot of questions. Are you digging up answers to report back to Harrington?" Malik stared at her pointedly.

"You're being ridiculous," Tygre answered coolly. "I was just curious."

"Don't overwork your brain too much, but if you must know, these seat inserts are specially molded for each driver," Malik volunteered.

"Nice thick wool...must be comfortable. It looks expensive."

Malik rolled his eyes upward. "Only a silly and shallow woman like you would notice the fabric."

Tygre wondered why Malik had both of the seat inserts in his possession. Why was Khalil driving without one? Or was he? As if reading her mind, Malik answered promptly, "We always keep a few spares on hand."

Tygre shrugged her shoulders and walked away from Malik toward Khalil's personal trailer. "Whatever! I'm leaving," she said and dismissed him unceremoniously.

"And where do you think you're going?" Malik demanded.

"Now look who's so curious." Tygre said steadily, trying to remain confident.

"Just answer the question," Malik demanded.

"Herve du Bois of Tele-Mondial wants to interview me," Tygre lied. "I'm going to freshen up before I meet with him." Without waiting for a response, Tygre slowly walked from the pit area toward Khalil's trailer. Malik watched her closely. But to Tygre's relief, he remained in pit lane.

After a few moments, Martin's voice resounded in Tygre's ear. "Good job, Tygre. He's not following you anymore. You are getting close to the line with Malik. I wouldn't push him too much more if I were you. He is an unpredictable son of a bitch. Now, let's get on with the job. Are you ready to place the listening device I gave you earlier in the trailer now?"

"Yes, I think it's time. I'll do anything to expose Malik and the rest of them.

"Stay calm, Tygre, and focus!" Martin said. "You're doing a great job."

Tygre pursed her lips and headed directly for the trailer. With one last look to make sure Malik was not following her, she stepped inside and locked the door. She quickly scanned her surroundings. The walls and the cabinets of the trailer were slick and ultra modern. The lack of crevices, openings, or shelves presented Tygre with a real challenge.

With trembling fingers, she tore open the envelope. The remote microphone, a silver-colored object the size of a pencil eraser, with an adhesive strip attached to the back, was tiny and clearly easy to conceal. But if it were discovered that the trailer was bugged, there would be little doubt that Tygre was the culprit.

"I'm in the trailer. I told Malik I'm getting ready for an interview. I have to hurry," Tygre reported to Martin.

Against her better judgment, Tygre placed the device under a large-screened laptop, one of many. It was not an ideal hiding place but, in her haste, she couldn't find a better one.

"Doug, there are a lot of personal computers in here. Shouldn't most of this equipment associated with the race be in pit lane or in the garage?"

"I would think so. Good observation. But, for now, just place the device and get out of there."

"It's done!" Tygre took one last look at the small microphone to make sure it was secure.

As she turned toward the door, she noticed a silver-framed snapshot of a young man with Khalil in the background propped on a shelf. Tygre froze. With a full head of hair and without his glasses, a younger Malik looked joyful as he smiled and embraced Khalil in the Saudi desert.

A wave of distaste swept over her. A strong suggestion of sensual affection between the two men emanated from the photograph. At that moment, Tygre recalled with dread her own sexual encounter with Khalil and the guilt-ridden aftermath that haunted her for months.

Malik's joyful face in the photo was quite the departure from the demeanor he had exhibited with her and in the pictures shown to her by the FBI in Florida. *"Youssaf is a terrorist. Intelligence tells us he trained with Al Qaeda and its explosives experts. He is well-known to the FBI for this skill set and for his electrical engineering expertise."* Tygre well remembered Martin's briefing.

"Doug, can you hear me? I see an old photograph of Khalil with Malik. I hardly recognized them! They look so different."

"Different you say? How and in what way?" Martin snapped.

Tygre quickly glanced at the photo of the attractive couple. "It explains why Malik hates me so much. Maybe I'm interfering with a personal relationship he has with Khalil," Tygre said.

"That's inconsequential, Tygre. These people are ruthless! Given any opportunity, Karim and Youssaf will strike without regard for each other or for you. I have no doubt about it," Martin stated without hesitation. "For God's sake, Tygre, stay focused!"

"I'm doing my best, Doug. But I'm still trying to come to terms with all of this..." Tygre took a deep breath as she reflected on the depth of their deceptions. "Gay, I understand. High on each other, yes. But ruthless terrorists! I cannot believe that I got involved with this man."

"Don't beat yourself up. How could you have possibly known? Take it easy, and concentrate."

"I should have known..."

"Tygre! Stop it!" Martin's abrupt tone startled Tygre, almost causing her to drop the picture. She snapped back to attention and carefully placed the frame back on the shelf.

"The reception from the listening device is not clear on our end," Martin said. "You need to reposition the bug and get the hell out of there."

"I'm on it," Tygre said. As she reached behind the computer, she heard footsteps on the gravel. "Someone's coming! I have to go and unlock the door. It's always left open when the trailer is occupied! Khalil's rules!"

Seconds after turning the lock, Tygre sprinted over to the banquette on the far side of the room and quickly dropped herself down onto it, reaching for a magazine. The door swung open and Khalil entered looking worn and tired. He reached for an ice pack and placed it on his back. Deep dark circles lined his bloodshot eyes.

"Greetings, my dear Tygre. What are you up to?"

"Nothing much," Tygre responded, quickly closing the magazine and praying Khalil wouldn't detect her heavy breathing. "How did you do?" she asked coolly, moving over to the bed where Khalil sat taking off his driving boots. He stretched his body and leaned back, watching Tygre intently. He hated to admit his failures, especially when they were tied to Brad Harrington's successes.

"That bloody New Deal is in the lead. I was two seconds behind Harrington! But it's still early in the race and anything can happen. Wait until it starts raining. I'll catch him then without a doubt."

Tygre forced a smile. "This is a nice surprise. I wasn't expecting to see you so soon. Who is driving now?"

"Pierre took over. I am very tired. I need to get some rest." He pulled Tygre onto the bed next to him and laid his head in her lap. Tygre patted his head softly and waited for him to doze off.

In less than five minutes, and much to Tygre's relief, Khalil fell asleep. It was a restless sleep and, Tygre noticed, it didn't seem to bring much peace or respite to Khalil. His body periodically contorted in a series of involuntary twitches. Tygre saw it as an opportunity to exit the trailer. She gently rolled Khalil's head onto the pillow, quietly slipped out from under him and tiptoed across the trailer to the door. Just as she was about to open it, a jubilant Malik burst in, screaming triumphantly. "Praise Allah! Khalil, wake up!" Malik walked immediately to the bed and shook his sleeping co-driver.

"What's going on?" Khalil mumbled, lifting his head from the pillow.

"I have wonderful news! There was a serious, multiple-car collision at *Arnage.* I just heard on the crew channel that one of the New Deal cars is involved. It skidded in some fluid and hit the barrier. I can't get any more information at this point."

Khalil sat straight up as Tygre leaned against the banquette and swallowed hard. Malik glared at her with delight while pressing down on Khalil's shoulder, giving him a gentle massage as he spoke. "Look at her! Look at her, Khalil! What more proof do you need? Does she look as if she is over Harrington? When will you believe that she is here for ulterior reasons? She is a fucking spy for Harrington's team. I know it! "

"What happened on the track?" Tygre asked, ignoring Malik's outburst.

"Sweat it, blond woman! That's all I am going to tell you!"

Malik washed his hands before unfolding his prayer rug. He knelt down and began chanting the *Shahada.* "*There is no God but Allah, and Muhammad is His messenger.*"

Khalil, now fully awake, knelt beside Malik. In a state of grateful euphoria, they exuberantly embraced their faith. As the two, now prostrate terrorists, joined forces in prayer, Tygre looked on helplessly, barely able to hide the dread she felt building inside her. How on earth had she come to such a place in her life? How?

Chapter 10

Seven Years Earlier
Lobby of the Hotel Bristol
Warsaw, Poland

In 1901, when it became a hotel, the Bristol was the meeting place of high society, artists and international dignitaries. Through the years, ownership of the hotel changed hands in a familiar fashion, which was not unlike the fate of the Polish nation. Poles became used to it. In the early 1980s, after a massive renovation, the Bristol's grand re-opening once again established the former estate as one of the most prestigious hotels in Europe.

Its characteristic art nouveau silhouette graced Warsaw's skyline for years. Beautifully complementing the royal route of Poland's capital, it was one of many stunning exemplars of architecture ranging from the 16th Century to present day and within walking distance of Old Town, the Royal Castle, the National Theatre and the Presidential Palace. The five-star Hotel Bristol had always been the place to stay, and to be seen, when in Warsaw.

The staff of the Bristol was well-versed in handling discreet appearances of high-profile guests as well as organized commotions associated with frequent visits of celebrities and heads of state. But even this notoriously unflappable team could be seen exchanging anxious glances and knowing nods on the day their most tightly wound guest entered in her usual flourish of frenzy.

"Vite, vite! I haven't a moment to spare!" she barked over her shoulder to the attentive girl following closely at her heels. The woman was Madame Marie-Laure de La Sable, a slender Parisian brunette in her mid-fifties.

Attired in La Dolce Vita's latest haute couture, a chic, pale gray, wool dress and understated silver jewelry, she emanated confidence and determination. She peeled the gloves from her impeccably manicured fingers and tossed them toward her assistant's face. "Claire, dépêchez-vous, vite! My coffee is cold again," she snapped. "Bring me another cup tout de suite!"

Madame de La Sable was the director of marketing for La Dolce Vita's line of beauty products in Europe. She had become the tireless epicenter of LDV's quest for a new face. Since she had issued LDV's announcement for its new model search two weeks ago, dozens of young girls queued every day outside the Bristol, hoping for the chance to meet Madame de La Sable personally and possibly change their lives in the process.

She walked briskly past the throngs of hopefuls lining up at the hotel's main lobby entrance and pushed her way past the Bristol's bell captain, dropping her keys carelessly on his stand without a word of greeting. "That's my car out front," she said as she passed.

The front desk manager hurried toward her with an outstretched hand. "Welcome, Madame."

"Has my room been properly set this time?" she asked.

"Yes, Madame, it..."

"And my Evian?"

"At room temperature as you requested." The hotel's general manager walked briskly beside her as she sashayed down the long hallway to her usual meeting room. He opened the door and extended an arm to welcome her in.

"Does Madame desire anything else?"

Madame de La Sable's eyes traveled to each corner of the room and back again before, to the manager's relief, she nodded her approval. "This will do."

"Thank you, Madame, very well."

"Where's that girl with my coffee?" Madame de La Sable demanded.

"Here! I'm here!" Claire hurried past the general manager carefully balancing a tray of fresh brewed coffee along with a china cup and saucer, creamer and sugar bowl. She placed the tray on the desk next to Madame de La Sable. "I'm sorry for the delay," she said through quick breaths.

Madame de La Sable eyed Claire's shaky hands as she poured the coffee and added just the right portions of cream and sugar to the steaming brew. Madame paced back and forth in front of the desk, inhaling deeply on her cigarette. "Think we'll find any gems in today's batch of dreadful hopefuls?" she asked.

Claire knew better than to answer. Madame de La Sable had searched for weeks to find the new face of LDV. The prize was a million-dollar contract, and it had attracted thousands of optimistic contenders from many different cities. But, to date, none had proven themselves worthy of the distinction. No Eastern European beauty queen or teenage model could meet Madame de La Sable's criteria. She wanted an innocent beauty with sex appeal and personality with a modicum of maturity; someone who could penetrate the global market for a line of high-end beauty products for teenage girls.

Madame de La Sable planned to reverse the trend of hiring well-known actresses as spokeswomen. *"Where's the challenge there? Where's the innovation?" She had raised the rhetorical question in her presentation to LDV owner, Sir Ari Beafetter, and was met with an agreeable nod.*

"Why conform when I can transform?" she had proclaimed spontaneously in what she would later refer to as her stroke of sheer marketing brilliance. "LDV doesn't need an actress. LDV needs the real thing. I will transform an unknown beauty into a spokesmodel extraordinaire! I will create the new face of LDV."

Sir Ari Beafetter mentally calculated the cost of an unknown versus the price to retain a celebrity actress and decided Madame de La Sable's idea was much more attractive to his bottom line.

The hum of teenage chatter lured Madame de La Sable back to reality. She glanced at the long line of young girls in their off-the-rack department store fashions now lining the hallways just outside the door. She watched doubtfully as Claire vigilantly checked their names against her list before breezing back into the room. "Ready, Madame," she said.

"Oh, Claire," Madame de La Sable sighed tapping her cigarette against the side of a glass ashtray, "how many more of these dull faces must I endure?"

"We're seeing 38 today, Madame," Claire answered.

"I already know these girls simply will not do. They are ordinary and provincial looking. You need to screen them better. Weed out the plain ones."

"But, Madame, I am doing my best," Claire protested.

"Your best is simply not good enough! We are running out of time and I am running out of patience. Send these half-wits home and try again!"

"What are you waiting for?" Madame snapped at Claire. "Send these girls away and watch me do your job for you! Take note as I handle this myself. Maybe you'll learn something." Madame snatched her wrap and gloves from the desk and whisked through the doorway.

"You must be hoping for a miracle," she muttered to the last girl in line as she breezed through the corridor. Madame secretly enjoyed the sea of confused faces and shattered dreams she left in her wake. It reinforced her degree of self-importance, which occasionally waned with the passing years.

With a one-week deadline approaching, Madame de La Sable knew how to fall on her old stand-by. Ransacking the latest fashion publications in search of a photogenic beauty had proved to be successful in the past. It took her a scant five minutes to scoop up an armload of magazines from the newsstand across the street.

Madame de La Sable returned to the Bristol triumphant, armed with her "research materials." She tossed the stack on the desk where Claire sat frantically pouring through A-List files and VIP contacts. The issue of MODA landed cover-side-up on the desktop, narrowly missing Claire.

Madame leaned in for a closer look at the blonde beauty featured on the glossy MODA cover. "Voila! I told you! I knew I would find her! Madame de La Sable clapped her hands and lit a second cigarette, not realizing she was already smoking one. "If I need something done right, I always have to do it myself." A broad grin graced her face, lifting the lines from her brow, as she held up the latest edition of MODA. "Who is this girl?"

Claire picked up the magazine and glanced at the cover, then flipped it open to find the answer to her employer's question.

After a moment, she glanced up. "Her name is Theresa Topolska. A nobody from Warsaw. Dismissed from a convent for sneaking out on a date with this playboy." Claire brandished the cover, which depicted Tygre on the arm of a dashing looking older man.

Madame de La Sable stared back at her assistant as if she were mentally defective. "Well, she is a nobody about to become somebody. Find her. Tout de suite! She is perfect!"

—

The next morning, armed with all the beauty and youth her mother had come to resent, Tygre arrived an hour early for her appointment with Madame de La Sable.

The million-dollar-dream maker looked even more sophisticated and polished in person than she did on the society pages Tygre–now back at home and living miserably with her mother–had read on her morning bus rides. Madame de La Sable sipped coffee and smoked continuously as she sat grandly in a makeshift photo studio in Old Town Warsaw. She was surrounded by half a dozen stylists, hair dressers, makeup artists and assistants.

The bouncing strobe flashlights of several cameras ricocheting off the white walls of the studio temporarily blinded Tygre as she walked in. The room was warm and sparsely furnished. Tygre's felt a wave of nausea mixed with despair sweep over her. Somehow she had managed to show up to the most important meeting of her life looking like a world-weary street tart. But perhaps it should not be such a surprise, for in fact, that is exactly what she felt like.

When she had first returned to Warsaw from the convent, she had been an obedient child, anxious to obey her parents' dictum that she never lay eyes on Roman Zajda again. Though secretly she hoped that Roman would find a way to scale the veritable castle walls that surrounded her, after months passed without a word from him, she began to tell herself that those were only childish fantasies.

And meantime, she had discovered a silver lining in that dark MODA cloud. After her appearance in the magazine, she had been contacted by several local modeling agencies. They were anxious to meet the young woman whose beauty radiated straight off the publication cover. Tygre had often been told that she was beautiful, but she had been reluctant to believe it.

Soon, however, she was taking on a steady stream of modeling jobs for Warsaw businesses, fulfilling not only her mother's requirement that she earn her keep but also Tygre's own need to validate herself. She began to feel more confident in her beauty and in her sexuality, and she took on an even more extraordinary glow. Tygre appeared on several more magazine covers and soon became Moda's favorite model.

"Your good looks and lack of experience could attract undesirable company," Adam warned his daughter. "You must always protect our family name and your own reputation. You survived one brush with scandal," he reminded her, "but you might not be so lucky the next time."

"I understand, Daddy. I'll be careful, I promise." Tygre assured him.

And she was careful, until one day, a few weeks after her 18th birthday, when she glanced up from a magazine she was reading while waiting for a photographer on the set of her latest shoot. When she saw Roman striding toward her, she thought at first it was a vision. She could not move or speak, but simply watched as he moved toward her, keeping his gaze fixed on hers.

She smiled as he approached, but neither one of them said a word. Roman brushed up against her, silently slipping his business card into her open palm. "I'll be waiting for your call," he purred into her ear as he swaggered quietly away.

Tygre's hands shook as she dialed his number later that evening.

"What are you doing this weekend?" she bravely asked.

As she sat on the back of his purring Vespa with her arms wrapped around Roman's waist, she couldn't help recalling how many times she had dreamed of that moment.

She wore a short black evening dress and her mother's pearls. They sped through a large square of Warsaw's Old Town toward a scarcely lit, scenic and cobblestone mews that led to the steep and cozy stairway of Roman's flat, a quaint, top-floor garret. He kissed Tygre as they made their way through the doorway.

"I can't wait to be with you," Roman uttered as he pulled her toward him, closing the door behind them. He led Tygre in and pressed her up against the wall just inside the hallway. With one hand, he caressed her hips. With the other he placed Tygre's hand on his erect penis. "I've been aroused for hours."

Tygre grinned with anticipation. "I want you, too."

Roman guided her into his living room where the Vistula River glistened with distant lights just outside the picture window. Chopin's *Raindrop Prelude* played softly in the background as Roman embraced her.

"Roman, I have been waiting for so long!" Tygre murmured.

"Ah yes, my own Lolita!" he whispered back. He led her to a large, pillow-covered bed, handing her a glass of wine.

"Have a little drink. It'll help you relax," he said. He slowly removed Tygre's pearls and placed them on the bedside table.

"Turn around, darling." Roman gently kissed the back of Tygre's neck as his hands skillfully unzipped her dress. "Your skin is so soft," Roman whispered into her ear.

As her dress fell to the floor, Tygre turned to face Roman. They locked in a kiss, while Roman expertly unhooked Tygre's black satin bra. Seconds later her panties were at her ankles, and Roman paused briefly to take in his prize before he laid Tygre on the bed and gently lowered himself on top of her.

Tygre folded into his arms with a moan. Her eyes closed. The room began to spin. She clung to Roman tightly, her body trembling as it never had. She had yearned to be with Roman and wanted to feel his body next to hers for a very long time. And now that she was 18, she considered Roman a birthday present to herself.

She loved the smell and the feel of his fit and muscular body. She burned with passion for him. His penis was hard and forceful while his lips were soft and tender. Tygre had never seen a naked man before, let alone one in a fully aroused state. But Roman was exquisite. She could not wait for her climax.

"Oh Roman, I have never been kissed like this before," Tygre softly confessed in his ear.

"Just enjoy it," he told her. "Have another sip of wine."

Tygre obliged. She already felt intoxicated. *Was it the wine or Roman or both?* Tygre smiled, deciding that she no longer cared. All she wanted was to enjoy the moment, enjoy Roman, and enjoy all of it.

So this is what it feels like to be loved by a man, Tygre thought. *This is the real thing.* With all the optimism of adolescent infatuation, Tygre began to plan her future with Roman. *We will be a couple, and my life will be changed forever. Roman will take care of me.*

Tygre reveled in her fantasy. Roman moved swiftly. He could not stop kissing her, peppering her neck with small, bite-size marks. Her desire soared, heightened by Roman's indisputable skill. She felt, in truth, as if she were entering a trance.

It must be love! she kept convincing herself. Tygre's body glistened with perspiration. She reached out to touch Roman's hand, but he placed it instead on his throbbing erection.

"Make it wet. Kiss it." He spoke softly and placed his thick penis in Tygre's open mouth, nearly choking her.

"Move your lips, up and down…careful…with your teeth," Roman instructed Tygre. She stared at him with moist, eager eyes.

"You're doing a wonderful job. Don't stop. It feels so good," Roman encouraged her. His voice trembled as he stroked Tygre's vagina.

"Oh God, you are so wet," he whispered.

"I want you, Roman. Take me now. I want to be yours. We belong together," Tygre exclaimed.

No longer able to contain himself, Roman swiftly parted Tygre's legs and penetrated her forcefully. He moaned with delight. She cried out, but he kept on going until he climaxed. Almost immediately, he became erect again and penetrated her once more, moving determinedly until he came a second time.

Finally satisfied, Roman lay exhausted by Tygre's side and looked at her as if he saw her for the first time. When he noticed the tears of pain running down Tygre's face and the red stains beside her on the bed, Roman grimaced and let out a sigh. He quickly got up from the bed, covered himself with a towel and paced around the bedroom, staring at Tygre. He looked confused, even angry.

"How could you not tell me you were a virgin? Look at the blood. Those are my best Italian sheets."

Tygre was stunned. "I am so sorry. I love you, Roman. I wanted you to be my first, to surprise you."

He remained silent. Tygre looked up at him, disbelieving the chill that had come to replace the passion between them.

"You love me, don't you?" He stared back as if irritated by the question. "Roman, do you love me?" she asked again.

He looked at Tygre and shrugged his shoulders, smiling lightheartedly. "Oh, Tygre, you are such a child! This is sex, not love. I already have a girlfriend."

"Girlfriend?" Tygre's throat tightened. "Did you say girlfriend?"

"I don't keep secrets," Roman said, curtly. He reached for his wallet and handed Tygre a photograph of a stunning brunette in a red convertible parked on a beautiful sunny beach. She looked glamorous and rich.

"Her name is Isabella," Roman explained flatly. "She is coming here for Christmas."

"Why didn't you tell me about her?" Tygre managed.

He stared at her as if she were the stupidest pupil in a miserable convent school. "Tygre, listen to me. What you and I have… had…it was nice, but that's all it was. It's over now." He raised his palms as if he could not believe her naïveté.

For a moment, Tygre thought she might vomit, all over Roman's precious Italian sheets. And then, just as quickly, the nausea left her, replaced by a steely fury. She trembled as she dressed herself in, feeling violated and confused, unsure of whether she was angrier at Roman or at herself.

One thing was certain, she told herself: She would never feel this way again. She walked out of Roman's apartment without uttering a word, though she was already mentally repeating the words that would become her mantra for so very long a time: *I don't need love.*

She had been no better than a tart that night with Roman Zajda, Tygre thought, and despite her resolve, the experience had taken its toll on her.

"Come in! Come in! Step forward, girl," Madame de La Sable barked at Tygre, startling her back to reality. She examined her from head to toe, clearly enjoying herself. A smile broke across her thin lips as she pointed her finger saying, "Who is this fool? Look at her clothes and her hair! I cannot believe it. What have you done with yourself? Your MODA cover was stunning! Why do you wear so much makeup? Look at those fake nails and lashes. You'll need to lose some weight!"

Tygre caught her reflection in the window. Madame de La Sable was right. She cringed at the sight of her overdone makeup and underplayed clothing. Tygre stood motionless. Her stomach churned as she contemplated how badly she'd blown her one opportunity to escape the confines of her life in Poland.

Then, in an instant, fueled by her anger and her deep desire to move forward in her life, Tygre found a simmering courage inside herself. She stood tall and responded bravely to the intimidating dragon lady in front of her, "I am Tygre, Madame, and I am not a fool."

Madame de La Sable, visibly impressed by Tygre's composure, reached for another cigarette and walked toward her. Most of the girls she routinely criticized would be in tears by now.

"You certainly look like one. Your makeup is ridiculous. Take it all off and wash your face. Your clothes need to go too. Burn them, and this hair … it is too long, au nom de dieu!"

"Ooh la la, that's enough. Let's give this girl a try." Webb Douglas, who had just entered the room, rescued Tygre with encouraging words and a broad smile. The tall stranger sporting blue jeans, a baseball cap and a leather jacket, was LDV's renowned makeover expert and photographer. He was the first black man Tygre had ever met, and his ebony-colored skin fascinated Tygre.

"Hello, Tygre. Call me Webb. Just try to relax." His handshake was firm and swift, and he focused on Tygre with undivided attention. "We have a lot of work to do. Let's get you into some decent clothes and makeup and get you started on some test shots."

Tygre followed, eager for the possibility of a pleasant interaction with this exotic man.

The several hours in his presence were the most interesting and enlightening she had ever spent. He was a man with a natural gift for visual artistry and the most eloquent way of expressing himself. Tygre was fascinated by his talent and captivated by his kindness.

When she emerged some 16 hours later at four in the morning, Tygre evoked the stunned silence of the crew. Under the expert guidance of Webb, Tygre had undergone a magical transformation from a reserved and unsophisticated teenager to undeniable supermodel material. Webb urged her forward as he stepped back to let her receive her accolades. The room slowly erupted in oohs and aahs followed by enthusiastic applause. Tygre smiled as she caught her reflection in the window. This time, she barely recognized herself. *This is so surreal,* she thought, *but it's really happening!*

The moment Webb took the first picture of this timid, provincial young girl, a love affair between Tygre's face and the camera began to form, putting an end to La Dolce Vita's weeks-long search for perfection. Madame de La Sable took one look at Tygre's illuminated features and knew it instantly.

The crew shared a couple of bottles of Taittinger champagne for breakfast, and it tasted sublime. Tygre could not believe the young woman in the smiling photographs was actually her, but she did not say a word.

She only wondered how long it would take her to get used to this exotic, innocent, yet very sexy image of herself.

Tygre carefully watched as Madame de La Sable's wrinkled face scrutinized, one by one, the hundreds of photos and spoke of Tygre as if she were not in the room. "The shorter hair emphasizes her eyes. Yes, the pale blue eyes are stunning," she muttered. "The camera loves her, c'est fantastique!"

Webb and the crew chimed in to agree, turning their heads vigorously as Madame spoke and Tygre listened.

"Yes, this is indeed the beginning of a very promising career," Madame proclaimed, lighting another cigarette. "You are exactly who we have been searching for!"

Tygre wondered if the hot blush that fell over her cheeks was noticed by Madame or the crew. "Thank you, Madame de La Sable," she uttered with a smile. Tears of joy filled Tygre's eyes as she was struck by the emotion of the moment. *I won't cry in front of Madame.*

"You've got it, Tygre, you've got what it takes," Webb interjected with enthusiasm.

"Now listen and follow directions," Madame de La Sable demanded. "Are you ready for a new adventure?"

"Yes, I am, Madame. I can't wait to get started!"

"Très bien, let's keep your name the way it is. I like it. How old are you, Tygre?"

Tygre smiled and answered resolutely, "I'm almost 19 years old, Madame de La Sable."

Madame snapped her fingers as everyone watched. "Then let's go to Paris."

Chapter 11

Le Mans
8:30 p.m. Saturday

After they had finished their prayers, Malik and Khalil walked briskly toward pit lane. Absorbed in a discussion about New Deal's accident, they ignored Tygre who was desperate to know if Brad was involved. She tried her best to disguise her concern over Brad's safety, straining to overhear their conversation without being obvious. She could see Malik's lips moving, but his teeth were clenched, making it nearly impossible to get the answers she wanted.

"It sounds like there wasn't much damage to the New Deal car," Malik whispered to Khalil as he concluded another cell phone call.

"What luck for them," Khalil replied.

Malik nodded and then turned to point at Tygre, who paced nervously, biting at her knuckle. "Look at that woman. She can barely resist running to see Harrington. Khalil, you have to get rid of her."

"To the contrary, let's use her. If you are right she will slip. Now tell me what happened. Who was driving?" Khalil inquired while gently massaging his lower back.

"Sonny Hicks was driving their No. 2. Too bad it wasn't Harrington's car."

Malik's phone rang again and he held it quickly to his ear. He listened intently for a moment, then rang off and quietly reported his findings to Khalil. "They're calling it a minor collision, but at 120 mph, you know what that can do to a car. The front left side is damaged but the car is still functioning. I'll know more in a minute."

Malik pointed toward the end of pit lane, "Look, Hicks is on his way in."

New Deal's No. 2 car pulled into its stall. As soon as Sonny Hicks stepped out of the racer, the ever-present photographers and reporters descended upon the car and snapped away.

Hungry for news, Tygre stepped forward only to be quickly scolded by Karim Racing's technical manager. "Tygre, get out of the way right now! Get out!"

"Sorry," Tygre said jumping back.

"Every year, someone gets badly injured in pit lane by an incoming car. You have to be careful. Never cross this white line. They come in and out very fast."

"I was just trying to see who…"

"It's Sonny Hicks. He just pulled in the damaged New Deal racer. Looks like he's okay."

"That's good," Tygre said in a forced tone of indifference. *Oh thank God!* She thought as she began to breathe freely again. The tightness in her chest slowly subsided. Brad was okay, and that was all that mattered. "So what happened?"

The technical manager shrugged his shoulders and carefully studied the New Deal LMP1 prototype. "Well, the car is still operable. They're lucky they didn't rupture the radiator. Outside intervention is prohibited. If the driver is unable to bring the car in by himself, that car is taken out of the race."

The New Deal crew pushed the racer into the garage and their team swarmed over the damaged vehicle. Remarkably, the No. 2 car was back in the race within 19 minutes as if nothing had happened.

Meantime, Khalil's technical manager turned his attention to Malik. "Get ready, Malik. You're up next!"

"I thought it was Khalil's turn to drive," Tygre said, glancing at Khalil, who was standing off to the side with a Karim Racing crew member.

"There's rain in the forecast according to our radar system. Khalil is fearless on the wet track. We need to save him for that. Besides, his back is acting up again," the technical manager explained.

Tygre checked the time. It was almost nine o'clock, and night had just begun to fall on Le Mans. The semi-opaque darkness was interrupted only by the shrieking roar of straining engines and the bright headlights of competing cars racing by. Tygre shuddered, sensing an eerie feeling in the air.

"At Le Mans when it grows dark, the magic is at its strongest," the technical manger said.

"You're right. It definitely feels different at night," Tygre managed.

Malik stood by impatiently, listening to their exchange. From beneath his helmet's visor, his eyes followed Tygre's every move until his attention was diverted by the racer pulling in. Pierre Auter quickly got out of the car as Karim Racing's team mechanics and an engineer rushed to perform routine maintenance.

"It's all yours, Malik," Pierre said. "She's running like a charm now."

To Tygre's relief, Malik got into the racer and roared away. She watched his car disappear, until, quite by surprise, she met with Khalil's stare. He stood on the other side of pit lane waving her over to join him. Tygre forced a smile and began moving toward him. Khalil walked to meet her halfway.

"Tygre!" Without warning Agent Martin's voice came ringing through her ear. "You need to check the listening device you placed in the trailer. It's not working properly. All we hear is static!"

Tygre turned and put her hand over her mouth pretending to cough. "Not now. Khalil is walking toward me! I can't move. Everybody is watching!"

"I can't impress on you enough...you need to do this right away. It is imperative."

"I understand," Tygre whispered. Then, out of the corner of her eye, she caught sight of Herve du Bois. "Oh Lord, and now the TV crew is headed my way. I have to go."

"What a lucky break for the New Deal team." Herve du Bois approached Tygre with a smile, his microphone arm extending outward.

"Tell us, Tygre, did you panic when you heard Brad's team had been involved in an accident?"

"Well, I was obviously concerned..." she began as she nervously glanced in Khalil's direction. "And I'm very happy that no one was hurt."

"By 'no one,' you must mean..."

"I mean no one," Tygre chimed in. "No one deserves to get hurt."

"Is it difficult dating a race car driver, especially one who happens to be the son of the U.S. President?"

"Uh...I..." she began. Tygre glanced toward Khalil. He was almost within earshot now. He was accompanied by the mysterious Middle Eastern man. "Yes," Tygre said with a smile, "but I'm doing my best to get used to it."

"Tell us, Tygre, how is the new La Dolce Vita campaign coming along?"

"Oh, it's wonderful," Tygre said, relieved by the change in subject. Khalil was getting closer. She glanced from Khalil to his familiar-looking friend before quickly returning her focus to Herve.

"Monsieur du Bois, that's all I have time for right now," Tygre blurted as she made a quick exit. "I must run."

Becoming accustomed to Tygre's fast disappearances, Herve continued unflinchingly. "That was the beautiful Tygre!" Then, as Khalil approached, Herve seized upon a new opportunity, "And here comes Khalil Karim of Karim Racing! Monsieur Karim, may we have a word...?"

With Khalil diverted by Herve du Bois, Tygre made her escape, stepping inside the narrow alleyway that separated the team's stalls. The cool cement walls hid her from Khalil's view.

"Doug, I only have a moment. That man I saw earlier...he's with Khalil right now."

"Go on..."

"I remember who he is. His name is Adis Gabir! I met him at Khalil's house in D.C."

"How does he know Khalil? What is their connection?"

"Let me think," Tygre paused as she tried to reach deep into her memory. "If I remember correctly, Adis is a research specialist. He was born in Bosnia but grew up in Saudi Arabia. He was working on some project for Malik."

"What kind of a project? Can you remember any details?"

"I'm trying, Doug. Oh my God, what does this mean?"

"Calm down, Tygre. Where are they now?"

"I'm not sure. I can't see them from here. Last I saw, Khalil was talking to the TV reporter and Adis was standing nearby."

"Okay, go find them. If you can't go back to the trailer now, I want you to engage Adis. Try to find out what he is doing here. Just remember your distress code is UNIQUE…and we have you covered."

Tygre started quickly around the corner of the wall. "They can't be far. I'll take care of it."

Pit lane was filled with brightly colored Porsche 997s, Audi and Peugeot LMP1 diesel prototypes, Ferraris, Bentleys, Aston Martins and Corvettes, all with different sponsorships, all proudly displaying their logos. Team mechanics and managers swarmed around the cars as they pulled in and out of their stalls. Every minute counted, especially at nightfall when the vision was somewhat blurred by the shadows of changing lights.

To Tygre's relief, she found Herve du Bois still involved in his interview with a preoccupied and tired Khalil. "Karim Racing is the first Arab-owned team at Le Mans. As the sole owner, you have obviously spared no expense in hiring the best and most experienced motor racing talent money can buy."

"I am flattered you noticed," Karim replied. I always insist on the very best. Pierre Auter and Michael Jacques are brilliant additions to my team. Auter is our third driver. And Jacques, our team manager, happens to be a two-time Le Mans winner."

"It is well known that all your non-performance items are custom made in leather and display your team's trademark colors. Is there any significance to navy, yellow and red?"

Khalil flashed a broad smile that showcased his perfect white teeth. "They compliment my olive skin, don't you agree?" He shot a knowing glance in Adis' direction.

Herve laughed and continued, "The cost of participating at Le Mans has been known for years to be the highest in the racing industry. You don't have any sponsors. Care to comment?"

"I am indeed fortunate to have accrued a degree of personal wealth. I praise Allah five times a day to thank Him for my blessings. The cost to enter the race and run two cars and two spare cars' worth of parts, and everything else involved, comes to well over a million dollars. But, racing is second to my true calling."

"Please tell us more," encouraged Herve who was clearly excited at this opportunity to get an impromptu in-depth interview with an Arab billionaire. "What is your true calling?"

"My wealth belongs to Allah, and I plan to spend it worshiping Him and bringing others to my Faith. Through the Khalil Karim Foundation, my ultimate goal is to provide all Muslim children with computers so that they can easily access the teachings of the Koran."

"Well, that certainly sounds like an admirable intention," Herve said.

"Indeed," said Khalil. "Thank you for your time," he added as he firmly shook Herve's hand and brought the interview to an abrupt end.

"Thank you, Monsieur Karim, and best of luck to you," Herve said, then turned to face the camera lens. "I'm Herve du Bois reporting live from Le Mans for Tele-Mondial."

Khalil didn't wait for Herve to finish his sign-off. He immediately rejoined Adis who was standing by patiently, his face all business and his expression deadly serious. Khalil squinted as he observed Tygre approaching.

"Khalil, Khalil, there you are. I've been looking for you everywhere." Tygre ran straight into Khalil's arms.

"Darling, you missed my TV interview," Khalil said. "Do you remember Adis? I believe the two of you met in D.C."

"Oh, yes, of course. Hello, Adis." Tygre extended her hand, but Adis ignored the invitation, keeping his hands firmly at his sides.

"Very well, I'm going to let you two get to know one another while I go and get some rest before it starts raining." Khalil walked away, leaving Tygre alone with Adis.

"So, Adis…what brings you to Le Mans?"

"Malik warned me that you ask a lot of questions. I am here to watch the race, what else!"

"Adis, I didn't mean to offend you. I was just surprised to see you here." Tygre turned on the charm, but her radiant smile was wasted on Adis. He coolly stared her down.

"Likewise, I am equally surprised to see you with Khalil. I thought you'd be here with the young Harrington." Adis turned his back on Tygre and headed in the direction of Karim Racing's stall.

Tygre took out a handkerchief and pretended to wipe her nose. "Doug, I tried. You heard me. Adis is just like Malik…crass and very calculating. I don't know which one of them is worse. I tried Doug…I tried."

"Perhaps you'll have another chance later on. Focus on the bug in the trailer for now."

"It's been impossible to get away. I'll get it done, Doug!" Tygre assured him.

She walked slowly toward the pit area, wondering exactly how it would all end. The grueling 24 Hours of Le Mans endurance race was only in its sixth hour. In a race of such duration, still every minute is an eternity. *Life is a team sport, Tygre. No one can play it alone.* Tygre remembered Brad's words as she watched various team mechanics, engineers and managers swarming around the cars that pulled in and out of pit lane.

"I wouldn't admit this to anyone else," Brad had told Tygre one rainy afternoon at the Harrington Ranch, "for a recovering alcoholic – and that's who I am, Tygre – solitude and isolation are detrimental to beating this disease."

Brad's words reverberated in Tygre's mind, taking her back to that time and place when she felt safe in his arms. Tygre knew Brad's alcoholism made him even more vulnerable, and that terrified her. Le Mans would test Brad's determination and push his endurance to the limit. He needed strength now more than ever, and Tygre felt tremendous guilt for leaving him vulnerable and alone.

Ironically it was Brad's struggle with alcohol that endeared him most to his fans worldwide. Five years ago, Brad experienced a well-publicized, near-fatal plane crash in Florida. Miraculously, all of the passengers on his Aerostar 99040 walked away. But Brad Harrington, the national headlines reported, "could hardly stand up."

His blood alcohol content was 2.1. It was the last time the son of the President flew legally drunk. He stopped drinking and using drugs cold turkey and willingly enrolled in a rehab program. At first, he greatly resented his father's presidency for limiting his AA anonymity.

In AA meetings, where participants shared with each other openly and in private, Brad always felt exposed by his last name. Eventually, it isolated him from the program. While the solitude had been extremely hard to overcome, Brad had remained clean ever since. Escaping death changed his life, but it was not until he met Tygre that Brad realized how much he had to live for.

"Your curiosity, your courage and your love for life have inspired me to stay sober," he had told Tygre. *"You help me to rise above my own challenges. I don't know what I would do without you."*

Tygre took some time to relive that tender moment in her mind before quickly refocusing on her mission.

Daydreaming about Brad won't help him now, she reminded herself. *I have to stay focused.* She glanced around Karim Racing's pit looking for clues to validate her mission and wondered why nothing appeared out of the ordinary nor seemed suspicious.

"Tygre!" Agent Martin's voice never failed to startle her.

"Listen carefully. We've learned that Karim is about to transfer a vast amount of his money. You mentioned earlier seeing several laptops in his trailer. Are they still there?"

"Yes, I think so." Tygre confirmed. She casually removed her La Dolce Vita shades from the top of her head and placed them in her small designer shoulder bag.

Agent Martin's voice remained calm and steady, "That's good. We need to understand why, during the race, he is planning to fund his so-called 'charities.' Our intelligence tells us that they might in fact be tied to terrorist sleeper cells. We have recent confirmation through satellite and electronic intercepts of Karim's meetings in Saudi Arabia. It is inconclusive but very suspicious. Tygre, be very cautious. It is critical that we find out what's going on. We are depending on you."

Tygre walked slowly away from Karim Racing's pit and, once she was sure she was out of the mechanics' earshot, spoke rapidly, "I told you I remember seeing maybe five laptops in Khalil's trailer."

"Then we need you to go back there and look again. Tell me, where did you put the bug?"

"It's underneath one of the computers."

"Not a good place. It could be too easily spotted there, and the transmission signal is weak. That is probably why it's not working. Look for a better location. Tygre, they are up to something big. Be very careful. Keep in mind President Harrington and the First Lady are arriving in 18 hours."

"Doug, I understand, but Khalil is in the trailer, and Malik is due in very soon! It is impossible now. Let's wait for the next change of drivers." Tygre's voice shook. She felt a chill come over her.

She paused to listen to the announcer's voice coming over the loud speaker: *New Deal LMP1 is leading over all, followed by the LMP1 of Karim Racing, confirming Brad Harrington in the lead. Karim Racing's car No. 7, driven by Malik Youssaf, is comfortably in second place.*

Tygre watched intently as Malik's car entered pit lane and passed closely by her. He revved his engine, which sounded off song. Their eyes met for an instant, and the hatred exchanged was palpable. Malik didn't bother to conceal it. He sat in the car, glaring at Tygre as his team's mechanics flocked around to fix a minor mechanical issue.

"Malik, you need to slow down." The team's technical manager and strategist shouted at Malik through his radio headset.

"You must conserve fuel, and not push so hard. We can't take any unnecessary risks this early in the race. A 3:25.00 lap time is the pace I want you to keep."

Within seconds, Malik roared out of the pit. Relieved by his departure, Tygre headed for Khalil's trailer, preparing to undertake the next task in her mission.

"Doug," she spoke discreetly into her pendant, "All this strikes me as so ironic. Khalil is filthy rich, smart and charismatic." Tygre paused, "I don't know this for a fact, but it seems inconceivable to me that such a narcissist would risk himself in the process of a terror plot." Tygre looked around and lowered her voice, "If anyone is going to risk his life in the name of this...mission, it must be Malik. But how could he get anything past such tight security? Le Mans is swarming with police! Malik can't possibly pull this off by himself. He must be working for somebody who is telling him what to do."

"Tygre, the FBI's field agents and the Joint Terrorist Task Force are working on it. Relocate the bug and together we'll make sure it's functioning properly. This is *your* priority. You need to do this... now!"

"I'm on it."

When Tygre entered the trailer, Khalil was sitting at the computer with the bugging device underneath it. His eyes shone with that all-too-familiar sign Tygre noticed in Washington, D.C. Khalil Karim was high.

Tygre froze with fear as Khalil welcomed her with a pleasant smile. "My dear Tygre, what have you been up to?"

"Not a thing," Tygre muttered softly, dreading the thought of what Khalil would do to her if he discovered the bug.

"I was hoping you were on your way to see me."

"I've been glued to the race," Tygre said, switching to a cheerier tone. "It's so exciting. Malik is in second place!"

"Harrington won't be in the lead for long. I'll take care of that."

"How? What do you mean?"

"Wait and see," he said glibly. He ran a hand through his hair and added in a more controlled tone, "Your curiosity is beginning to irritate me."

Tygre composed herself and put on her bravest face. She quickly took inventory of her surroundings. A dozen white pain pills – the kind that Malik frequently served Khalil – were carelessly scattered on the table.

"How is your back?" Tygre, asked barely audible.

"It's much better now, thank you."

"Are you safe to drive taking these medications?"

Khalil flashed a terrifying smile. His dilated pupils darted aimlessly, shadowed by a canopy of black lashes. He looked stoned out of his mind. *God help the other drivers,* Tygre thought, horrified. She tried her best to cover her anxiety with a smile.

Khalil's eyes danced with joy. He moved closer to Tygre. "I appreciate your concern, my darling," he said with a tinge of sarcasm, "but there's no need to worry. I am used to it. These pills make me fly, Tygre. I love the feeling."

Raindrops fell quietly at first and then cascaded in a steady stream that streaked the trailer windows with sheets of water and obstructed the view. As darkness fell on Le Mans, the rain fell harder. Khalil's eyeballs rolled heavenward. "And suddenly…" he moaned in a forced foreboding tone, "the dynamics of the race have changed."

Tygre's heart sank. "What do you mean, Khalil?" she asked.

"Suffice to say…the rain and the high speed inspire me, Tygre! I have no fear..."

A call from pit lane interrupted him: "Khalil, you're on in 15 minutes!"

"Praise Allah," Khalil rejoiced and jumped up.

The three-hour-per-driver time limit was approaching. It was time for both a change of drivers and a change of tires.

"Let's go and catch Harrington," Khalil said, reaching for Tygre's hand. "I can't wait one minute longer to knock him out of first place."

Tygre concentrated hard to keep herself from shaking. "I'm tired suddenly. I'll stay here and rest," Tygre sat down and forced a yawn.

"No," Khalil responded firmly. "I want you to come with me. So far you have brought me good luck. And you'll enjoy watching how efficient my team has become. Depending on what the weather necessitates, it takes us less than nine seconds to change the tires from dry to wet."

Khalil grabbed Tygre's hand and swiftly pulled her closer to him. "By the way, Tygre," he said, watching intently for a change in her expression, "tell me again why you broke up with Brad?"

With Khalil inches away from her ear insert, Tygre knew she had to take drastic action. She was loath to do it, but she kissed him passionately on the lips and said coyly, "Because you are a better lover."

Khalil beamed with pride and, for an instant, his ego interfered with his logic. His eyes turned black again and became deadly serious. Khalil spoke flatly and without a smile, "You had better believe it, Tygre. I'll show you again after the race how right you are!"

Tygre could not resist covering her bases. She flatly challenged him, "Is this why you took me back, Khalil? Tell me. I need to know."

"No. Your belief system and your values are weak. I am convinced I can change them. You belong with us." Khalil's eyes darted crazily before landing on her with a forceful stare. "Do you belong with us, Tygre?"

Tygre held his glance with all the intensity of a girl who knew that her life depended on it. "I am here with you, aren't I?"

Khalil's body inched closer to Tygre's. His hand brushed against the silver pendant. He held it up, twisted it, and repositioned it between Tygre's breasts.

"You have some serious convincing to do, my dear."

Chapter 12

Le Mans
11:55 p.m. Saturday

"Due to the heavy rain and fog, visibility is extremely poor and the yellow caution flag is being waved near Virage de Mulsanne." The voice of the announcer mixed with the howling pack of racers. *"The disabled Ferrari No. 83 has been pushed away from the track by the corner marshals and is out of the race. Karim Racing's driver, Malik Youssaf, I am told, is coming in for a scheduled change of drivers and to fix a problem with a malfunctioning radio."*

Tygre held onto Khalil's hand as they ran through the rain, trying to escape a good drenching as they made their way to Karim Racing's pit. She didn't need to hear the rest of the report. Brad was alive, not involved in the earlier New Deal No. 2 car accident, and that was all she cared about. But Tygre could not dismiss the fact that she was deeply embroiled in a situation that was becoming more complex and terrifying by the second.

"Rain at Le Mans turns the track into an ice rink," one of the team mechanics said as Tygre entered the pit. Khalil let go of her hand and lingered for a moment in the entryway shaking the rain from his hair.

"That it does," a voice answered in a matter-of-fact tone. It belonged to a middle-aged man with a graying dark blond ponytail. "The clouds shift, the sky opens up and – *bam!* – we can't see a bloody thing," he added. "Racing at maximum speeds in near-zero visibility… I'll tell you this is the kind of thing that separates the men from the boys."

As Khalil stepped inside and made eye contact with the ponytailed stranger, a smile spread across his face. The stranger spoke first. "Ah, there he is."

Tygre watched Khalil's reaction. He reached out to give the man a friendly handshake, which turned into a warm hug and a firm pat on the back.

"Tygre, I want you to meet Pierre Auter, a local legend and my co-driver."

"I'm pleased to meet you," Tygre said, managing a smile as she wiped dripping rain from her face. "I have heard a lot about you." She extended her hand.

"Pierre is one of the best drivers in the world, and I am very lucky to race with him."

Dressed in Karim Racing's signature navy, yellow and red driving gear, Pierre Auter, one of the oldest drivers in the competition stood all of 5' 9." He raised Tygre's hand and gave it a European-style air kiss before stepping back to take in the image of Tygre. His expression suggested that he found her an undeniable beauty even soaking wet.

"Mon plaisir aussi," he said with a flirtatious tone. He turned his head toward Khalil. "Professionally speaking, I am his partner in the race from hell."

Tygre smiled, detecting something refreshingly honest in Pierre.

"Mademoiselle Tygre," he said with a wink that made Tygre wonder if he'd just read her thoughts, "Please try not to distract this man too much. There are very, very tough driving conditions out there now. Khalil needs to keep his wits about him."

"I'll try not to," Tygre said with a quick laugh. She was well aware that her raison d'etre at Le Mans was perceived to be limited to her appearance. And, judging by the look on Pierre's face, he viewed her simply as a pit lane groupie. Doing her part to help expand Khalil Karim's larger-than-life ego felt degrading, but Tygre was willing to do it for Brad.

And then, as thoughts of Brad seeped into her mind– and as impossible as it seemed–the man himself stepped into her line of vision. Tygre had been staring into the distance, lulled into a daydream of better days as Khalil and Pierre's conversation faded to a far-away drone behind her. Just as Tygre's mind took her briefly back to the Harrington Ranch, Brad appeared in front of her. He walked slowly in Tygre's direction. Her pulse quickened. Tygre blinked in disbelief, not sure if the vision before her was real.

She desperately wanted to call out his name and run into his arms, hold him and never let go. But judging by the look on his face, it was clear he would not have opened them to receive her even if she had been free to do so. Her heart ached as she recalled a time not so long ago when Brad wouldn't open his arms to let her out of his embrace.

"You're not going anywhere," he'd said as his naked body pressed up against her back, his arms wrapped firmly around her shoulders and breasts. His body provided a warm contrast to the cool cotton sheets on that crisp morning at the Harrington Ranch.

"Am I in heaven?" Tygre had asked him.

"No, my angel, you're in Florida," Brad teasingly answered.

"Brad..." Tygre looked over her shoulder so she could see Brad's eyes as she asked the question.

"How did you know I love tiger lilies?" she asked, recalling the superb bouquet Brad had presented when he met her at the airport the day before.

"I didn't know," he answered. "But they reminded me of you."

"Because of the name?"

"More than that," Brad stroked Tygre's hair and kissed her shoulder. "The tiger lily is a flower that is both strong and fragile. It has to endure some very harsh elements as it grows. But when it manages to thrive, it's magnificent." He kissed her again. "But even for all its strength and tenacity, the tiger lily is soft..." He kissed her again. "... and delicate..." and again, "... and beautiful."

This time Tygre turned her body around to face him. She met his waiting lips, which devoured hers in a passionate kiss. She felt his erection grow hard against her thigh as she reached her hand down to guide him inside her.

To Tygre's surprise, Brad moved her hand away from him and looked longingly into her eyes. "There's one more little-known fact about the tiger lily," he said with a serious tone.

"What's that?" Tygre asked.

A devilish smile spread across Brad's face. "They're completely edible."

Tygre let out a squeal as Brad planted his mouth against her neck, and helped himself to a long, passionate nibble. He worked his way down to her breasts, where he stopped for another, before finding his way down to the warmth between her thighs.

Tygre's body rose and fell as Brad brought her to a slow, deep orgasm that sent tremors through every part of her body. He gave her only a moment to recover before sliding himself firmly but gently inside her.

This is my soul mate, she thought. He knows me. He gets me. He completes me. We are one.

But at that moment at Le Mans, the intense bond she felt with Brad just a few short weeks earlier, was replaced by cold indifference. As he walked toward her with the look of a stranger, Tygre's heart stopped. He was striking in his New Deal uniform. Even among all the other similarly clad racers at Le Mans, Brad Harrington stood out. His body was fit and muscular. His face was tanned and handsome. But his once-glistening eyes were empty. He looked briefly in Tygre's direction. His glance was cold and unforgiving. Still, Tygre couldn't help smiling at the sight of him even as her heart was breaking.

She longed to remind him that she was his soul mate and would be forever. And to proclaim to everyone in the crowded area that he had been her one true love all along. Instead, she held her breath and Brad's gaze, praying that some glimmer of affection would appear in his eyes to let her know he still loved her.

But his eyes remained resentful and empty. As he passed her, he quickened his pace until he was swallowed up by an excited crowd of fans, eager to get a close-up glimpse of "Mr. Le Mans."

Tygre turned away, Brad's apparent indifference too painful to bear. As she lowered her eyes, she felt a body press up behind her and two strong arms wrap around her. Khalil's voice purred in her ear. "Ah, now that was interesting," he said.

Tygre's throat tightened and she began to feel queasy. "What do you mean?" she asked.

"For a moment I am thinking perhaps Malik was wrong about you. Perhaps you were telling the truth about Harrington after all."

"What exactly do you mean, Khalil?" Tygre squirmed in his powerful embrace.

"It's clear the young Mr. Harrington wants nothing to do with you." Khalil said releasing his hold on Tygre and triumphantly reaching down to pat her behind. "You might as well have been a stranger to him." Khalil let out a hearty laugh and turned his attention to the video screen on the wall.

Tygre took the opportunity to collect herself. "I need to find a jacket," she said, stepping away from Khalil. "It's getting chilly. She did her best to hide her tears.

As she walked down pit lane in the direction of the garage, Agent Martin's voice caught her by surprise. "Hang in there, Tygre."

"You'd better be right about all of this. The FBI is ruining my life!" Tygre said, stepping behind a wall of stacked tires to escape Khalil's line of vision. The rain, which now fell in a light drizzle, helped to conceal her tear-streaked cheeks.

"It's well past midnight, Doug. I have nothing out of the ordinary to report to you." Tygre's voice broke as she spoke, "No evidence of any plot has materialized, except the horrible consequence of Brad thinking I've betrayed him. Do you have any idea how hard this is for me?" She choked on her words. "He wouldn't even look at me!"

"I know this must be very difficult for you, Tygre. We all appreciate your efforts. And Brad will know the truth soon enough," Agent Martin's voice reassured her. "You will be his hero forever. This I promise."

"I hope you're right." Tygre's tears kept streaming.

"Trust me, Tygre. Brad will understand, and he will love you all the more for what you've done. "

"That's the only reason I'm doing this!" Tygre snapped back.

"Tygre, where are you?"

Tygre shuddered, startled by the sound of Khalil's voice shouting at her from Karim Racing's stall. She turned quickly to see Khalil pacing frantically, waiting anxiously for his turn to drive.

"I'm right here!" Tygre called, running to join him just in time to see Malik pulling into pit lane.

The toad-like Malik got out of the car, removed his seat insert and threw it into the stall. As he reached for another, Khalil gave Tygre a quick wave, then ran to facilitate a quick change of drivers. Tygre watched as Malik, holding Khalil's black seat insert, leaned toward him. In a swift maneuver he placed the insert behind Khalil's back and helped him into the car.

Pierre Auter stood by calmly observing the frenetic scene. In a few short hours, it would be his turn at the wheel.

"Faster! Let's go! Let's do it!" Khalil ordered the crew from behind the wheel of the racer where he sat impatiently waiting to leave pit lane. After fueling, it took barely nine seconds for two of Karim Racing's crew members to install a new set of full-cut wet tires, which were necessary for maneuvering in such heavy rainfall.

As soon as the onboard air jack system dropped the car to the ground, and despite warnings from his team that he was driving too fast, Khalil peeled out of pit lane in a blur. His car slid and then recovered in an audacious but skillful maneuver. A shower of sparks ignited an otherwise dark corner at the end of pit lane as Khalil's car sped away, kicking loose stones and gravel. In an instant, it was out of sight.

As if watching a gripping tennis match, Khalil's pit crew immediately swung their heads simultaneously in the direction of an explosion that erupted in the next stall.

"What happened?" Tygre gasped, watching a flurry of crew members spraying a blazing car with fire extinguishers.

Pierre was at her shoulder, pointing in the direction of the clamor. "The number 5 Audi driver started his engine while the hose was still attached to the fuel hose," Pierre explained. "Some fuel spilled to the ground and when the driver spun his wheels the friction blew it up.

Tygre turned away, raising her arm to block the heat of the explosion. In a matter of seconds, it was all over, with one Audi team crew member suffering burns. Two fire engines and an ambulance approached pit lane with sirens blaring. They picked up the injured fueler and, moments later, they were gone.

Pierre shrugged casually and reached out to console a horrified Tygre. "No one will die, Tygre. It happens. C'est fini." He gently patted her shoulder.

"Why do you do it, Pierre?" Tygre asked. "It's so dangerous. You are a champion already." She realized that she was sharing a moment with Pierre that she wished she could be sharing with Brad.

"You mean driving?" Pierre looked at Tygre surprised.

He motioned for Tygre to join him, and they walked over to a pile of spare tires. They sat down and leaned into them. Pierre Auter looked every bit of his 53 years. He appeared tired and stiff as he shifted his position and settled in to answer Tygre's question.

"To most drivers, motor-racing is just a job, another way of providing a living for themselves and their families. In most cases, we are risking our lives for money. Some drivers do well for a couple of years, then quit."

"So it's just about the money?" Tygre asked.

Pierre shrugged. "For some. For others, it's about the competition. If a driver doesn't make it in today's world championship competitions by the time he is 35 or so, the odds are he won't make it all."

"What about you? What does all of this mean for you?"

"It's not about the money, that's for sure. For me, it's about competing. Karim Racing is a new entry. It is a challenge for me to be a part of such a well-organized and well-funded team. Both Khalil and Malik are competent drivers, but they need more practice here. I can drive the Le Mans circuit with my eyes closed. Any experienced driver can, as long as he has the right combination of skill, a good team and good luck."

"Do you feel lucky today?" Tygre asked.

Pierre hesitated only briefly before answering. "Lady Luck will decide that for me. I'm just a driver," Pierre said matter-of-factly and without expression as he slowly rose and walked away.

Tygre watched him leave. Pierre, she thought, appeared to be a genuine competitor, truthful and honest. He was a refreshing departure from all the others Tygre had met in Karim Racing's pit. She smiled as she contemplated Pierre's words. He had somehow managed to leave her with a rare moment of calm amid the chaos and frenzy of Le Mans.

And then, as if on cue, Malik slid quietly up behind Tygre, startling her with an accusatory growl. "Always so carefree," he said. "You models have nothing to occupy your small brains!" he added in a wicked tone.

Malik glared mockingly at Tygre, ignoring the ring of his cell phone for several seconds before stepping aside to answer it. Even as he became immersed in intense conversation, he kept Tygre constantly in his peripheral view.

"Tygre, did you relocate the bug in the trailer?" Martin took the opportunity to cut in. "Is Youssaf at a safe distance?" His voice seemed rushed, but sounded clear.

Tygre took a few careful steps away from Malik. "I haven't been left alone for hours, but I think I can do it soon enough." Her ear insert worked almost too well. She feared being overheard by Malik who stood just a few feet away. In one quick motion, she pulled her hair over her ear, turned casually around and began to make her way out of pit lane, careful not to look back or catch Malik's attention.

As soon as she was out of his sight, Tygre ran through the pouring rain until she reached the trailer. Fearful of what she might find inside, Tygre slowly stepped in and pulled the door shut. Her hair dripped water on the floor and left a small trail behind her as she started moving around, frantically searching for a place to reposition the bug. The sleek interior provided her with few options. *Where?* Tygre whispered to herself. *Where, where, where can I put this thing?*

"There aren't many choices, Doug," she said into her pendant.

"First remove the device from underneath the laptop computer," Martin instructed her. "There must be a light fixture or a flat table surface. Find it quickly, Tygre. We don't have a visual on

Youssaf. You've got to get back to the pit before he comes looking for you."

Tygre's hands shook as she peeled the bug from the laptop and carefully placed it on the back of a small ceiling fan. "I'll be done in two seconds," she told Martin.

"Tygre…!"

"Shhh!" Tygre cut him off. She heard footsteps outside the trailer door. She instantly slipped down onto the banquette and closed her eyes. Her heart pounded relentlessly as she waited for her fate, which soon came in the form of Malik bursting through the door.

Tygre opened her eyes in time to see him closing in on her. "Malik!" she screamed as he approached her with flaring nostrils and an expression of sheer rage.

"I warned you what would happen if I caught you nosing around in things that don't concern you, you blond bitch!" Malik placed a hand on Tygre's neck. "Who were you talking to? I heard you through the window!" he demanded. "Tell me now or you'll never speak again."

"I'm lonely. I was talking to myself." Realizing how odd that must have sounded, Tygre quickly tried to recover with an improvised explanation. "It seems I have an acute shortage of friends here, so I have no choice but to rely on my own company. You never talk to yourself, Malik?"

Malik's suspicions were not appeased. He tightened his grip around Tygre's neck. She felt his body tense as a ringing sound blared loudly from her pocket. It was Tygre's cell phone. She prayed silently that the panic she felt did not show on her face. In an attempt to avoid an instant tip-off that her Bluetooth was a fake, Tygre anxiously tapped on the device.

"It isn't working." Tygre was quick to cover her tracks, "It probably needs to be charged." She removed the fake Bluetooth and slipped it into her pocket.

"Answer your call right now, or I will." Malik ordered.

Tygre reached into her pocket and flipped the phone open on the third ring. "Hello…?"

Malik removed his hand from her throat as she spoke.

"Daddy?"

Malik shook his head. "Nice try, blond woman. Who is it?"

"Oh, I'm so glad to hear from you," she continued, trying her best to ignore Malik as his hot breath dampened her face. "Yes, I'm fine, Daddy." Tygre fought back tears.

"I don't believe it!" Malik grabbed the phone and barked through clenched teeth, "Who is this?"

"Hello ... hello ... Tygre?"

The gentle voice of Adam Topolski was enough to calm Malik's doubts. He reluctantly handed the phone back to Tygre. "Make it fast," he ordered and paced loudly to the other side of the trailer.

Tygre took the phone and forced a smile, "I'm having just the best time at Le Mans, Daddy. I wish you were here."

"Tygre who is that with you? Was that Brad?"

"Yes, Daddy," Tygre lied. Then she lowered her voice to a whisper, "Everything's fine. He sends his best."

"Tell him he better take good care of my baby."

"I will, Daddy," Tygre said sadly. "I'll do that."

Malik shot her a look from across the room. "Wrap it up, bitch," he snapped, twirling his index finger mid-air in a fast-forward motion.

"You take care of yourself, Daddy," Tygre said. She turned her back to Malik as he again advanced toward her.

"Don't forget to take your tea," she said quickly, as Malik grabbed at her phone.

"And don't worry about me...I'm doing fine...everything's great ... I'll visit soon...I promise...I have to go now...I love you..."

Malik snatched the phone from Tygre's hand and slammed it shut. "You're through, bitch!"

Chapter 13

Six Years Earlier
En route to New York City

Sir Ari Beafetter's Gulfstream V left Charles de Gaulle Airport bound for the United States. Tygre sat quietly next to her boss, the fabulously wealthy owner of LDV, staring out the window. As she soaked in the beauty of Paris from midair, she blinked away a tear.

"Are you feeling all right, Tygre?" Sir Ari asked.

"I was just thinking about my father. I miss him." Tygre said. "He taught me so much…including how valuable it is to stay true to yourself."

"You certainly are valuable in my estimation…a million dollars and counting!"

"Oh, Ari, stop teasing. You know what I am talking about!"

Until now, with the exception of a few kisses and his affectionate pats, Tygre had managed to rebuff Sir Ari's sexual advances. However, once in New York, she imagined he would mount a determined effort to change that. She doubted that it was wise to become sexually involved with Sir Ari, but she knew nothing was going to stop him from trying to claim his "prize."

Tygre wasn't technically Sir Ari's girlfriend…*yet.* Lady Beafetter made sure of that. Acutely aware of her husband's budding infatuation with the exquisite new face of LDV, she insisted on attending every social function where Tygre might be present on her husband's arm.

Sir Ari reached for Tygre's hand and held it firmly. "Everything will be different in New York, my darling. We'll be in our own territory. Manhattan is yours to claim, remember?" he promised.

"I'm still feeling conflicted, Ari." Tygre gazed into the darkness beyond the plane's window.

"Conflicted how?"

"I'm afraid I'm becoming…caught in your spell. You're a charismatic man."

"But that is a good thing, isn't it?"

She glanced at him. He was not physically unattractive, she thought. When he used his winsome smile, he even looked a bit like Michael Caine. "In some ways, yes, but you are also married. And I have been hurt before."

"Marriage creates a vacancy for a mistress, my dear Tygre. Besides, what man could possibly want to hurt someone as beautiful and delightful as you?"

"You'd be surprised." Tygre lowered her gaze.

"Tygre, life can be cruel, but it shouldn't stop you from taking risks. I didn't get where I am today by living in a bubble. This is going to be good for both of us. You are going to be rich and famous, and I am going to have some fun."

Tygre sat in silence for a few moments before speaking again. "While I am becoming rich and famous and you're having…fun… what will your wife be doing?"

Sir Ari laughed. "You are worried about the wrong thing, Tygre. Trust me, Mimi is used to it. It just gives her another excuse to drink more, and that's exactly what she likes. She embarrasses me publicly. I cannot stand it. She knows it, yet she does it anyway."

He seemed to contemplate the sadness of his relationship with his wife, then continued with a more serious tone, "For now, enjoy the ride, dear girl. Nothing lasts forever. When you meet the right man, and when it is time for you to settle down, you'll know. Meanwhile, I am a package at your doorstep, Tygre. Take it. I am the best for you for now," Sir Ari assured her.

"If you say so, Ari," Tygre whispered softly, gazing out the window.

"I know so," he replied, and placed his hand on her thigh.

Somewhat appeased by Sir Ari's pragmatic reasoning, Tygre closed her eyes, ready to doze off. She was a big girl and Sir Ari seemed sure of this arrangement. Why shouldn't she enjoy herself with an attractive man who could give her anything? So long as she was content with "fun."

"You don't want to miss this. Wake up darling," With a gentle nudge, Sir Ari turned Tygre's attention to the Statue of Liberty looming out of the wispy clouds beneath their plane. "I wish I were as young as you are," he proclaimed. "America was made for you, Tygre. Here it is! Grab every piece you can and enjoy it."

Fifteen minutes later, the Gulfstream touched smoothly down at JFK Airport.

"Promise to be a good girl and you'll never fly commercial again!" Sir Ari said as he pulled Tygre closer to him.

As they taxied to the gate, Tygre slowly gave in to the excitement of New York and all that it might mean for her. *Sir Ari is right! The time is right to take some risks, she thought. Just enjoy. Have "fun."*

The trip from the airport to Manhattan was a blur. Sir Ari traveled light, holding a briefcase with one hand and clutching onto Tygre's arm with the other. They were followed by the pilot who carried Tygre's luggage, as they made their way to the waiting limousine.

When they arrived at the townhouse, Sir Ari and Tygre were welcomed by four staff members waiting in an orderly line, wearing black-tie uniforms. "Welcome home, Sir Ari," their voices greeted him in unison and were acknowledged by Sir Ari with a smile. Without a moment's delay, he took Tygre's hand and hurried her upstairs to the master bedroom suite.

"Ari, what's the matter? Why are we rushing?" Tygre uttered breathlessly.

A mischievous grin broke across Sir Ari's face as he guided her to a seat in a chaise lounge near a fireplace.

"Do as I say now, Tygre, and close your eyes," Sir Ari commanded in a low voice.

"Ari…please..."

"Keep them closed until I say. Now, give me your hand." Tygre felt a small object, cold and light, drop into her palm.

Tygre's eyes popped open and, after a few involuntary blinks, she managed to speak. "Oh my God, Ari!!" Tygre stared in astonishment at the pink emerald-cut solitaire in her hand.

"Let me put it on," Sir Ari said, sliding the jewel on the ring finger of Tygre's left hand.

"Ari, what is the meaning of this?" she asked.

"This is a friendship ring, Tygre. It's a welcome-to-New-York present, darling."

Sir Ari was beaming as he led Tygre onto his gigantic, pillow-covered bed. Tygre was dumbfounded. "I've been waiting for you long enough, young lady. I can't wait any longer."

"Ari..."

Sir Ari pulled her to him and excitedly pressed his lips to hers. In moments he had removed Tygre's blazer and slacks and thrown them aside. As she lay there half naked, and watching him undress, Tygre hesitated. "We're doing the right thing, aren't we?"

"Oh, darling. It's a little late for that." Sir Ari said, removing her shirt. "Embrace the beginning of our time together."

In moments, Sir Ari had slipped her panties off and penetrated her gently. With each rhythmic movement of his well-preserved body, Tygre's doubts slowly began fading, but the excitement she felt seemed very different from her experience with Roman. Sir Ari cupped her breasts and moaned, then guided her into a change of position without interrupting the rhythm of their lovemaking. Now he moved behind Tygre, holding her shoulders as he penetrated her, gasping with excitement.

Why, she wondered, why was she making the comparison to Roman? Being with Sir Ari was nothing like being with Roman, she thought. And yet, in the end, the result was the same. The earth did not move beneath Tygre. Her breath remained even and her mind stayed clear. It was not at all the feeling she had read about from the great poets or heard about from hopeless victims of love.

"You are more thrilling than I ever expected," Sir Ari sighed after reaching his climax. He lay on his back, and pulled Tygre's hand to his lips.

"Thank you, Ari." Tygre's tried to mask the disappointment in her voice.

She understood why it hadn't felt right with Roman and she wished it would be different with Sir Ari, but it wasn't. Sir Ari had simply failed to reach her soul. Why had she hoped for anything otherwise? she wondered.

"We will fine-tune our lovemaking and, in time, you'll get used to me, my darling," Sir Ari reassured her.

Tygre smiled and silently touched her solitaire. *What have I done? She asked herself.*

She turned to look at him. "Ari, I can't accept this." She removed the ring and handed it back to him.

"Don't be silly, darling. Trust me, by the time you are done with me, you will have earned it!"

She stared back at him in astonishment, then noticed his smile. In the next moment they were both laughing.

It was not long before the LDV guest suite where she resided felt like home. Tygre also found her self embracing the anonymity that Manhattan provided her. In New York she was just another young "it" model on the arm of a middle-aged billionaire. In a city where anything was countenanced, there was nothing unusual about her relationship with Sir Ari. And, without Lady Beafetter scrutinizing their every move, they could both be anonymous immigrants. At least, Sir Ari and Tygre had something in common. They were alone together, in the big city and had the means to enjoy all it had to offer. In time, she decided, it was "fun."

The terrace of LDV's Upper East Side headquarters, where Tygre often sat with Sir Ari, looked more like the rooftop of a Roman villa than that of a Manhattan townhouse. The 40-foot wide Georgian mansion was architecturally inconspicuous and appeared appropriately unassuming.

Built of brick and limestone, this residence lacked curb appeal and looked its age, but that was just the way Sir Ari liked it. To the untrained eye it would have looked more like a private school than the residence of a billionaire.

Sir Ari gazed at Tygre fondly. "As Madame de La Sable most probably told you, my dear, unlike those who prefer the vulgar display of fortunes, I am obsessed with anonymity and privacy. I own almost nothing that bears my name."

Tygre smiled, recalling Madame's detailed briefing prior to Tygre's first meeting with Sir Ari.

"I am certainly no Donald Trump, and I despise publicity of any kind. Remember that, Tygre."

"Why the secrecy, Ari?" Tygre shifted in her chair. "What are you hiding?"

For a few thoughtful moments, Sir Ari stayed quiet. When he spoke, it was with an intensity that Tygre had not yet heard from him. "No country or government is going to gain access to my money," he began. "Most tax revenues are wasted on social programs I do not support. I am 51 years old, and I have taken many risks to accumulate what I have. I am not about to give it up to others. Tax-free living is my motto and the focus of my most recent investments. I intend that for generations to come, my offspring will not pay a dime of any taxes anywhere in the world."

Sir Ari stood and began pacing. "Considering the vast array of government resources used for tracking the movements of foreign and taxable capital in the U.S., it is a tall order indeed." He rubbed his hands together as a satisfied smile appeared on his face. "But it is a game I thoroughly enjoy playing, and one I never intend to lose."

He broke off for a moment and stared at her. "Come along, my dear. There is no time like the present." He reached down and pulled her from her chair. "Today you are going to get your first lesson on tax free living."

He led her to the upstairs library. If it were not for the string of computers flickering with real-time quotes of major stock indices worldwide, the room would look more like a museum, with its Renaissance masterpieces dotting the walls and with its fine sculptures cheek to jowl with glowing monitors.

Sir Ari paused, scanning Tygre's face. He smiled mischievously.

"What is it?" Tygre implored him.

"I will give you information as to when to buy stock in my company and, more importantly, when to sell it. It's simple to get on the train but you have to know when to get off." Sir Ari smiled knowingly. "Let me show you how to turn your first million into real money. We will do it in no time at all."

Tygre stayed quiet, mesmerized by the small screens with the moving numbers.

"You can always trust numbers," she murmured. "Numbers never lie."

"Splendid, my dear, on that we do agree!" He smiled. "The truth is that control of a publicly traded corporation is a license to print your own currency. For instance, I control 51 percent of Classic Resources, a Luxembourg-based oil company, located in Guatemala. The drilling is deep and expensive there, and the government keeps changing the petroleum code to limit my daily output of oil. That's why CRG – its symbol on the New York Stock Exchange – is trading at $14¾. That's a 15-month low." Sir Ari's face broke into a Machiavellian grin as he paused and asked, "Tygre, do you follow me?"

"So far!"

"Excellent," Sir Ari seemed genuinely pleased. "I will establish an offshore revocable trust for you in the Cayman Islands today. You'll be the sole beneficiary and will be able to identify the trust by your birth date and a secret password. Withdrawals can only be made by you, and in person, at the bank's branch in George Town. No phone calls, no e-mails, no paper trail. Standing instructions will be hand-delivered by a personal courier. Do you understand this?"

Tygre nodded.

"It's a perfect time for me to start buying shares of CRG for you with your LDV prize money…slowly, of course, so as not to raise the price of the stock. In total, however, a million dollars."

A pensive look crossed Tygre's face. "The whole million?"

"Yes, it's a trifle. Your expense account with LDV, is lavish, and your contract entitles you to an additional two million dollars to come. You'll be fine." Sir Ari waved his hand as if a million dollars were in fact a "trifle."

"And there really is no risk involved?" she asked.

Sir Ari winked. "Not as long as I am in control of CRG, my dear! With creative research reports, plenty of tequila and some pretty Guatemalan talent to entertain the analysts, I expect CRG to hit $50 in a few months. You will start selling then, little by little, not to lower the price, of course. If we buy at $15 and sell at $50, 67,000 thousand shares will generate a 2.3 million-dollar profit. Quite simple, darling, isn't it?"

Sir Ari turned away from the screens and looked directly at Tygre. His charming smile vanished and his eyes turned into icy emeralds. "You must tell no one. I mean no one can know. This is very serious business."

"I understand, Ari. Let's do it. I won't tell a soul."

"I knew I could trust you. You'll profit greatly if you play by my rules."

To Tygre, it seemed easy enough. She only wished she could say the same about the regular, between-trading, afternoon 'quickies' that Sir Ari was becoming addicted to.

And then, one afternoon, their regular 'quickie' took a different turn. Sir Ari refocused his attention from the stock market reports and looked playfully at Tygre as he began unbuttoning his shirt. He silently led her to the adjacent master suite, leaned back on his extra-large down-filled bed and swiftly removed his trousers. A reasonable-sized erection beckoned to Tygre as he parted his legs.

"Come to me, Tygre. I have been a bad boy." Sir Ari's voice grew deeper.

A faint thought of amusement crossed Tygre's brow. She didn't quite know how to respond.

"Did you hear me, Tygre? I said I have been a very bad boy, and you're going to have to punish me."

"What are you talking about?" Tygre asked.

"I never pay my taxes. That's wrong, very wrong and I know it. Come and arrest me." Sir Ari opened the nightstand. Excited and intensely aroused, he swiftly produced a pair of gold handcuffs, an official looking vest, a tie and a pair of tortoise-shell rimmed eyeglasses. "Here, take these. I want you to strip for me and then put those on."

"Ari…stop it!"

"Please, Tygre, humor me. Just this one time only, I promise." Sir Ari pleaded.

Tygre, in stunned silence, cautiously began to undress.

"You would look good in these glasses. Pull your hair into a bun."

"What's come over you, Ari? I've never seen this side of you before."

"I am sure you have never been an SEC compliance officer before either!"

"Ari, you can't be serious."

"Does this look serious enough for you?" He indicated his erection. "Come on, be a good sport and handcuff me to the bed. I need to be disciplined right now." Sir Ari rolled over onto his stomach.

Tygre was bewildered, but felt pressured to play along. Sporting nothing but a vest with the SEC emblem and a tie, she straddled him, grabbed his wrists and cuffed him to the bed.

"Slap me, Tygre. I want you to slap me hard." Tygre obligingly patted his buttocks gently.

"Harder Tygre, I've been a very, very bad boy. I need to be spanked." Sir Ari insisted, breathing heavily.

Tygre turned around, closed her eyes and gave his behind a series of solid slaps. Within moments he was bucking beneath her, crying out as he ejaculated. "That was incredible, Tygre. You're the sexiest SEC regulator I have ever met. I knew you could do it."

Tygre quietly climbed off Sir Ari, still unsure of what to think or feel. Such quirkiness left her more confused than ever. How long, she wondered, would she be able to put up with him?

Contrary to what Tygre had hoped, it did not get any better as the months went by. With time, Tygre became increasingly unwilling to satisfy his increasingly bizarre requests. Outside of the bedroom, their life together was pleasant enough. But Tygre longed for more. More than her illegally expanding portfolio could provide.

One midnight, in the guest suite of LDV's Manhattan headquarters, Tygre turned 20 years old. She was by herself, and could not stop crying. In the dead of night and choking on her tears, she made her decision.

The next night at dinner, Tygre sat pensively staring at her plate.

"You haven't been yourself these days, Tygre. Are you feeling old now that you're out of your teens?" Sir Ari's smile was light, but when she didn't look up, his tone became more serious. "You're still young. You have many more years of modeling ahead, and I have no doubt you will continue to do great things after that," he assured her.

Tygre shook her head and spoke without looking at him, "That's not it, Ari."

"What is it then, my dear?

"I feel trapped."

"Trapped?" Sir Ari's face showed no surprise.

"In our relationship," Tygre added.

Sir Ari casually shifted his weight and gently kissed Tygre's hand. He cleared his throat before speaking. "I know you have been loyal to me, Tygre. I am surprised it has lasted this long, considering our age difference."

"You have changed my life, Ari. And I am forever grateful," Tygre responded without hesitation.

Sir Ari took a deep breath and chuckled. "I think it's high time you had some fun with people your own age!"

"I don't know." Tygre answered.

"Your happiness and wellbeing mean a lot to me," Sir Ari added with a grin. "Let me propose an easy solution."

"You have an answer for everything, don't you, Ari?"

"Of course I do," he said. "And here's another. Provided you exercise discretion, I really don't mind if you take another sexual partner."

Tygre's head snapped up. "Did I hear you correctly? You mean to say you don't care if I have sex with another man?"

Sir Ari's smile faded slowly. "Isn't that what you want?" he asked.

She shook her head. "That is far from what I want. In fact, I find it disgusting. It's demeaning!" Tygre's voice trembled.

Sir Ari was unfazed. "Listen to me for a moment. Every woman I have ever known, including my wife, has been willing to share me. I am simply telling you that if it makes you happy, I am willing to return the favor."

"I am not like your other women!"

"Yes, you are, Tygre! You just don't want to accept it." Sir Ari tilted his head and tried to kiss her, but Tygre pulled away.

"Simply put, all I care about is that you choose well and avoid scandal." Sir Ari's expression was solicitous.

"Tygre, you are a young woman and, your life should be filled with all kinds of experiences. I've been too selfish keeping you all to myself."

He raised his wine glass and asked in a low, raspy voice, "Perhaps you already have someone in mind?"

"Stop it, Ari. That's enough!" Tygre cried.

"Well," Sir Ari said, holding his ground, "You are welcome to change that at any time. And when you meet this new person, I would like to know about it. Fair enough?"

She stared at him, truly flummoxed. "First you say it is okay to sleep with another man, and now you are telling me I need to let you know who it is!" Tygre's exasperation reached a new high.

"You might as well," he shrugged. "It is inevitable that I will find out. Besides, this solution is bound to improve our relationship." Sir Ari stood up as if to put an abrupt end to the dinner and the subject.

He paused as he stepped out of the room, however. "In fact, when you find this new man, please invite him home. I like to watch."

Alone in her LDV guest quarters, Tygre cried softly, and wishing she had someone to talk to. *Where do I go from here?* Tygre wondered. *Where do I go from here?*

Chapter 14

Le Mans
1:58 a.m. Sunday

Tygre stood in the doorway of Khalil's trailer pondering what to do. Heavy rain clouds loomed over the Le Mans track. In the distance, the vast parking lot leading to pit lane grew dark as mist descended.

"You're through!" Malik called again as Tygre stepped out into the damp night. "I'm on to you, you blond whore."

"Whatever you're hiding or whomever you're sneaking out to meet up with, it doesn't matter. It's just a matter of time until it's all over for you. Praise Allah, that moment is almost here!"

Tygre glanced back to see Malik pointing an angry finger in her direction, then hurried on.

As the rain intensified, she pulled a black weatherproof slicker over her head, walked on, drawn by the hopes of seeing Brad again. She braved the rain, running as quickly as her heels would allow on the slick pavement, negotiating between the sea of trailers and other support vehicles parked nearby. In the dark of night, the roaring cars, relentlessly striving to achieve their goal, were diminished to slivers of light passing at a hundred miles per hour or more.

"Mademoiselle, fait attention!" Pierre Auter called out as Tygre entered pit lane. The sleek body of the car moving quickly toward her was barely distinguishable in the low, dense fog. Pierre moved quickly to grab her by the arm and pull her forcefully into Karim Racing's stall.

They ended up on the floor with Pierre taking the brunt of the fall and Tygre landing straight in his lap.

"Ça va bien?" Pierre asked Tygre with a look of concern.

"I'm so sorry!" Tygre said. "I didn't see…"

"Don't worry about it," Pierre said sliding out from under her. "You seem so preoccupied. Pit lane is not a good place for that!" He reached out a hand to help Tygre to her feet as the ever-present voice of the announcer blared over the speaker system.

"A multiple-car collision at Arnage involving Brad Harrington has racing fans concerned…"

Tygre froze, clutching Pierre's wrist as she listened intently to the announcer.

"… but not to worry, the damage sustained to Harrington's car is minor, a very lucky break for the three-time winner known as Mr. Le Mans! The other car involved in the crash is a Ferrari No. 8 driven by Marc Proffacio…"

Tygre relaxed her grip on Pierre as the news sank in. "Ça va?" Pierre said, "You look like you have seen a ghost. Is there something the matter?"

"I'm fine," Tygre stammered. She brushed off her pants and pulled her hair forward over her shoulders, ever conscious of concealing her earpiece.

"Thank you, again," she said, and walked quickly away from Pierre to avoid having to give any further explanation. Tygre found a chair in a quiet corner and leaned against it for support. She felt weak from the recent string of trying events – the close call with Malik, the news of Brad's collision and the near miss with the racer. It was becoming more than she could bear. Tygre closed her eyes and listened to the announcer.

"The No.8 Ferrari driven by Marc Profaccio skidded in the rain, missing the downhill left turn and ran into the wall at Arnage. The car caught fire causing a minor explosion. The driver was pulled out of the wreck and is being taken by helicopter to the Grand Prix Medical Unit. Marc Profaccio's condition is unknown."

The announcer's voice faded. Tygre slumped deeply into the chair, listening to the noisy fury of the race, which continued on. She pondered the idea that, within moments of the Arnage crash, the fate of Marc Profaccio's racing career became old news. It could happen to any one of the drivers, including Brad. In a split-second, lives could change forever. And the race would go on. That was the nature of Le Mans, and the world of motor-racing.

"Mesdames and messieurs...I'm told Marc Profaccio has sustained severe burns to his body. His condition is serious. We will bring you updates as they become available. The yellow flag is still out but the fire is under control. The burned Ferrari is being removed from the circuit. Our prayers are with him and his family!"

"Horrible," Tygre muttered softly.

"...Marc Proffacio ran a perfect race...but no one can practice an accident like that. And an accident is always looking for a place to happen at Le Mans."

"He's right, blond woman." Malik's fetid breath preceded him as he crept up behind Tygre. "And accidents don't just happen on the race track," he snorted in her ear. Malik flashed his sinister smile before he passed her by.

Tygre moved to the concrete wall of pit lane and watched him walk away. She leaned across it, trying to clear her head.

"Okay, it's time, Tygre." Agent Martin's voice crackled in her ear. "Get back to the trailer before Karim comes in for a change of drivers. We may not have another chance at this. Go now!" Martin's tone was urgent.

"Check for anything suspicious. We're looking for plastic explosives. Even in small quantities they can cause major damage."

"Plastic explosives?" A shiver of dread ran down her spine.

"Tygre, can you hear me?" Agent Martin anxiously pressed.

Tygre coughed in acknowledgment.

"The garage was checked. It's clean. There's nothing there. *If* they have them and *unless* they moved them, which is highly *unlikely*, we think any explosives will be hidden in the trailer. Hurry, Tygre. I'm told Youssaf is pacing in the rain. He is on the phone and looks preoccupied."

Tygre knew it was time to act. Her hands became sweaty. She could not believe what she just heard. *Plastic explosives... major damage...*Martin's words echoed through her ears.

"Tygre, are you there? Say something! Can you hear me?"

Tygre couldn't answer. Malik stood not far away, watching her closely. He was drenched from the rain and apparently annoyed by his cell phone's poor reception. As his frustration mounted, he began shouting in Arabic, a rapid string of indecipherable phrases.

Tygre tried desperately to keep from shaking as she walked past him. Once out of Malik's sight, she broke into a sprint and ran all the way to the trailer. She estimated she had moments at best before he followed her inside. Inside the trailer door, she threw down her slicker and immediately checked the back of the ceiling fan on which she had placed the listening device. It was still in place.

She tapped on the device. "I'm in. Doug, do you hear me?" I repeat. Do you hear me?" Noticeable panic laced her voice.

"Roger that," Martin responded. "Stay calm, Tygre. The bug is working fine. You did a good job. Now focus, and look around!"

"Doug, what do I know about explosives? You must be kidding me!"

"I wish I were, Tygre. Plastic explosives can be shaped as blocks or rolled into tube-like forms. They can even be flattened into quarter-inch sheets. Just look around. Concentrate and hurry up." There was a palpable urgency to Martin's voice.

Tygre scanned the trailer's interior, paying close attention to the small objects scattered around the countertops. One in particular seemed out of place. It was a medium-sized antique cigar box.

"Doug, I'm looking at a strange box."

"See if you can get it open without leaving any sign that it's been tampered with."

"Right." Tygre carefully lifted the box and gently forced her finger under the lid. "I got it."

"What's inside?"

"I see two cell phones, some spare SIM cards, a couple of pagers, several walkie-talkies, a small garage door opener and three car keys."

"This is very important, Tygre! Some of those items could be transmitters, or bomb components," Martin said. "Take a picture with your cell phone and leave everything where you found it... exactly in the same place."

"Okay." Tygre pulled her phone from the pocket of her overalls and flipped on the camera button.

She took a deep breath to calm herself, but a wave of dizziness overcame her. She leaned against the wall for support. She finally managed to steady her hands, took a picture and forwarded it to Martin. Small beads of perspiration dropped onto the screen as she finished her work.

"Hold on a minute, Tygre," Martin said. He paused, interrupted by a rushed conversation in the background of his FBI post.

"What, Doug? What do I do now?"

"Hold on!" he repeated his irritation clear.

Tygre's heartbeat quickened as she struggled to make sense of the background conversation at the FBI command center.

"Okay, Tygre..." Martin's voice was a welcome relief. "I need you to confirm some intelligence we are currently receiving. What do you see on the screens of the laptops?"

"Let me take a closer look."

"Some transactions from Karim's accounts may be money transfers to suspected terror cell accounts. The timing of it doesn't make sense to us. Why now and why from here? Is there any movement on the screens right now?" Martin insisted.

"No, there doesn't appear to be anything going on. Just looks like a bunch of numbers to me, same as before. They look like digital bank statements."

"Good, good. Okay, that's what we need to know. Now listen, Tygre...let me tell you..."

"Wait ... Doug..." Tygre never stopped scanning the room. A small closet door caught her eye, and she moved quickly over to it.

"Hold on a minute, I see a closet that I missed before."

"What about it?"

"Give me a moment. There is something inside in the back of the closet," she said, opening the door.

A racing suit lay on the floor. *That's odd,* she thought. *All the other racing items are hanging neatly. Maybe Khalil had tossed it there in his hurry?* She picked up the suit and looked it over.

"What is it?"

"It's a racing suit, but for some reason it's on the floor of the closet."

Scattered along with the suit were a couple of fire-resistant Balaclavas used to protect the driver's neck and head, racing gloves and helmets. And then Tygre noticed a second suit lying partially hidden under the other. It looked like the first, except that it bore Malik's name, and it was considerably bulkier.

"There's another suit on the floor underneath the first. It belongs to Malik."

Tygre pulled it out of the closet and noticed immediately that it was much heavier than the first suit. "Something about it feels different from the first one." She said calmly.

"Describe it to me as best you can."

"Hold on ... I'm checking something." Tygre held the suit out in front of her. *This is strange,* she thought. Her focus was suddenly thrown by the startling noise of her ringing cell phone. Tygre jumped, almost dropping the suit.

"Tygre, what's happening? Is that your cell phone I hear?"

Tygre placed the suit back on the floor, pulled out her phone and looked at the screen. "I'm getting a call from Poland." she said.

"Tygre I'm afraid that call will have to wait. You must concentrate. This is of critical importance! I need your full attention. Please turn the phone off right now," Martin demanded.

"You're right, sorry," Tygre said, quickly disconnecting the call. She turned her focus back to Malik's suit and anxiously patted the slick fabric. *It feels far too bulky, she thought.* And then she reached beneath the fireproof lining and her heart began to thud.

There, between the layers of fabric were long, narrow blocks of a pliable, clay-like substance. The blocks, sewn into the vest panel, looked to be connected by a series of spaghetti-like wires.

"What do you see, Tygre?"

Tygre stuttered, searching for words. "The suit. I've found what you're looking for. I'm getting sick to my stomach, Doug. I'm scared...please, God, help me!"

"Tygre. Listen, I want you to take some deep breaths, count to four and exhale slowly through your mouth. Take a picture of the suit! You can do it, Tygre."

Martin's words had little effect on Tygre. "I...can't. I'm terrified, Doug. There are blocks of explosives and wires and some kind of box..."

"You must calm down!"

"I'm trying..." Tygre uttered, turning pale.

"Tygre, the suit. How heavy is it? Lift it up... very carefully."

She did as he told her. She felt as if she would vomit any minute. "About three or four pounds, I'd say."

Martin's was calm. Too calm, she thought. "Tygre, stop and listen to me carefully. Just follow my instructions and you will be all right."

"This is a bomb! Am I going to die, Agent Martin?" Tygre felt her knees about to give way.

"Tygre, you're not going to die. But you must listen to me carefully. I want you to get out of there immediately!"

"I can't move Agent Martin. I can't move...please help me... please!"

"Tygre, pull yourself together now. You've almost certainly located what we are looking for. Now put the suit back where you found it and get the hell out of there!"

Her cell phone was ringing again, unnerving her. "Shut up, shut up!" Tygre muttered, switching the setting to vibrate. She needed all the focus she could muster just to place the suit back in the closet. Tygre held her breath and lowered the suit to the floor. Then she closed the closet door and gently backed away.

She steadied herself, leaning against the trailer wall. Beads of sweat ran down her neck, yet she felt cold.

"Oh, God, please help me! Please, God, help me!" Tygre's voice was barely audible, "Doug, if I die, please tell Brad I love him," she pleaded.

Martin's voice came back. "Tygre, if the suit is back in place, get out of there."

On shaky legs, Tygre made her way to the trailer door. Her phone vibrated in her hand, but Tygre ignored it. "I'm on my way out...," she began, when suddenly Martin was shouting in her ear.

"Wait! Change of plans. Stop! Stop! Stop!"

Tygre froze as Martin continued.

"Tygre, listen carefully. Karim is right outside the trailer. He's coming in. You need to act as normal as possible. Stay calm."

Though she couldn't have believed herself capable of it, fueled by fear and adrenaline, Tygre sprinted to the banquette. She dropped herself onto the cushion and quickly positioned her body into what she hoped was a natural pose. She had barely crossed her legs and pasted on a smile before the door flew open and Khalil entered. He glanced at her, then paused to toss his gloves on the counter beside the box she'd pried open moments before. Then he turned and crossed the small room to sit down heavily next to her. She prayed he wouldn't detect the pounding of her racing heart against her chest.

"A bad night," Khalil said. "This diabolical weather is even too wet for me," He glanced at Tygre as if he expected some commiseration.

"You look tired. Why don't you come and lie down with me for a while?" Tygre offered. She tried to muster a seductive glance.

Khalil's eyes widened, his voice resonating with anger. "I just watched a man barbequed alive, Tygre. I don't want sex. I need to preserve every ounce of energy left in me to win Le Mans."

"I didn't mean sex, darling," Tygre said, trying to mask her nervousness. "I just want you to relax." Tygre reached to pull him toward her. His body smelled of smoke and burnt fuel. "Just put your head on my shoulder..."

Abruptly, some sort of switch seemed to flip inside him. He blinked and rubbed at his eyes. "I'm sorry," he said. "I'm tired and upset, that's all." He managed a weak smile and leaned to kiss her gently.

How could he have empathy for an injured driver if he and Malik were planning to use those the explosives? she wondered, as his lips met hers.

Khalil nestled his face into Tygre's neck. She turned her head to face away, stroking his hair in an attempt to hide her fear. She was surprised at how she was able to think and behave under the circumstances.

The door to the trailer opened abruptly again, and Malik appeared. The sight of Tygre and Khalil on the banquette seemed to infuriate him. "Do you want to kill him? Let him rest!" Malik shouted.

Khalil's face broke into a broad grin at the sight of his enraged cohort. He pushed himself upright. "Enough Malik! I won't let Tygre take advantage of me."

Tygre heard a strength in her own voice she could not have believed herself capable of just moments ago. "Worry about yourself, Malik," she snapped. "I always enjoy my time with Khalil! Now piss off and mind your own business!"

Malik's eyes bulged as if he couldn't find the proper words to address such an outrage. "Clam yourself, my friend," Khalil said. "Not another word from you."

Malik opened his mouth as if to reply, but shut it again, clearly exasperated.

Khalil smiled at Tygre and kissed her on the cheek. He rose from the banquette, then, and shook his head as he glanced outside. "Come on, Tygre. It's stopped raining. Let's get some air. I think Malik needs a nap."

"I'm fine," Malik insisted. He turned away, his eyes darting around the room before coming to a stop on the closet door. He looked down at the floor before shifting his gaze to Tygre. Her body tensed as their eyes met.

When Malik looked back to the closet a second time, Tygre took the opportunity to steal a glance in the same direction. She noticed a part of one of the racing suits peeking out from under the door. *Had it been like that before?* Tygre wondered. She felt a flutter of panic in her chest.

Malik glanced back at Tygre and cocked his head. "Something wrong, blond woman?" he asked.

"I'm fine," Tygre managed.

Malik started toward the closet when the sound of Tygre's phone vibrating on the countertop stopped him short.

"You and your phone calls! Who is it this time…the Polish Pope?" Malik grinned broadly, reveling in his own cleverness.

"It seems I get almost as many calls as you," Tygre replied dryly. She got up from the banquette and moved toward the counter where her phone sat flashing and buzzing. Malik dashed in front of her and snatched the phone from the counter.

"Yes," he said into the mouthpiece, and waited for the response. Upon hearing it, he rolled his eyes and told Khalil, "It's some woman name Helena. I can barely understand her."

"My mother…?" Tygre stared. She hadn't spoken to her mother in years.

"Give her the phone, Malik." Khalil said.

She made a fierce effort to control herself. She'd had no contact with Helena since she left Warsaw. *Why now?*

She prayed for strength as she snatched the phone from Malik's grubby hand. "Mother, I can't believe it's you!" Tygre's mind raced.

"Who answered your phone just now?"

"No one you know mother," she said, glancing at Malik. "Why are you calling?"

"Theresa, are you somewhere you can talk for a moment? There's a lot of background noise. I can barely hear you."

"I can talk, Mother. As a matter of fact, I am at Le Mans. The noise you're hearing is from the race cars."

"Oh, yes, I've been reading about the race in the newspaper."

"Mother," Tygre said. "What did you want to talk to me about?"

"Theresa…" Helena cleared her throat and took a pause.

"The fact is that your father died this evening."

"Died? I just spoke to him, a few hours ago. Mother, please, this isn't possible!" Tygre's knees caved. She collapsed onto the banquette, stared blankly at the wall across from her.

"Theresa, calm down." Helena's commanding voice had not changed over the years. *"I know this is a shock, but your father has been ill for some time."*

"I had no idea."

"He didn't want you to know. He wanted you to focus on your own life. He wanted to hear your voice once more before he passed away."

Tygre could not believe what she was hearing. She had to reach deep into her heart for the strength to ask the next question.

"Mother...how are you doing?" But before Helena could answer, Malik grabbed the phone from her.

"Who cares how she is?" Malik yelled. "I certainly don't! Stop this circus, blond woman." He snapped off Tygre's phone and tossed it carelessly to the floor.

"How dare you?" Tygre shrieked, going after him.

"The death of a Christian always warms my heart!" Malik proclaimed as Khalil inserted himself between them.

"You are despicable," she hissed at Malik. "I pray you rot in hell, you dammed hypocrite!" Tygre spat in Malik's face.

"That is quite enough, both of you!" Khalil pushed Malik away and turned to wrap a consoling arm around her shoulders. In the absence of another option, Tygre accepted what little comfort his gesture provided. She buried her head in Khalil's chest and sobbed. Malik stomped out of the trailer, slamming the door behind him.

Khalil murmured softly into her ear. "I am very sorry about your father. Is there anything I can do?"

Tygre shook her head and stared blankly at the wall.

"I don't care about anything anymore, Khalil. I have nothing to live for. My life is over."

Chapter 15

Four Years Earlier
New York City

On Sunday night, shortly after her 20th birthday, and as soon as Sir Ari and Tygre returned from a weekend in Southampton, Tygre stole away to the quiet of her bedroom to make a long-awaited phone call.

"Father, it's Tygre. I hope I didn't wake you up."

"Hello, darling. No, not at all. I've been up for quite some time." Adam's voice sounded weak and distant. It was not the hearty greeting Tygre had expected.

"Is something wrong?" Tygre instinctively backed into a corner chair and sat down. Her brow wrinkled with worry. "You don't sound well. Are you all right?"

Adam cleared his throat and erupted in a raspy cough. "I'm getting over a nasty cold, that's all. It's nothing."

"Well, you need to take better care of yourself..."

"Never mind me ... tell me your news, I've been waiting for your call. How is everything?"

"Daddy..." Tygre paused. "So much is happening with my LDV work. And, I will be moving out from LDV headquarters very soon."

"Moving?" Adam sounded surprised. "Is everything all right ... with the job ... with Sir Ari?"

"Yes, everything's fine," Tygre said half-heartedly. "It's just that it's time for me to be on my own!"

"That's wonderful news, darling."

"Yes, it is." Tygre said. Having her father's support in the matter made everything feel right. "This is something I have to do, for me."

"Of course you do, darling," Adam agreed. "You've always been an independent girl."

"It's not that I'm not grateful to Sir Ari..."

"So, Tygre, this relationship with Sir Ari...it's not entirely professional then, is it?"

Tygre paused before answering, ashamed at what her father might think of her, but still craving his guidance.

"No, Daddy, it's been more than that. But I've realized that my involvement with Sir Ari has been for all the wrong reasons," Tygre confided in her father. "I need to break it off."

"Tygre, you've finally gotten what you've wanted for so long – success and financial freedom," her father said. "Just keep in mind the larger implications those things have on your life. My darling Tygre, you cannot change the past, but you can learn from your mistakes."

"I'm trying," Tygre said softly. "I guess I thought I would be safe with a much older man...but I'm not."

"Tygre, are you in some kind of trouble?" Adam asked urgently. "Tell me honestly, Tygre. What can I do to help you?"

"No, Daddy, I'm fine. I just meant I'm not *emotionally* safe with Sir Ari. I'm afraid it will be a while before I can free myself from the hold he has over me. But that's why I'm getting this new apartment. I think it will be a good start."

"One moment, Tygre," her father said suddenly. Tygre felt a warm tear roll down her cheek as she listened to her father struggle his way through another coughing fit. When he returned to the phone, he spoke only in a whisper. "Tygre..."

"Daddy, you are not well. Have you seen a doctor?" Tygre sat up at the edge of her chair and waited intently for an answer. "Father?"

"I will, I promise, darling. It's nothing to worry about."

"You've had this cold for a very long time." Tygre said. "I can wire more money first thing tomorrow."

"You're a wonderful daughter, Tygre – so generous. I don't know how to thank you." Adam coughed again.

"I need you to get better," Tygre said, "so that you can help me manage all these twists and turns my life is taking."

"The sound of your voice always makes me feel better," Adam said. "Call me again, my darling. And arrange some time to come and visit me soon."

"I will, Daddy. I love you."

"I love you too, Tygre."

Tygre held the phone against her heart and swallowed hard through a lump in her throat. She longed for one of her father's warm embraces. But, for now, the conversation would have to suffice.

Two days later, Tygre sat in the dining room of Harry Cipriani, a fashionable mid-town restaurant, waiting for Sir Ari to join her for lunch. Tygre's cell phone quietly vibrated. The eagerly awaited message from her real estate broker registered on the screen. Tygre's face broke into a smile as she learned that her offer on the apartment she had seen earlier that day was accepted.

She was anxious to tell Sir Ari her news, and she had pondered a number of different ways of breaking it to him. As the minutes ticked by, Tygre found herself gazing out the window overlooking Central Park, her thoughts turning slowly. She thought of how she had been profoundly hurt by her two sexual partners to date. Roman had humiliated her. Sir Ari had brought her an even deeper pain by proposing to share her with other men. She wondered if it were possible to find closeness and affection with a man without having to suffer the inevitable heartache that came with it.

"Today is the day," Tygre said quietly under her breath as she placed the phone back on the table. "Today, I break free and live for myself."

"I'm sorry. I didn't hear you. Are you saying something to me?" Sir Ari asked as he leaned in to kiss Tygre's cheek. An attentive waiter pulled out a chair for him opposite Tygre.

"I was actually talking to myself," Tygre said with a nervous laugh.

"That's never a good sign, my dear Tygre. Why don't you talk to me?" Sir Ari observed as he took his seat.

Before Tygre had a chance to answer, he spotted the cell phone by her place setting. "Expecting a call?" he asked suspiciously.

"Not really," Tygre answered. "I received a message earlier, before you arrived."

"Oh?"

"It was from my real estate broker. She's found an apartment for me!" Tygre said. "Isn't that wonderful news?"

"I see. You are considering moving out then, are you?"

"Yes, Ari, I'm ready, and I'm old enough," Tygre declared in a strong voice.

"That you are, my dear, but don't rush into anything. There is plenty of room in the townhouse for both of us."

"But, Ari, that's not what I want. I need to have my own place. I need to live my life the way I want to live it!"

"There will be plenty of opportunities for that down the line. Meanwhile, take your time. Stay with me as you continue working for LDV. You can live your own life, my dear. We'll see each other occasionally – no sexual obligations and no strings attached. Just make sure you remain discreet."

"You see?" Tygre said. "That's exactly what I'm talking about. You say I can live my own life, and then you turn around and dictate to me how I must behave!"

Sir Ari smiled and lightly stroked Tygre's arm. But his charm was not going to work this time. She pulled her arm away and placed both hands on her lap. By now, Tygre had known Sir Ari to be a man who lived first and foremost for business, a steely entrepreneur with world-renowned deviousness and savvy. She inhaled and tried to find the courage to challenge her formidable opponent.

"I need to move on. I can't live with you anymore, Ari," she said visibly nervous.

"Of course you can, my dear. In fact, you must. We need time to bring your investments on shore and cleanse them." Sir Ari's stare turned icy.

"You're confusing the issue of the apartment with talk of business and offshore investments, and you are doing it deliberately!"

"Your intelligence, as usual, is quite compelling, my dear Tygre," Sir Ari smiled, but his voice oozed sarcasm. "Thus, I am delighted you understand that until your CRG stock is sold, we're stuck with each other."

"For how long?"

"Oh, come on, Tygre. You make it sound like a sentence!" Sir Ari's smiled faded away as he stated the obvious, "For as long as it takes!"

Having made a pre-lunch pact with herself to remain firm and unflinching no matter how Sir Ari tried to push her buttons, the CRG stock was a painful reminder of how much Tygre still needed Sir Ari's help to secure her financial freedom. With so much money at stake, Tygre couldn't simply walk away, and Sir Ari knew it. He watched Tygre intently as her face flushed red and her eyes became glassy with soft tears of frustration.

"No strings attached?" she finally said in a tone that betrayed her exasperation. "There is no such thing with you, Ari. Your strings are golden and I am just another acquisition in your gigantic vault."

"You have grown too cynical for your own good, my dear." Sir Ari chuckled. "I miss the lean years of my own life, Tygre. It was the only time I ever felt truly happy and satisfied. The long and short of it is that you remind me of myself when I was young. Your determination to make something of your life never ceases to amaze me."

Tygre remained silent. Sir Ari moved closer and pulled her hand gently off her lap. He placed it back on the table and began stroking it again. This time, Tygre allowed it.

"You're a fighter, Tygre, and I live vicariously through your struggles. You bring priceless excitement into my otherwise predictable existence."

"That's quite flattering, Ari, but it's not my life's ambition to be a nostalgic reminder of your leaner days. I'm not here to help you relive your happier days. It's time for me to find my *own* happiness."

"By all means, my dear," Sir Ari said sternly, "I am not here to prevent you from finding your happiness." He gave a sigh then. "Move to a new apartment if you must, but remember this: apart from LDV, you and I have other unfinished business… and you clearly understand that, don't you? It's the end result that is best for both of us."

He pulled her chair close to him, but Tygre leaned away.

"You can relax and be cordial. I promise not to bother you for any special favors," Sir Ari declared.

"Are you willing to put this in writing?" Tygre asked, giving him a tolerant smile.

Sir Ari broke into genuine laughter. "I taught you too well, my dear."

Tygre held his glance. "You most certainly did, Ari. And, for that, I thank you."

Chapter 16

Le Mans
5:50 a.m. Sunday

"Let me cover you, Tygre. You're shivering." Khalil wrapped a thin wool blanket around her shoulders and opened a bottle of wine. "Here, drink a little," he said taking a seat next to her. "You need to get some rest. Your father would want you to." Khalil leaned to kiss her, but Tygre ignored him.

She stared straight ahead, lost in her thoughts.

"Drink your wine, Tygre. It will do you good!" Khalil held the glass in front of Tygre until she finally took hold of it.

"I should have been by my father's side," she said. "I should have spent more time with him. Instead I'm stuck here in Le Mans being humiliated by that bastard, Malik!" Tygre took a sip of wine and shook her head exasperated with herself.

"I am sure you were a wonderful daughter. Take it easy, Tygre. The race has us all exhausted and emotional. And now the death of your father."

"Yes," Tygre said softly.

Khalil added more wine to her glass. "Malik gets very intense at times like these," he said. "I am so sorry for his outburst. Karim Racing has a lot at stake here. Le Mans is not for the faint of heart."

She slumped back, and quietly sobbed. *Not for the faint of heart,* she thought. *If he only knew.*

Khalil observed Tygre's solemn expression and decided to try another approach. "I am sorry about your father. Truly I am."

Tygre remained silent. After a few moments, Khalil stood up. He ran his hand through his hair, looked at her again, then turned to glance about the trailer. He first focused on the countertop, then moved across the room. She watched anxiously as he approached the closet.

"Ah, here they are," he said. He opened a small compartment next to the closet where he found his white pills. He popped one, crushed it with his teeth and swallowed it without water.

He leaned against the wall and looked up toward the ceiling. "I don't remember my father very well," Khalil volunteered to Tygre's surprise. "We spent very little time together when I was growing up. It's my mother whom I shall always miss. A day doesn't go by that I do not think about her. She always motivated me in everything I did. She still inspires every day of my existence."

"What happened to your mother?" Tygre asked. Anything to distract him from that closet.

"She died tragically in Palestine when I was thirteen."

"I'm sorry," she said, finding in fact that she was. "How did it happen?"

"My mother and all my siblings were killed by an Israeli raid." He turned to her. "I blame the Americans for her death." Khalil's voice was controlled but she could see the iciness in his eyes.

"Is that why you hate Brad Harrington so much?"

Khalil shrugged. "I hate his father even more," he said. "President Harrington uses democracy as an excuse for his attempts to control oil supplies and territories that do not belong to the U.S. It has to end!"

Tygre stared at him. What was there to say to such ravings?

"Don't look so surprised, Tygre. Short of Syria and Iran, the U.S. controls the oil production of the entire Muslim world already. Harrington was elected on a promise that the flow of cheap oil would continue forever. It's that simple."

Tygre tried to appear interested. She doubted that any of this would surprise Agent Martin.

"Americans are spiritually bankrupt heathens," Khalil continued. "As long as they can afford to fuel up their SUVs, all is well."

"I think those pills cloud your judgment. President Harrington is a good and peaceful man," Tygre protested. "For one thing, he is on the same page with the Saudis. I know that for a fact."

"And how do you know that?" Khalil inquired evenly.

"President Harrington is a good friend of Crown Prince Abdullah bin Farid and his family. I saw them together at the Harrington Ranch!"

Khalil's eyes sparkled with interest. "Oh, did you? When was that?"

"About a month ago," Tygre answered matter-of-factly. "I have to admit I was intrigued to meet a prince."

"I am quite certain you were! You're not the only one. To us, he is a modern day Saladin."

"Saladin?"

"Saladin the Great was a charismatic leader who united the Muslims under one nation and rid our lands of the infidel crusaders." Khalil's speech was rushed now, his eyes glittering.

Tygre watched him carefully. The not-so-subtle effects of the pain killers were all there – the enlarged pupils, and the loss of focus, the violent gestures and, worst of all, the anger. She knew she should neither agree nor disagree with his statements at this point.

"Harrington is blinded by his ego in thinking that America can do no wrong. The U.S. hasn't been number one for decades, but he doesn't want to accept it."

Tygre remained pensive as Khalil continued his tirade. Her mind was back on Prince Abdullah's visit to the Harrington Ranch. She had overheard the Prince speaking on a late-night phone conversation, something that nagged at her, something that seemed to connect with the things Khalil was raging about. *It will come to me,* she thought to herself. She was sure it was important, but in her exhaustion, Tygre found it impossible to concentrate.

"Harrington's power was handed to him by his father and his cronies!" he blurted out.

"What about you, Khalil? Didn't you inherit your wealth as well?" Tygre said mildly.

Khalil blinked, as if the question had reminded him that there was indeed another person in the room. "It is true that I did, but my fortune belongs to Allah. That is the difference. I spend *my* wealth to glorify and worship Allah, spreading the one true faith and the teachings of the Prophet Muhammad." He broke off to sweep his arm about them. "Even my being at this race is part of that plan."

He was nose to nose with Tygre now. "For God's sake," she said, drawing back. "You need to stop taking those pills. You're scaring me."

Khalil jabbed a finger at her chest. "Harrington's imperialistic ways and his support of the Jews *killed* my family," he snapped." We want to control our own destiny, our lands, our oil, and our governments. We want to bring about an era of *Muslim* control in the Middle East *without* foreign interference...and we will."

Tygre's hand went to her chest. She felt her fingers brush the silver pendant. She gripped it instinctively. Was his rage apparent to Agent Martin? she wondered. Khalil stared at her hand and for a moment a paralyzing fear gripped her.

"I am sorry," he said, drawing back abruptly. "I'm not myself."

He walked to the refrigerator, snapped the top off a canned energy drink and raised it to his lips. Silence filled the trailer as Khalil's rage subsided. Finally, he turned back to her. "You look absolutely exhausted," he said. "And I could use a catnap myself."

She gave him a shrug, but Khalil was already headed toward the banquette, where he collapsed as if he'd been struck. In moments, he was snoring soundly. As for herself, she did not think she could fall asleep in a trailer filled with explosives, on the day of her father's death, while racing cars screamed outside like so many angry hornets. But eventually, Tygre's body and mind gave in to exhaustion and turmoil of the day and she began to doze.

Chapter 17

Le Mans
8:30 a.m. Sunday

"Let's go, Tygre. You've slept long enough." The sound of Khalil's voice startled Tygre. Thinking she was having a nightmare, she blinked several times before coming to. *Oh, God, the explosives in the closet!* came the troubling thought, followed immediately by a wash of terror.

"I have some business to take care of with my tire rep at the Michelin tent," Khalil said in a low tone. "Let's try to find him, before my turn to drive."

Khalil checked the closet door, pushing against it to make sure it was latched tightly. He motioned Tygre out the trailer door, then pulled it shut and locked it, looking over his shoulder to survey the area.

The two had stepped out into bright sun on an early Sunday morning at Le Mans. The dark, heavy clouds that hovered just a few hours ago had departed, taking the rain with them and leaving the drivers, pit crews and fans with a sense of relief. But it brought no reprieve for Tygre. Beleaguered by the dread of her discovery and by her father's passing, Tygre silently prayed, *Lord, please help me and don't abandon me now!*

The grounds about them, the very Woodstock of racing, gleamed now in the sun. The track had begun to dry and the noise of grinding engines, both diesel and petrol, came at a higher pitch, as the race regained its ferocity after the long wet night. Cars once again whipped past the stands in a blur, though as mechanical failures and crashes mounted, there were fewer of them.

Khalil held Tygre's hand as they walked silently to Le Mans Village. Sponsors' restaurants were crowded again. Against the backdrop of roaring cars, the drivers awaiting their turns were chatting with sponsors, comparing lap charts and discussing mechanical failures. Khalil secured the only available table in the Michelin tent and glanced around looking for the tire rep. He seated Tygre and took a chair next to her, then watched her keenly as he sipped his coffee. "You are very quiet, Tygre."

Tygre didn't answer. Her mind darted from the images of her father's face to the plastic explosives in Malik's suit.

"You should take comfort. Your father has gone to a better place."

Tygre looked away, not wanting to discuss it. She took a sip of freshly squeezed orange juice.

"There is nothing you can do about it anyway," Khalil persisted.

Tygre wished he would stop talking. The only person Tygre wanted to share her sorrow with was Brad Harrington. She craved the comfort of his strong embrace now more than ever. But with Brad out of reach, she longed for the next best thing, a quiet place to mourn her father's death in peace.

That will have to wait, Tygre thought, trying her best to gather her courage. *The sooner I get this over with, the sooner I can move on with my life.*

"I need to call my mother to discuss the funeral arrangements for my father," she said firmly. "I left my cell phone in the trailer." Tygre started to rise from the table, but Khalil quickly stopped her.

"You can call her after the race. Your father won't know the difference."

Tygre blinked anxiously. She knew Khalil was inherently cruel, but his insolence still caught her off guard. She stared at him in amazement. *I hate this man!* She nearly said it out loud.

"Do you disagree with me?" Khalil inquired.

"My father is dead," she said. "I loved him! I should have been there for him!" Tygre said, choking back tears, "I'm so far away from home, and I'm surrounded by tragedy…!"

Khalil looked at her curiously. Tygre stared into his emotionless eyes and felt chilled to her core. "My father has just died! You saw another driver incinerated. That could have been you or

Malik in that car…or Brad." Tygre instantly regretted her words, but she had been unable to control herself.

Khalil considered her statement for a moment before he spoke. "So you are still thinking about Brad Harrington, even when he doesn't care about you anymore?"

Tygre looked away.

"I thought so," Khalil added.

"I didn't mean…" Tygre tried futilely to explain.

"Brad won't win Le Mans, Tygre. And I can assure you that he won't have you back. His ego would not allow it. He is an arrogant son of a bitch, the son of the President no less."

"I'm not looking for Brad to take me back," Tygre lied.

"Then snap out of it, and stop crying about what might have been, and who may or may not have been hurt in that accident. You attach far too much meaning to life. The concept of dying does not frighten me in the slightest. I embrace it. That's why I race without fear!" Khalil paused. "I love to live on the edge, Tygre. You should know that about me by now."

Khalil glanced at his watch then and took another look around for the Michelin rep. Tygre took the opportunity to check her own watch. 9:05 a.m., six long hours until the checkered flag would signal the conclusion of the race. *Will I live to see it? Will I follow my father to the grave?* she wondered. Her mind raced back to suit in the trailer and she shuddered at the thought of having to go back there again.

"Do you believe in life after death?" Tygre asked even though she already knew the answer.

"Of course, and I look forward to a life that promises to be so much more fulfilling than this one."

Tygre stared at Khalil as he turned from her to smile cheerily at a group of sponsors seated at a nearby table, sharing an elaborate champagne brunch. They waved back enthusiastically at the handsome and sophisticated driver who looked almost like one of them.

The crackling of the team's handheld radio suddenly attracted Khalil's attention. His forced smile faded as he listened to an update from the pit. He held the phone to his chest for a moment and looked at her.

"Go back to the trailer and make your calls," he said, dismissively. "Use your own key." He quickly gathered his belongings and rose from the table.

Tygre nodded. "Is there something wrong?"

"I have to run to the garage. One of the sensors on the car that feeds the data to the electronic control unit has failed. Malik is coming in for an unscheduled pit stop. This is not good news." Khalil threw a few crumpled euros on the table and walked away.

Tygre watched him move through the crowd until he was out of sight, then she left the tent and hurried toward the trailer. She was just a few yards away when she heard Agent Martin's cautious voice whispering in her earpiece. "I am told Khalil left the tent. The crowds are out again and surveillance is a bit challenging. Are you still alone? Can we talk?"

Uncertain, Tygre remained silent as she reached the trailer. The thought of facing a closet full of explosives petrified her. Barely able to steady her hands, Tygre unlocked the door and stepped inside to find the space unoccupied.

"I'm here, Doug. I'm back in the trailer."

"Tygre stay away from the explosives, do you hear me?" Martin's voice crackled.

"Don't worry about that much, Doug." Tygre said. "But listen to me. That conversation I had with Khalil a couple of hours ago about Prince Abdullah. I think this could be important. How much of it did you hear?"

"We heard all of it. What are your concerns?"

"Something is not making sense to me, but I can't put my finger on it."

"What is it, Tygre? Hurry up," Martin said.

"I think Khalil looks up to him. They share the same beliefs..."

"So what?"

"I think Prince Abdullah is somehow connected to Khalil's plan!"

"That doesn't square, Tygre. Abdullah is one of the closest allies of the President. You're right about one thing though. Malik is not acting alone. We've intercepted several conversations between Youssaf and his accomplices. We are still not sure who is in league with Khalil, but we doubt very much it is Prince Abdullah."

"My intuition tells me otherwise," Tygre persisted.

"The FBI doesn't act on intuition. Do you have any concrete facts to back it up?"

"I don't," she admitted. Was it possible she'd fixed on the Prince simply because Khalil's interest piqued when she mentioned his name? Or because the Prince had leered at her whenever Brad Harrington's back was turned?

"Leave the facts to us, Tygre, and listen carefully," Martin replied. "It seems apparent that Youssaf is part of a conspiracy to cause an explosion that looks like an accident. We don't know when, how or where. But he has a back-up plan to use two or possibly three remote control devices. We know that much for certain."

The shrieking noise of a passing racer interrupted him.

"Tygre, can you hear me?"

"Yes, Doug, I…"

Martin cut in. "Right now the most important thing is to determine the location of the other explosives. There's little doubt that Youssaf and his men are definitely going after the President. It's imperative that we find out exactly where the explosives are and when he's planning to detonate."

"Why not just cancel the President's arrival!"

"Negative, Tygre. The President has been informed about the plot. William Harrington stated emphatically that he won't duck his meeting because of a terrorist threat. He is on his way to Le Mans as we speak."

Like father, like son, she thought as Martin continued.

"We need to secure the remote control devices. They are probably among the items you found in the cigar box. Grab that box and leave at once. Don't try to open it, just grab it. And do it fast, Tygre. You need to get out of there. Right now!"

Tygre ran quickly to the counter and grabbed the box. "I'm on my way Doug..."

"Good. We'll have a man meet you at..."

"Oh, my God," Tygre cried as she yanked the door to the trailer open and found Malik's frame blocking the opening.

He shoved her backward into the room and strode inside, slamming the door behind him.

"Malik!" Tygre cried.

He snatched her free arm and twisted it firmly behind her.

"You're hurting me!" Tygre cried.

"What are you doing with my cigar box?" Malik demanded, "Don't you ever touch it again."

Tygre placed the box carefully on the counter. "Sorry, I was just..."

"Shut up!" Malik cut her off. "Who were you talking to, you infidel trash?"

"I don't know what you mean. I wasn't talking to anyone."

"Tell me who it was or I will break your arm!" Malik screamed.

"I wasn't..." Tygre said. "Let go!" She struggled to free her arm from Malik's grip, but it was hopeless.

Malik shouted in her face, inches from the earpiece. "Who are you working for?" He paused and then asked her in a gravely serious tone. "Did Khalil send you to spy on me?"

Tygre was shocked. Of all the things Malik could have suspected, it never occurred to her that he would have considered a betrayal by Khalil among them.

"Khalil is your best friend, Malik," she said, doing her best to plead with him. "He would never betray you."

"You think I believe you?" Malik cried. "But it doesn't matter. There has been a change of plans, blond woman. I don't love *him* anymore! Khalil is going to die, not me," he boasted scornfully.

"What are you talking about?" Tygre twisted in his grasp.

"Khalil has become weak. He abandoned his faith in Allah and, more importantly, his faith in me. Once Khalil is gone I will live his life."

Tygre saw tears welling in Malik's eyes. She had no choice but to take advantage of the vulnerability. "I love Khalil and you tell me you are planning to kill him? Have you lost your mind?"

Malik released her arm and slapped her hard across the face. "You lying piece of shit, you don't love him. You are not capable of loving him like I do."

Tygre put her hand to her cheek to stop the stinging. She stared at Malik in disbelief.

"How Khalil could betray me with a whore like you, I will never know. I will never forgive him for it, never! You fucking bitch!"

"I love, Khalil," Tygre lied. "And I can see that you do too. But I never meant to hurt you, Malik." Tygre infused her voice with all the sincerity she could muster. "I didn't know that you and Khalil…"

"Shut up," he cried. "You are nothing but a liar!" He pulled Tygre close and spat in her face. Malik's eyes followed the trail of his saliva from her cheek to her chest. She trembled with as Malik settled his gaze on the pendant.

"What's this?" Malik said. "Might it be what I think it is?"

"It belonged to my mother!" Tygre lied.

Malik pulled an instrument the size of a Blackberry from a nearby drawer. It beeped as he waved it wildly around Tygre's upper body. "Do you know what this is, blond whore?" he said maliciously. "It's a high-frequency signal emission detector."

"I don't know what you mean," Tygre said.

He snatched her arm and pulled her close to him. "Let's see what happens when I hold it…here," he said waving it in front of Tygre's pendant. The device beeped relentlessly.

Tygre squirmed and tried to back away.

"I knew it. You are wired!" He looked at Tygre astounded. "I should have known!"

He yanked at Tygre's hair and pulled it back from her face. "And what do we have here?" he ripped out Tygre's earpiece and threw it to the floor, then snapped the pendant from her neck and threw it down as well. He ground the two devices under his heel until they were crushed into pieces. So much for her lifelines to Agent Martin and the FBI.

Malik let her go and began to pace about the small space like a deranged madman, waving the emission detector. "What else? What else?" he repeated over and over as he tore about the place in a mad rush. It took him less than a minute to locate the listening device Tygre had placed near the light fixture. She stood motionless as Malik peeled it loose. He smiled at her, placed it into his mouth, and then bit down. She heard the splintering of plastic and watched in amazement as Malik swallowed the shards.

Next, he reached out his hand. "Give me your cell phone! Now!" She gave it do him, and Malik deftly removed the battery, then tossed the pieces onto the countertop. "That should take care of your employer, whoever it might be. No one can track you now!"

Tygre stared back in horror. Unless Martin had his men racing pell-mell toward the trailer, she suspected that the end of her life was near.

"It's just you and me now." He reached his arm to the small of his back and quickly produced a semi-automatic Glock 20. It was compact, but it was as terrifying as a cannon.

Malik aimed the gun directly at her forehead. She walked slowly backward as he inched toward her wearing an evil grin, beads of perspiration pouring down his face and hers.

"Who are you working for?"

"No one," Tygre tried to keep her voice steady.

Malik's lip twisted in a sneer. "Doesn't matter...you'll be joining your father soon enough!"

Malik moved steadily toward her until Tygre fell backward, landing on the banquette. She gasped.

"Put this on." He peeled off a plain rain jacket he'd been wearing and tossed it at her. "We need to go somewhere. I have work to finish. Without taking his gaze from Tygre, he scooped up the contents of the cigar box and placed them in his pockets.

"Wear this too," he added, tossing her his ball cap. She slowly slipped into the jacket and adjusted the fastener on the cap to fit her head. She prayed silently, hoping the FBI was waiting outside the door. But something told her that chances of the FBI intervention were slim at best.

A stark realization dawned on Tygre, one that made her shudder. *I am expendable,* she thought. *No one really cares.*

Malik motioned her up and shoved her toward the door. "Just remember I am not afraid to die for Allah! I'll kill you in a fucking second. In fact, I look forward to sending some cold lead through your tiny empty brain. Now bitch… let's go!"

Chapter 18

Three Years Earlier
New York City

When she awoke on a quiet morning, just three days before her 21st birthday, Tygre's heart felt hollow and her stomach felt like lead. Her eyes had been open long before her alarm clock rang. After staring at the ceiling for several minutes she rose and made her way to the bathroom to splash cold water on her face.

No matter how many times she washed her face or cleansed her body, she thought, Tygre still felt dirty. Just being in Sir Ari's presence demoralized her on a daily basis, stripping her of pride and robbing her of joy. She dried her face and went back into her room to sit dispiritedly for a moment on the chair across from her bed. She glanced at the several world-renowned works that adorned her walls, uninspired by their beauty. She had been forewarned about the lengthy board approval proceedings involved with the purchase of her new co-op, but still she couldn't wait to move.

A museum-quality Utrillo landscape hanging above her desk reminded Tygre of the countryside in Poland. She pulled her knees up to her chin and shuddered, thinking how mortified her father would be if he knew the truth about her association with Sir Ari. She had never intended it to be so, but she nonetheless had allowed herself to become trapped in Sir Ari's web of power. A wave of sadness washed over her, followed closely by a burst of Polish pride that, for a long time, had lain dormant within her. Thoughts of Adam and his unwavering, unconditional love gave Tygre a much needed shot of adrenaline.

She rose from the bedroom chair, donned a robe and marched downstairs where she knew she'd find Sir Ari already in his office.

She dispensed with knocking and pushed the door open to find Sir Ari already glued to his computer screen, just as she suspected. The markets in Europe and Asia had been open for some time and he was following the dancing figures on the screen with keen interest. Tygre cleared her throat.

"Don't you look enticing, my dear Tygre?" Sir Ari said as he turned to find her in the doorway. "To what do I owe the pleasure of such an early visit?" Sir Ari rose from behind his desk and greeted her with open arms and a smile. Tygre stood firmly holding on to the doorknob.

"Come here and give me a kiss."

"I'm not here for that," Tygre said firmly.

"Have you taken a new beau my darling? I told you that good sex would improve your mood...and our relationship. Now, obviously, you can't wait to see me this morning."

Tygre stared back at him. Even if she had allowed herself an indiscretion, it was not anything she intended to take up with Sir Ari. "I want you to sell my Classic Resources stock today," she blurted. "I would like to have my money back."

Sir Ari's face lit with joy at another chance to torture her. Tygre recognized it instantly and braced herself for what was to come. "You want to sell 67,000 shares in one trade?" Sir Ari laughed. "That's impossible!"

"All of it," she said, unfazed, "as soon as the market opens."

"Well, my darling Tygre, I wish it were as simple as that. But it is not."

"I don't care about your tactics and your schemes. Never mind the millions in profits. I just want my original investment back. That shouldn't pose a problem."

"But I am afraid that it does, given the latest fluctuations in the market. I am afraid that it will be quite some time until you're able to do so, much as break even." He turned back to the computer and tapped a few keys. "You can see for yourself. When we bought your stock, CRG was trading in a range between 12 and 18 dollars per share. Let's say your average cost is 15. If we are lucky, CRG will open today at 7."

A momentary look of dismay crossed Tygre's face, but Sir Ari went on unfazed. "Don't forget, my dear, oil was trading at $147 a barrel then. Today it is at $80. I'm sure you realize what that means."

"I'm very good at arithmetic, Ari. You're telling me that my one million dollar investment is worth about half of that. But I want to sell it anyway. I don't care."

"You should care, Tygre. You have worked very hard to earn that money."

"You're not kidding!" she said without humor. She remembered the lashes she'd had to apply to his bare backside. For a moment, she wished she had a whip in her hand again.

"It would be suicide to sell at these prices." Sir Ari said, smiling.

"I want to sell," Tygre uttered through clenched teeth.

Her anger had finally caught Sir Ari's attention. He looked up from his computer screens, leaned back in his chair and folded his hands in his lap. "Come on, Tygre, lighten up and tell me what's really going on."

"Lighten up? Everything is a joke to you. I can't stand it anymore!"

"And now you want to leave me?" Sir Ari remained cool and unruffled. His tone annoyed Tygre all the more. She was fully aware that he was expert at manipulating her, and still she couldn't help herself.

"Stop patronizing me, Ari," she warned.

"Don't be in such a hurry to leave me," he shot back. "I assure you a dollar bill is not any greener elsewhere. Besides, I won't let you go that easily! You amuse me too much."

"I am tired of being your bedroom clown!"

Sir Ari's warm voice dropped several degrees. "That was harsh and unbecoming."

"How can you stop me from selling my shares?"

"Very easily, Tygre," A smug grin returned to Sir Ari's face. "CRG is a very thinly traded stock. It cannot be sold in one block. It might take months, perhaps a year, to dispose of it without further devaluing shareholder equity."

"I don't care about shareholder equity. Sell it now."

"I can't let you do that, Tygre." Sir Ari's golden screws took one more turn. "I owe it to the other stockholders."

Tygre wanted to strike him, but in the next instant, she was struck with an idea and softened. "If you think CRG will do well in the future," she said in a reasonable tone, "why don't you buy me out? Give me my money back."

"This is priceless!" he said, clapping his hands together. "I love you dearly, Tygre, but I cannot buy back your stock."

"And why is that?"

"Well, let's set aside the fact that the shares are worth half of what you paid for them and no good businessman would do such a thing. More importantly, as the chairman of CRG, I am legally prohibited from doing so." He raised his hands as if to say 'what a pity,' before he continued. "Perhaps I'll find someone who would be interested in such a large block. But I repeat that you would lose a lot of money. You should wait until the stock market stabilizes and CRG stock goes up again." Sir Ari turned his attention away from Tygre and became absorbed once again in his computer screens.

"I should have known this would happen," Tygre said forlornly. She sat down in another chair and looked at Sir Ari in despair.

"Investing carries risks, Tygre," he said, his eyes still on the screen, his fingers dancing across the keys. "It's a learning process. Your LDV contract calls for an additional two million dollars at the end of the year. You'll be fine."

"Every month is an eternity!" Tygre blurted. She stood angrily. "Just let us be clear. Do not plan to make any additional investments with my earnings!" she demanded.

"Tygre," Sir Ari said calmly, leering at what he could make out through her opened robe. "If you want out of CRG, I will make it happen, eventually. But you have to be prepared to wait."

"Do I have a choice?" she asked. She turned quickly from his hand that had snaked to her thigh.

"I'm afraid not," he said, as he flipped her robe open. "Have you had something done to your breasts?"

Tygre pushed his hand away and clutched her robe shut. "I swear, Ari, I am beginning to seriously dislike you."

"How wonderful, Tygre. Hate is always followed by love." He turned his chair to show her the throbbing erection that he had somehow managed to free from his trousers. "I'm afraid I'm going to be out of town on your birthday, my dear. As long as you're up so early, let me offer a little something to tide you over until my return." He waggled his penis and gave her his most engaging smile.

"You're disgusting," she said, and turned on her heel.

On the night of her 21st birthday, Tygre wandered alone through the LDV headquarters apartment, oblivious to the lavish amenities and expensive works of art that graced the walls. She glanced at the distorted face of a woman in a Modigliani and sighed softly, thinking that she felt equally misshapen. She had acquired far more than she'd ever hoped or expected to have by the age of 21. But she still felt empty inside.

Tygre picked up her cell phone and absently dialed the missed-call number displayed on her screen. But the moment she heard the high-pitched keening of her mother's voice, her temples began to pound. "Mother....? Mother...? I can't hear you. The connection is terrible. I'll call you back." She snapped the phone off and tossed it into her purse.

She collapsed onto the bed and lay staring at the ceiling, recalling an image in her mind from long ago, blowing out the candles on her eighth birthday cake, which she had baked with her father. In her memory, her father was smiling adoringly, clapping for his little girl as she blew out that last stubborn candle.

"You got them all, my darling!" he cheered. "I knew you could do it."

Tygre could hear her father's voice in her head as clearly as if it had been yesterday. *He always encouraged me,* she thought. *He always believed in me. He always loved me.*

"Today, I am 21," Tygre said out loud then burst into tears. "I'm going to turn things around," she promised herself. "I know I can do it!" she said, biting her lip in determination. "I must!"

Chapter 19

Le Mans
10:10 a.m. Sunday

Tygre's moved in slow motion, anesthetized by the sheer terror she felt inside. Malik held her tightly in a protective, lover-like grip. His gun was well concealed in the pocket of his jacket, but Tygre felt the hard steel pressing against her body. Although they were now surrounded by throngs of enthusiastic spectators, without her transmitter and earpiece, Tygre felt frighteningly alone. Where were Agent Martin and his men? she wondered.

In an attempt to reason with her abductor, Tygre turned to Malik. "There is security everywhere. The U.S. Secret Service, the French Police, paratroopers....Malik, listen to me. You'll never get away with this!"

"Shut up and walk," Malik ordered quietly, forcing a grin. She knew that to anyone watching, they would seem like an ordinary couple having an ordinary conversation.

Tygre might have pleaded with him further, but the voice of the announcer over the loud speakers interrupted her.

There has been an accident at the corner of Tetre Rouge. There is smoke coming from the tail pipe of Ferrari No. 29 and there is a large oil spill on the track, just after Arnage. The yellow flag is being waved. The drivers are slowing down as several cars have gone off track. Brad Harrington's car No. 1 is coming in for an unscheduled pit stop. His car was just behind the Ferrari and is covered in oil from the spill. We're speculating that the oil has presented a visibility issue for Mr. Le Mans!

Malik jabbed the pistol in her ribs. "You'll never see that son of a bitch again, so stop the drama and keep walking. We have a ways to go."

"Just where are you taking me?" Tygre replied, but another jab from the blunt point of Malik's pistol reminded her who was in charge.

"Just move forward, Mata Hari," he said through clenched teeth. "Keep smiling and shut up."

The announcer's voice was back on the loudspeakers again: *Car No. 1, The New Deal, has had its windshield cleaned of that oil spill. Meanwhile, Francois Cevet's No. 99 Ferrari is out of the race, putting New Deal's No. 1 car driven by Brad Harrington back in the lead followed closely by Karim Racing's car No. 7 driven by Khalil Karim. There are just two seconds separating them. These two have been challenging each other from the beginning of the race. It promises to be a very exciting, hard-fought battle down the stretch, messieurs and mesdames…*

The murmur of the crowd rose, and Tygre slowed, straining to hear the last of the announcement. Malik tightened his grip about her shoulders.

"I swear to Allah almighty I will kill you right here," he said. "You will drop and I will keep on walking and no one will be the wiser."

She did not doubt that he was right. They were pressed by a mob equally exhausted by a night without sleep and numbed by drink and raucous excesses of every kind. The noise of the crowd and the engines were overwhelming. What would it mean if there were a muffled pop and a young woman slumping to the ground? Just one more spectator who'd had a drink too many.

"I must use a bathroom." Tygre ventured.

All she needed was a second of his lost concentration. She could pull away and disappear in the milling crowds. *Don't turn around at Le Mans, you'll never find your partner again,* Tygre recalled Brad's words. He had issued them as a warning, but she now hoped to use the advice to her advantage.

Malik laughed. "Soil yourself, then," he said, amused at the prospect of Tygre's discomfort. "When you die it will happen anyway."

"You are a barbarian," she hissed.

His smile didn't waiver. "I think that is how the Americans say, 'the pot calling the kettle black.'"

He prodded her forward through Le Mans Village, now a crush of spectators absorbing the ambiance of a massive advertising spectacle. The race was entering its final stretch with a maddening scream, with 600 horsepower engines straining beyond the point of fatigue. For the teams anywhere near the lead, less than 270 minutes left put a win very nearly in sight.

Tygre suddenly heard the shout of a familiar voice and turned to see two friendly faces bobbing through the crowd, hailing her from a distance. The two crewmen from Tele Mondial, she realized, pushing their way through the crowds in her direction.

"Turn, look away," Malik warned her sternly, his arm tightening. "I'll fucking break your neck right now, and they will never know what happened."

"The weather has finally decided to cooperate!" Another familiar voice caught Tygre's ear. She looked over her shoulder to see Herve du Bois standing with a microphone, giving a report to the camera. "Here at Le Mans, the air is infused with the smell of barbequed foods smoldering on portable grills mixed with the potent smell of hot oil and burnt rubber. It is Sunday, mesdames and messieurs, and the circuit is alive again. Le Mans at its best!"

Herve waved his arm about the crowds, his gaze sweeping over Tygre as if she were not even there. "Just take a look at the excitement-filled packed paddock and pit lane. Everyone wants to see the winner cross the finish line and stand on the podium."

Just take a look at me, you bombastic fool, she thought, willing the self-obsessed reporter to notice her.

But as du Bois babbled on about the thrill of Le Mans, joined now by the two crewmen who had been struggling toward him, Malik dragged Tygre steadily away.

Tygre realized she was quickly running out of options. How could it have come to this? It seemed only yesterday she had been enjoying the sanctity of her Hay Adams suite, careening through LDV promotional tours and being wined and dined by Washington's elite. Now she was on the arm of a crazed terrorist with a gun in her ribs and nowhere to turn. She inhaled again and swallowed hard trying to hide her fear. The last thing she wanted was to grant Malik the satisfaction of knowing how frightened she was.

The announcer's voice brought her back to reality: *Ladies and Gentlemen, it is the great honor and pleasure of Le Mans to announce that the President of the United States, William Harrington and his wife Barbara, the First Lady, will be arriving shortly. The Harringtons are avid supporters of their son Brad's New Deal team, and are making their fourth visit to Le Mans. In his youth, President Harrington raced at Lime Rock Park in Connecticut and successfully competed against the late great actor and driver Paul Newman.*

If the French held any residual ill will toward the United States, it was not evident in the raucous cheering that greeted the announcement.

"Praise Allah!" Malik cheered along with them, but for a different reason. "This appearance will lead our way in jihad today!" A look of malevolent glee spread across his face.

The announcer continued: *President Harrington will join Le Mans organizers at the finish in waving the checkered flag from the Rolex Bridge. The British Prime Minister, Sir Anthony Sprake and our own President, Jean-Jacques Pellier, await them in the presidential box. It is an historic moment for Le Mans. We are celebrating today the European Union and 78 years of racing which has united so many participating nations.*

"Praise Allah!" Malik muttered again.

Tygre felt drops of perspiration beading on her forehead. "The FBI is aware of your plans. They're on their way to you right now. Malik, listen to me, you're dreaming. Give it up. You'll never pull this off! Let me go. You don't have a chance!"

"Just watch, you mindless slut. Your miniscule brain cannot comprehend what is about to take place." To reinforce their lover-like pose, Malik pulled Tygre close and smashed his mouth painfully against hers. He drew back and addressed in the tone a lover might use. "No one can help you now."

He pulled one of the garage door openers that had been in the box she'd found and waggled it at her. "This is one of my transmitters, the very best to be found. They've been tweaked and extended and no stray radio frequencies can block them. So sorry you won't have a chance to say goodbye to Khalil."

"Where are we going? Where is Khalil going?" Tygre's head spun with questions.

"There are enough explosives in the seat insert of his car to obliterate the Rolex Bridge. It is all taken care of."

"But I thought you loved Khalil" Tygre cried.

"Khalil can no longer be trusted. He will die with the infidels."

Tygre wanted to speak, but she couldn't find the words. Her mind had gone numb, even as her body shook. She felt herself slipping into a trance-like state, an abyss of white noise, devoid of any thought.

"Yes, it is your fault, bitch. Of course, the FBI wants to bring us down. I warned Khalil about you, but he wouldn't listen." Malik pushed the gun deeper into Tygre's side as he spoke. "I am the only one with a brain. Khalil simply provides the money and listens to Al Hajal orders. He doesn't..."

The ring of Malik's cell phone cut him off. He answered quickly and spoke slowly and clearly in Arabic. The only words Tygre understood were *Abdullah* and *Adis,* but it was enough for her to fit the last piece of the puzzle into place.

"So you are all working for Prince Abdullah."

Malik snapped off his phone. "You ARE a genius, aren't you?" he said, his voice dripping with sarcasm. "What a shame the world will never learn the size of the brain that lurks behind such a beautiful face."

"Prince Abdullah would betray President Harrington...?" Tygre breathed, shaking her head in amazement.

"Ahhh, quel dommage! Or, as the American phrase goes... what a bummer!" Malik smirked. "You, the Harrington family, and all their infidel friends, are about to be shredded into scraps." He glanced down at Tygre's breasts. "Console yourself," he said. "Perhaps you can prostitute yourself with the young Harrington in the next life, if Allah sees fit for him to carry along his pitiful equipment, that is."

Tygre longed to have a weapon of her own at hand. If she could grasp a pistol in her hand at that moment, she would empty it into Malik without an instant's hesitation.

"What kind of faith dictates the killing of innocent people to make a political point?" she said, trying to keep her seething hatred under control.

"Innocent? Oh, you blonde cipher. I should kill you right here." He dragged her along more quickly now, elbowing his way through the crowds long since anesthetized to pushing and shoving. Tygre felt her tensed muscles beginning to spasm. It seemed as if a bullet had penetrated her already.

"Please give this up, Malik. Please!" she begged.

"We have been planning this for years," he replied mildly. "Prince Abdullah has acquired everything we need from Khalil now. Harrington's war in Iraq is over, and, after his death the government *we want* will be put in place. We will finally cleanse the Muslim world of infidels such as Harrington and his puppets. The British Prime Minister and the French President will die in the process." Malik's black eyes glittered with the joy of unbridled hatred.

Such ravings only confirmed to Tygre that she was in the hands of a madman. Reason would never work with such a creature. *If she only had a weapon,* she thought...*and where was Agent Martin? Where is the FBI?*

Helicopters roared overhead, part of the massive security sweeps conducted in anticipation of the U.S. President's arrival. French Police swarmed the grounds near the Rolex Bridge, abetted by armed security forces. But they were of no help to Tygre.

She thought briefly about simply making a wild break from Malik. She could scream, strike him, cry for help...but what were the chance anyone would take notice before she was dead? No, she told herself, she had to stay alive. As long as she was alive, there was hope that Agent Martin and his men might find her, of that she might find some way to escape and warn officials of what was about to happen. Indeed, the fate of the free world's leaders and the lives of thousands were in her hands.

"I can feel you getting jittery," Malik said. "But try a move and you'll be gone in an instant. Besides, if you behave, perhaps I will change my mind and leave you behind to explain it all. I might enjoy the spectacle of your tearful face on television, telling the world how Brad Harrington really died. Play your cards right and I just might do it, despicable whore."

Malik began to cackle at his own cleverness when the announcer's voice broke in: *Ladies and Gentlemen, it is 11:10 a.m., less than four hours left in the race. All unauthorized personnel, including the members of the press are asked to stay clear of the designated areas as President William Harrington's helicopter approaches the stands. Three-time Le Mans winner Brad Harrington in car No.1 is in the lead. New Deal's second car, Car No. 2, driven by Sonny Hicks is in second place. Karim Racing's entry, driven by Khalil Karim just completed another unscheduled pit stop and has fallen into third place...*

"Not now, Allah, not now! I need him to cross the finish line!" Malik growled. His face contorted as he processed the news.

In the next instant, the announcer was back on the loudspeaker and Malik was grinning again: *Disregard the last bulletin, mesdames and messieurs. The Karim Team car has passed through the pits and is back on the track. I repeat, Khalil Karim is back on the track and gaining ground.*

Malik smirked with satisfaction and gestured at the Rolex time clock that loomed in the distance, the seconds flickering rapidly off its dial.

"See that, infidel trash? You and all the rest of them are almost out of time."

Chapter 20

One Year Earlier
The Four Seasons Restaurant
New York City

While awaiting the liquidation of her CRG stock, Tygre did enjoy one amenity: for a time she was able to live alone in Sir Ari's spacious townhouse. Careful not to exceed the 183 day residency limit imposed upon non-citizens by the U.S., Sir Ari had been away for several weeks. Still, his self-imposed absence was coming to an end, and Tygre anticipated his homecoming with much trepidation.

Still, she was hardly prepared when, without warning, he appeared one morning in her bedroom doorway, moving toward her with open arms. "I'm home at last, my dear, and how I've been looking forward to this moment. You look more ravishing than ever!"

"Hello, Ari," Tygre said, her expression neutral. She gave him a quick hug and a chaste peck on the cheek.

"I've made arrangements for us to have lunch at the Four Seasons today. We'll have a chance to catch up with each other!"

"That will be nice, Ari." Tygre managed. How sad that she had allowed herself to be a prisoner of money, she thought. There had been a time in her life when having nothing was a blessing.

Sir Ari retreated back down the stairs leaving Tygre alone, but it seemed only seconds had passed before he was calling up the stairs. "Are you ready to go, my dear?"

She glanced at her watch. "It's only 11:30, Ari. Give me a few moments please."

Tygre walked to her mirror and placed a wide-brimmed straw hat trimmed with ribbon on her head three or four times until she was satisfied that it was set at just the right angle.

Ari appeared in the doorway to watch her. "The doorman tells me you were out this morning," he said, brightly.

She glanced at him. Soon he'd be keeping tabs on her trips to the bathroom. "I was advised by my real estate broker to keep on looking while I'm waiting for board approval at the coop, just in case I should get turned down. I had an appointment to see a few additional apartments this morning."

"Oh, are we talking that nonsense again?" Sir Ari said, shaking his head as he entered the room. "That hat becomes you. Now put something on that's sexy from our latest LDV collection. We have to move along. I have a very busy afternoon." He turned and left, missing the venomous look she shot him.

Precisely at noon, Tygre met Sir Ari in the downstairs library. Sir Ari took her arm and guided her to the waiting town car parked outside. They rode to the restaurant in silence. The cordiality they'd once shared, along with their playful banter, had long been exhausted.

Sir Ari had reluctantly allowed their relationship to fall into a platonic co-existence mainly sustained by Tygre's contract with LDV, but he still enjoyed promoting the idea that Tygre was his girlfriend. Tygre, on the other hand, did all she could to keep the focus on her role as LDV spokesperson, but the lingering perception that she was Sir Ari's young mistress infuriated her.

The rumor surrounding Tygre's supposed intimacy with Sir Ari was largely accredited to his reputation as a world-renowned womanizer. The fact that Tygre was still living at LDV headquarters, which happened to be also one of Sir Ari's residences, did little to dispel the malicious gossip around town.

But Tygre was intent on establishing her emotional and physical distance from Sir Ari, to free herself from his financial stranglehold and start building her own life. It couldn't happen fast enough as far as Tygre was concerned. In the meantime, she would have to endure Sir Ari's company and the knowing looks that came from New York gossipmongers every time she appeared with him in public.

"You know, Tygre," Sir Ari began, finally breaking the silence that permeated the back seat of the town car. "If you're not seated in The Grill Room of the Four Seasons, you simply don't count in the *Who's Who* of the world's most successful and accomplished individuals. Getting in requires either a standing reservation or major corporate status, and I have both!" Sir Ari beamed as Tygre silently listened, looking out the window of the town car.

As they entered The Grill Room, Sir Ari continued to lecture Tygre on the topic. "You may not realize this, Tygre, but being seen here, and being seated at the 'right table,' has great significance and can often make or break a deal."

"Why is it that all powerful men seem to be obsessed with the right tables?" Tygre said innocently, as they stepped up to the maitre d' stand.

"You'll see why, Tygre. Trust me, I know it firsthand. At 12:30 on any Tuesday or Thursday of any given week, no other restaurant in the city represents more financial power," Sir Ari continued while slowly scanning the room.

Tygre discreetly glanced around to see for herself. There was a sea Armani-clad businessmen speaking passionately, using their hands to punctuate a point, waving designer watches through the air as they gestured – that is until they caught a glimpse of Tygre's eyes upon them. It seemed the only distraction capable of pulling attention from their business at hand. Tygre suppressed a grimace and turned her focus back to Ari.

"There are extremely important connections being made right at this moment, even in the midst of a financial turmoil. I find it fascinating to watch," Sir Ari continued.

"Anything to do with making money gives you a hard-on." Tygre laughed.

"Welcome, Sir Ari. We are ready for you." The headwaiter led them to the LDV table, a position that Sir Ari had long ago approved as "prime real estate" in The Grill Room. He took his usual chair – the one that provided him with a near-complete view of the room's goings on – and looked around to make sure he was being noticed. Sir Ari was the only man in the room without a tie. Very few patrons were afforded this privilege, she understood.

"Miss Tygre will start with the main-course-size Four Season's lobster salad," Sir Ari told the waiter. "In fact, I'll join her and have the same."

"Certainly. Would you like to see the wine list, sir?"

"No, thank you, bring us some iced tea," Sir Ari ordered.

Before the tea arrived, a parade of business acquaintances began filing by their table. They stopped, one by one, to shake Sir Ari's hand and get a close-up view of his stunning lunch date, his presumed girlfriend and the current face of LDV.

Tygre was keenly aware of the glances that converged on her from every table. *This is all just a part of my job,* she kept reminding herself. She graciously extended her hand and a warm, obligatory smile to each passing admirer. She always did her best to present the perfect LDV image.

"You travel well, my dear," Sir Ari concluded with an approving nod. "The LDV product line is enjoying record sales. Well done, Tygre." Sir Ari leaned in close to steal a kiss, but Tygre drew back. Pleasant smiles and gracious handshakes for business associates were part of her job. Kissing Sir Ari, she had decided, was not.

Sir Ari went on unfazed, "Our LDV stock seems to be immune to the downturn of the economy. Given the low cost of our products, LDV earnings are up 7% in this quarter alone. Imagine that!"

Sir Ari laughed then took a slow sip of his iced tea. He would have gone straight on patting himself on the back had he not caught sight of an old acquaintance across the room.

"That's Senator Lloyd Owens. I know him from D.C. He is a Rhodes Scholar from Oxford. He also went to Harvard Law School. Owens is extremely well-educated for an American politician. Such a shame."

Tygre's interest piqued as she looked across the room. "Why do you say it's a shame? What's the matter with intelligence? He's quite nice looking too."

"That's another of his problems," Sir Ari responded while placing his hand on top of Tygre's. "For one, Owens is from Nebraska. Too few electoral votes! If not for his close relationship with the

President, no one would take him seriously on Capitol Hill, even though he is a member of the Foreign Relations Committee."

"Why does the President like him?" Tygre asked politely.

"Owens is a staunch ally and supporter of Harrington's unpopular Middle East policies and his friendship with Prince Abdullah bin Farid." Ari answered, his gaze still across the room.

"Why would he support the President on those things? What does Nebraska care about the Middle East?"

"Oh, it's quite simple, Tygre. Owens doesn't have any personal money to speak of. I bet you right after his term expires, Harrington's Argyle Group will offer Owens a seat on its board of directors. Jackpot – isn't that what the Americans would call it?" Sir Ari chuckled as he watched Owens.

"What is the Argyle Group?" Tygre hated to admit it, but she always enjoyed Sir Ari's mini-educations, this time about United States politics.

"The most powerful company you've never heard of. These boys sitting here might be important on some level," Sir Ari said, waving about the room, "but they are insignificant in the big scheme of things and especially in comparison to the board members of the Argyle Group."

"What do you mean?"

"Argyle is a privately owned corporation. Its partners, directors and advisors are the most powerful men in America and, indeed, around the world. Members of the Saudi Royal family, including Prince Abdullah, are on the board as well. But this information is not readily known, and you won't hear about it on the six o'clock news." Sir Ari paused as the all-too-familiar mischievous grin, returned to his face.

"That's interesting. Tell me more," Tygre said as she sipped her iced tea. Maybe he'd let something slip that she would be able to leverage against him someday, she thought. In any case, she was happy to have him talking about something other than himself.

"Some of Harrington's critics," he began, "– and let me assure you, he has many – have been looking into Ron Harrington's role in Argyle's Strategic Investments Group. Since Ron Harrington is the President's brother, and he sits on the Argyle board, there is a perception that this private organization has been financially benefiting from America's military actions in the Middle East for years."

Sir Ari paused before going on in a somewhat hushed tone. "Argyle invests in the sort of companies that profit from the business of war, Tygre. It's a massive conflict of interest!" Sir Ari winked, pleased with his own knowledge. "Impressive fortunes are being made by these entities. And the conflicts in that region continue and are likely to do so for years to come."

Sir Ari moved closer to Tygre and said in a low voice, "Mark my words, the Argyle Group's profits during the wars in Iraq and Afghanistan will pale in comparison to what they stand to make in the aftermath of it."

"How do you know this?" Tygre asked, just as the waiter approached with their dishes. She and Sir Ari put their conversation on a brief hold while the waiter served their lobster salads.

As soon as the waiter moved away, Ari continued. "Have you noticed how little has been publicized in America about the oil reserves in Iraq? Saddam Hussein nationalized the oil industry in Iraq decades ago. The new government, supported by the presence of the U.S. military forces in the region, is denationalizing it to help Iraq revive its oil production, which has suffered from years of war and neglect."

"I haven't been following that story too closely," Tygre said. If Sir Ari noticed any irony in her voice, he chose to ignore it. He enjoyed his role as her mentor too much.

"Trust me, my dear Tygre, I have followed it. The conflicts in the Middle East always have been and always will be largely about the control of oil. And since I know a thing or two about the oil business, I find it intriguing!"

"Does this have anything to do with CRG?" she asked, hopefully.

He chose not to answer her directly. "Iraq is thought to have one of the world's largest supplies of crude oil, with 115 billion barrels of proven reserves. That oil is easy to extract, unlike our own CRG's fields in Guatemala which are deep and very expensive to drill. Oil contracts on Iraq's six fields are being auctioned off to foreign companies as we speak."

"Will CRG take part in these auctions? I'd like a little good news on the company's score, Ari."

His face broke into a genuine smile. "That's my Tygre – always focused on the bottom line, aren't you, my dear? I wish we were able to bid. Sadly, CRG is a peanut compared to the likes of BP, Exxon, Royal Dutch Shell, Lukoil or Sinopec. We wouldn't make the cut to qualify to enter the auction or profit from the other related businesses, unless, of course…" Sir Ari lowered his voice, "I had been able to involve myself with the Argyle Group years ago!"

"You tried to and couldn't?" she asked, genuinely interested. "Why not?"

"Being a Jew, I wasn't invited to participate in their deals." Sir Ari's tone seemed to carry a bit of greed, regret and anger all at once. "But I am not crying into my lobster salad. I have managed to make my billions all by myself in spite of it. No markers to collect from me!"

In this rare instant, pride and satisfaction graced Sir Ari's face. He flashed a broad smile at Tygre, and then, looking around the room, caught sight of Senator Owens. "Besides," he continued, "politics is like swimming in a contaminated fish bowl. I would not like it. For one, I couldn't enjoy the sexual freedoms I have become accustomed to," he paused to bestow a momentary leer at her cleavage before continuing, "although that seems to be a hobby for most politicians on Capitol Hill."

Tygre glared at him, "Don't start, Ari. I was beginning to enjoy this conversation. Don't spoil it! I'll leave right now."

He reluctantly lifted his gaze from her breasts. "I'm simply saying that most politicians have to compromise most, if not all, of their principles to get elected. Before long, they lose touch with what is real and why they are serving in the first place. Politicians simply turn me off."

Tygre glanced at Senator Owens, who was now moving closer to their table. A faint smile flashed across her lips.

"What do you think about him?" Sir Ari asked.

"You mean Senator Owens? Nothing," Tygre shrugged her shoulders.

"Well, my dear, you haven't taken your eyes off of him." Sir Ari chuckled with enjoyment.

"Okay, this time I stand corrected, Ari. Your recent revelations about the Senator and the Argyle Group have me somewhat intrigued."

"You're not the only one!" Sir Ari assured her. "But for the record, you do have two things in common with him. For one, Owens is a Roman Catholic, just like you. And, for another he is single."

Tygre tried to keep herself from glancing Owens' way at that, but it didn't work. When her eyes darted to the table where the Senator had been seated, she realized he was approaching their table, and was looking directly at her.

Sir Ari too had noticed. "Well now, here he comes to say hello." He winked at Tygre mischievously. "Don't get too excited, my dear. Rumor has it he might be gay. Lloyd is nearly 40 and has never been married."

Tygre scarcely paid attention. She did not imagine a United States Senator would look anything like Lloyd Owens, but there he was. Though tall and slender, Owens' preppy clothes were outdated and made him look older than he was. His dark blond hair was uncombed and the tortoise shell-rimmed glasses he wore on the bridge of his nose were askew. If nothing else, Senator Lloyd Owens certainly looked like he needed a wife to care for him or a good night's sleep, or both. And yet, despite his disheveled demeanor, in this room filled with the most powerful men in New York, Senator Owens was clearly regarded warmly and with respect.

"People love to touch Washington power," Sir Ari said in a low voice.

Tygre frowned, but Sir Ari continued with a hint of sarcasm in his voice, "Lloyd Owens is the epitome of Washington D.C. power. Just imagine the prospect of walking on his arm into the White House. Wouldn't you like that, my dear?"

Tygre seriously considered kicking Sir Ari under the table, but simply smiled instead. The Senator was now looming above their table.

"Forgive me, Sir Ari, I don't mean to interrupt, but I'll be honest." He gave Tygre a radiant smile. "I could not resist the pleasure of meeting your young lady friend. Who is this lovely creature?"

Sir Ari smiled back. "By all means, Senator, let me introduce you to Tygre, our new La Dolce Vita girl. Why don't you join us?" Owens, who had not taken his eyes of Tygre, finally gave Ari a downcast glance.

"I would like that very much but I only have a moment. I am on a three o'clock shuttle back to D.C. There is a vote that I can't miss," he had refocused on Tygre, as if she were the only person in the room. "Tygre, is it? What a beautiful, unusual name." His voice was smooth and disarming, "I'm Lloyd Owens."

He sounds much better than he looks, Tygre thought to herself. "How do you do, Senator Owens?" she greeted him warmly.

"I detect a lovely accent, where are you from, if I may ask?"

"I was born in Warsaw."

"In my youth, I studied for a semester in Krakow, at the Jagielonski University. I was a Marshall Scholar."

"Why my father studied there!" Tygre found herself blurting, excitedly.

"The beauty of Poland pales in comparison to the magnificence of its people!" Owens said, with a bow.

Sir Ari chuckled pleasantly, enjoying their interaction.

"Senator, don't let this pretty face fool you. She is quite a tiger when it comes to getting what she wants."

Senator Lloyd Owens was elected and remained in power for 10 years, against all odds. He wasn't about to pass on this kind of opportunity. "Tygre, is there anything special I can do for you?"

Tygre found herself blushing beneath Owens' gaze. For a moment she was speechless.

"You're going to Washington for LDV soon, my dear," said Sir Ari. "I'll wager the Senator could arrange a tour of the White House for you."

Tygre blinked. "Why yes, of course, that would wonderful," she managed.

"I'll see to it," Owens said. "I'll just give you my personal card and you'll call...," he broke off, patting at his coat pockets. The search went on and was almost comical to watch, Tygre thought. How was Lloyd Owens able to manage in the Senate...or was it all done by his staff?

Unable to produce his card, Owens wrote his office number on a paper napkin and handed it to Tygre. "I'll be very flattered to be your personal White House guide. Call my office when you get to Washington. They will find me. So long, Sir Ari. It was good to meet you, Tygre."

Tygre watched him walk quickly away, each step measured in haste. Just before he disappeared from their sight, Owens stopped, turned, and waved goodbye to Tygre, mouthing *see you soon.*

Tygre waved back tentatively then looked at Sir Ari puzzled and asked, "Are you sure he is gay?"

"Who knows and who cares, Tygre? Being seen with Senator Owens is not bad exposure for you or LDV."

At that, Sir Ari dismissed the subject and refocused on his lunch. Tygre had to fight the urge to stab him with her table knife. No matter what, Sir Ari's arrogance always prevailed, leaving her feeling used. It only confirmed that her significance in Sir Ari's life was limited to how she made him look, period.

As she watched Sir Ari poke away at his lobster salad, oblivious to her feelings, Tygre decided then and there to put an end to their exclusive public appearances. She would discover this world with persons other than Sir Ari. And, she had a feeling that she would begin this adventure during her promotional tour's next stop, in Washington, D.C.

Chapter 21

Le Mans
11:25 a.m. Sunday

Sean Ives sat alone in the New Deal pit, visibly detached from the excitement of the race. But as Brad Harrington's Secret Service agent, Ives had little choice.

"One man's thrill ride is another man's ennui," Ives grumbled cynically to himself as a veil of fatigue began to overtake him. His eyes, burning with exhaustion, fought to stay open while his mind craved a second wind.

Trying to fend off sleep, Ives stood slowly, shook his head and sucked in a gulp of cool air. He made his way to a cooler and reached for a Red Bull. Dressed in pit-regulation fireproof overalls, he leaned against the wall of the garage to support his shoulders as he cracked open the drink and gulped it down. With little more than three hours left in the race, he knew certain he could make it through to the end—he was a Secret Service Agent, after all. But he didn't have to be happy about it.

His head ached. He closed his lids momentarily but, within seconds, they popped open as a call came through his earpiece, connecting him immediately to the encrypted channel of the Joint Terrorism Task Force.

"Sean Ives, this is Doug Martin," the voice said hastily. "Do you read me? Where are you?"

"Loud and clear. I'm in New Deal's garage. What's going on?" Ives raised his hand and spoke into his wristwatch transmitter.

"This is urgent." Agent's Martin's voice was clear and decisive, "Your director advised me that you have been detailed to the JTTF relative to any potential terrorist threat involving the President and his son."

"That's right," Ives answered, his exhaustion beginning to burn away.

"I need your help immediately," Martin continued.

"Go ahead," Ives said.

"We're trying to locate a young European model by the name of Tygre Topolska. She has been assisting us undercover in investigating a possible terrorist action to take place on the grounds at Le Mans. We believe she had located an explosive device in Karim Racing's trailer. But we've lost contact with her."

Agent Ives pressed two fingers against his earpiece, listening intently now. "Was she wired?"

"Yes, and we've been in regular communication with her all along. But one of the suspects, a Muslim who goes by the name of Malik Youssaf, surprised her in the trailer. He's one of Khalil Karim's co-drivers."

"I know the name," Ives said.

"It's likely that Youssaf discovered Tygre's communications devices and disabled them. We believe she has been taken hostage by Youssaf. You said you know the suspect. Can you I.D. him?"

"Negative. I only know the name from listening to the race coverage. I haven't had any contact with him, none at all."

Martin thought he detected an unusual note in the Secret Service agent's tone. Years of experience in reading voice inflection should have sent up the red flag immediately, but he was short on time.

"I'm sending you a photo of Youssaf right now by text message," Agent Martin said. "Check your phone."

"Will do," Ives answered. He felt his phone buzz in his pocket, but he left it there for the time being.

"What about the girl? Do you remember Miss Topolska from the time she spent with Brad Harrington a few months back?" Agent Martin asked impatiently. "Can you I.D. her?"

"No problem on that one. I remember her well."

"Good," Martin answered. "You're the closest agent available and your director has authorized you to assist. This is a Code Beta protocol, Ives. Do you register?"

"Roger that," Ives responded. Apparently he recognized the interagency designation validating extraordinary field measures.

"Good," Martin said. "Listen carefully. I need you to proceed immediately to the trailer located behind Karim Racing's pit. It is imperative we find them both. Use extreme caution as you approach. Youssaf is armed and dangerous. Advise me ASAP of your findings. There is no time to waste!"

"I'm on it," Sean Ives replied as he moved calmly toward the pit exit.

"It should take you three to four minutes to get there. I'll expect to hear from you then."

"I'm already walking out of the garage," Ives said. "I'll get back to you as soon as I reach the trailer, over." And with that the connection broke.

—

Agent Martin pulled a neatly creased handkerchief from his back pocket and blotted his forehead. He took a swig of cold coffee from a two-hours-old cup and winced as he swallowed it.

Since September 11, 2001, he had been directly responsible for dozens of undercover operations and FBI investigations of terrorist activities, activities which had led to numerous arrests. For his work, Martin had been highly praised and decorated. Yet, with what was facing him now, Martin could easily imagine tomorrow's headlines naming him the man responsible for the largest international security disaster in history.

Martin blotted his forehead again and sighed audibly. But there was no time to wallow in his anxiety. He had to find Tygre.

"Agent Ives, where are you?" he shouted into his own wrist communicator, exactly four minutes after Ives signed off from the New Deal pit.

No answer.

"Ives! You should be there by now. I need an update."

Agent Martin looked nervously at the analog clock on the wall of the FBI's command center in the trailer, then to his digital watch and back again. *Four and a half minutes. Way too long...what the fuck is going on with this guy?*

"Ives!" he shouted again.

Agent Martin tapped at his watch as if to make sure it was transmitting. Stupid, he knew. He could fall into lava and be vaporized, the communicator would survive and keep on ticking. "Ives, for Christ's sake, where are you?"

"I'm inside the trailer, Agent Martin," Ives finally responded. "There's no one here."

"Damn it!" Agent Martin shouted. "What *do* you see?" he demanded.

"There's a cell phone on the countertop. It's pink. It might belong to Topolska."

"Make sure it's on. I'm calling her number." Before Ives could speak, he could hear Tygre's phone ringing, confirming his worst fears.

"That phone is Tygre's GPS tracking device. She would never have left it behind!" Martin shouted.

"I also found shattered bits of an earpiece on the floor. It's likely the one the young lady was wearing." Ives continued.

"Do you see a small closet in the back of the trailer?" Martin asked impatiently. He glanced at the clock on the wall.

"Affirmative. What do you want me to do?" he asked calmly.

"There should be a couple of racing suits inside – are they still there?"

"I see the suits," Ives answered.

"I believe that you'll find that one is packed full of plastic explosives, Agent Ives. Use caution."

Martin heard rustling sounds, then a sharp intake of breath. "Affirmative, Agent Martin. You'd better get a bomb squad over here."

"It's happening as we speak. Now listen to me. Do you see a wooden cigar box on the countertop?"

"I already checked it. The box is there but it's empty."

"I was afraid of that. We believe the box held two, perhaps three, remote detonators. We also believe that additional PETN is planted elsewhere on the grounds. We have a team on the way to secure the trailer and the explosives," Martin said.

"What else can I do here?" Ives answered.

"Finding Tygre is our top priority at this point," Martin said. "Your orders are to canvas the grounds. Keep your eyes open and let me know at once if you should spot her."

"Roger that," Ives acknowledged, "over."

Martin ended the conversation with an impatient tap on his communicator. Ives seemed marginally competent at best to Martin. No wonder he's been repeatedly passed over for promotion on the Presidential Protective Detail, Martin concluded. He took his Sig Sauer P229R 9 mm from a drawer in his desk and holstered it under his jacket. As he stepped out of the unmarked trailer, a voice from the command center came over the line.

"Seven to ten minutes until agents reach the Karim Racing trailer, sir."

"Copy that," Martin responded. He paused for a brief second to let his fatigued eyes adjust to the bright sunshine outside before he began to push through the eager crowds that separated him from the trailer. It would take a bit longer to arrive. Maybe Ives could pull off a miracle in the meantime, he was thinking, when the race announcer's voice cut over the omnipresent speaker system:

"Ladies and Gentleman, may I have your attention please. I have this just in." Martin hesitated, as if expected the announcer to declare that there'd been a kidnapping, with a bomb threat added in the bargain.

"Karim Racing's Pierre Auter is out of the race," the announcer continued. "I repeat, Auter is out of the race. A well-known Le Mans veteran, Auter was reportedly blocked by another driver traveling at a slower speed and was forced into a spin to avoid a collision at Mulsanne corner. Auter hit the metal barrier at a very high speed. He has survived the crash and was able to bring the damaged car back to the garage."

Applause drowned the announcer's voice. Martin continued to brave the crowds and the deafening noise as deeply troubling thoughts flashed through his head.

"Ives!" he shouted into his transmitter. "Any luck?"

"Negative, sir. I'm set up outside the trailer, but no sign of either the girl or the suspect."

Martin snapped off the connection, exasperated. The crowds seemed to have reached the consistency of slow-setting concrete. If he pulled out the Sig Sauer and emptied it into the cretins in front of him, it wouldn't gain him ten feet.

Suddenly, Agent Martin heard the voice of his supervisor, Ben Hartley, coming through his earpiece from FBI headquarters in Washington, D.C.

"Doug, it's Ben. Listen closely," even from thousands of miles away, the voice came through clearly. "We have every agent at Le Mans looking for the young model and her abductor. They couldn't have gone far and the young woman should be easy to spot."

"Got it, sir." Martin replied.

"I need you to forget about the woman for now, and pay close attention," Hartley said. "As we speak, millions of dollars are being remotely and simultaneously wire- transferred from Khalil Karim's Islamic Foundation accounts into several so-called charitable trusts controlled by Malik Youssaf. It suggests that, whatever else is going on, Youssaf may be planning to leave Le Mans. I want you to take possession of the computers in Karim's trailer where the transfers were initiated. We need to shut down the flow of funds and secure the hard drives as evidence."

Martin glanced at the hoards that moved like untroubled zombies before him. "I'm still several minutes away from the trailer, sir. These transfers could be finished by the time I get there."

"No one's close by?"

"There's a member of the Secret Service detail staked out there. A guy by the name of Ives."

There was a pause on Hartley's end. "We know Ives. Is there no one else?"

"I'm afraid not," said Martin.

"Let's take help wherever we can get it," Hartley replied.

"I'm on it, sir. Can you hold for a moment?"

"I'll be here," Hartley answered.

Martin tapped his watch to switch the connection. "Ives, do you read me? I need you to get inside the trailer immediately and shut down the computers. Do it at once...over."

The response came back more quickly than Martin expected. "Shut down the computers, sir? Not my area of expertise, but I'll see what I can do."

"You don't have to be a computer geek, Ives. Just pull the fucking plugs, but get it done!" Martin screamed into the transmitter.

"I got it. Will do, sir." Ives clicked off.

Martin shook his head in exasperation, then switched back to Hartley. *Where the hell could Youssaf have placed the additional explosives without the elaborate Le Mans security apparatus finding them?* he wondered.

"Are you there, Ben?" he asked.

"Right here," Hartley answered.

"Ives should be inside the trailer by now," Martin said.

"That's a good thing," Hartley said.

"I've got a sinking feeling these lunatics are timing their attack with the end of the race." Martin said. He rubbed his throbbing temples. "But Youssaf probably plans to be gone by then. I suspect he's intending to use the girl to aid in his escape somehow."

"The important thing is to find the explosives, Doug. It only stands to reason that they're holding the detonation to coincide with the arrival of President Harrington and the other heads of state."

"I don't even want to imagine the collateral damage in pit lane and the paddock area...or near the podium..."

"No chance of start clearing that area, I suppose..."

Martin cut in. "Not without an announcement that would create pandemonium! Hundreds of people would die in the stampede!"

"We're going to have to dispense with the notion of collateral damage, Doug."

Martin heard the tone in Hartley's voice. Not only did he understand, but he agreed, callous as some might find it. "We're going to have to divert President Harrington and the other dignitaries to a secure location. At the same time, we'll do what we can to find the explosives without raising an alarm." Martin paused. "But unless I find Youssaf, I'm afraid a lot of people are going to die."

"I wish you luck, Doug," Hartley's voice came over the line, and then the conversation was over.

Martin was still thinking about his last words to Ben Hartley when he found himself jolted backwards. He staggered back, his hand going instinctively under his coat. An enormous fat man—400 pounds if he was an ounce—stared angrily at him. "Fait attention! Ca vas pas? You're going in the wrong direction!" the fat man barked at him.

Martin nodded, stepping adroitly around the mound of flesh that chastised him. "You're probably right," he replied to the puzzled man, and pushed on.

Chapter 22

11 Months Earlier
Washington, D.C.

Sir Ari's early morning call from London took Tygre by surprise. She was still curled up in bed in her suite at the Hay Adams. "How is your relationship with the good Senator progressing, my dear?" There was a hint of mischief in Sir Ari's tone.

"As a matter of fact, Lloyd is taking me to the Senate Dining Room for lunch today. He's a bit busy, so we're saving the White House for another day."

"Perfect! That will be the ideal setting for the two of you to be seen."

"Ciao, Ari," Tygre said with a tone she hoped would indicate that, she was more than finished with the conversation. "I'll see you back in New York."

"Remember, Tygre, keep an open mind *and* an open heart."

"Goodbye, Ari," Tygre said sweetly.

She moved to the window and gazed across the landscape. The first thing to catch her eye was the White House, looking austere under the early morning sun. But somehow, with Ari's cynical prattle in the back of her mind, the White House looked more like an ordinary building than a presidential residence.

As she emerged from the front lobby of the Hay Adams, Tygre turned the heads of every doorman, hotel guest and bystander. Dressed in an LDV couture pale blue suit, high heels and her mother's pearls, Tygre was the embodiment of fashion.

Senator Owens opened the door of the waiting taxi and greeted her with a smile. "Hello, Tygre, you look amazing!" He offered a hand and tucked her carefully in the backseat, then hurried around to the other side to join her. "I am so delighted you accepted my invitation, Tygre," he said.

"What girl wouldn't jump at the opportunity to have lunch at the Senate Dining Room?"

"With an actual Senator," Owens added proudly.

"I must admit, Lloyd, I was hoping it would be to the White House." Tygre's signature smile perfectly masked her slight disappointment.

"I'm working on it," Owens assured her. "But you should realize that the Senate Dining Room isn't open to just anyone."

"I did a little research on it."

"And what did you learn?" Senator Owens took the tone of a satisfied school teacher quizzing his prize pupil.

"That only Senators and their wives and children and special guests are admitted."

"Right you are," Owens said. "What else?"

"And that every Thursday, the food is representative of a different state." Tygre said.

"Right again, though I'm afraid Nebraska's turn has recently come and gone."

"A shame," Tygre said playfully, before adding, "I also understand that lunching there is less about the food and more about seeing and being seen."

"Bravo! You've done your homework, Tygre," the Senator said.

"I have to admit I got that last part directly from Sir Ari," Tygre confessed. She laughed.

"Well, I have to admit that I'm excited about being seen there with you." The Senator looked directly at Tygre until she grew uncomfortable and looked away.

"I'm looking forward to it too," she said, though she knew her enthusiasm did not match the Senator's.

As they entered, it was clear that the two of them quickly became the central focus of the dining room. Owens could not have looked more pleased with himself. "I skipped a roll call and missed a vote to secure the center table. It's not every day this place is exposed to someone of your beauty." Owens glowed as he looked around the room.

"Well…I'm flattered, Senator."

Owens guided her to what he whispered was the most coveted table in the room. The headwaiter greeted them with a smile while placing a chilled glass in front of Owens. "Welcome Senator, here is your wine, sir." Next he turned to place an amber-filled glass in front of Tygre. "And your iced tea, miss."

"See, Tygre. I already know what you want." Owens gently touched her arm.

"Thank you Lloyd," Tygre said and lowered her voice with a smile. "I have to admit, Senator, you look pretty sharp today."

"Ah, thank you for noticing," Owens said proudly. "I couldn't have done it without the help of my staffers. Actually, I am color blind. They knew this was an important occasion for me so they gave my wardrobe a little extra thought."

"Well, it's certainly getting you noticed," Tygre said, observing the blatant stares from the high profile room.

"No legislation that I managed to pass through the United States Senate has ever given me this much attention," an elated Owens joked.

Tygre leaned into him and said, "I have to admit, it's a little intimidating. Look at all the familiar faces. I'm used to seeing them in the newspapers or on television. But…here they all are… in person!"

"These are my colleagues, Tygre. There is Senator John McGrath, the ranking Republican from Texas," He exchanged a polite wave with McGrath and continued scanning the room for more well-known politicians. There were more shared waves and approving glances as he took a sip of his wine.

"I do thank you for bringing me here," Tygre said politely, drinking the iced tea while observing the room.

"It's my pleasure, Tygre. I thought this would be a good introduction to the world I inhabit."

Owens took another sip of wine and, after a brief moment of silence, cleared his throat and began to speak as if he were addressing a colleague about an item of pending legislation. "The fact is that I see us blossoming…into something much more…serious. I wonder what you might think about that."

Tygre stared back in amazement. Could Ari have known about this when they spoke this morning?

Owens sat up straight and took two more sips of wine. He swallowed, then plowed ahead with what sounded like a speech he'd been practicing in front of a mirror. "I would indeed like to get to know you better. Perhaps one day even marry you, Tygre."

Owens spoke clearly, but his voice was subdued. There was not a hint of emotion on his face. Nobody looking on would have guessed the conversation at this table concerned a marriage proposal.

"You mean…us…you and me?" Tygre arched her eyebrows. She could not have anticipated anything more unexpected. Still, Owens stuck to his script.

"Yes, I think we would make a great team, and we could have a very interesting life together. We are both Catholics and that's a good start, don't you think?"

"But…I…Senator this is too much!" Tygre uttered in disbelief.

Owens went on unfazed. "And I think a Nebraska Senator and a European beauty like yourself would make quite the pair! This is a country of immigrants, and we'd be the perfect representatives of the melting pot." Owens didn't seem to notice that Tygre was frozen in her seat, dumbstruck. "Besides, I need to be married in order to get re-elected. It doesn't look right for me to be single." He took a sip of water.

"I'm forty years old. It just doesn't look right."

Tygre couldn't have imagined a marriage proposal to be more farfetched. She had actually been looking forward to today's lunch. And she'd had to admit that she'd been intrigued by the notion of being a Senator's "date." But this? It made her wonder for the man's sanity.

"Well, Senator…" she began, still unsure of whether she would allow pity or frustration to govern her tone. She suspected a little of both were apparent.

"Lloyd. Remember, I asked you to call me Lloyd."

"Lloyd," she said, trying to keep the exasperation out of her voice. "I am very flattered," she said, taking a deep breath. "And one day, I do envision myself being married. But it will be to someone who shares my dreams and my passions. Someone who will be my soul mate, someone who loves me for who I am–not for what I can bring to the political table."

A thin smile spread across her lips as she attempted to soften her response so as not to insult her eager suitor. She tried a more professional tone. "Right now, as you know, I am fully committed to my LDV contract. Any relationship would be a very serious step for me, and I just don't think it would make sense given my current career focus."

The Senator was silent, so Tygre continued with her attempt to explain her feelings without crushing his. "Keep in mind that you may be 40 but, Lloyd, I'm only 23. I'm not working on the same timeline that you are." Tygre studied his face to see how her words had affected him.

Owens appeared disappointed, she thought, but not surprised. Tygre touched his hand and chuckled playfully. "Besides, Lloyd, I did not leave Poland to live in Nebraska."

Owens tried to force a laugh, but it came out as more of a snort. "I imagine you get marriage proposals like this all the time," he said in a dejected tone.

"Not at all," Tygre said in a cheerful tone and took Lloyd's hand again. It was the first time that Tygre had been asked to marry, but, sadly, it was for the wrong reasons and by the wrong man. She wondered how many more such proposals she would have to endure before the right man would step into her life.

As if the gods were tampering with her emotions, at that very moment, the most handsome and exotic looking man Tygre had ever seen walked into the Senate Dining Room. He was tall, dark, and tanned to perfection, in stark contrast to the room full of pale-faced politicos and their staffers. Wavy dark hair framed his exquisite, bordering-on-beautiful face. He beamed with a broad smile revealing a set of flawless white teeth.

His piercing dark brown eyes slowly scrutinized the room and focused for a split second on Tygre. With her attention fixed on this striking stranger, Tygre slowly pulled her hand away from Senator Owens.

"Have you ever met such a fool before?" Owens asked.

"Excuse me?" Tygre snapped momentarily out of her trance and looked at the Senator. He was staring down at the table, slowly shaking his head.

"I've made such a fool of myself. Can you ever forgive me?"

Tygre looked beyond the Senator to catch another glimpse of the mystery man before turning her attention quickly back to Owens.

"Yes, of course. I mean…no, you didn't make me uncomfortable. And, yes, I forgive you."

"So we can still continue our friendship?" he asked looking up at her sheepishly. He noticed Tygre's focus was elsewhere and turned to see what, or who, had caught her eye.

"Yes, Lloyd," Tygre said, quickly trying to pull his focus back to the table. "We can definitely stay friends."

Owens leaned into her, "Thank you, Tygre," he said, then paused, noticing her gaze. "You see something interesting over there?" he asked.

"Oh…no, I'm just people watching," Tygre said nervously. Isn't that what the Senate Dining Room is all about?"

Owens motioned to Tygre's mystery man, knowing full well he was the object of her undivided attention. "There's a suit for you, huh?" he said offhandedly.

"What? Oh, yes, I suppose it's very attractive," Tygre answered casually.

There was no denying the man was impeccably dressed. With ease, he sported a Seville Row gray pinstriped suit that fit him to perfection and a pale pink handmade silk shirt. A lavender tie completed his ensemble.

In comparison to the conservative suits worn by most of the men in the room, the newcomer's attire struck her as fabulous. He sported an exquisite watch and a pair of soft leather Belgian loafers that Tygre recognized. One of the male models in a recent shoot had worn those very shoes, and the sponsor had snatched them off the poor young man's feet the second the last shot had been taken. "No scuffs on these babies," the assistant had said. "Five hundred bucks a pair."

"Seems a little out of place here, don't you think?" Owens suggested.

"I suppose so," Tygre said smiling, happy now to have an excuse to look in the stranger's direction. He stood tall as he stole another glance at Tygre before redirecting his attention to the stunning, petite brunette who accompanied him.

"His name is Abdul Khalil Muhammad Abu Karim. They call him Khalil Karim," Owens offered.

"Oh?" Tygre tried to act less interested than she was.

"He'd like to pose as a playboy, but trust me, he's not. Grant you, Khalil Karim is extremely rich, which allows him the luxury of being a major player in D.C. But the rumor has it that he finances some very questionable 'religious' activities."

"Hmm....really? In that case, what is here doing here?"

"Deep pockets can bring even the Karims of the world to the inner circles of Congress and the White House." Owens quickly checked his wristwatch. It was after 1:00 p.m. He looked up, signaled the waiter, and ordered a second glass of wine.

"Wait a minute, Lloyd," Tygre said. Something didn't seem quite right. "According to you," she said, "seated in the Senate Dining Room on Capitol Hill next to the most powerful men in Washington is a man suspected of financing suspicious terrorist activities!"

"I didn't say that!" Owens protested.

"You're most certainly insinuating it, Lloyd." Tygre looked at the Senator and asked him point blank, "Are you telling me all of this because you're jealous of him, Lloyd?"

"Me? Jealous of Khalil Karim?" Tygre watched his face carefully as it registered irritation and then full-blown exasperation.

Owens paused to carefully choose the right tone. "Listen," he said "Karim's mother and all his siblings died during a visit to Palestine. They were killed by an Israeli raid."

"That's terrible," Tygre said. The look of compassion that flashed across her face was exactly what Owens feared.

"Tygre, don't be fooled by Karim's façade. He has nothing but hatred for Americans and Jews."

"But, can't you understand why?"

Owens took Tygre's hand and looked at her in earnest. "Tygre, I am a United States' Senator. I sit on the Senate Foreign Relations Committee and I have access to classified data."

"And…?"

"A lot about Karim and his so-called 'charitable' activities is available on his Web site. Let's leave it at that."

Tygre glanced again at Khalil, who still stood surveying the room, waiting for the maitre'd, who was involved ushering an elderly man to a table. Khalil smiled back at her daringly as if to indicate he knew he was the topic of her conversation with Owens. Suddenly, he was making his way toward their table.

Owens sat up straight in his chair and breathed deeply, as if readying himself for an assault.

"I just wanted to stop by and say hello, Senator." Khalil seemed to know better than to attempt to shake Owens' hand.

"And who is this lovely lady?" He looked into Tygre's eyes. Tygre blinked and smiled, trying to maintain her poise. She feared her attraction to Khalil Karim was more than obvious. "I'm Tygre Topolska," she said, extending a hand.

Khalil took it eagerly. "My name is Khalil Karim." His silky voice and pronounced British accent fascinated Tygre. She noticed how soft his hand felt against hers.

Owens looked again at his wristwatch. "We were just leaving, Khalil. You will have to excuse us." Owens hastily rose from the table and took Tygre's free hand. Her right hand was still in the possession of Khalil Karim.

"Let's go, Tygre," Owens said, forcing a tight smile.

A palpable tension filled the room as the lunch crowd watched the drama: one angry red-faced Senator from Nebraska and one impeccably dressed smooth-talking playboy from the Middle East, each holding the hand of a Polish supermodel, was clearly more excitement than the Senate Dining Room had experienced in some time.

It was Khalil who elegantly ended the standoff. "Very nice to meet you," he said with a bow, releasing Tygre's hand, if not her gaze. Tygre stood silently, smiling back at him, her eyes dancing across his face from his eyes to his lips and back again.

"Surely we will meet again," he said and, taking two steps back, motioned to Owens that he was free to exit with Tygre.

The silent cab ride with Senator Owens back to her hotel reminded Tygre of the tense ride home she shared with her father when she was expelled from the convent.

As the taxi pulled up to the Hay Adams, Owens made one last attempt to convince Tygre.

"I hope you never see Khalil Karim again," he said. "Any involvement with that man would prove to be a serious error, trust me."

"I understand, Lloyd," she said as she exited the cab.

"I don't think you do," the Senator replied, pulling the door shut between them.

Tygre waved to Owens as the cab drove away, but he did not look back.

Several hours later, as Tygre was reliving the day's events in her mind, the phone in her room rang. She knew who it was before she picked up the receiver.

"Tygre, it's Khalil Karim. I am downstairs in the lobby. Come down. I want to show you D.C. my way. Are you willing?"

Am I ever! Tygre thought. After that mind-boggling lunch date with an insane Senator, the thought of getting to know an irresistibly attractive and single billionaire sent her spirits soaring. Tygre took less than three minutes to change her clothes, refresh her makeup and adjust her hair in the mirror before dashing from her suite. In the elevator, on the way down from her room, Tygre checked herself again in the mirror and noticed she was shaking. She had three floors to decide her destiny-it occurred to her-whether to turn a page on everything that was familiar to her and descend into what Lloyd Owens swore was danger, or return upstairs and stay safe. Tygre stared at the flush in her cheeks and knew it would be a quick decision.

Tygre's mobile phone suddenly rang and Senator Owens' number flashed on the screen. She switched off her phone and dropped it into her bag. When the elevator doors opened, Khalil was standing directly in front of her, smiling with soft lips and penetrating eyes. This time, he skipped the handshake in favor of a gentle hug. Up close, she found his scent intoxicating.

"I couldn't resist this impulse. Forgive me, please," he said.

"I'm definitely curious to see D.C....your way."

Karim held the lobby door open for Tygre to step through. He watched her from behind as she made her way toward his silver Maserati. Karim gallantly helped her into the car, and then slipped in behind the steering wheel, watching her intently as he revved the throaty engine. Tygre smiled back at him, and they sped swiftly away from the hotel, headed toward what she was certain would be adventure.

Tygre felt an overwhelming sense of devilment as Khalil ran through the gears of the powerful machine that carried them away. The rich exhaust echoed in their wake, and passersby stopped to gape at the exotic car and its equally exotic passengers. Despite all of Lloyd Owens's pontificating warnings, Tygre was brimming with delicious anticipation of what was to come with her charismatic suitor.

Within minutes of leaving the Hay Adams, however, it seemed that fate had other plans. Tygre's eyes widened and she shrieked. A blue Volkswagen convertible had appeared from nowhere, blowing through a stop sign and crossing directly into the path of the speeding Maserati. Khalil slammed on the brakes and swerved but, despite his evident driving skills, the two cars met with a soft thud.

"Are you okay?" Khalil asked a shaken Tygre.

"I think so," she answered softly. "Are you?" She was lightheaded with relief.

"I'm fine." Khalil stepped out of his car and approached the driver of the Volkswagen—a college student, from the looks of him. The young man sized up Khalil and moved back tentatively.

"I am so sorry," the driver apologized as he pulled out his driving license from his wallet. "I didn't see you."

Tygre watched the scene through her window, her breathing still ragged.

"Listen young chap, I'm actually on a rather important date, so let's not make too much out of this," Khalil glanced in Tygre's direction. "No one was hurt and the damage is minor." He pointed to a scrape on the Volkswagen's bumper.

"I'll call my insurance company," the young man said, fumbling for his cell phone. "They'll probably want a police report."

"That will not be necessary. I would prefer we settle this here and now," Khalil peeled off twenty crisp one hundred dollar bills as the other driver gaped. "I am sure this will more than cover the damage." Without waiting for a response from the stunned driver, Khalil quickly returned to the car, flashed Tygre a smile and sped away.

"Where are you taking me?" Tygre asked, "And why didn't you let that kid's insurance cover your damage? It was clearly his fault."

Khalil was quiet for a moment. His eyes shifted back and forth between the rearview and side mirrors of his speeding car.

"I prefer to take care of things myself, Tygre. The last thing I need is police and bureaucrats getting involved in my affairs." Tygre silently nodded, noticing that Khalil was glancing nervously into his rear view mirror. *Is someone following us?* she wondered, but she didn't feel comfortable asking the question. Khalil accelerated and slipped effortlessly into the next lane. He checked his rearview mirror once again.

Too curious to sit still, Tygre shifted in her seat and leaned forward to take a peek out of her passenger side mirror. She immediately spotted a black sedan skillfully maneuvering through the traffic and trailing them closely.

She turned to Khalil with the question already formed, but he smile and pointed over her shoulder.

"Take a look, my dear. We are on Embassy Row, now, and this is the Islamic Center of Washington." She followed his gesture toward a limestone building with a minaret that reached high into the early evening sky. Soft lights illuminated its exterior, making it a slender ribbon of white against the cobalt sky.

"It's remarkable," Tygre said politely. But the beauty of the mosque was overshadowed by her fear that they were being followed. She glanced out of her mirror again to find the black sedan pursuing closely behind.

"It was designed by Italian architect Mario Rossi," Khalil said. "It's the largest mosque in the United States."

"I've never seen anything like it," Tygre responded, still preoccupied by the sedan.

"Then it's time you had a closer look," Khalil said invitingly. He pulled the Maserati into a parking space alongside the broad avenue and turned off the engine. "I'd like you to come inside."

"Is it safe?" Tygre asked.

Khalil's smile faded instantly. He glanced up at the soaring tower, then back at her. "Tygre, this is a place of worship. Why would it be unsafe?"

"No, I mean...them," Tygre turned to indicate the black sedan that had pulled into a spot only a car length behind them. "Why are we being followed?"

Khalil turned and stared bluntly in the direction of the sedan for several moments. When he turned back to her, he gave her a weak smile. "You might as well get used to it, Tygre. I've had to." He stepped out of the car, walked confidently to the passenger side and opened the door for Tygre. He ushered her out with a flourish.

"Are you sure about this?" Tygre said taking another peek at the black sedan.

"Come," Khalil said reaching for her hand. "Don't pay any attention to the FBI."

"The FBI?" Tygre's face registered bewilderment and fear. She suddenly regretted not listening to Senator Owens. For an instant she imagined snatching her phone from her purse and calling him back. *"Lloyd, you were right. Come save me!"*

"Don't worry," Khalil was saying, reaching for her hand. "Once we are inside the mosque, you'll be inspired. Worshiping Allah gives me purpose. It teaches me how to embrace dying without fear and promises paradise to come."

The lines of stress had disappeared from Khalil's face. He looked relaxed and peaceful in sharp contrast to Tygre who felt her own face pinched with concern.

"But if they follow you there must be a reason," she said.

"They have absolutely no reason, Tygre. Nothing, but their own paranoid suspicions." He glanced at the parked sedan again, as if daring the men inside to come forward. "Come."

She hesitated, then gave him her hand. What was going to happen with a carful of FBI agents, right there, anyway? She gave another quick glance in the direction of the sedan.

"Ignore them, Tygre." This is what the FBI wants to do," Khalil said. He adjusted his sleeves in as if to indicate that those who watched them were of little significance. "They are determined to reduce my life to constant fear and concern, but I am even more determined not to let them."

Khalil held out his arm for Tygre and moved her toward the mosque. She took a quick glance over her shoulder to see two men in dark suits, stepping from the sedan to stand at the curb, watching.

"Tygre, do you know what Islam stands for?" Khalil asked attempting to redirect her focus.

Tygre shook her head.

"I didn't think so," Khalil said answering his own question. Islam simply means 'submission' and derives from a word meaning 'peace.' I submit to the will of my God, Allah every day. The FBI means nothing." Khalil spoke dynamically and punctuated his last statement by planting a gentle kiss on Tygre's cheek. The faint smell of his cologne lingered on her skin. As she breathed deeply, it made her lightheaded.

"Perhaps, we should go back to the hotel," she said. "I just don't feel comfortable here. I don't like them watching us like that. It scares me."

Khalil sighed and glared angrily over Tygre's shoulder at the FBI agents. "I wanted you to experience the serenity and beauty of this mosque," Khalil said keeping his eyes on the agents. "But that will have to wait for another day." He turned her around and walked her back to the car. "Let's go to my home in Georgetown where we can be in peace."

When they pulled from the curb, the black sedan followed them for several miles. Finally, at a stop light, the sedan accelerated abruptly past them, making a show of breaking off their surveillance. Khalil offered up a cheery wave as the sedan sped past.

"How can you live like that?" Tygre asked once the sedan had disappeared.

Khalil glanced over. "I'm afraid I don't have a choice, Tygre. And I'm sorry about that for your sake. I understand that the FBI can be very intimidating, but it takes more than that to rattle me."

They drove on in silence for a bit until he parked the car on the corner of 33rd and P Streets. Without so much as a second glance at the dent in the sleek machine's bumper he hurried to help Tygre step down onto the cobblestone pavement.

"Is this your place?" she asked, glancing up at a distinguished brownstone that loomed over them.

He smiled but shook his head. "My home is nearby. But I thought we might walk. It is a beautiful evening. Let's not waste it. Georgetown is the most coveted and prestigious, civilized square mile of cobblestoned real estate in the nation."

As if on cue, Tygre's heel became caught between a pair of paving stones. She felt herself lurch forward, heading facedown toward the pavement. And just as suddenly, Tygre found herself in Khalil's arms, inches away from his face. The scent of Khalil intoxicated her, and Tygre felt a pounding at her temples.

"Thank you," she managed after a moment. It was getting to be too much for her, she thought. One instant, she was frightened to be in this man's presence, and in the next, she was palpitating like a schoolgirl. She managed to pull herself away, smoothing at her dress.

Khalil smiled as if he was aware of every thought in her head. "I was in the midst of a geography lesson, wasn't I?" He pointed down the street in front of them. "This is the Northwest quadrant of the District of Columbia, and the Potomac River is just down the hill. In its early days Georgetown was a thriving port, Tygre."

"I'm fascinated," she said.

Khalil nodded as if he might have believed her. "George Washington, Thomas Jefferson and Franklin D. Roosevelt have all lived here. Everyone of any standing in the halls of power and diplomacy, have resided here. JFK not only lived in Georgetown but also maintained a mistress who lived on an adjacent street very near my house."

"Now that's very interesting," Tygre said, a bit surprised at her own brazenness. It was as though, with the departure of the dark sedan, all of the mystique and allure of the man before her had rematerialized.

"And here we are," he said, suddenly waving his hand at the home that appeared in front of them. "My own home in Georgetown." Like a child in front of a lighted Christmas tree, Tygre stopped to gaze up at what seemed a stately home from the pages of an architectural magazine.

"It was built in 1810, but it doesn't look that old, does it?" Khalil laughed genuinely amused by Tygre's reaction. Her eyes sparkled as she absorbed the immaculately maintained federal-style red brick mansion that spread over nearly an acre of the most expensive real estate in D.C. Judging from the expression on his face, Khalil was introducing her to his most prized possession.

"It has an impeccable pedigree," he told her. "And, I don't mind telling you, the highest price tag ever attached to a home in the District." Khalil shook his head. "As I wrote the check, even I was having second thoughts."

Tygre smiled politely. "It looks very impressive."

"I'll tell you why I went through with the purchase, Tygre." He sighed before he continued. "Many felt 1717 35th should have remained in the hands of a U.S. citizen. So, needless to say, its impending sale to a supposed Arab playboy outraged some of my neighbors." He gave her a wistful glance. "When I learned that, I knew I would have to live here, just to prove to everyone that in fact the Devil has no horns." He opened his palms and gave her his most guileless smile.

"No, no horns," she said. In fact, she thought, he was one of the most impressive looking men she had ever seen. He was gorgeous, and wealthy beyond reckoning, and single. And yet still something seemed wrong. "Well," she said after a moment. "Are we going inside, or do we just stand out here and look?"

Khalil leaned in to kiss her cheek as he guided her through the front door to an appropriately unassuming entryway, one which soon led them to a high-ceiling rotunda with an exquisite marble floor. Its walls were stenciled and adorned with Arabic art works and mosaics.

"The Renaissance painters are a bit too nouveau for my collection," Khalil teased Tygre, who followed him through the house.

The superbly appointed grand drawing room was filled with ancient Byzantine art and oversized furnishings that spelled ease and comfort, combined with *Town and Country* sophistication. A tall pair of French doors opened to a manicured lawn and adjacent garden lit to jewel-like radiance.

"This is the most romantic setting I have ever seen!" Tygre exclaimed.

Khalil nestled against Tygre's ear then planted a gentle kiss on her lips. "Let's go outside."

As they stepped into the garden, Tygre's attention was drawn to a nook where oval swimming pool with a cascading fountain shimmered in the evening lights. They stood quietly in the serenity of the gathering nightfall and Khalil pulled her closer. Tygre felt something loosen inside. He bent to kiss her and she returned it with a passion that exceeded all of her expectations.

The strap of her silk camisole fell slowly off her shoulder revealing one of her cherubic breasts. Tygre's heart quickened as she felt Khalil's arousal pulsing against her. She was becoming slowly and deliciously mesmerized by the thought of making love to him and fought to keep from giving into the impulse altogether

The faint noise of a distant conversation drifting from inside the house broke the spell of the moment. Tygre tried to let go of Khalil's hand to adjust her fallen camisole, just as a bespectacled young man appeared at the opened set of French doors. "Dinner is served," he announced, a chilly tone in his voice.

Tygre turned, startled. Khalil put a comforting hand on her shoulder. "Tygre," he said. "Allow me to introduce Malik Youssaf, my trusted assistant."

Tygre would have spoken, but the young man advanced past her, his jaw set and his eyes flashing. He presented to Khalil a white napkin-covered silver tray, which held several white pills. Khalil, who seemed not to notice his assistant's manner, picked up a pair of the pills and swallowed them down without water.

"Give us a moment, would you Malik? I would like to show Tygre my collection before it gets dark. By the way, I left the Maserati on the corner of 33rd and P. We had a minor fender-bender earlier. Would you mind seeing to it that it gets parked and fixed properly?"

Malik gave his boss a curt nod and turned on his heel. Tygre watched him march off.

"Is he always so friendly?" she asked.

Khalil turned to her with a tolerant smile. "Pay no attention, Tygre. Malik is never certain about those who are strangers to him." He sighed. "I'm afraid we have an array of people here in this country to blame for that."

"Maybe you should let him know that I'm not with the FBI," she said.

Khalil laughed and took her hand. "Come. I've got something else to show you."

As he tugged her along to a garage at the back of the property, a thought occurred to Tygre. "What about those pills Malik brought. You're not sick, are you?"

Khalil turned to flash his most spectacular smile. "It's nothing serious, Tygre. I need painkillers from time to time. I've had some issues with my back since I was young – an old motor racing injury."

He turned then to usher them through a door into the sizable garage in front of them. "Come along," he said as he stepped inside, groping for the light switch. As she joined him, Tygre could see that the cavernous pupils of his eyes shone and danced like distress signals.

"Here's the switch," Tygre said, turning on the lights.

"Ah, most grateful thanks, Tygre!" Khalil said, with an unusually slow and deliberate inflection. "Look around, now." Tygre stared at a line of half a dozen meticulously kept vintage cars before her. She recognized a Ferrari, a Porsche, and a staid Bentley. The others-impossibly sleek and imposing in their gleaming nickel and brass accouterments-seemed like vehicles that had never graced an actual street. Perhaps they'd been handcrafted in some machine shop by Valkyries and carried directly here, she thought. The garage walls themselves were lined with trophies and photos of Khalil in racing gear. Here and there were pictures of Khalil and Malik hoisting trophies together.

"Malik races with you?" Tygre asked in surprise.

Khalil seemed almost puzzled by the question. "Of course he does. Why do you ask?"

"It's nothing," she said. "I was just surprised, that's all."

Khalil bent to brush an invisible speck from the gleaming hood of the Porsche before them, then polished the spot with the elbow of his coat, leaving Tygre to take in the spectacle of this shrine to the automobile.

Banners and posters proclaiming the dominance of Khalil Racing dangled from the rafters. This was no garage, she thought. This was a temple. "These cars bring me nearly as much joy as racing itself," Khalil murmured, risen to stand beside her now.

"Remarkable," Tygre managed. Her mind was back on the surly Malik. Hardly the picture of hospitality, she was thinking.

"Khalil, dinner is served."

Tygre jumped as Malik's unmistakable voice crackled over an intercom.

"He's everywhere," she told herself.

"Did you say something?" Khalil asked.

"It was nothing," Tygre said.

Khalil stepped to the speaker set in the nearby wall and pressed a button. "We're on our way in, Malik," Khalil guided her outside, pausing briefly to turn off the lights and close the door.

"Does Malik live here with you, Khalil?" Tygre asked as they strolled back to the mansion.

"Of course he does," Khalil told her. "Malik is indispensable to me. He oversees the house and the servants and the car collection. As you saw, he also races with me. When I am in town, we dine together. I hope you don't mind if he joins us."

"Not at all, Khalil," Tygre replied evenly, hoping to conceal her disappointment. "How long have you been racing cars, anyway?"

Khalil's face brightened. "For a very long time, it is my way of relaxing. And it is my passion."

With that, they walked back to the dining room in silence where Malik sat at one end of the long table, sorting through a stack of documents.

"Malik." Tygre cautiously acknowledged.

Malik ignored her. When Khalil showed Tygre to a place at the opposite end of the table, Malik stood abruptly, dropping a napkin to cover the documents.

"We're having an excellent wine, Tygre. Opus One, Baron Philippe de Rothschild, 2001. It was a great year for me too," Khalil said, raising a glass. "I received my green card in 2001."

Malik stared silently at Tygre as another casually attired young Muslim man walked into the room with a bottle and placed it on the table. Malik nodded to him and the man nodded in return.

"Tygre, this is Adis Gabir," Khalil said, pointing with his wine glass. "He is one of my research specialists from Saudi Arabia." Adis' stern-looking face broke into a hesitant smile.

"Tygre," Gabir said, with the trace of a bow.

Before Tygre could respond, Khalil motioned to Gabir. "Would you care to join us?"

"Not tonight, Khalil," Malik interjected sharply. "Adis is working on a project." Khalil seemed about to say something, then signaled his acceptance with a wave and reached for the wine.

Adis silently disappeared from the room. Within moments the meal commenced, with two young Arab servants bringing in a series of Middle Eastern dishes.

"So Khalil," Tygre asked as she took a sip of her wine. "How can driving at high speeds be relaxing?"

"If I could explain it, I would," Khalil said. "All I can tell is that it is true." He took a sip of his own wine, seeming to drift for a moment before fixing his gaze on her again.

"Against my mother's wishes, I started motor racing in the Saudi desert at age 13. I wrecked my car and I suffered serious back injuries, but I still race. We did very well this year at the American Le Mans series, didn't we?" Khalil said, directing his last question to Malik.

"We did," Malik answered, curtly.

Tygre looked over at him then turned quickly away from his belligerent stare.

"Actually, Malik and I are scheduled to race at Le Mans, the 24-hour endurance race next June. Perhaps, you would like to join me in France?"

"Perhaps," Tygre answered casually. She suspected Malik would rather that she had a car crash of her own. "It sounds exciting. I'll see what LDV has planned for me and let you know."

If Malik's eyes could kill, Tygre would be dead. But if Khalil noticed, he chose to ignore their tense interaction. "There is very little more exhilarating than what goes on at Le Mans, Tygre. For me, racing is as stimulating as the sexual act itself, perhaps even more."

Tygre fought to keep a blush from her cheeks. Far-fetched as Khalil's statement seemed, she could not keep the image of Khalil's naked body from her mind. "I believe it," she uttered under her breath.

Malik stood abruptly, dragging his chair noisily. He left the dining room without a word and without having touched the food on his plate.

Tygre watched him leave, then turned quickly back to Khalil with a puzzled look. He returned the look with a disarming smile, and with a wave of his hand dismissed the other servants.

"Why don't we take our dessert and champagne upstairs, Tygre?"

Tygre smiled at Khalil and the two of them left the dining table hand in hand. On the way out from the room, Khalil stopped her. "I want to kiss your beautiful lips every time I look at you," he said.

As he brushed his lips across her cheek and moved in to taste her mouth, Tygre heard a distant conversation. *It's him again,* she thought. She pulled back for a moment. "What about Malik?" she asked breathlessly.

"He has work to do." Khalil placated her between kisses.

"But why is he so upset?" Her eyes peered over Khalil's shoulder, certain she would catch sight of Malik nearby.

"Don't worry about him. I'll talk to him later."

Tygre found herself walking silently toward what she was sure would be Khalil's bedroom. She wished she hadn't finished her third glass of wine at dinner. It weakened her resolve and clouded her thinking.

"Are you all right?" Khalil asked, as he guided her inside the dimly lit room.

"It's nothing," Tygre answered. "I'm just a little nervous, that's all."

"What do you have to be nervous about?" Khalil raised an eyebrow and smiled.

"We are playing with fire, aren't we, Khalil?" Tygre uttered, barely able to articulate her words.

"Yes, but I find you irresistible."

Tygre breathed heavily as Khalil's lips ran along the side of her neck. "Why do I feel so drawn to you and so frightened of you at the same time?" Tygre asked.

Khalil lowered his voice. "Such a thing is erotic, isn't it?"

"It is," Tygre said. "But I don't understand it."

"You don't need to. Just enjoy the thrill of it!" Khalil pulled her closer.

His hands were on her hips, now. He leaned in, pinning her against the wall just inside the door. As he thrust his aroused self against her, Tygre trembled with excitement. The wine had lowered her inhibitions and her doubts were scattering like so many motes of dust.

There was an exquisite scent of Casablanca lilies in full bloom filling the room, and an Italian tenor's rich voice drifted from hidden speakers. The giant fur-covered bed was turned down.

Egyptian cotton sheets waited to caress her in lavish comfort. Several dozen white candles flickered on a breeze that wafted through the French doors overlooking the flower garden. It all seemed to Tygre to add up to the most sensual experience she had ever known.

Khalil kissed Tygre again tenderly on the lips. When she closed her eyes and fell into his arms, he carried her to the bed, set her down on the sheets and quietly began to undress himself. He meticulously unfastened the sapphire and diamond cufflinks and set them on the dresser. His eyes lingered on Tygre as he opened his shirt, revealing a perfectly sculpted chest. He slipped his flawlessly manicured feet from the Belgian loafers and worked the carefully tooled buckle on his belt. The pants dropped silently to the ancient Aubusson rug.

He was posing narcissistically for Tygre, she understood, but it only brought a faint smile to her face. Certainly it didn't stop her from soaking every inch of his god-like physique.

Tygre reached for him, but Khalil grabbed her hand and whispered, "Wait, Tygre. Take one of these. It's ecstasy. You'll love it, trust me." He swallowed one, broke another in half and placed it in her mouth. Tygre did not protest although she found it decidedly unromantic.

Khalil lay next to Tygre and slowly, piece by piece, began to remove her clothing. He slipped the straps of her camisole off her shoulders and expertly used his tongue on her breasts and nipples.

Tygre leaned in to kiss him, but he stopped her. "Wait, Tygre," he said. "It will get better if you wait. I promise you!"

Tygre looked at him, confused. Khalil reached for an opened bottle of champagne and poured himself a large glass. He took a sizable gulp and, moved towards her. As their lips touched, he allowed the champagne to drizzle inside her mouth. In a daze now, Tygre swallowed.

"Now repeat after me," Khalil said, smiling, gently stroking her breasts. "There is no God apart from God; Muhammad is the messenger of God."

"Khalil, stop. I don't want to pray right now." There was a part of her that was revolted by his words, but there was also a part of her that was on fire at his touch.

Khalil swiftly slid down her body and pressed his face between her legs. His lips were soft and he moved slowly. Tygre moaned with pleasure and reached to pull him even closer.

He looked up at her, his face glistening, gasping the words. "There is no god apart from Allah. Say it, Tygre. You must say it now! Muhammad is the messenger of God."

Tygre's mind was repulsed, but her body screamed to feel Khalil inside her. The heat of her desire was aflame with the drug and the champagne. It did not really seem to matter, she told herself. And in the next moment she was repeating the words.

"There is no god apart from Allah...."

She felt Khalil moving up her body. He was forcing her legs wide with his knees. He was plunging into her.

"Muhammad is the messenger of God..." he said. "Say it after me."

"Muhammad is the messenger of God," she heard herself repeating.

Her hips rose to meet his. "No god apart from Allah," he reiterated, and she answered again, their bodies pounding against each other for what seemed forever, the words pouring out of his mouth and hers in an unending litany, until finally she felt herself falling toward the earth as lightly as a cloud, every nerve ending on fire.

"No god but Allah," she repeated, the words slurred, her lips rubbery.

Khalil was thrusting wildly toward his own climax, his head thrown back, the cords of his neck bulging...until suddenly he was screaming, "Zahara, Zahara, my love, my mother. I love you. Why did you leave me?"

There was a madman thrusting, emptying himself inside her, Tygre knew. Had she one iota of human will remaining, she would have flung him off her body and run wildly for all she was worth. But instead, she felt her hips slamming back against his, trying to quench the fire...and in the next moment all was black.

When she woke up, Khalil was not in the bed with her. Nor was he anywhere in the room, something told her. She pressed a hand against her forehead to try to make her head stop throbbing. After a few deep breaths she managed to make her way into the vast bathroom and splash cold water on her face. She made her way silently downstairs dressed in Khalil's shirt, which still smelled of Eau de Toilette *Egoiste* and the underlying hint of sweat and sex.

Daybreak fell on Washington and peeked through the massive French windows leading to the garden. The house was still and quiet, yet Tygre did not find it peaceful. The marble floor beneath her feet felt cold and suddenly she was overwhelmed by nausea and loneliness.

She trembled. The sense of guilt and shame, and the aftereffects of the alcohol and drugs wracked her body, but nothing came close to the emptiness and sadness she felt in her soul. Tygre tried to make sense of last night, but Khalil felt more like a stranger now than before she had slept with him. She felt a sudden sense of urgency to get back to her suite at the Hay Adams, as far away from Khalil's mansion – and Khalil himself – as possible.

"Khalil?" she called softly as her head continued to throb.

She suddenly heard hushed voices coming from the grand wood-paneled library he'd showed her about last night.

"Khalil?" she called again. But there was no answer, only the sound of soft laughter of two men. Tygre stepped into the doorway of the library. There propped on pillows on a fur rug in front of the smoldering fireplace, Khalil and Malik lay side by side, fully clothed, holding hands.

Tygre gasped and quickly threw a cupped hand over her mouth.

Khalil raised his head to see Tygre standing in the doorway. He waved and smiled lazily. "Come and join us!"

Tygre stood speechless, staring at them and shaking her head.

"Come now, Tygre," Khalil said, raising himself on an elbow. "It's not what you think. We are like brothers. We love each other. We have a common God. And, after last night, you are a part of this bond as well."

"You're so wrong!" Tygre cried out.

"Tygre, you simply need to learn more about me," Khalil said.

"I know more than I need to," she managed, her stomach heaving. "You drugged me and used me, that's what I know." Tygre felt her face burning with anger. She staggered back from the doorway, then turned and vomited onto the cold tiles of the hallway.

The image of Malik's triumphant grin followed her all the way upstairs to Khalil's bedroom where the smell of alcohol and raw sex nearly overwhelmed her again. Tygre fell to her knees at the bedside and began to pray. *God, please forgive me. Help me find myself. I am not a Muslim. I promise, I will never to betray you again.*

After a bit, Tygre felt her breathing begin to come under control. She wiped away tears and stood unsteadily, trying to find her bearings. She gathered her belongings and got dressed. With no intercession from Khalil, she made her way quietly out the door and onto the street, desperately searching until she found a taxi.

At her hotel she took a shower that never seemed to end. *I am so sorry,* Tygre repeated again and again, as hot water streamed down her shivering body. *God please forgive me for my actions. I'm sorry!*

The time to take control of her life was long overdue, she understood. *Something has to change,* she vowed, *so help me God!*

Chapter 23

Le Mans
1:08 p.m. Sunday

Doug Martin wiped a layer of sweat from his face as he squeezed the last few yards toward Karim Racing's trailer. It was in his sight now, at the far end of a parking lot near pit lane. Each step he took was part of a nerve-shredding journey through a minefield of terror. The thought of the imminent destruction that could erupt at any second was mind-numbing and left Martin exhausted.

"Anything new on the search for the girl and that scumbag?" he barked into his wristwatch transmitter.

Ben Hartley responded immediately. "We've got several agents deployed Doug, not to mention the JTTF, Secret Service, French military and police. How close are you to that trailer?"

"I'll be there in a couple of minutes, sir."

"The Secret Service explosives detection detail is on the way. They've been informed about the explosives in the trailer. I'm sending a Weapons of Mass Destruction team along with the bomb technicians. Meet them there immediately and brief them accordingly. After you deal with the computer issue, get the hell out of there."

"Yes sir," Martin responded as he glanced at his wristwatch. "It's 1:11 here."

"I know what the fucking time is! You don't have to remind me. Now hurry up for God's sake!" Ben ordered.

The drivers were nearing their final stretch. The crowds started pushing toward the podium where the winning teams would be appearing to bask in glory.

Their moment of victory, Martin thought, *could be a moment of doom… for them and for all the rest of us.* Acutely aware that at any second, the entire scene before him could be reduced to a pile of dust and flying body parts, Martin felt his pulse quicken and his breathing become shallow. As he maneuvered past the back of Karim Racing's garage, the sound of screaming brakes cut through the din of the crowd, and he turned to see a car entering pit lane for a last-minute refuel. In seconds, a fuel nozzle was attached to the racer, while other mechanics swarmed under the hood to attend to the car's engine.

The smooth voice of Herve du Bois boomed over the loudspeakers, with yet another update on the imminent conclusion of an intensely fought race. *"For those of you who have just joined Tele Mondial, you are lucky to be tuning in to what promises to be yet another exciting finish. The No.1 car, New Deal's LMP1 prototype, driven by Brad Harrington is comfortably in the lead followed by New Deal's second car, driven by Chris Summers, in second place. On Summers' heels is Khalil Karim of Karim Racing in third place, with only four seconds separating them. These three competitors have been challenging each other from the start. Brad Harrington could be well on his way to claiming his fourth consecutive win. Bien fait, another splendid effort by Monsieur Le Mans."*

Martin cringed at the mention of Brad's name. Even if they were able to find and disarm the explosives, the prospect of explaining Tygre's disappearance to the son of the President was beyond comprehension. Better not to think of that, Martin decided, and pushed forward, praying that Malik did not intend harm to Tygre.

Hardly had he completed the thought than the excited voice of Herve du Bois was back, delivering his next update.

"*Mesdames et Messieurs! Attention! Another crash has been reported. Can you imagine? With barely an hour and a half left, Ferrari No. 81 is being towed away! Let's see if the organizers will flag Porsche No.19, the car responsible for the accident. Unfortunately, the flag won't make a difference for Ferrari No. 81. The car is out of the race! Just another example of the danger that is Le Mans.*"

"And it's becoming more dangerous by the minute," Martin blurted.

Numb to the unrelenting fury of the race, Martin plodded on, wincing when he caught sight of Agent Ives pacing outside of Karim Racing's trailer.

"Ben, I've located Ives. I'm at the trailer," Martin said into the transmitter. "Now, where the hell is the bomb team?" Martin scanned the parking lot as he covered the last few steps toward Ives, who looked to be chatting on a cell phone.

"They are coming from the far side of the track, Doug. They can't fly, can they?" Ben raised his voice.

"I need them now, sir!" Martin approached Ives, who was speaking intently into his cell phone, waving a hand wildly. He didn't notice Martin advancing until the last moment. Abruptly, Ives snapped his phone shut mid-sentence and shoved it into his pocket.

"Who were you talking to?" Martin demanded.

"I was checking with New Deal's manager on Brad's lap time."

"Everybody knows Harrington's in the lead! What fucking difference does it make? That should be the last thing on your mind right now." Martin's jaw jutted toward Ives.

"The President's son is *my* priority." Ives said mildly.

Martin shook his head. "There's no time for quibbling. Did you get those computers shut down?"

Ives shook his head. "I took a look. I didn't think I should do anything until you got here."

Martin gave him a murderous look, then stormed inside the trailer, followed by the Secret Service agent.

Martin hurried to check the monitors where it appeared that real-time financial data flashed in multi-colored sequences across the screens. "These could be new wire transfers," he said in a voice filled with rage. "Goddamn it, Ives, you were given orders to disable the computers!"

"I'm not a computer expert," he told Martin. "This isn't my detail and I wasn't about to screw something up. I went outside to wait for you and keep an eye out for the Muslim and the girl."

Martin gave him a sidelong glance. "We don't need terrorists. We have you," he said, beginning a methodical shut-down of the laptops. "What the hell is the matter with you, anyway?"

"I told you..."

"You're an idiot, Ives!" he growled. "Who knows how much cash went spiraling off down the terror pipeline thanks to you!"

As the last screen went black, Martin lifted his watch to his mouth and spoke into his transmitter. "The computers are down, Ben. Hard to tell how much damage was done..." He broke off before Hartley had a chance to answer.

"Ives! What the fuck are you doing?"

Martin lunged forward just as Ives raised one of the laptops and was preparing to smash it on the countertop. Martin quickly blocked Ives' arms and forced the laptop back on the edge of the counter.

"You said you wanted to disable the computers," Ives said.

Their eyes met in a tense standoff of mutual suspicion. "What the hell is going on here, Ives? I know you saw those wire transfers in progress. I briefed you very clearly. Why didn't you stop them?"

Ives appeared oddly calm. "I didn't see any activity on the screens when I arrived. Everything was quiet."

"That's not the point. You had specific instructions to disable the computers." Martin spoke with deliberate clarity, aware that every word of their conversation was being transmitted to FBI Headquarters.

Ives shrugged shoulders and spoke evenly. "I am telling you again nothing was going on when I got here. As far as I could tell the computers had already been shut down."

It wasn't going to get him anywhere badgering Ives, Agent Martin concluded. Either the guy was the most incompetent Secret Service Agent, who had ever been minted, or something else was going on...and he had little time to wonder about that. Abruptly he switched gears.

"All right Ives, our intelligence indicates Youssaf has at least two remote control transmitters connected to explosives...perhaps three. We can't assume they were all in the cigar box. Anything else, like a diagram or written materials may provide us with help as to where the explosives themselves are hidden."

"I've already searched the place. I haven't turned up anything," Ives said.

Martin turned away in exasperation. After a moment, he tapped his wrist communicator. "Any luck on the search for the explosives, Ben?"

Ben's voice came back in seconds. "We've got a dozen trained operatives out there, but it's a madhouse. Trying to accomplish anything without starting a panic is practically impossible."

"Any leads on the whereabouts of Youssaf and Tygre?"

"Nothing."

Martin sighed. "Anything from the bomb squad?"

"Moments away, Doug. Just sit tight."

"Look, Ben, why I don't have a look at the suit that's packed with explosives here. I can determine the location of the battery, the arming and firing circuits and the detonator...I don't have the necessary tools to disable the battery and the circuitry, but at least this would be a start." As he spoke, Martin saw that Ives was listening intently.

"You realize we'll have to deactivate on site, Ben. No way can we transport anything through these crowds. Youssaf can detonate this thing at any second." Martin used the back of his arm to wipe the perspiration from his forehead. "We're too close to pit lane, Ben. We're running out of time here."

As if on cue, Martin saw the door of the trailer open. Special Agent Lawrence Russell climbed into the trailer accompanied by a group he introduced as a French Special Service Agent, four other FBI Agents, the Secret Service explosives detection detail, and a couple of additional bomb technicians.

There was little ceremony. Martin indicated the explosives-packed suit and Russell and his men went quickly to work. Martin turned aside and got Ben Hartley on the line.

"Russell's here, Ben. They're working on the suit. Keep your fingers crossed, and meantime, I am certain that Youssaf has an escape plan. He's not planning on blowing himself up. He's going to use the girl or he would have killed her on the spot. You need to have a team checking for a chopper or even a small plane. Anything connected with Karim Racing, needs to be tracked."

"We're already on it," Ben answered.

Martin cut the connection with Hartley and turned his attention back to Agent Russell and the team working on the suit. "What do you think, Agent Russell?"

Russell glanced up. "We've found the power source for the detonator, and the wiring seems pretty straightforward. But whoever did this knew what he was doing. We need to make sure there's not a backup power module. If there is, and we attempt to cut the primary circuit, we're all going to be brake dust."

As Martin moved in to get a better look, Ives started toward the trailer's exit.

"You going somewhere, Ives?" Agent Martin stopped him short.

"I need to get some air." Ives said.

"We need you here. Suck it up. And put your cell phone on silent." Ives stared back at him for a moment, then reluctantly complied.

The distant noise of the race and the approaching helicopter seemed to belong to a world Martin might never be a part of again. He intently watched Agent Russell's steady hands. He checked his own. They weren't shaking, but they felt like they were. He vividly recalled his wedding day and the birth of his daughter Eliana, as the events had happened moments ago. Martin took a quick look at Agent Russell, who glanced at him and smiled.

"Wish me luck," Russell said.

He raised a small pair of cutting pliers and severed a wire. The snap of the clipped copper was instantaneous. Time stood still, punctuated by a momentary silence… which lingered, than stretched into two and then three more seconds. Panicked eyes were the only body parts that moved. A second later, it seemed to Martin that every man in the room exhaled at once.

Martin opened the line to Ben Hartley. "The explosives in the trailer have been rendered safe," he said.

"Good work, Doug. Give my congratulations to Agent Russell and his team." Martin nodded, exhaling a chest full of air that he had been holding onto for longer than he would have thought possible. But relief was nowhere on the horizon.

Ben's voice cut through his earpiece. "Negative on the search for other explosives, Doug. The French WMD team hasn't turned up a thing. Nothing near the paddock area. Nothing in the presidential stands. Nothing in pit lane either."

"So…you think we're wrong. There are no additional explosives?" Martin asked. But the moment he spoke, he caught a look on Ives's face that made him wonder. He studied Ives intently. *What does that sonofabitch know? What is he hiding?*

"Wishful thinking Doug, but we can't take that chance. We are back to square one," Ben concluded.

A feeling of dread washed over Martin. "Back to square one," he repeated. *But wasn't one better than nothing?*

Chapter 24

Eleven Months Earlier
New York City

Who have I become? Tygre pondered the question as she stared dolefully at the stranger in her bathroom mirror. The drawn face belonged to someone Tygre would have been ashamed to know, a person who had committed treason against her own soul.

Well, what should I expect? she thought to herself as she blamed her mother for instilling in her a distorted sense of self and a fascination with the wrong kind of man. She cursed Helena's name to the heavens and, feeling immediately guilt-ridden, quickly said a prayer asking God's blessing for her parents and forgiveness for her own transgressions.

She had returned from Washington some time ago, but she still suffered from disturbing flashbacks of Khalil and Malik lounging affectionately on that fireside rug. The thought of having shared Khalil's bed made Tygre physically ill, but she couldn't stop the image from replaying over and over again in her mind. Once again, she thought, she had overlooked the obvious shortcomings of a man's character. *This is becoming a pattern,* she chided herself. Then she broke into tears at the thought of what her future would be like if she didn't learn how to free herself from her own predilections.

Thankfully, Sir Ari hadn't been in town when she returned from Washington. Tygre couldn't possibly have stomached another dose of his lecherous inquiries on top of everything else. She cupped her hands under a stream of cool running water and splashed it against her face, hoping to suppress the feelings of disgust that wracked her.

As if in a trance, Tygre stepped into her closet. She slipped into jogging clothes and bent to tie her shoes. Even while engaged in such a menial task, her mind shifted back to the image of Khalil's naked body and bulging erection beckoning to her, alternating with the image of Khalil and Malik on the rug.

She forced her mind to clear and hurried from her suite. Outside at last, she crossed Fifth Avenue for her early afternoon jog, staring straight ahead, unaware of her surroundings. Central Park's beauty was lost on Tygre. Now and then a sweet flowery smell carried by the fresh breeze would tickle her senses and cause her to long for home. She ached to talk with her father, nearly dialing his number a couple of times before deciding against it.

What would I say to him? Tygre wondered. *Guess what, Daddy, I slept with a drug-addicted bi-sexual Muslim playboy, a suspected terrorist whose every move is being tracked by the FBI...do you have any advice for me?* Tygre fought back tears as she considered how ashamed her father would be if he knew even half the story.

It tore her heart, but she had no choice but to keep her secret from him. How could she possibly own up to such a reprehensible lapse in judgment? But just as bad was the pain of not being honest with the one man in her life who had always given her comfort and unconditional love.

As she reached the heart of Central Park, neither the famed Bethesda Terrace nor the view of the lake afforded her any relief. Finally, overcome by a feeling of hopelessness, Tygre collapsed on the steps of the Bethesda Fountain and began to sob.

Hidden behind her La Dolce Vita cap, and dark sunglasses, she allowed the tears to flow. In the shadow of the Angel of the Waters, and bathed in the comfort of the early afternoon sun, Tygre allowed the tears she'd kept bottled up inside to gush forth in a cathartic release. She shed tears of self-loathing for falling for Khalil's exotic charm and for allowing herself to abandon reason and judgment in favor of sensual curiosity. She shed tears of guilt for allowing her faith to be compromised even if only for an instant while in the arms of a Muslim playboy. She shed tears of loneliness because she was so far from home and missing the comfort of her father's reassuring voice of reason. She shed tears of sadness for her inability to find genuine love with a man of integrity and honor.

Maybe I don't deserve someone honorable, she thought as she watched a young couple jog in perfect rhythm past the fountain. *Maybe God is punishing me for my foolish mistakes and selfish behavior. Maybe I'm greedy to think I deserve true love on top of everything else I've been blessed with.*

As Tygre shifted her sunglasses to wipe away her tears, she caught sight of a young schoolgirl strolling past on her father's arm. The child looked up at her father with loving admiration. The father returned her gaze with an affectionate smile. The happy pair laughed as they passed by, and Tygre couldn't help but smile through her tears as she watched.

As if sensing a secret bond with the heartbroken young woman on the fountain, the little girl turned to look over her shoulder, still clutching her father's hand. Tygre smiled back, sharing the silent bond with her for a few serene moments before the girl disappeared from view.

"You are my wonderful Tygre. I love you, my darling. Remember that always and forever." The comforting words of her father from so many years ago rang through Tygre's mind as the image of the little girl's smile faded from her thoughts. Adam had spoken those words to Tygre the night he broke the news that he and Helena were divorcing and that Tygre would be sent away to the convent. She remembered the feeling of dread as if it were yesterday. Life seemed so hopeless in that moment, but, still, Tygre reminded herself, she had survived.

"And you're stronger for it," Tygre's father had reminded her years later.

He's right, Tygre decided. She stood up and inhaled the humid air as she bent at the hips and gave her legs a good stretch. *I've been through tough times before,* she vowed, *and I'll get through this too.* She stepped back onto the path and continued her jog, pushing herself farther and harder than ever before.

By the time she returned to her suite at the LDV headquarters, she was tired but also invigorated and eager to find the strength that had eluded her since returning from D.C.

Tygre enjoyed a long, warm shower, then slipped into a robe, picked up her cell phone and discovered five missed calls. One was from Sir Ari. He would be returning to New York next week. One was from Senator Lloyd Owens. Something about high school French. Two idiots, she decided. She would call both of them back later when she was in a better frame of mind.

The three remaining calls were from Khalil. The sound of his voice instantly turned Tygre's stomach. "You left in such a hurry! I didn't have a chance to explain. I would like to see you again…" he began. Delete message. "Where are you? Have you left for Europe? I can meet you in London or Paris." Delete message. "Tygre, surely you are not avoiding my calls…"

As Tygre was deleting the third message, her phone rang in her hand. Khalil's number flashed on the screen. She hit the *Ignore* button and tossed the phone on the bed as if it burned her fingers to the touch.

It wasn't until later that night when Tygre was slipping into bed that she looked again at the phone. Two more calls had come in from Khalil. She deleted both messages without listening to them. She planned never to speak to him again.

One afternoon a few weeks later, as Tygre was working at a La Dolce Vita photo shoot in a downtown Manhattan studio, she received a follow-up call from Senator Lloyd Owens.

"Forgive me for not having called you back yet," she said. He was completely out to lunch, but he meant well, and she knew his feelings for her were well-intentioned.

"I was worried that maybe you were avoiding me," the Senator said good-naturedly.

"Not at all," she told him. "I've been terribly busy with work. I'm glad to hear from you. What's this about high school French?"

"Ah, yes," the Senator said with a chuckle. "I'm afraid my French skills are pretty feeble. I haven't retained much from my two semesters in high school. But I imagine a refined European sophisticate such as you would have a much better handle on the language of love, am I correct?"

"I do speak French, Lloyd... but I'm not sure why you're asking," Tygre answered.

"If you would care to join me at the White House tomorrow evening," he said, "you'll have a chance to practice your French. President Harrington and the First Lady are hosting a State Dinner for the French President and his wife."

Tygre gasped with childlike excitement. "Why that sounds wonderful. I would love to attend. How exciting, Lloyd!"

Yes, Tygre thought, *this will be a good thing, a new chapter in my life that will not involve shame or guilt or heartache or sex. I can feel it.*

"Oui!" she said excitedly.

"So that's a yes?" Senator Owens confirmed.

"Oui! Merci bien, Lloyd!" Tygre's impeccable French might have been lost on Owens, but he was able to gauge her enthusiasm without a problem.

"So you'll finally get your tour of the White House," he added. "And, moreover, you'll be a guest of the President when you do! You'll need a special clearance. My office will contact you right away. I've got to go. Time to vote!"

"Wonderful!" Tygre said, smiling as the connection closed. She felt better than she had in months. "Thank you again, Lloyd," she added into the empty phone.

Tygre had promised herself a quiet, date-free year to purge the Khalil experience from her body and soul, and to re-establish herself as a woman of strength and principle. However, Senator Owens was offering an invitation that no one of sound mind would decline. And, of course, it would be viewed by Sir Ari as a sound business move. Furthermore, Senator Lloyd Owens felt more like a brother or a cousin than a prospective date. After his brief and disastrous attempt at courtship, Lloyd seemed to have abandoned all hope of winning Tygre over as anything but a friend.

As soon as the phone screen went dark, Tygre dialed her father's number and blurted the news to him. "Daddy, you'll never believe it," she began, then filled him in on all the details.

"I was just reading about President Pellier," her father said, when she had finished gushing. "He's divorced his second wife of a year and half and married his pregnant girlfriend."

"Yes, but I'm not interested in any of that, Daddy. I am going to meet the President of the United States. I am focused on important things, my career. I've decided to look beyond all that superficial gossip and nonsense. I want to find happiness."

"Good for you, my darling. May I ask what inspired this new philosophy?"

Tygre hesitated, still too ashamed to mention the fiasco with Khalil Karim. "Let's just say your little girl is growing up."

"You are indeed, Tygre," Adam said with a chuckle. "By the way," he teased. "The son of the President, Bradford Harrington, is said to be quite the eligible bachelor. Is he expected to be at this event?" Adam asked.

"I have no idea, Daddy. I don't really know much about him. Lloyd didn't say anything about Bradford Harrington."

After a pause, Adam continued with a slightly different tone. "You seem very comfortable with Senator Owens now. Am I detecting a new level to this relationship?"

"If you mean that we've shifted from courtship to friendship, then yes. The Senator is not for me, Daddy. But I do enjoy his company."

"I can hear it in your voice," Adam said, genuinely pleased for his daughter. "In any case, you sound very happy, my dear."

"Yes, Daddy," she said, though she still winced inwardly at the thought of what she had done with Khalil Karim. "I'm ready, to come out in D.C. in style...in my own time and on my own terms."

"I wish I could see you there, darling." Adam's voice betrayed a hint of sadness.

The beeping of another incoming call cut into Adam's words.

"It's Sir Ari, Daddy. I'd better take his call. I love you, too!"

"You make me a proud father," her father said. "Have fun! I love you…"

Tygre brushed a tear from her eye as she switched to the other line. How wonderful it would be, in fact, to have her father with her. One day, she thought, when her life was once again her own, she would make such a thing happen.

Meantime, she thought, there was Sir Ari to deal with. Before she could even speak into the phone, Sir Ari's voice boomed across the line. "I am curious to know which gown you are planning to wear to the White House reception."

Tygre closed her eyes at that. Had he tapped her phone line somehow? The man was simply insufferable. "Well greetings to you, too. How did you hear?"

"Well, how do you think, Tygre? Owens called to ask my permission to escort you. I told him absolutely, dear boy! This is a fantastic opportunity for you and LDV. I'd suggest you wear the pale celadon strapless from this spring's haute couture collection," he plunged on. "Accessorize it with a pink shawl, I think. It will not only be very appropriate attire for the State Dinner, but the press will love it. The color photographs very well on you."

Tygre shook her head. Sir Ari could not care less about her excitement, of course. He had simply gone straight to the business calculations. Not only had he already dressed her as if she were his private doll, he probably had attached a dollar figure to the value of her appearance at the event.

"I'm glad we agree on something," she told Ari wryly. "I was just thinking about that very gown."

"Furthermore, I'll arrange to have something exquisite sent over from Cartier. You will need eye-popping jewelry for this occasion, Tygre." Sir Ari chuckled. "By the way, we just got some of the early sales numbers in. Your signature collection is on its way to becoming a best seller. You have done an excellent job, Tygre. I'm very proud of you. I'm not surprised, mind you."

She was sure that he was not surprised. In his mind she was just a business asset. A beautiful one, with parts he liked to push and prod, of course, but a business asset just the same. "Thank you, Ari," she said. "That fits right in with my new approach to life."

"And what new approach is that?" Sir Ari asked. His tone suggested she had just announced the determination to learn to play the piccolo.

"I'm going to focus on being true to myself," Tygre stated, careful not to give too much away. "I'm no longer going to allow myself to be co-opted by other people's agendas."

"Ah, well stated, my dear. Your beauty is wisdom in a very fortunate form, Tygre. It should give you strength." If she didn't know better, she thought, Sir Ari's tone might have sounded sincere. "You're growing up, maturing, learning to say no," he broke off, into knowing laughter. "Unfortunately, even to me!"

"Very funny," Tygre said, determined to get past his reptilian tendencies. "I want you to know that I'm very excited about this White House visit, Ari. I think it could be the beginning of something for me. A new Tygre...."

"Don't change too much, my dear," he cut in. "Some of us love you just the way you are. You have a unique flair that has meant a great deal to La Dolce Vita, in cosmetics, clothing and accessories worldwide. That's a massive achievement, even in my book!"

Just like him, she thought. Sir Ari was always focused on the bottom line. "Don't worry," Tygre assured him, "I plan to keep LDV going strong. My public image isn't what I'm talking about..."

"There are millions of young women who want to emulate you," he gushed on. "When you go to the White House on Friday night, you'll be going armed with your own success. Be sure to make the most of it..."

"Without question, Ari," Tygre said. She was finished with this conversation. Listening to him blather about the importance of keeping LDV profits up under the pretense of caring about her well-being was the last thing she needed.

"And I don't want you taking a shuttle tomorrow, Tygre," Sir Ari asserted. "I'm sending my plane for you. You need to travel to Washington in style. And you do deserve it...even if you're no longer being generous with me!"

"That's very nice of you, Ari. Thank you," Tygre answered. She could only imagine what constituted "generosity" in his mind. Perhaps he envisioned himself buckled into a leather saddle, while she rode him like a pony about the townhouse flailing him with a whip.

"Perhaps the plane ride will reignite the flames of our forgotten passions. What do you say, Tygre?"

"Ari, I would rather take a middle seat on the shuttle."

"Now, now, Tygre, you can't blame me, given the things we've done together. Just remember, I'll be ready when you are!"

"Goodbye, Ari."

"Goodbye, my dear."

Tygre sighed as she set her phone aside. She could live with such ignominious conversations, she told herself. For in her heart was the certainty that the days of enduring Sir Ari's advances would soon enough be coming to an end.

On Friday morning, Tygre was awakened by pangs of anticipation and excitement. She carefully picked out her wardrobe, packed her bags and ran downstairs to meet the LDV car. "We're going to La Guardia…the Delta shuttle. The noon flight," Tygre told the driver, who turned to regard her in surprise. She held up a hand to forestall his question, then took out her cell phone and dialed the number of Sir Ari's personal assistant.

"Please call Sir Ari's pilot and tell him to cancel my flight to Washington. Thank Sir Ari for me, but tell him I have decided to fly commercial today."

One hour later, as she boarded her flight, she was beaming inside and out, pleased with herself for having successfully snapped one of the many strings tying her to Sir Ari. She settled comfortably into her seat and made a mental note to ask him during their next conversation how many shares of CRG he had managed to sell so far.

On the final approach to Reagan Airport, Tygre glanced out the window at the D.C. landscape, thinking that the city looked different somehow. Recognizing her own strength gave her a new perspective on everything, she thought, with satisfaction.

A text message from Senator Lloyd Owens flashed across her cell phone screen as she rode to the Hay Adams. "Here's to your return to Washington. I'll pick you up at six."

"I'll be ready!" she texted back.

When Tygre appeared downstairs a few hours later, Owens was not the only one who stopped short at the sight. She noted with an undeniable sense of accomplishment that the entire lobby of Hay Adams hotel guests and staff discreetly stopped what they were doing to catch a glimpse of what she had done with herself. Though she'd disdained Sir Ari's plane, she'd been willing to don the dazzling Cartier pink and white diamond necklace he'd sent, along with the matching earrings. And she was well aware that the strapless celadon gown perfectly accentuated her figure. She had twisted her blond hair up in a chignon to frame her face, which she well knew glowed with excitement. The Senator took several moments fumbling for words.

Tygre helped him snap out of his trance. "Let's walk, shall we?"

A puzzled look crossed the Senator's face. "Walk? To the White House?"

"Why not?" she asked, pointing through the lobby doors. "It's one of the perks of staying at the Hay Adams, Senator. We're right across the park!"

"Well, sure, I guess...why not," he said finally finding his wits. "It's a beautiful evening." Senator Owens gallantly offered an arm to Tygre. His smile was pasted on his face for the entire ten minutes of their walk through the balmy evening.

"You are a picture of perfection tonight," Senator Owens told Tygre as they strolled under the portico of the White House. He gently kissed her on the cheek, as Marine guards held the doors aside for their entry.

"Thank you, Lloyd. I'm honored to be here," she answered quietly. "Thank you so much for your invitation."

Hardly had they entered the foyer than the Senator began scanning the area to point out colleagues, other dignitaries and guests to her. Every few seconds he turned to check Tygre's reactions.

"This is simply fabulous, Lloyd," she told him. She squeezed his arm in excitement, resisting the urge to squeal. "It's much more than I ever dreamed."

"That's usually the case, Tygre, for anyone who comes here for the first time," Owens slid his arm around Tygre's waist and guided her gently forward in the long, slow-moving receiving line.

The queue of guests spoke in hushed tones while patiently waiting to be introduced to President William Harrington and the

First Lady as well as the French President and his new wife, all of whom radiated a stately and dignified demeanor as they shook hands and greeted their guests one by one. But, it was William Bradford Harrington, II that Tygre noticed most.

In addition to his good looks and the stature he held as the President's son, there was something about him that set him apart from every other young man in the room. His relaxed demeanor emanated warmth without a hint of arrogance or ego. Their eyes met for a few seconds and lingered with a curious spark as they looked each other over.

He was an inch or two over six feet, she saw, well-built, with sun-streaked, wavy blond hair framing his angular, tanned face. His eyes were pale blue, with soft, golden flecks. She thought they offered a portal into kindness and unpretentiousness.

Tygre allowed her eyes to linger on the young Harrington for only a moment or two. She was well aware of the lure that wealth and power held for her. Senator Owens smiled and shook his head knowingly. "Almost there," the Senator said with a quick squeeze on Tygre's hand.

"This is exciting, Lloyd," Tygre whispered. Tygre couldn't help thinking that Bradford Harrington looked like a man who had spent most of his thirty years outdoors, either on a farm or on a beach, most certainly somewhere far away from Washington, D.C. No formal black tie attire could hide it.

He belongs somewhere else, Tygre thought watching him patiently fulfill his duties as the first and only son of the President and First Lady. He greeted each guest with ease, apparently unfazed by the display of White House pomp and circumstance about them.

"Look at Brad, what a handsome young man he has turned out to be," an older lady in the line behind Tygre whispered to her husband.

Tygre took a deep breath, as she and Lloyd took their place as the next in line to be received. The Senator suddenly pulled her closer to him as their names were formally announced. *"Monsieur Le President, Mademoiselle Tygre Topolska escorted by Senator Lloyd Owens."*

All present focused on Tygre as she greeted the French President and his wife Giselle with a perfect Parisian accent. "Comment allez-vous?" she heard herself say as she shook their hands.

"Enchanté," President Pellier responded, pleased. His wife stood by his side, apparently a bit nervous despite what must have been repeated crash courses in protocol and etiquette. Tygre was nervous too, but she hoped she managed to mask it with a smile.

Next Tygre shook hands with President Harrington and his wife, Barbara.

"How do you do, Mr. President? Mrs. Harrington?" Tygre asked.

"Hello, Miss Topolska, Lloyd." The President acknowledged them before swiftly refocusing his attention on the next guest, while the First Lady looked on.

The last to welcome her was the President's son. Senator Owens steered Tygre to an open space in the receiving line directly in front of Bradford Harrington, II. As she lifted her gaze slowly upward, Tygre was greeted with that dazzling smile. She was not surprised to discover that it was even more powerful now that it was intended specifically for her.

Tygre tried her best to maintain her composure-had she not had enough bad experiences with the rich and powerful? Then, as Bradford Harrington took her hand, Tygre felt strangely calm and relaxed.

"You are even more beautiful in person than in your photographs. It's a pleasure to meet you, Tygre."

Tygre paused for only a moment. "Thank you, sir. It is a pleasure to meet you too." Her polite tone masked the undeniable rise she felt…Brad Harrington knew who she was. She truly was hopeless, she told herself.

"Come on now," Brad laughed heartily, "I am not *that* much older than you. Call me Brad, please." They stared at each other for a split second, then lingered, oblivious to all else.

Tygre quickly shook herself free of the moment. "If you insist, I will, Brad." She felt her cheeks flush. And, in the next instant, she was being ushered by Lloyd Owens down the receiving line and out of Brad's sight, wishing their introduction hadn't been quite so rushed.

"I have no doubt he'll want to see you again," Lloyd said as he guided Tygre to the State Dining Room.

"I'm sorry? What did you say?" Tygre said, lost in her own thoughts."

"He was impressed, Tygre. I could tell," Lloyd said. "I've known him for a long time."

"He seems very natural and warm." Tygre ventured, but by then they were being escorted to their table.

All around them, elegantly dressed couples approached their pre-assigned, flower-adorned tables. Gentlemen pulled out Empire-style chairs for their ladies who invariably marveled at the crystal candelabras and the extraordinary place settings. The large gold charger plates had been manufactured by Lenox during the Eisenhower Administration and there was no end of commentary on those and all the other accouterments of the table. Dinner included superb crab with dill sauce and tenderloin of veal with rosemary, all served on the Roosevelt china.

In truth, the food was sumptuous, and the conversation was inspiring. The entire evening was sheer perfection. Yet Tygre, who was without a doubt the most beautiful woman in the room, felt a sense of emptiness, which could not be dispelled even by this extraordinary experience.

Senator Lloyd Owens proved to be a poor substitute for a real date, something which Tygre might have predicted from the start. Still, she hadn't thought she'd mind as much as she did now. She couldn't help looking over at the French President and his wife with a hint of envy. They were obviously in love, dancing closely with each other, oblivious to the crowd of seasoned Capitol Hill cynics scrutinizing their every move.

She watched handsome men affectionately focused on their plain-looking wives and the crowd of emissaries, politicians and industry leaders wowing their dates with the exquisite dinner and stimulating conversation. Tygre sat at her table in silence, exhausted by the polite small talk with her dinner partners and the Senator.

A few times throughout the evening, Tygre glanced over at Brad Harrington, who seemed preoccupied with his table guests. To

Tygre's surprise, despite the momentary connection she thought she felt earlier when they first met, Brad never again looked in her direction. *So much for Lloyd's hunch,* Tygre thought as Owens led her stiffly through a dance or two, before they finally called it a night.

In the weeks following the State Dinner, Tygre spent her days fully focused on her work, tirelessly promoting LDV's products and her own name brand. The schedule was demanding and exhausting, but it grounded her and kept her mind off of her feelings of loneliness and self-pity.

Back in New York, amid the nonstop frenzy of her hectic lifestyle, Tygre managed to enjoy one small victory. The long-awaited, coveted board approval to purchase her East-side cooperative apartment was finally granted. She spurned Sir Ari's vehement objections and pleas and finally moved out from the LDV headquarters townhouse. It was a long overdue accomplishment that gave Tygre a newfound independence and a renewed level of confidence. *Why did I wait so long?* Tygre asked herself. She treasured her solitude, her freedom and her early mornings in Manhattan. Every day after completing her jog, she sipped coffee at the foot of the Bethesda Fountain and simply sat to watch the passersby in the park.

On one such coffee break as she was enjoying the best of a New York fall morning, her cell phone rang.

"May I speak to Tygre Topolska?"

"This is she."

"Hi, Tygre, this is Brad."

"Brad?" Tygre was truly puzzled for a moment.

"Brad Harrington."

Tygre paused. In all honesty, Bradford Harrington, II, was the last person in the world Tygre expected to receive a call from. Still, the days of making a fool of herself were over. "I remember the name," she said, playfully.

Brad's genuine laughter confirmed that he liked what he just heard. "I would have called before this," he said. "But I wanted to make sure I was not interfering in any relationship you may have with Senator Owens."

So he was interested, Tygre thought. How many girls could say they had received a call from the son of the President, she wondered? And in the next instant, she asked herself the question in a different way. Just how many girls HAD the son of the President called? "Lloyd and I are just friends," Tygre heard herself saying.

"Are you sure?"

"I'm not dating anyone at the moment," Tygre said. She saw no reason for disguising the truth.

"That's good to know because, if you allow me, I would like to change your present circumstances."

"How so?" Tygre asked playfully.

"The truth is that I've been thinking of you since we met the night that President Pellier came through. I was hoping we might see each other again."

"That was quite a night," she said.

"It was," he said, an earnest tone in his voice.

"I thought you looked a little out of place, if you want to know the truth."

It brought another laugh from him. "You're not only beautiful, you're a mind reader too," he said. "In fact, that brings me to the reason for my call."

"Oh... what is it?" she asked. She couldn't help but feel a surge of anticipation.

"Listen, Tygre, I hope this doesn't sound too forward," he cleared his throat before going on. "It's not much notice either, but I am going to my family's ranch in Florida and I was wondering if you would like to join me." Brad's voice was calm but she thought she detected a bit of nervousness there.

Tygre took a moment to let Brad's invitation sink in.

"Do you mean alone?"

Another laugh. "Of course not. I'm never alone. My secret service detail will be there and who knows who else, but it's a more natural setting than the White House. I'd like to get to know you better. That's why I'm calling."

There were a million questions fluttering through Tygre's mind. *Is this proper? Is this really the son of the President I'm talking to?* She dismissed them all, answering with as much reserve as she could muster, "that sounds wonderful. I would love to join you."

"Great," Brad said. "Where are you now?"

She glanced around. "I'm in Central Park enjoying a day off. It's beautiful here today," Tygre answered.

"Well, I'm in D.C. How about if I pick you up in the morning at the Westchester County Airport? Ten o'clock, let's say. Just ask for my plane. And pack light. It's informal down there. All you need is a pair of jeans and a bathing suit."

"Tomorrow sounds perfect, but I don't own a pair of jeans!" Tygre said, laughing. The idea of abandoning the haute couture she had been wearing for the last twelve months became suddenly irresistible.

Brad laughed, genuinely amused. "Maybe you can pick up a pair."

"I'm sure I can," she said.

"That's great," he said. "I'm looking forward to seeing you."

"Same here."

When Tygre flipped her phone closed, she realized her heart was racing. So much for reserve and restraint, she thought ruefully. She immediately dialed her father's number. "Daddy, you're not going to believe who just called me for a date."

Her father did not skip a beat. "And who is that, my darling?"

"Brad Harrington," she said, hearing the undeniable excitement in her own voice. "The son of the President of the United States!"

Chapter 25

Eight Months Earlier
The Harrington Ranch
Vero Beach, Florida

The next morning, dressed in white linen slacks, a pin-striped shirt and a navy blue blazer, Tygre hailed a taxi to the airport to meet Brad Harrington. Having left behind the plethora of La Dolce Vita gowns, couture outfits and accessories that usually followed her in steamer trunks around the world, Tygre felt oddly liberated. This morning, she carried nothing but an overnight bag, a small LDV pocketbook and her mobile phone.

As the taxi made its way, she relived something of the phone conversation she had had with her father. She'd been thrilled, of course, but soon enough he'd given her a bit of perspective on her enthusiasm.

He listened patiently as she explained what had happened, then cleared his throat. "Well, darling…I know that you are most excited, but why do you think you should be doing this?"

She was astonished by the question at first. "Why I, well, he's the son of the President," she said.

Her father paused. "And that makes him the man of your dreams, the man who understands you, who will love you for who you are?"

"I didn't say anything of the kind, father…"

"You didn't have to," he replied. "I heard it in your voice."

Tygre immediately felt sheepish. She was so transparent. Her father knew her well. "You're right. It's probably too early to know for sure. But it is just a date. And I do have a good feeling about him.

"Tygre, I'm going to give you a bit of advice, slow down, my dear. Why do you think he is so special?" Atypically, Adam raised his voice, "just because he is the son of the President of the United States?

"I saw it in his eyes and I heard it in his voice! I feel it, Father."

"You hardly know this young man! Besides, haven't those 'good feelings' failed you in the past?"

"You're right, it's just that..."

"Tygre, listen to me. My darling, you are so generous with your heart that you have a tendency to give it away very quickly...too quickly sometimes."

"I know...."

"And that's how you get hurt."

"Yes, I realize that, but..."

"It seems to me, Tygre," Adam cut in, "that rather than choosing the men in your life..."

"Yes? Go on..."

"It seems to me that you allow yourself to be chosen by men. Tygre, you're so intelligent. You have found a wonderful career. But when it comes to men, you tend not to do the choosing at all. These men latch on to you immediately – and there's no doubt as to why; you're a gorgeous and talented woman, Tygre – but you sometimes mistake their infatuation with you as...well, as true love."

Tygre was silent for a moment.

"Tygre, if I've said something to hurt you..."

"No, Father, you're absolutely right! I need to hear this. I tend to rush into love – or what I think is love – because I'm so eager to find happiness, you know?"

"And, my dear, you often do so at a cost."

"You're right, father. Perhaps this trip isn't the best idea, after all."

"I'm not saying that, Tygre. You should certainly take this opportunity. How many young women could be so fortunate? Enjoy yourself. But, please, keep your wits about you. And when the weekend is over, call me, and tell me all about it."

Tygre played and replayed her father's sage advice for every mile of the journey to the Westchester Airport. She could only pray that for once she HAD made a choice, and a good one. She desperately hoped so.

Though it seemed she had traveled from one dimension to the next, the taxi ride to the airport had actually taken less than an hour. It was a stunningly beautiful fall day, and Brad's plane, an Aerostar with New Deal scripted in blue lettering on its tail, sat gleaming on the sunlit tarmac looking to her like a miniature Air Force One. It's white body was trimmed with red and blue stripes, and seemed to Tygre to be aching for takeoff.

Despite her assurances to her father that she would indeed keep her wits about her, Tygre felt as giddy as a schoolgirl about to meet up with the most popular boy in school. The butterflies in her stomach had become a mad swarm, and when she stopped to consider that her schoolgirl crush was on the son of the President of the United States, she became immediately humbled by the magnitude of it all. It was real-life but a fantasy beyond her wildest dreams at the same time, and it filled her with an anticipation that both excited and terrified her.

As Tygre's taxi pulled up to the plane, she noticed the main door to the cabin had been left open in invitation. Waiting on the tarmac beside the folding steps, was a tall, dark-haired man in his forties. He wore a business suit with a white shirt and a black tie, and seemed preoccupied by a conversation with someone on his cell phone, waving his free hand about as he spoke. When the taxi approached, he abruptly ended his phone call and came to open Tygre's door.

"You must be Miss Topolska. We've been expecting you." He said with a nod.

"That's me," she said. "But please, call me Tygre."

"I'm Sean Ives, United States Secret Service," the man said as his cell phone vibrated in his hand. "Excuse me, ma'am, I'll be with you in just a moment," he added holding up a finger and turning his back to take the call.

Tygre stood silently, looking around, waiting for Agent Ives to complete his conversation.

"Not now!" He barked irately into his phone. "I'll call you back!"

Taken somewhat aback by the intensity of the agent's exchange with his caller, and a bit put off by the terse welcome, Tygre busied herself with paying the cab driver, tipping him generously. She stood next to her overnight bag and glanced at her watch. Ives continued his call, talking angrily into the phone using a hushed tone.

Three minutes seemed like a long time to leave a guest standing aimlessly on the tarmac. Ives' reception was a far cry from the cordial greetings Tygre had become used to while traveling on the LDV corporate jet. After begrudgingly allowing two more minutes to pass, she cleared her throat and approached him. "Excuse me Mr. Ives, I don't mean to interrupt, but could you please tell me where Brad is?"

"He should be here momentarily. He's running a last-minute errand." Ives said. He broke off to redirect his attention to yet another incoming phone call.

Tygre looked at her watch again then scanned the scene, anxiously hoping to catch a glimpse of Brad.

"There, all done. I'm sorry about that." Agent Ives said, slipping his phone back into his jacket pocket.

Tygre watched him cross his arms and stare in the distance. Everything about Sean Ives, from the irritated look in his eye to the tense body language and unfriendly tone, seemed to indicate that he'd rather be anywhere else but here.

"So, Mr. Ives, how do you like protecting the President's son?" Tygre offered, attempting to chip away at the agent's icy persona. It seemed like a good idea to get on the good side of the man, she reasoned.

He gave her a tight smile. "It's my line of work, and it comes with its ups and downs just as you might expect." He turned his attention to an oncoming vehicle, a hunter green convertible that rapidly approached the plane. "Look, he's here." Ives said.

She thought it was a rather reserved response, but maybe Secret Service men simply had to play it close to the vest. In any case, as the green convertible maneuvered closer, Tygre's initial uncertainty about Ives was replaced by her own trepidations regarding Brad Harrington's arrival.

His car screeched to a quick stop just a few feet from where Tygre stood. Brad's dark-blond windblown hair was a handsome contrast to his deeply tanned face. With one hand on the wheel, he shifted his car into park then extended his right hand toward Tygre, holding a bouquet of tiger lilies. Tygre felt herself blush.

"It's so good to see you, Tygre." He took a moment to take her in.

"You look great!" Brad said finally.

"So do you," Tygre answered flashing her trademark smile.

"Now! Are you ready to have some fun, young lady?" Brad asked excitedly.

"Oh, yes! I'm ready." Tygre assured him.

"Then, let's go." Brad took her hand and guided her toward the Aerostar.

Tygre was filled with anticipation as they boarded, her smile fading for only a moment as she noticed Sean Ives pensively watching them from the co-pilot's seat.

"You're not nervous are you?" Brad asked as he indicated a seat for her.

"I'm ready whenever you are!" she confirmed as she buckled herself in.

Sean Ives sat quietly in the cockpit next to Brad, preoccupied with the flight charts and seemingly oblivious to their exchange. Brad held Tygre's gaze for a few more moments, before turning his attention back to the cockpit, going through the pre-takeoff checklists.

"Be careful, and take it slowly!" On cue, Adam's voice echoed in her head as Tygre watched Brad Harrington run confidently through the pre-flight routine.

I will, Daddy, I promise, Tygre thought.

"Are you all buckled up, Tygre? Just two minutes 'til takeoff!" Brad called over his shoulder.

"Let's go!" Tygre answered.

Brad turned his attention to the control panel and began speaking with the tower. He was a man in charge and looked the part.

"We have strong headwinds all the way to Florida," Brad called back to her over the sounds of the now-revving engines. "It's going to be a slow ride."

"I don't mind."

"There's a bit of bad weather in the way, but we'll try to dodge the worst of it," he said calmly. "We'll be busy up here, so feel free to put your feet up and take a nap if you like."

"Oh! I'll be fine. Don't worry about me."

Despite Brad's warning about the impending weather, Tygre remained calm. Something about Brad's demeanor allowed her to feel at ease. Soon they were aloft. As Tygre had had little rest the night before, the steady drone of the engines soon lulled her to sleep.

Three hours later, Tygre awoke refreshed from her nap, realizing that the plane had begun its descent. She looked curiously around the interior of the plane and marveled. *I'm flying in a plane with Brad Harrington.*

"Are we here already?" Tygre stretched like a cat, spreading her body across two seats.

"We're about to land. Make sure your seat belt is fastened."

As the wheels touched the runway, the butterflies in Tygre's stomach fluttered once more. She peered out the window, admiring the palm trees swaying in the breeze.

Brad taxied to the Customs and Immigration terminal designated for private aircraft. "We cheated death again!" he exclaimed with a chuckle.

"That sounds very dramatic. What do you mean? Were we in danger?" Tygre asked.

"Every landing is a controlled stall I'm grateful to be able to walk away from!" Brad turned the engines off then moved to the back of the plane to help Tygre gather her belongings. Sean Ives, still detached, went through the motions of closing the flight plan.

As they stepped outside, Brad pressed Tygre against his chest. "That's your first Florida hug," Brad said with a smile.

"Just where in Florida are we?" Tygre asked Brad as a second agent walked up to meet them. "I know where Miami is."

He laughed. "Vero Beach is a long way from Miami," he said. "But I think you're going to like it here!"

"I already do!"

Brad laughed, and guided her to a waiting jeep. As the two of them slipped into the front seat and drove off, two more Secret Service Agents and Sean Ives followed in a dark SUV.

"We'll be home in 20 minutes," Brad said.

Tygre smiled. She liked the sound of the word.

Home for Brad turned out to be the Harrington Ranch. As she would learn, with breeding cattle and horses, polo, steeplechase, skeet shooting and acres of open space abutting the Atlantic Ocean, it had been a family cornerstone for three generations. Located just an hour north of the social resort of Palm Beach, the secluded backcountry wildlife ranch, all 10,000 acres of it, might as well have been on another continent.

"Descendents of my grandfather Nathaniel have been coming here since the early 1920s." Brad broke the silence as Tygre took in the picture perfect scenery.

"The ranch hands and cowboys are a part of the family and live on the premises. They protect the place and livestock as if they were their own," Brad said. They were maneuvering along an unpaved dirt road, now. Dark clouds formed ahead with a promise of a good drenching.

"This is a working ranch, Tygre. It strengthens our lives and those around us. It grounds me every time I come here."

"I can sense that," Tygre said, a bit surprised by the depth of emotion in his voice.

A few drops of rain fell onto the front windshield as they continued along the dirt road, and within minutes, the rain was coming down in torrents. The ever-present agents followed them along the wet, rough terrain. She couldn't help but think of riding with Khalil, being followed by the FBI. Yet it seemed so much different in this case.

They rode in silence until the track ended at the foot of a small rustic house on the eastern side of the ranch. The front yard was lush with high, uncut grass. The thick foliage was cut through by a small stream and scented by the pines that rose high out of the tangle.

Brad parked the jeep on a stretch of grass adjacent to what looked like a combination barn, then came to open her door and usher her into the farmhouse. Inside, she found herself in a great room, which ran the entire length of the first floor. The 19th-century beams gave it a pronounced western feel. The dark wood and old leather furnishings were complemented by hand-crafted log cabin quilts, hickory chairs, and a New England-style bench table.

"Welcome to my world, Tygre." Brad watched her intently as he spoke. "You look surprised."

Tygre stood silently, smiling and absorbing the ambiance of the room. "Not what you expected?" he asked.

She shook her head. "I love it here!" she exclaimed.

"I was hoping you would."

"It's a pretty simple life, here, Tygre." Brad said, observing her closely.

"You call this simple?" Tygre asked.

"I'm grateful for the serenity," he said.

Tygre nodded. Perhaps Brad Harrington, II truly was what he seemed to be: goodhearted, unpretentious, humble, and down to earth…simply a good person.

She had never imagined that being thousands of miles away from everything she knew would feel this familiar and comfortable. She felt suddenly at home here…in this place…with this man.

"Hungry?" Brad asked.

"Starving," Tygre replied.

Brad led her to the dining area. The rustic, dark oak table was already set with a lunch for two. He pulled out a heavy wooden chair for Tygre before taking his own seat across from her.

"What was it like growing up in Poland?" Brad asked as he ripped the corner off of a large round of sourdough and placed it on Tygre's plate. "That's where you were born, right?"

"Well, to tell you the truth, except for the palm trees, your ranch reminds me of the countryside just outside of Warsaw. My childhood was…" Tygre paused, searching for words.

As Brad awaited her answer, he noticed a veil of sadness fall over her face. "Do you miss your family?" he asked.

"I miss my father terribly." Tygre tried hard to contain her tears.

Brad thought about this. "Does he know you're visiting the ranch… with me?"

"Yes, he does."

"Well, then let's surprise him and give him a call. What's his number?" He handed Tygre his cell phone.

Tygre looked at Brad. Her hands shook slightly as she dialed her father's number. She held the phone up to her ear and, after hearing the first ring, handed the phone back to Brad. "It's ringing," she said, smiling excitedly.

Brad changed the setting to speaker mode. "Mister Topolski?" he said, with a quick glance at Tygre. "I would like to introduce myself. This is Brad Harrington. Your daughter and I just called to say hello."

As Tygre's father murmured a polite greeting, Tygre broke in, "Hello, Daddy! The ranch is so beautiful! You would love it here. It reminds me of stories you used to read to me!"

"It's so good to hear your voice," her father replied. "And thank Mr. Harrington for calling me, please."

Brad gazed fondly at Tygre as she rambled on, stopping only to catch her breath every once in a while. "Good-bye, Father! I'll speak to you soon! I love you, too." When Tygre ended the call, the room became immediately quiet.

"I'm glad you made that call," she said, after a moment.

"Well, it just seemed like the right thing to do," Brad said, flashing a knowing smile at Tygre. "Now let's eat."

Their lunch was hearty and wholesome – coleslaw, potato salad, baked beans, and barbequed beef, all homegrown, he assured her.

The simple meal was a welcome departure from the ostentatious lunches and dinners Tygre was accustomed to sharing with Sir Ari and others.

After lunch, Brad and Tygre moved back into the great room where she noticed the many framed photographs of exotic-looking, motor-racing prototypes bearing the New Deal logo.

"Why 'New Deal'?" she asked.

"FDR is one of my heroes," he said. "I thought it would be the right name for my motor racing team."

Tygre's heart sank momentarily as she thought of Khalil Karim's passion for fast cars. *Please don't let them have anything else in common,* she thought.

"So you drive yourself?" she asked.

"This ranch, polo, and motor racing are my passions. They keep me away from politics, Washington, and booze."

"I see," Tygre said, not sure if she understood the force he gave to his statement.

"I am first and foremost a racecar driver," he said. "My base of operations is right here in Florida. It's close to Sebring and the St. Petersburg racetrack. Right now, I am developing and personally financing my own LMP1 prototype for the American Le Mans Series. In the States, it's the closest thing to Formula 1 car racing."

Brad's face lit up with excitement as he continued enthusiastically. "The New Deal team has three drivers, including me. The cars are made entirely in the United States. The American Le Mans Series includes 9 races here in the U.S. and several in Europe. All of them lead up to the biggie, the 24 Hours of Le Mans, in France."

Tygre had little idea of what he was talking about, but she listened intently.

"I've won at Le Mans three years in a row," he said.

"You did? That's great." Tygre said, wishing she knew more about the accomplishment. Obviously, it meant a great deal to Brad.

"God willing, I plan to make it number four this year. We've been lucky so far."

"I'm sure it takes more than luck," Tygre said.

Brad nodded. "It's tough, but it's the top of the racing world. Le Mans is 24-hours of flat out endurance. I'm hoping my parents will come to watch me race there next June."

Tygre became pensive, recalling Khalil Karim's plans to race at Le Mans at the same time. She worried that her brief encounter with Khalil would haunt her forever. And, at a moment like this, it was the last thing she wanted on her mind.

As if he had read her thoughts, Brad pointed out the window. "That's enough of me going on about racing," he said. "It's stopped raining," Brad said as he stood and walked over to one of the large windows. "Why don't you change into those jeans you said you'd bring and we'll go riding?"

"Perfect!" Tygre agreed and went to change.

Within minutes, they were outside again, where a ranch hand turned over the reins of Brad's sturdy stallion. Brad effortlessly mounted the cumbersome-looking western-style saddle and extended his hand to Tygre. She looked up apprehensively. The ranch hand gave her a knee-up to help her mount the horse. She slid into the saddle behind Brad and wrapped her arms around his waist.

"Hold on tight," Brad said. He pulled back on the bit, urging his horse to walk steadily along until they found their stride, finally allowing the thoroughbred to break into a trot. Tygre glanced over her shoulder and caught a glimpse of a jeep that was following at a safe distance behind them. Inside, Sean Ives and a second Secret Service agent in the passenger seat were watching dutifully.

Brad and Tygre gracefully cantered away from the ranch and, before long, came upon a sandy pathway with tall grass and bushes on either side. It led them directly onto the beach revealing a breathtaking view of the ocean.

"It's beautiful!" Tygre called out.

"You haven't seen anything yet!" Brad promised.

Tygre was struck by the splendor of her surroundings. But as she tried to revel in the joy of the moment, an unwelcome memory flashed through her mind – the image of her rides on Roman's

Vespa, speeding through the streets of Old Town in Warsaw. Tygre shuddered, trying to shake the painful recollection.

Brad looked over his shoulder and asked, "How are you doing back there?"

"Couldn't be better," she said. She leaned in close, shedding the memory of Roman and allowing herself to become accustomed to the rhythm of the ride.

Except for the low-flying seagulls hunting for their dinner and one lonely fisherman, the miles of beaches ahead of them were deserted. The sand was white and pristine and it seemed to her like the coast of some remote island. As they rode on, the wind started to pick up and, far off in the distance, dark, low clouds signaled another rapidly approaching thunderstorm. Soon large drops began pelting them, followed by claps of thunder and flashes of lightning, forcing Tygre's face against Brad's back. Within moments, they were both soaked.

"Brad! Let's go back," Tygre pleaded.

"There's a small cabin about a mile up the beach," he called through the clamor of the storm. "Hold on. We'll be there shortly," Brad said.

He dug his heels into the horse's side, breaking him into a faster pace. As they rode along the beach, the skies opened up anew. Sheets of water slapped against their faces and flashes of lightning raged all around them. Tygre buried her face deeper into Brad's back to shield herself from the storm. "Brad! I'm terrified of thunderstorms! Please hurry!"

"We're here," Brad announced as they arrived at the cabin.

Brad lifted her from the stallion and placed her onto the covered porch. The cabin, once the lodging of migrant farm workers he explained, was tucked into a grove of trees adjoining the beach.

"The door is open," Brad said. I'll be with you in just a minute. I need to take care of my horse."

She entered the cabin, dripping from head to toe, finding the interior lit by the dim rays of light peeking through the small windows and skylights. Tygre moved to the window and wiped the condensation away so she could watch Brad outside. He led his stallion to an adjacent shed where he removed the saddle and put water in a drinking trough. Sean Ives and a second Agent parked their jeep on the other side of the porch and remained inside the vehicle.

Moments later Brad walked into the cabin. "That was a lot of fun, wasn't it?" he joked as he noticed Tygre's troubled expression.

"Can we put on some lights?" she asked.

"We can do better than that," Brad said, making his way to the large fireplace in the center of the room. He pulled some logs from a stack and placed them onto the rack. He struck a wooden match against the wall of the hearth and within minutes a warm fire was blazing.

Tygre looked around at the interior of the cabin, now bathed in the warm glow of the flames. It was sparsely furnished but comfortable. A large daybed with colorful blankets and pillows was arranged in front of the fireplace.

"It'll just take a few moments to warm the place up," Brad said.

Tygre stepped toward him. "Brad, hold me, please. I'm cold."

He grabbed one of the blankets from the daybed and wrapped it around Tygre's shoulders. Pulling her close, he held her tightly in his arms. Brad's finger traveled to Tygre's face. He gently removed a strand of wet hair from her forehead and smiled. "You did well for a city girl. I'm impressed," he uttered softly into her ear. Tygre smiled and pressed her face against Brad's chest.

"As a child I used to come here to hide from my parents and all the guests they would entertain," Brad said. "It was a sanctuary for me. When I was in college, a brush fire leveled it to the ground."

"Oh no," Tygre said, keeping her face pressed against Brad's chest.

"So I decided to rebuild it," he said.

"By yourself?"

"With my own two hands," Brad said proudly.

A bolt of lightning illuminated the sky followed by a sharp clap of thunder. Tygre shuddered and buried herself deeper in Brad's embrace.

"Don't worry. We get a lot of thunderstorms in Florida, but they don't last long."

"It can't go fast enough," Tygre said softly.

Brad pulled her away and looked at her face. "Why does the thunder scare you so much?"

"An unpleasant childhood memory," Tygre answered.

"Hey," he said. "What if I promise to make you forget all the bad things you've had to endure?"

Tygre looked up at him with a doubtful smile. "Promise?"

Brad nodded and slowly lowered his gaze. He placed his mouth on hers, kissing her gently at first, then passionately. Their embrace tightened as Tygre pushed her mouth against Brad's.

"I've never met a girl like you," he said pressing his lips into her scented hair.

Tygre took Brad's face in her hands and guided his mouth back to her waiting lips. She felt him become aroused as she leaned her hips into his.

"We should get out of these wet clothes." Brad said with a smile. "I have some dry shirts in a drawer."

When he turned away, Tygre dropped her blanket to the floor, inviting the crackling flames to warm her body as she slowly began to undress. Her fingers moved steadily along the buttons allowing her blouse to fall open as each one came undone. She stopped when she caught sight of Brad staring at her.

"Let me help you with that," he volunteered, moving closer to her and reached inside the blouse. His fingers unsnapped the hook of Tygre's delicate lacy bra. The blouse fell off her shoulders and slid down to her waist, exposing Tygre's breasts. Brad paused, then lowered his head.

"Oh, God!" Tygre gasped with a passionate sigh. Her voice became barely audible as Brad's lips touched her flesh.

"Tygre, I've wanted to make love to you from the first moment I saw you." Brad wrapped his arms firmly around her.

"Me, too," Tygre said as she lowered her hand and unzipped his pants.

Brad kicked off his boots and stepped out of his jeans.

As he stood naked, Brad Harrington, II had a drop-dead body, powerful erection and kind, passionate eyes.

Soon he had removed Tygre's wet jeans and let them drop to the floor. Brad lifted Tygre effortlessly and placed her over his hips. Her long legs wrapped around his waist. Their bodies moved as one as he penetrated her.

"Brad!" she cried breathlessly as she felt him push deep inside her.

"I must be dreaming," Brad whispered.

"You feel so good," Tygre let out a cry of passion that became quickly muffled by the deep kiss that Brad pressed against her mouth. Without parting their lips or bodies, Brad lowered himself onto the blanket with Tygre positioned on top of him. Her long, damp hair brushed against his chest each time he lifted her on and off in rhythmic thrusts until she quivered.

Brad then sat upright and gently placed Tygre down onto her back. As he rose above her, Brad looked down into Tygre's eyes. She was ready to belong to him, and Brad welcomed her. In that very moment, the connection between them was born.

I'm safe now, Tygre thought to herself and, for the first time in her life, she believed it. She believed it enough to abandon all of her inhibitions and give herself over fully to this experience. Her body trembled and shuddered as her first orgasm washed over her, leaving her with a tingling sensation from head to toe. As Brad climaxed with her, Tygre cried out in a shrill voice that she was sure could be heard outside the tiny cabin.

She never felt more satisfied, or at peace. The years of what she now knew to be empty, unfulfilling sex, with the likes or Roman, Sir Ari and Khalil, were all along missing one key ingredient. With them, it had been only an act of sex. With Brad, Tygre was experiencing intimacy.

"This was my first Big O," Tygre looked up at Brad who held her tenderly, caressing her face and stroking her hair.

"I'm so happy to be the one."

"So this is how it's meant to be?"

"You may as well get used to it," Brad promised.

Late that night, after the storm subsided, they returned to the farmhouse. Tygre was awakened the next morning by the sound of Brad's raised voice. "Karim Racing received an invitation to Le Mans? I can't believe it!"

Tygre's eyes popped open.

"Sorry, darling," Brad said, cupping his hand over his phone's mouthpiece. "It's my team manager. I have to take this. It's about one of my competitors. A guy I despise." Brad changed his tone as he continued his phone conversation. "Khalil has obviously bought his way in! I've seen him in action! People like that bring bad publicity to racing!"

Tygre, now fully awake, began to process what she was hearing. Her worries about Khalil resurfaced. *Should I tell him about knowing Khalil now or wait until later? Would he love me enough to understand my past association with a man like Khalil?* Tygre had barely been able to forgive herself for her appalling lapse in judgment. And now that she knew how Brad felt about him, her indiscretion with Khalil suddenly felt more distressing than ever.

As she pondered her past transgression, Tygre began retreating inside herself, waiting for Brad to complete the call.

"No daydreaming without me, darling." Brad jostled her gently, bringing her suddenly back to reality as he returned to bed.

When a man first falls for you, Tygre, you can do no wrong. Tygre remembered her mother's pearls of wisdom. Perhaps this is the time I should tell him about Khalil? "Brad…," she hesitated to muster the courage, "there is something I would like to tell you..."

"Hold that thought until later, darling. We have more pressing matters to tend to." Brad smiled as he rolled on top of Tygre.

Still, she hesitated. "I'm developing feelings for you, Brad," Tygre said, "I promised myself to never feel like this…"

"Like what…?" Brad paused.

"I feel… vulnerable." Tygre's eyes swelled with tears.

"Don't push me away, darling. I won't let you."

"We're going too fast," Tygre insisted.

"But that's the way it should be, love at first sight."

"You hardly know me, Brad." Tygre looked away.

"It's a little late for that, wouldn't you say?" Brad's attempt to humor Tygre fell short.

"You know what I mean Brad. Besides, I have done some things in the past..."

"I don't want to hear it. Not now. My past isn't exactly pristine either."

"You're a man, the son of the President, no less. You can get away with it. I've been hurt before."

"So have I, Tygre."

"Easy for you to say, you probably have women stashed all over the country."

"Don't tell me, you of all people, believe in what you read in the tabloids?"

"No... But..." Tygre hesitated.

"Darling, it's just us here now. Be happy. Don't let the past ruin this wonderful moment. Give our future a chance, please."

"If you say so..."

The rest of the weekend at the Harrington Ranch had passed in a blur of moments that might have been snatched up from any young woman's most ardent romantic fantasies.

Instead of turning cold and distant the moment their love making was over, Brad became all the more attentive and interested. They rode, swam, ate, laughed, and made love together and when it came time for Tygre to return to New York, she felt as if she were leaving a piece of herself forever.

Chapter 26

Eight Months Earlier
New York City
Washington, D.C

The morning after Tygre's return from the Harrington Ranch she awakened in her new Upper East Side apartment. She lingered in bed, on the sheets she had washed and ironed herself, rejoicing in her good fortune. At last, she was living on her own. And even though the apartment lacked the abundant luxuries of LDV headquarters, none of that mattered in the least.

LDV had once provided Tygre with an escape from her pain and loneliness. Now, this small and cozy pied-à-terre had become her haven, a place she could relax, meditate, grieve and heal from emotional wounds and past mistakes. Surrounded by nothing but the essentials, and with nothing to distract her, Tygre faced her own feelings as painful as some of them were. To be loved had always been her goal, and she was finally willing and ready to accept it with honesty and openness.

These thoughtful reflections played out in her mind as she slowly opened her eyes and stretched under the covers until a sudden realization jolted her out of bed. *Oh my God!* Tygre clasped her hands and grinned at the thought – *I'm in love!*

"I love him," she said out loud, timidly at first. "I love Brad Harrington! I love him!" she repeated louder this time.

Tygre snatched up her cell phone and quickly dialed her father's number.

"Daddy, I have something to tell you!" Tygre cried out, "I'm in love with Brad Harrington!"

"I was expecting a call from you," her father said mildly. "So I take it everything went well?"

"Daddy, this weekend, we both…oh, where do I start?" Tygre searched for words, "We realized, at the same time, we want to love and to be loved! Brad is perfect! I couldn't have asked for anyone better."

"And you don't think you're rushing things this time?"

"Not this time, Father! I asked Brad the same question last night."

"And what did he say?"

"It felt right, for him too."

"I'm so happy to hear that, darling. Didn't I say that love would find you, so long as you were open to it?"

"You did!"

"When are you going to see this young man again?"

"I don't know yet. I have a very heavy schedule before the end of the year. I'm promoting my new line of après-ski clothes and accessories all over Europe."

"Aha. Does that mean you will be able to come and see me for Christmas?"

"I would love to, Father! Let's plan on it!"

As Tygre ended the call, she was suddenly overcome by a feeling of happiness and a sense of calm and fulfillment that had eluded her for years. Suddenly the sunlight coming through her window looked brighter. She ran into her small kitchen. The tall cup of coffee she poured herself tasted richer than ever before. The morning-after torments that haunted her previous experiences with men were conspicuously absent. As she recalled the events of her weekend, the doubts in Tygre's mind whether Brad Harrington, II was right for her in every possible way, slowly subsided. So far so good, Tygre smiled.

Following her conversation with her father, Tygre returned her focus to the screen of her computer to find several e-mails from Sir Ari. He was in New York this week and requested an urgent meeting. If it had been about sex, he would have used a far different tone, she understood, and without a moment's delay Tygre dialed his private number at LDV headquarters.

"Ari, I'm back. I hope everything is all right…"

"Tygre, my dear. Thank you for getting back to me so promptly. I need to speak with you as soon as possible, sometime later today."

"Can't we talk on the phone?"

"Believe me, this is something you'll want to hear. Let's make it five o'clock, shall we?"

"Very well then, I'll be there." Tygre sat down, a welter of feelings mixing inside her. The fact that Ari was unwilling to be specific made her hope that the call had something to do with the sale of her holdings in Classic Resources. Untangling Sir Ari's financial stranglehold had become Tygre's utmost priority. But still she worried that he would never follow through.

Tygre decided to use the time before meeting with Sir Ari to catch up on her correspondence. As she scanned the dozens of e-mails in her inbox, several unwelcome entries caught her attention. They were from Khalil. No matter how often Tygre had deleted his steady stream of e-mail messages over the last few weeks, Khalil persisted. But as tenacious as he was about re-inserting himself in Tygre's life, Tygre was equally tenacious about keeping him out of it. She tapped her delete button over and over until all traces of Khalil Karim had disappeared. It felt good to systematically erase him from her screen. If only she could erase him completely from her life...and from her memory.

Such troubling thoughts danced through her mind for the rest of the day, until the very moment that Tygre rang the bell at the front door of the LDV headquarters.

To Tygre's surprise, Sir Ari answered the door himself. He was accompanied by his newest paramour, a Russian beauty who held on tightly to Sir Ari's arm.

"My dear Tygre, how lovely you look!" Sir Ari oozed his trademark charm. He opened his arms to hug Tygre, removing himself momentarily from his young protégé's grip.

Tygre extended her hand, limiting their greeting to a formal handshake. "Hello, Ari. It's good to see you."

"Indeed, indeed. Far too long!" Sir Ari concurred. "Let me introduce you to Natasha," he added.

"Hello, Natasha." Tygre smiled politely.

The leggy blond pursed her collagen lips and silently sized Tygre up with an icy stare.

"Let's go upstairs, shall we?" Sir Ari proposed, breaking the awkward moment.

Tygre watched Natasha follow Sir Ari to the library. She felt a great sense of relief that her function as LDV's spokesperson had become limited to promoting their products. *In a year, when my contract with LDV is up, Natasha will be ready to step in and take my place.*

"Give us a moment, Natasha dear," Sir Ari said, dismissing the young model before she could enter the library. "Tygre and I have some important matters to discuss."

"I hope this is not another one of your games, Ari," she said, as he moved to close the door of the library behind them.

"I'm just making sure we're left alone," he said as he snapped the lock on the door. He paused then and fixed her with a self satisfied smile, making sure he had her full attention. "The fact is that a Saudi Prince has agreed to purchase your stock in CRG."

"Really? And who might that be?"

"Suffice it to say he is a very good friend of mine who lives in London. We studied together years ago at Eton."

"Have I met him?"

"Definitely not, which is a very good thing considering the delicate nature of this transaction."

"How delicate?" Tygre gave him a wry smile. "Is the Prince planning to pay me at least ten cents on the dollar?"

"Oh, come now, Tygre. You've become a cynic. I wouldn't let him take advantage of my favorite girl! His offer is fair."

Tygre glared silently at Sir Ari with distrust.

"When all is said and done, you're going to make a million dollars. Not bad at all, I'd say."

"That's a lot of money," Tygre agreed, "But as I well remember, I almost lost everything."

"Life is a risk, my dear. And you've come out quite well in the end. In any case, this is the best I can do for you. Just say the word and it'll be done." He waved at the bank of blinking computers behind him.

Tygre remained silent.

"You're getting what you wanted, Tygre. And you'll be helping me out. I have long-term plans for the expansion of CRG. The Prince is willing to participate, but he needs a substantial stake in the company to make it worth his while."

"Then I should get paid *more,* Ari, not less!" Tygre stated emphatically.

"I taught you too well for your own good, my dear Tygre." Sir Ari said with his usual deprecating smile. "But as I've told you before, you cannot just dump your block of stock on the market. The Prince's discretion in making this acquisition is reflected in the price of the offer. To put it bluntly, we can trust him to keep the source of these shares confidential. It's an extremely important consideration." Sir Ari's charming smile vanished.

"It's the next thing to blackmail, Ari."

He shook his head wearily. "I'm trying to do you a favor, my dear. If you're not interested, I'll try to find someone else who would like to make a million dollars without so much as turning a hand upside down."

"As I recall it involved a lot more than turning my hand upside down, Ari."

He smiled. "Ah yes," he said, "You do have artful hands."

"I've had about enough of this, Ari."

"Then make a decision. The SEC is not very keen on individuals making tax free profits based on insider information, my dear." Sir Ari's translucent eyes turned stern. "You can wait for another buyer who might one day pay more for your stock." He shrugged his shoulders and paced near the fireplace. "Take it or leave it. If you choose to take it, your money will be wire transferred to your offshore trust account in the Cayman Islands tomorrow."

As usual, Sir Ari had the upper hand. But Tygre no longer found his icy glare intimidating. She saw the warmth in Brad's Harrington's eyes every time he looked at her. By contrast, Sir Ari's frosty stare, fixed on her now, was simply manipulative and cold.

"I am certain you could get a better price for me, but I'll take the offer, Ari," Tygre stated firmly. "Tell the Prince to wire the money." Tygre stepped closer to the desk, producing the gold pen

Madame de La Sable gave her in Paris when she signed her contract with LDV. "Where do I sign?"

Sir Ari pointed to the documents neatly arranged on his Louis XVI desk. With a simple stroke of the pen, Tygre freed herself from Sir Ari's financial grip. She had never felt more relieved.

—

Tygre's six-week long promotional tour of Europe was anything but glamorous. Though she was used to covering three different countries in a week, this time her schedule seemed more exhausting and tedious than usual. The myriad of hotels and cities became a blur as she counted down the days until she would be with Brad. Tygre couldn't wait to fulfill her contractual obligations with LDV and return home to him.

There was one highlight of the tour that she was looking forward to, however. The whirlwind would culminate in Warsaw where she would finally visit with her father again.

"Two more days, Daddy," Tygre said excitedly ringing him from Vienna.

"Forty-eight hours, darling, and you'll be here! But bundle up, darling! It's very cold."

Her father's warning was an understatement, she thought as she stepped out of the plane and onto the snow-covered tarmac of the Frederic Chopin Warsaw airport. The icy cold air outside reminded Tygre of the many winters she had spent there. *This place used to be my home,* she thought. Tygre wiped away tears as she slipped into a chauffeur-driven car waiting for her at the curbside. *But it doesn't feel like home anymore.*

"The Bristol Hotel? Miss Topolska?"

"No," Tygre said, "I'm making a stop on the way." She handed the driver the address to the pre-war building where Tygre grew up. As he pulled up to the Topolski home, a flood of memories held Tygre pinned in her seat. She leaned back against the soft leather and took a few moments to prepare herself for her first reunion with her father since leaving Poland.

Inside the building, Tygre was admitted to the apartment by an elderly housekeeper she did not recognize. As she peered beyond the woman's stocky figure, Tygre caught sight of her frail-looking father, waiting for her in the living room. The image of his thin body and ghostly pallor sent a rush of concern through Tygre.

"Daddy!" Tygre cried. She rushed hug her father.

"Here you are, my darling… finally!" Adam rejoiced. "Don't cry! Wipe your tears, and let me look at you. Oh my! How you have grown up!" Adam marveled. "We have so much to talk about. How about some tea to warm you up?"

"That would be great, Daddy! It is so good to see you! I love you so much."

"I love you too, my darling." Adam held her tightly. "Tell me about you and your new friend, Brad. I want to hear everything!"

"At first I was worried about the timing of this whole tour," Tygre said after taking a few moments to compose herself, "I had to leave right after that first weekend. But he has been so wonderful and understanding." Tygre sat down next to her father and took his cold hand in hers. "He calls me sometimes twice a day even with his own busy schedule."

"That's the way it should be, darling," Adam answered with a raspy voice. "I truly hope that one day he'll take care of you the way I haven't been able to." Adam's voice trailed off into a whisper.

"Daddy, you're worrying me. What's the matter? You look so tired." Tygre studied her father's drawn face.

"It's nothing, darling. I'm just getting over a cold. I'll be fine. Tell me about your new apartment."

"I love it, Daddy. I wish I had moved sooner."

"What matters the most is that you did it. I'm so proud of you." Adam stood slowly and reached for a book, one of many neatly lining the shelves of the Topolski living room.

"Here, Tygre, I want you to have this," he said, handing her a copy of *'Famous U.S. Landmarks.'* "It's your early Christmas present, darling."

Warm tears welled in Tygre's eyes. As she took the book from Adam's shaky hand, Tygre recalled the many hours she had spent on his lap, paging through her favorite books. "Daddy, I…"

"Take it with you to New York. This is also my house- warming gift for your new apartment."

"Thank you, Daddy!" Tygre smiled and hugged him. "And I have something for you too." Tygre she reached into her purse to hand him a leather-bound first edition of Daphne Du Maurier's '*Rebecca.*'

"My favorite book!" Adam said as his eyes brightened, momentarily masking his frailty, "How thoughtful of you to remember. Thank you, darling, but I'm thinking that this was very expensive…"

"I sold my stock in CRG." Tygre blurted out. "I've got plenty of money."

"Oh?" Her father's face turned serious.

"I couldn't talk to you on the phone about this. It was one of Sir Ari's 'tax-free' schemes. But it's over now. The money is in my bank account and I'm free."

"Free from Sir Ari?'

"Yes, Father!"

"And how about the authorities?" Adam asked with more than a hint of concern.

"I wish I had never let Sir Ari talk me into doing anything illegal. I didn't fully understand. I was naïve and got greedy, but I learned… and it is behind me now. Let's hope the SEC never finds out."

"I hope so, darling."

Tygre stood and walked to a bookshelf behind her father. She picked up a silver-framed photograph of her mother. "Mommy always got away with her various escapades. As long as I don't talk about it, I'm sure I will too." The look of concern on her father's face prompted her to change the subject. "But look, LDV is going very well! My collections and accessories are selling …even in this difficult economy!"

"Your contract expires next year, doesn't it? What are you going to do after that?" Her father asked.

"I don't know yet. As mother would say, let's cross that bridge when we come to it." Tygre looked at her father as he turned away and fixed his gaze outside the window. "I hope you don't mind," Tygre said, "but I have to ask. How is she, Father? Do you talk to her?"

"She is away right now. Otherwise I'm sure she would be here to greet you." Tygre remained silent as she watched her father struggle to come to terms with his ex-wife's behavior. "She came to see me when I was…sick." Adam instantly regretted mentioning his illness.

"Sick? What do you mean? Are you okay, Daddy? You don't look well."

"I'm fine, darling. Please don't worry."

But throughout the remainder of her stay, Tygre continued to worry. She had longed to take daily walks with her father like she did as a child, but Adam wasn't well enough. So they spent her two-day visit playing gin and telling stories and reading to each other. All the while, Tygre watched Adam closely, looking for clues as to his health. She was certain he wasn't telling her the whole story.

Tygre hated the thought of leaving her father, but with Christmas only three days away, she had to go.

"Goodbye, my darling daughter. I hope to see you soon."

"Daddy…I love you so much." Tygre held Adam's frail body in her arms as she choked on her tears.

"Don't worry about me. Your visit has me feeling much better, Tygre. Your happiness keeps me healthy."

Adam's selfless words echoed in Tygre's mind as she boarded her plane for New York. Her feelings of excitement over seeing Brad were tempered by her feelings of dread. The very real possibility of never seeing her father again cast a dark cloud over her upcoming Christmas visit with Brad.

Except for confronting the continuing stream of annoying e-mails and calls from Khalil Karim, her return to the U.S. was uneventful…until she reached her New York apartment. She smiled as she caught sight of a huge bouquet of tiger lilies on her doorstep. An accompanying, hand-written note read, *"Welcome home, darling. Longing to see you in Washington, Brad."*

She booked her flight from New York to D.C. several hours before the White House party. She had important business to take care of before she could enjoy her reunion with Brad and celebrate Christmas. She had the feeling that if she were to personally confront Khalil, she could put an end to his calls, and more importantly, face the devil she had been hiding from for months. Until she did that, she knew, she would never truly be free of him.

The next morning she rushed to make her morning flight from La Guardia. As soon at the Delta shuttle landed in D.C., Tygre dialed Khalil's private number.

"Hello, Khalil, this is Tygre."

"Tygre! She finally graces me with a call. I can't believe it!" Khalil sounded livid or high, or possibly both. "Where have you been? I must have called you dozens of times."

Tygre ignored his question. "I would like to see you, Khalil. I am in D.C. now."

"Very well. Why don't you come to house at eight, and we'll have dinner."

"I already have plans for dinner, but I can stop by right now."

"So be it." Khalil replied. The phone went dead.

Tygre loathed her return to Khalil's life, even for a few moments, but it had to be done. Tygre glanced at her watch, calculating the time she had. If she finished quickly all would be well.

Though the traffic was heavy, the car arrived at Khalil's Georgetown mansion promptly at five. With a wine glass in hand and a silk scarf knotted at his throat, Khalil greeted her himself at the door.

"Tygre, you look absolutely marvelous," Khalil said through a broad smile.

"Hello, Khalil." Tygre said stepping back from his extended arms.

He turned his attention to a servant waiting attentively in the foyer, "Make sure the outdoor heaters are on in the gazebo so that we can enjoy the garden," he told the servant, who scurried off.

Khalil turned back to Tygre.

"Please come inside. You upset me with your disappearance from my life." Khalil came right to it. "I'm hurt, Tygre, I truly am."

"A life full of drugs and alcohol, not to mention sex sprinkled with a few prayers?" Tygre mocked him. "Yes, Khalil, that was certainly hard to resist." She felt disgusted at the thought of it all.

"I remember your moans of pleasure quite vividly." Khalil stared directly at Tygre.

Tygre fought the wave of self-loathing that washed over her. How had she let it happen? "I'm not coming inside, Khalil. I just came here to tell you to stop calling and e-mailing me. It is over between you and me. There was never anything there to begin with."

"Those are harsh words, Tygre..."

"I've met someone," she continued. "I'm in love with him and I want you to leave me alone."

Khalil's expression turned into a sneer. "Are we speaking of President Harrington's piteous whelp? He is nothing more than a rube."

"How could you know...?" Tygre began, feeling violated.

"Don't underestimate me, Tygre. There is nothing you do that does not reach my ears. So you spent one weekend with the privileged son of a capitalist swine and you tell me you're in love?" Khalil broke off with a laugh. "Next you'll tell me is that he's in love with you!" Khalil's laugh became a roar.

Tygre felt as if a giant weight was pressing against her chest. It seemed as if she were being suffocated. "You are horrendous," she managed. "I don't know why I thought I should have come here."

She turned and ran back down the sidewalk toward her car, tears blinding her.

"Wait," she heard Khalil's voice calling. "Tygre! I am sorry my words were cruel..."

She jumped into the back seat of the car and called to the startled driver. "The Hay Adams," she said, fighting to stop her tears. "Quickly, please."

The driver nodded, pushing the button that snapped the car's locks just as a wild-eyed Khalil reached the car. They peeled away from the curb as Khalil's shouts echoed in the otherwise peaceful neighborhood.

Tygre never saw the men in the black Chrysler parked across the street. A Nikon D40, set on the no-flash function, quietly and inconspicuously shot every moment of the encounter. As her car drove away, the man in the black sedan secured the cover on his lens and put his own car into gear, following after.

—

Back in her room at the Hay Adams, Tygre collapsed on her bed in despair. She had hoped to feel a sense of freedom and relief after meeting with Khalil, but clearly the man was far too addled for such a logical approach. There was only one option left, she realized. *I will tell Brad about Khalil tonight,* she promised herself. *I just have to trust that he will know my heart, my love for him... and he will understand.*

She was looking forward to the evening of course, but the rush she felt upon seeing Brad standing in the lobby next to the graceful Hay Adams Christmas tree still surprised her.

"Brad!" Tygre said. "I'm so happy to see you!" Tygre threw her arms around his neck.

They lingered in a passionate kiss that provoked jaw-dropping reactions from the hotel's guests. "I think we're causing a commotion, darling!" Brad took Tygre's hand and led her out of the lobby.

Tygre rested her head on Brad's chest and lingered, inhaling the scent of his body. She'd meant to tell him immediately about Khalil, but it was impossible for her to spoil the moment.

The intimacy between the young lovers didn't go unnoticed, of course. The man in the passenger seat of the black Chrysler pointed his lens at the stylish couple and began clicking away... again and again.

Satisfied with the pictures, the driver of the Chrysler slowly pulled away from the curbside and merged with the oncoming traffic. It stopped briefly to yield the right of way to Brad and Tygre as they crossed H Street to Lafayette Park toward Pennsylvania Avenue on their way to the White House.

"I insisted that my Secret Service shadow Ives wait to meet us at the reception," Brad told her. "I wanted to greet you at your hotel without him looking over my shoulder."

"I'm glad," Tygre said with a grateful smile.

"I assured him I could get us both safely across the park, but he wasn't too happy about it."

"I hope you don't mind me asking something..." Tygre paused.

"Go ahead."

"It's just that Agent Ives doesn't seem very happy with his work. Protecting you, I mean."

Brad laughed. "That's an understatement. A few months ago, Sean was dropped from my father's detail. He has yet to get over it. He thinks he's overqualified to be tagging around after me."

"So why do you put up with his attitude?"

Brad paused before he answered. "Ives and I go back a long way, Tygre." They'd arrived at the east gate of the White House by then and Brad gave a nod at a group of presidential protective detail standing on the grounds a few yards away. "He's right over there. I'll tell you more about it some other time."

Tygre agreed. In seconds, escorted by Ives and a second Secret Service agent, they were swiftly whisked inside.

As Tygre would discover, the White House Christmas party is possibly the only time of year when bipartisan differences are set aside in Washington. Politicians from both sides of the aisle were more than willing to let down their guard and celebrate the holiday season. Dressed in festive attire, members of Congress and their spouses congregated around the massive Christmas trees, placed strategically in various quarters.

The reception rooms, each with its own contingent of carolers, smelled of fresh pine and gingerbread. Tygre was struck by the magnificence of the Christmas decorations and the 800-plus ornaments dating back to the first occupants of the White House, John Adams and his wife, Abigail.

She recalled her own two-foot-tall Christmas tree in Poland, barely decorated and lit with real candles, and also fondly remembered her first-ever Christmas present, a red bicycle that her father had saved for months to purchase. Tygre, five years old at the time, had insisted on riding the bike in three feet of snow.

What a difference 19 years made, Tygre thought, looking around at the White House staff and beautifully attired guests. Distinguished visitors mingled with Senators and US Congress representatives and freely exchanged holiday greetings with President Harrington and his wife, Barbara.

"It looks like one big happy family," Tygre said.

"Until the next filibuster!" Brad said drily. "Come on, let's say hello to my parents." As they walked to meet the President and the First Lady, Ives followed them closely.

Tygre couldn't help but feel nervous. *This was not an LDV promotional tour,* she kept reminding herself. *This is my life!*

The First Lady discreetly waved at her son and Tygre, beckoning them to cut the receiving line.

"They look so busy." Tygre's heart fluttered as she pondered the idea of seeing President and Mrs. Harrington again.

Brad laughed and kissed her, "Forget it," he said. "I want to show you off."

For his part, President Harrington greeted her warmly. "We met when we entertained the French President and his wife. Brad has told me so much about you!" William Harrington hugged a stunned Tygre.

"It's wonderful to see Brad so happy," The First Lady said in Tygre's ear as she leaned in for a hug. "He can't stop talking about you, Tygre! I've never seen him so smitten. Take good care of each other!" Barbara Harrington added.

Tygre was glowing as Brad led her away from the meeting with his parents. She'd heard that they had not always been easy to please when it came to Brad's previous relationships.

"Tygre, this place is starting to give me the heebie-jeebies," Brad said, leaning in close to her. "How would you like to see the Oval Office?"

"The Oval Office?" she said. "Are you serious?"

"Serious as a heart attack," he said. "Hurry up while Ives is trying to suck up with my old man."

Tygre gave a glance back at the receiving line where it seemed that Sean Ives was trying his best to cut in for a word with his old boss. She took Brad's hand and the two of them quickly scurried away through the crowd.

The room seemed as quiet as a bank vault when they entered. Flanked by both the United States' and the President's flags, William Harrington's desk was empty, except for two silver framed photographs, one of Barbara and one of Brad in his colorful New Deal prototype race car.

"I can't believe I'm seeing this in person," Tygre finally spoke. "I saw pictures of this room in a book I used to page through as a little girl, sitting on my father's knee."

"I'm happy to be the one to show you." Brad said, smiling at her. "I have mixed feelings every time I walk in here."

She glanced at him. In her own excitement, she hadn't given much thought to Brad's feelings. "I suppose it isn't the easiest thing to be the son of the President," she ventured.

"My parents were never around," he answered, with a shrug.

"Just like my mother," she told him. "Something else we have in common."

"I haven't really told you much about it, Tygre. But there was a long time where I turned to alcohol to fill the void."

He hadn't told her of course. She hadn't seem him take a drink, but then again, she'd been so caught up in the whirl her life had become in his presence, she hadn't really thought about it.

"I'm sorry you had to go through that," she said. "I became addicted to my work to prove myself. It doesn't seem to mean much to my mother, though."

Brad stood, seemingly lost in thought as he stared at the desk before them.

"Would you like to be President one day?" Tygre suddenly blurted.

He turned to her with the hint of a smile on his lips. "No way," he answered flatly. She felt relief at the certainty of his tone.

"Why not?"

Brad led her to a small settee. They sat close, the muffled noises of the Christmas party barely audible in the distance.

"The truth is that I try to distance myself from my father's job. He and I disagree about a lot of things. Politics is a global business, full of compromises. I've seen my father's principles get twisted by our dependence on foreign oil and a whole raft of other circumstances beyond his control. Occasionally I feel my father's decisions are not entirely his own. That's bad enough, but it's even worse when he gets criticized when things go wrong."

Tygre nodded. "Everyone just assumes the President of the United States has all the power..."

He gave her his knowing smile. "I respect my father, but I'd hate to have his job."

"What do you want to do, besides race?" Tygre asked.

"Racing is just part of a bigger plan," he said. "I know I can make a difference by developing and manufacturing prototypes and eventually the road cars. That would make for a lot of jobs and saving energy and a lot more," he said. "But, hey, that's enough about changing the world. Right now I want to spend my time with you." He stood and pulled her gently up to meet him face to face.

"What do you say we run off to the Hay Adams before Ives finds us?"

"That sounds like an Executive Decision to me," Tygre said, and they were gone, quietly closing the doors to the Oval Office behind them.

"Thank God you don't want to become President," Tygre said, kissing him tenderly on the cheek.

"Why, darling?"

"Because I want you all to myself!"

Chapter 27

Le Mans
1:50 p.m. Sunday

"Walk faster and keep smiling, infidel whore!" Malik barked, his patience apparently wearing thin. She was moving as slowly as possible amid the sea of bodies, hoping to stall for time until she might escape. At the very least, she desperately wanted to catch the eye of someone who might detect her fear and seemed capable of reaching out a helping hand.

She heard the trill of Malik's cell phone behind her and the press of the gun barrel in her ribs as he answered. "Yes," Malik said, lowering his voice, "How did you get away from the trailer?"

Tygre was instantly on the alert. *Who could he be talking to about getting away from the trailer?*

"I have the bitch with me. Yes, you don't have to tell me. She's been in bed with the other side. But I assure you, she is done sleeping around! I'll be at the airport shortly. Tell the pilot to have the helicopter ready."

Tygre fought to hear above the clamor of the crowd.

"I will light all the remaining candles simultaneously. The big cake is still in place, is it not? And Khalil is on the track in No.7?" Malik paused and glanced over his shoulder.

"Excellent! Praise Allah!" Malik's face lit up. "No more chances, Ives. Essential calls only from here on out," he ordered and flipped his cell phone shut.

Tygre turned to Malik in astonishment. "You just said, 'Ives.'"

"Indeed I did. It is the man's name."

"Sean Ives? Brad Harrington's Secret Service agent?"

He stared at her. "I see why Khalil is attracted to you. When your brain struggles to operate, you become a most inviting victim."

"What possible connection could scum like you have with a Secret Service agent?"

Malik gave her his most satisfied smile. "I shall so enjoy ending your life," he said. "I can go to my grave content that I have wiped out a strain of stupidity that might have doomed the human race."

"How do you know Sean Ives?" Tygre demanded, trying to ignore the chill that ran through her.

"It's quite simple. Ives is a discontented failure. An alcoholic and a closet gambler. The American Government does not pay Ives nearly enough to cover his debts. Because of his connection to Harrington, Khalil bought his debt from the Russian mafia!" Malik gloated. "In addition Ives is getting another two million dollars to go and squander once all this is over, or so he thinks. Almost unfathomable motivation, isn't it, miss rocket scientist?"

Tygre's heart seemed to be pounding through lead. "This cannot be happening!"

"Ives hates Harrington and his old-boy network! He's been repeatedly passed over for promotion. "He hates being detailed to your lover—SP, as Ives calls him."

"SP?"

"Stupid prick. The younger Harrington's two most notable assets," Malik added with what passed for a smile. "As I am sure you have noticed."

Tygre swallowed hard. "I can't believe Ives would go this far… to become a traitor…?"

"Depends on which side of the fence you're sitting on. To me, Ives is a hero. Now, put that model's smile back on your face and keep walking!" Malik ordered.

"You're hurting me," Tygre said trying to jerk her arm away from Malik.

"I can see my car," Malik pointed at a distant corner of a crowded lot stretching out in front of them. "Not much further to go, my sweet."

Malik shoved her on as the crowds about them surged on toward the finish line, oblivious to everything else around them.

Malik laughed at the irony of it. "Hiding in plain sight," he said, taunting her.

She turned away, fighting her fear. Amazingly, her gaze fell upon a uniformed French policeman only a few yards away. He glanced in Tygre's direction and, for a few seconds, their eyes locked. *Help me,* her eyes silently beckoned to him. But the officer seemed not to notice. He smiled politely and turned away.

"Kiss me!" Malik demanded. She felt the stab of the pistol at her ribs. "Right now! Kiss me." He forced himself on Tygre with lips that were chapped and tart. His breath smelled of garlic and tasted of salty sweat. Tygre's stomach turned.

"Don't look at that cop," Malik ordered. "Keep kissing me and act as if you enjoy it."

Malik's gun moved up to Tygre's breast just inches from her heart. Tygre closed her eyes and wondered how quickly she would die if Malik pulled the trigger. Would there be pain or just a sudden end of everything?

She closed her eyes and listened to the sound of accelerating engines, which heralded the arrival of the racers near pit lane. The race was almost over. *Will I live to see Brad's victory?* Tygre wondered. *Will I see him ever again?*

When Malik felt confident that the police officer had safely passed, he peeled his lips from Tygre and guided her toward the parking lot. Lightheaded, Tygre dragged her feet. She could only pray that someone might catch up with them before she was forced into Malik's vehicle.

"Ladies and Gentlemen, the No. 1 car, driven by Brad Harrington is nearly one minute in the lead, followed by New Deal's No.2 car, driven by Chris Summers in second place. Khalil Karim is in third position, nearly 90 seconds behind. The No.1 car's average speed is 135 mph. Harrington is on pace to break last year's speed record here at Le Mans."

"Let's go, bitch! Don't you dare pass out on me or I'll have to shoot you right now!" Malik pulled Tygre toward his waiting car.

"I've just been informed Karim Racing's driver, Khalil Karim, is having trouble with a shifter and an overheating engine," the announcer's voice cut in. "Karim remains in the race, but has fallen behind into fourth place."

Tygre shuddered as Malik began swearing angrily in Arabic. "Zarba! Kanith! Elit air ab tizak!" He squeezed her arm so tightly she thought it might break.

But the pain meant nothing to Tygre. "If Khalil's car doesn't make it to the end of the race, what happens to your plan, you asshole?"

She reached to pull off the hat Malik had forced her to wear.

"Don't do it. I'll kill you!" Malik warned.

Tygre quickly opened her hands in surrender, leaving the hat untouched on her head. The feeling of dread returned just as quickly as it had waned.

He pulled her toward a compact Volvo sedan parked beside a large van. She glanced around, desperately looking for any chance to escape, but Malik swiftly unlocked the car. The Volvo's tinted windows were opaque and dirty, and the interior reeked of stale food.

"Get in!" Malik demanded.

"I won't!" Tygre protested.

"You will," Malik said cocking the pistol and prodding her into the driver's seat.

"I'm going to be sick," Tygre said as he climbed into the passenger's seat. "I swear I am." She slumped forward in her seat. "I'm going to throw up."

"If you want to stay alive, you'll start this car and begin driving." Malik closed the door as a policeman hurriedly walked by, glancing for only a moment in their direction. Malik tensed and leaned toward Tygre with a forced smile.

"Don't try anything foolish!" Malik slid his hand to the nape of Tygre's neck and pulled sharply on her hair turning her face close to his. "Don't you love me any longer, darling?"

"You repulse me!" she said, turning her face away.

Malik was smiling as the policeman made his way into the milling crowds and away from the car.

"Now drive!" he demanded once he was satisfied the officer was gone.

Tygre turned the key and started the engine. She held the steering wheel with shaking hands and lowered her head as tears streamed down her cheeks. After taking a moment to collect herself, she picked up her head and asked resignedly, "Which way?"

"When you get out of the lot, turn left. At the first stop sign, you will go right." Malik ordered.

Tygre put the car in gear and began moving it as slowly as she had ever driven a car, hoping someone in the parking lot would stop them.

Malik's cell phone rang again. He answered while checking his wristwatch. "Perfect timing, Ives. Tell the pilot I'll be there shortly. Praise Allah."

Malik closed his phone and forcefully dug his elbow into Tygre's side. "Get going, bitch!"

Tygre gasped at the blow, and jerked the car forward in second gear, while Malik anxiously scanned the parking lot.

"I really don't know how to drive a shift," Tygre lied, frantically searching for any sign of help.

"Learn fast, or you'll die."

Tygre slowly shifted gears and sent up a quick, silent prayer. *In the name of God, where is the FBI? Where are the French authorities? They promised me this would never happen! Where is everybody? Please, Lord, help me!*

Malik reached under his jacket and pulled out two devices — one that seemed to be a gray cell phone, the other, a black garage door opener. She'd seen them both in the box she'd gone through in the trailer. He waggled them both at Tygre before placing them back in his breast pocket.

"Get it through your head, Ms. Mensa," he said. "Those devices are going to blow your boyfriend and his precious prick and his father and mother into the next world." He paused and pulled out another small cell phone from a side pocket. "And with this I can explode Khalil's chopper and the rest of Le Mans Airport in the blink of an eye," he boasted proudly before placing it by his side.

"And what do you think that would accomplish?"

"Never mind," he said. "Your useless existence is of no interest to me! You and these transmitters are my ticket to freedom. That is all. Just keep driving. If I don't make it, no one at the airport will either...including you!" Malik grinned with delight at the prospect.

She pondered the idea of jerking the car forward, catching him off guard and digging her fingernails into his eyes, but she realized the risk of him detonating the explosives was too great.

Malik glanced at his wristwatch. "Praise Allah! At 3:00 p.m., the Rolex clock will signal the end of the free world here at Le Mans!" Malik laughed hysterically, choking on his own words. "Just wait and see."

"What do you mean about the Rolex clock?" Tygre asked.

Malik abruptly stopped laughing. "What do you think?" he asked. "The Rolex clock is the perfect centerpiece for this great tribute to Allah!"

Tygre stayed silent.

"If the French police, the FBI and all your government agencies, including the Le Mans officials, couldn't figure it out, why should I expect a stupid bitch like you to get it?"

"Oh my God," Tygre uttered. "The explosives are in the clock."

"Ah! So she does have a brain!" Malik laughed cruelly. "And now she is beginning to panic," he added as he watched Tygre's face flush with horror.

"You warped bastard!" Tygre cried. "How can you live with yourself?"

"Quite nicely," Malik answered with a laugh. "*You,* on the other hand, I can live without. You're about to find that out soon enough."

"You're despicable!" Tygre shrieked.

"And *you* are pathetic," Malik countered. "You underestimated me, bitch, just like all your FBI friends. And now you expect them to find *you*? Good luck with that!"

Malik was right. The FBI had failed her. If there was a way out of this, Tygre would have to find it on her own. And, the best way of making that happen, she decided, was to keep Malik talking. "How were you able to hide the explosives without the bomb-sniffing dogs finding them? I'm just curious, Malik."

Malik looked at her suspiciously for a moment, then relented. "It doesn't matter if I tell you now. The explosives are sealed in a sanitized plastic box filled with diesel-fuel-soaked rags! With the activity on the race track, no bomb-sniffing dog will ever come near it!" Malik's eyes danced with glee.

"What about….."

"That's enough for now," Malik said. "Turn here," he pointed the way out of the lot.

Tygre pushed on the accelerator to appease Malik. "Why don't you kill me? What's the point in keeping me around?" She was terrified to know the answer, but convinced it might help her plan her own escape.

"I'll take care of you when I'm good and ready," he said. "Just be happy that you're more useful to me alive than dead right now! And keep in mind that could easily change."

They were on the road that paralleled the race grounds now, moving slowly in a line of traffic leading to the entrance of Arnage Airport. Malik seemed oddly calm, muttering prayers under his breath. He reached into his pocket and withdrew his Karim Racing's driver credentials, pinning them to the front of his jacket in anticipation of their arrival at the private airport grounds.

Tygre thought through the details of Malik's plan in her head. She tried to remain calm as a flash of clarity came over her. Perhaps *Malik needs to be airborne,* she thought. *He needs that aerial view in order to pinpoint the exact location of Khalil's car so he can detonate it. And he's planning to synchronize the explosion with the additional explosives in the Rolex clock!*

As they approached Le Mans Airport, Tygre noticed that the vast array of private aircraft was guarded by any number of French police, paratroopers, and military-looking security forces. Her heart filled instantly with hope. *They must know about my abduction,* she told herself as she pulled through the barbwire-topped gates. The executive jets of sponsors and mega clients were carefully lined up near the runway. A few uniformed pilots walked past, casually inspecting their planes and helicopters, readying them for the post-race departure. But to Tygre's dismay, no one looked in the direction of the Volvo. Their arrival went completely unnoticed.

"I need some air," she said and started to roll down her window.

Malik jerked forward ready to lean over and stop her if she went too far. "Don't try anything stupid!" he warned.

"Just a little crack," Tygre said through quick gasps, somehow managing to satisfy Malik that all she wanted was air. He relaxed and leaned back into his seat.

The sounds of the conversations outside the window mingled with the roar of the distant cars. A sense of doom rolled over her. *The end is near,* she thought, as she deeply inhaled the fresh air.

"At the check point, slow down and smile," Malik ordered as he removed Tygre's sunglasses and handed her a handkerchief. "Clean your face right now. Hurry up!"

Tygre kept one hand on the steering wheel as she wiped her face with the back of her other hand, leaving the handkerchief untouched.

Malik's phone rang again. "Adis?" he answered, speaking quickly in Arabic. When Malik began intermixing English with Arabic, Tygre was finally able to fit together the last few pieces of the puzzle. "Rolex....Khalil...chopper...Prince Abdullah..."

Of course, she thought. *It all fit. The things she had overheard between Ives and Brad during their last trip together...her meeting with Prince Abdullah that same weekend...she had been steps away from the masterminds of this entire plot. If she had only known then...*

Malik spoke louder into the phone, sounding agitated by whatever he was hearing from Adis.

Tygre didn't have time to decipher their conversation. She placed her hand on the door handle and, for an instant, contemplated jumping out of the moving car. As if reading her mind, Malik tugged harshly on her hair as he continued his Arabic rant. The corners of his mouth moved upward to mimic a smile, but his eyes remained stern with unwavering purpose.

"Put them on," Malik ordered.

Tygre winced.

"Right now!" He shoved the sunglasses back on her face.

As a French officer approached the car, Malik slammed his phone shut and quickly tucked it into his pocket. “Drive slowly,” he ordered Tygre with a grin plastered on his face. “And when the officer speaks to you, do what you do best…show him your tits and smile.”

“One wrong word and you’re dead. Just wave and smile,” he warned. “I’ll do the talking!” he said. Tygre nodded quietly, and rolled her window down. She could only pray that the French officer would recognize her behind the dark sunglasses. Or that the end would be merciful and quick.

Chapter 28

One Month Before
The Harrington Ranch
Vero Beach, Florida

When Tygre arrived at the airport in May for a long-planned trip to the Harrington Ranch, she found Brad frantically dialing his cell phone. As he approached, he closed his phone for a moment to give her an absent-minded kiss.

Tygre was puzzled. It wasn't like Brad to be so preoccupied in her presence. She'd been so looking forward to this trip, one of several in the last few months. This time the President and Mrs. Harrington would be there, and there was even a bit of political intrigue. Brad had told her that his father would be hosting Prince Abdullah, a key player in maintaining an uninterrupted flow of oil from the Middle East to the U.S.

"What's the matter, darling?" she asked.

"Sean Ives requested a personal day yesterday. He asked me to keep it from his supervisor. But he was supposed to meet us here at eight this morning. He's late. I have a bad feeling about it. I should never have agreed to it."

"Why did you?"

Brad took a deep breath. "Do you remember in Washington when you asked me if Sean liked his job?"

Tygre nodded.

"I told you that Sean and I go back a long way."

"I remember." Tygre said.

"Well, that was only half of the story." Brad paused, and then confessed, "Ives used to gamble heavily, and, like I told you, I used to drink...a lot. He covered for me when I flew and drove under the influence. In return, I turned a blind eye when he placed bets. It worked for both of us. We were each other's enablers."

"Oh Brad..."

"There's more. Ives claimed he had been at the controls one time when I had a little incident during a landing in Vero. I clipped a parked plane, and there'd been hell to pay if anyone had given me a sobriety test. I owe him, Tygre." Brad nervously checked the time. "But if he doesn't show up soon, we'll lose our spot for the take-off." Brad began pacing. "The bad thing is, I think, Ives has been gambling again."

"He's certainly seemed preoccupied." Tygre stated evenly.

"I've tried to help him," Brad said. "But like any other addiction, it's a very hard habit to break."

"Maybe this is him," Tygre pointed at a Yellow Cab rapidly approaching across the tarmac.

"Finally!"

"I'm sorry," Ives said as he clambered out of the taxi. "The traffic on FDR Drive was backed up all the way to the Cross Bronx Parkway." Ives looked haggard and tense.

"I was about to cancel our flight plan!" Brad said, his anger, thinly veiled.

"I'm really sorry…" Ives began.

Brad cut him off. "Let's get going."

Tygre kept a careful eye on the pair as they boarded and began the pre-flight preparations. Even though Brad had let him off the hook, Ives seemed impatient and irritated as Brad led them through the routine.

"We need to talk, Sean," Brad said as the plane leveled at 30,000 feet. "What is going on with you?"

Tygre closed her eyes and strained to hear their voices above the sound of the Aerostar's engines.

"I have it under control," Ives said quietly. He turned around to make sure Tygre was asleep as usual. Satisfied by her closed eyes, he reiterated, "Don't worry about it, Brad. I'm taking care of it."

"By looking at you, you're not taking care of it very well." Brad snapped.

"You don't need to get involved," Ives said.

"I already am involved! I need to know what you're up to, right now!" Brad demanded.

"An old gambling debt reared its ugly head, that's all." Ives sighed. He softened his tone and tapped Brad's shoulder to reassure him. "I'm dealing with it, I swear to you."

"Protecting you isn't helping either one of us. Get help, man, and get it now...or you're not coming to France with me. You and I both know you need to straighten out your life!" Brad said, his voice firm.

"I promise, Brad. I won't let you down at Le Mans."

"Just get it together!" Brad warned and turned his attention to the flight charts.

When Tygre and Brad arrived at the Harrington Ranch three hours later, the mid-day picnic was fully underway, and the President and the First Lady were just finishing up a ride. The fragrant smells of barbecued beef, corn on the cob and freshly baked ham lingered in the air.

"Happy Mother's Day!" Brad called to the First Lady, blowing her a kiss as she dismounted her horse. Brad hugged her tightly then watched as Barbara turned to Tygre and greeted her with a warm embrace. "I'm so happy to see you, my dear!"

The President looked on, holding the reins of his own mount. "Good to see you both," the President waved to Brad and Tygre. In Levi's, a long-sleeved shirt and a cowboy hat, the President looked as if he'd stepped out of a Norman Rockwell painting. If not for the Secret Service Agents standing nearby, no one would have taken him for the leader of the most powerful nation in the world.

"You're just in time for lunch," Mrs. Harrington said. She handed the reins of her horse to a ranch hand and urged them all toward a table groaning with food and surrounded by dozens of joyful ranch hands, cowboys and their families.

Barbara looked at Tygre while the others were lost in the commotion, "I wish I looked as good in my jeans as you do in yours! It must be LDV."

Tygre laughed. "You look wonderful," she assured the First Lady, who gave her an affectionate hug in return.

"Pretty peaceful down here," Brad said to his father as he watched the interchange between Tygre and his mother.

"Not for long!" President Harrington interjected. "Prince Abdullah and his entourage arrive later this afternoon. Why don't you and Tygre join us all for cocktails around six? I want to show you kids off."

"We'll be there, Father, thank you."

"I've never felt so full in all my life!" Tygre said taking one last bite of her barbecue.

"I think that's our cue to go!" Brad told her. "I could use a nap. How about you?"

"I thought you would never ask!"

Later, they lay in each other's arms in the bedroom of the farmhouse where they'd shared their first close moments together. The late afternoon sun filled the room with glimmering light. The sound of the birds, carried by the balmy breeze, filtered through the open windows. Brad tucked his chin atop her head. "I love you, Tygre. I'm so happy you are a part of my world."

"You have become a part of me too, Brad. I love you very much."

Brad looked at Tygre. "I think my grandfather had us in mind before he died."

"Oh?"

"I inherited this ranch from him, you know. My grandfather was shrewd and ruthless, but I always knew how much he loved me."

She felt him take a deep breath before he began again.

"It was my grandmother who brought me up, especially when my father ran for Governor of Florida. She drank a lot…alone… and, eventually, so did I." Brad paused, "after that accident with the plane, I quit cold turkey and haven't had a drink since. To this day, it's very hard for me to accept that I'm powerless over alcohol."

"I'm proud of you, Brad. I hope I never let you down."

"You couldn't if you tried." Brad moved so that they were facing each other. "Listen, I want you to come to Le Mans with me this June."

"I would love to," Tygre tried to smile, but she knew that her face betrayed the turmoil that filled her mind at the very mention of Le Mans.

"What is it, sweetheart?"

Tygre fought back thoughts of Khalil Karim and his participation in the race. *I have to tell Brad,* she thought. *If I'm going to be completely open with him, I need to tell him about my involvement with Khalil.* But she simply couldn't find the words. Brad, meanwhile, relented. He took her hand and pulled her up from the bed after him.

"It's settled, then," he said. "Let's go and watch the sunset."

He led her onto the deck of the second story room and pointed westward at the purple-red glow that blazed across the tropical sky. And then, in an instant, the sun was gone.

"Look, here comes company," Brad said, spotting several black SUVs slowly negotiating the unpaved approach to the ranch compound.

"This must be Prince Abdullah," she said. "It looks like he has more security than your father!" Tygre laughed.

"He travels with a dozen bodyguards, not to mention all his aides and advisors," Brad said. He sighed and glanced at his watch. "I guess we better get ready. We need to be on time for this one."

A half hour later, Tygre entered the library of the main house at Harrington Ranch, smiling proudly, holding onto Brad's arm. President Harrington and the Prince courteously stood as they walked in. Tygre had chosen a pale green gingham summer dress, flat shoes and a light pink shawl to drape over her shoulders

Mrs. Harrington smiled signaling her approval. "Your Royal Highness," she said. "You know my son Brad, I believe. May I introduce my son's girlfriend, Tygre Topolska?"

The Prince, who looked quite Western in a navy blue gabardine blazer, a pair of perfectly fitted tan slacks and a green and white pin-striped dress shirt, bowed as he took Tygre's hand.

His picture in the *New York Times* didn't do him justice, Tygre thought, a bit surprised at the Prince's debonair demeanor. But as his lips lingered on Tygre's hand, the feeling of admiration, quickly turned to discomfort.

After a moment, the Prince released her hand. "I am honored, mademoiselle," he announced with a pronounced British inflection. "Your LDV photographs do not accurately portray your exquisite beauty!"

Sensing Tygre's unease, the President redirected the attention of the spellbound Prince. "Of course, your Highness remembers meeting my son last year?"

"Yes…yes, of course! Good to see you, young man." The Prince shook Brad's hand firmly. "I understand that you are defending your title once again at Le Mans next month."

"Indeed I am, your Highness. And I expect spirited competition from the Saudi team," Brad replied.

"I hope they will be up to it," the Prince said.

"Brad is ready for the challenge, I assure you," President Harrington broke in with a wry smile. "And I am going to be at Le Mans to watch him win!"

"I am certain that it will be an extraordinary event this year," the Prince replied.

Once champagne had been served, the Prince turned again to Tygre. "Have you ever been to Saudi Arabia, my dear?"

"I haven't," Tygre politely answered.

"Should your assignments take you there in the future, I would like to extend an invitation for you to visit me at my palace."

"Thank you so much. That's very thoughtful of you, Your Royal Highness," Tygre said.

"You'll never know where your travels may take you," the Prince added. "Just in case, I want you to have my private number." The Prince motioned to one of his guards who handed Tygre the Prince's card. Tygre could imagine no circumstances under which she would call this man, but she placed the card in her purse.

Brad eyed it all with some amusement, then finally took Tygre's hand. "It has been a pleasure, Your Royal Highness," he said pulling Tygre close to his side, "But I know you have business to discuss and Tygre and I have dinner plans. I'm glad you could see the ranch," he added, as he ushered Tygre out.

As they stepped outside the library, Brad quickly apologized to Tygre. "I'm so sorry you had to endure that, darling. The Prince is a lecher."

Tygre pulled the Prince's card from her purse, tore it up, and handed the pieces to Brad. "I've endured worse," she said.

"I'd have been within my rights to deck him," Brad said, smiling. "If I was still drinking, I probably would have."

"And start a crisis in the Middle East?" Tygre said with a smile as they stepped outside.

"If you're hungry, I'll make us a light dinner." Brad asked as he put an arm around her shoulders.

"I'll settle for a walk on the beach," Tygre said, leaning into him.

"Let's go," Brad jumped into the jeep and started the engine.

Moments later, closely followed by Sean Ives and a second Secret Service agent, they reached the cottage. They got out of the vehicle and walked the hundred yards or so to their favorite place on the ranch in silence, then spent another half hour in a peaceful stroll along the gently crashing surf. When they returned to the farmhouse, Brad began to doze off while Tygre regretfully began packing-she would have to leave early the next morning for a photo shoot in Miami.

"Oh dear," Tygre said. "I must have left my cell phone in the library. I put it down when the Prince went to kiss my hand."

"I'll get it for you," Brad mumbled, clearly half asleep.

"Just rest," she said. "I know where I left it. It won't take me more than a couple of minutes." Tygre slipped into a robe and left the farmhouse.

"I'll be right here," Brad called sleepily after her.

As Tygre walked briskly toward the main house, a Secret Service Agent appeared out of the shadows. "Miss Topolska, can I help you?"

She was startled, but told herself she should be used to it by now. At least it wasn't Sean Ives. He would have probably demanded her identification. "I left my phone in the library earlier. I'm just going to get it."

"Go right ahead, miss."

He turned to speak into a communications device, his voice too low for her to hear. She rolled her eyes and moved along toward the house where another of the presidential detail and one of the Prince's bodyguards looked on as she entered.

As she walked down the hallway to the library, the sound of hushed words spoken rapidly in Arabic drifted from the door to a guest bedroom where another guard stood like some figure from a movie. It was the bedroom given to the Prince she realized. A sliver of light fell through the door, which sat slightly ajar. *Le Mans* and *Al Hajal* were the only words she could make out before the Prince's bodyguard turned and closed the door.

Tygre quickly retrieved her phone then walked back to the front door and quietly stepped out of the house. Both the Secret Service and the Prince's security detail looked on as she ran back to the farmhouse. Happy to be inside and out of their view, Tygre slipped under the covers next to Brad. When she gave him a kiss, he stirred momentarily.

"I hate seeing you go…more than you'll ever know!" Brad said, wrapping his arms around her. "But I will see you in Paris in less than a month. We'll take the town by storm, and after that, we'll take over Le Mans."

Chapter 29

Le Mans
2:08 p.m. Sunday

As he darted from Khalil Karim's air-conditioned trailer into the sticky air outside, Agent Doug Martin was fuming. He scanned the chaotic scene before him and shook his head. He felt helpless and overwhelmed as he called back in to his supervisor. "Ben, I don't see how we could find anyone in this mess."

"Goddamn it, Doug! That's not what I need to hear."

"There are over two hundred thousand people here! We're doing the best we can, Ben!"

"Try harder! I'm taking a lot of shit from the seventh floor. I need some answers! Just get it done!"

Ben's harsh response was not what Agent Martin wanted to hear, but he understood. He turned to a pair of fellow agents, who along with two members of the French Special Forces, had arrived to assist.

"Washington wants answers! They don't care that we're looking for a needle in a haystack..." he began, when an urgent voice in his earpiece stopped him abruptly.

"Doug? I can barely hear you!" It was Ben's voice again. Martin re-keyed the encrypted code card in his wristwatch transmitter and answered, expecting another earful.

"Yes, Ben."

"Okay, listen up. The French Special Forces just reported that a helicopter owned by Khalil Karim is standing by at the Le Mans Airport. It is registered in the name of one of Karim's off-shore corporations. It took awhile to trace it, but it has been confirmed."

"Roger that. We are headed to the airport, then."

"You do that, Doug. That's got to be where Youssaf is planning to take the girl. We're on the line with the airport authorities right now. Our Hostage Rescue Team and the French commandos have been dispatched as well. They will secure the perimeter. How far are you from the airport?" With the deafening background noise of the passing race cars exploding like thunderbolts, Ben's voice was barely audible.

"We're heading for my car on foot," Martin said, "but with the crowds it's impossible. If you could get a chopper to the main parking area, that'd be our best bet."

"I'm on it!" Ben replied. "Get to the lot as quickly as you can."

"We're on the way," Martin assured him.

Martin led his men zigzagging through the crowds toward the parking area, paying no attention to the sporadic radio reports or the crescendo of excitement building among the crowds around them. Just outside the parking area, he spotted a detail of French Special Forces and elbowed his way to the little guy who was clearly the squad leader. *A little Napoleon...* thought Martin, but at least this Napoleon had transportation.

"I'm Special Agent Doug Martin, FBI." Doug displayed his credentials to the little guy, whose name tag identified him as Pullet. "This is Agent Russell and Agent Ives," Martin said, pointing at the nearby van marked with the Special Forces insignia. "We've got to get to the Le Mans airport."

"We are aware of the situation," Pullet acknowledged. "Tres bien. Let's go! Vite!" Pullet wasted no time in leading them toward the van.

"There is a plot to assassinate President Harrington and detonate explosives," Martin told Pullet, as they climbed inside the van.

"I know this," Pullet said. "We have been briefed and advised accordingly. All high-level dignitaries have been evacuated or taken to a safe location. But I am told that your President Harrington has overruled the recommendation of his Secret Service protective detail to evacuate. He insists on attending the victory ceremony on the Rolex Bridge."

Martin shook his head. "President Harrington is not known for giving in to terrorist threats," Martin explained. "On top of that," he said, pointing toward the crowds converging on the finish line, "his son is about to win Le Mans. This is personal for him. In any case, we've got to get to the airport and get our hands on the terrorist who's the key to it all."

"I understand," Pullet shrugged his shoulders. "As you American's say...let's do this!"

Pullet turned to his cohort behind the wheel. "To Le Mans airport," he said. "Try your best not to run over anyone, but don't worry too much about it either."

The driver nodded and dropped the van into gear. He leaned on his horn and the vehicle lurched alarmingly through a snaking line of spectators and toward the exit of the race grounds. As they passed through the gates, the driver took them onto the sidewalk, scattering a knot of spectators who cursed and shook their fists as the van sped by. As they press on down the sidewalk past a line of slow-moving vehicles on the adjoining highway, the driver slapped a magnetic bubble light on the roof and flipped on a deafening siren.

Martin glanced at his watch. "I figure it's all planned for the end of the race. We don't have much time."

"Oui! I know this," Pullet sighed.

The speeding van veered through a swale and bounced violently onto a narrow unpaved service road that paralleled a stretch of the race track. Everyone in the van held grimly to their seats as the van swerved, threatening to topple for a moment before righting itself.

"Your driver ought to be out there on the track," Martin said.

"He is the best!" Pullet replied.

"Youssaf is armed and dangerous and must be approached with extreme caution," Martin explained. "We believe he is carrying a number of remote control detonators. The FBI has already confiscated and disabled a suicide bomber's suit found in Karim Racing's trailer."

"We are aware of that," Pullet confirmed as he keenly surveyed the crowds surrounding the van.

"Our recent intelligence tells us there are additional bombs somewhere along the race circuit, but we don't know where the hell they are."

Pullet shook his head. "How credible is your intelligence?"

"Rock solid," Martin responded.

"I don't see it," Pullet took off his cap and scratched his head. "Every inch of the track has been searched! There are no explosives."

"I wish you were right," Martin said. "Let's just get to the airport and find Youssaf."

With the mad Frenchman behind the wheel of the van, weaving through traffic, cutting into the on-coming lanes at will, it was less than ten minutes until they approached the regional airfield. As the van rushed toward the perimeter that the FBI's Rescue Team and French commandos had set up, Martin heard Ben's voice resonating in his earpiece.

"Doug, listen to me. We just received a translation of Youssaf's last call to one of his men, an individual he called 'Adis.' Explosives are located in Khalil Karim's car. His seat insert is full of PETN, several pounds of it. Apparently, he is being set up by Youssaf."

"The explosives are in Karim's car?"

"Affirmative, Doug. It's been confirmed."

"Karim is sitting on the stuff?" Martin said, still trying to wrap his mind around the concept. Surely, Khalil Karim had no idea what was in store for him.

"Yeah, pretty ingenious, isn't it?" Ben's voice trailed off.

"Unbelievable," Martin said. Visions of the Khalil Karim's car exploding in a gigantic fireball before a packed throng of spectators filled his mind.

"Doug, listen up!" Ben promptly interrupted, "We've got a photo obtained during FBI surveillance of Khalil Karim in Washington D.C. U.S. Customs identifies 'Adis' as Adis Gabir. His photograph is being sent for distribution to our agents and to the French police as we speak. He should be considered armed and dangerous."

"I got it." Martin confirmed as he turned to Pullet. "Our latest intelligence confirms a man named Adis Gabir as Youssaf's accomplice. He's here at Le Mans. Tygre saw him earlier in Karim Racing's pit, disguised as a mechanic. His photo has been transmitted."

"Bien sur!" Pullet responded. He pulled out his own cell phone to check.

Martin turned back to the conversation with his supervisor. "Let's focus on the explosives in Karim's car, Ben," Martin continued. "To minimize the carnage we have to terminate Karim while his car is on a remote section of the track. We'll need a sharpshooter, Ben. The best we've got."

"Doug, he is in a car going 150 mph!" Ben shouted.

"Not everywhere," Martin replied. "Besides, we've got to take him out. It's the simplest way."

"Where do you suggest, Doug? I've got a map of the course pulled up in front of me."

"According to Pullet, the slowest corner is Virage d'Arnage at 45 mph, and the second slowest is Virage De Mulsanne at 55 mph. They're both wooded areas so any collateral damage should be minimal, no matter what."

"It seems we don't have a choice." Ben agreed. "I'll get it set up immediately."

Martin paused, pondering the wisdom of the plan he had just set in motion. Khalil Karim would die and so might other drivers if his car should careen into someone's path. But those losses were nothing compared to the alternative. As he thought, he noticed Sean Ives staring at him with a surly expression on his face. Once this was over, he would do his best to see this loser drummed off the rolls, Martin decided.

Ives glanced away and opened his cell phone as if checking for messages.

"Expecting a call?" Martin asked.

"I'm on duty," Ives replied. "Do you mind?"

"Save it!" Martin cut him off and tapped back into the connection with headquarters. "Ben, patch me through to Brad Harrington in New Deal car No.1 radio ASAP. Tell his team to switch Brad to the backup low band frequency, B-5, and then shut down all other access to B-5."

"Harrington's moments away from finishing the race, Doug. I'm informed that he's in the lead."

"It doesn't matter, Ben! Karim is seconds behind him. There is no way of knowing when Youssaf will detonate the explosives. He'll most likely try to take out Brad if he can."

As he waited for the connection, doubt once again crept into the mind of Doug Martin. *How did I allow this to happen? Get it together and do what you've been trained to do your whole life! Failure is not an option!*

Ben's voice interrupted Martin's internal pep talk. "Doug, I have Brad Harrington for you. You can go to channel B-5 and brief him."

Martin leaned back and cleared his voice. Nothing could have adequately prepared him for delivering such news. *Don't sugarcoat it!* he told himself. "Mr. Harrington, this is Agent Doug Martin of the FBI."

"Agent Martin," Brad said briskly, his voice carrying about the whine of his car engine. "Any chance this can wait until the end of the race?"

"Unfortunately not. You're in danger. Khalil Karim and Malik Youssaf are involved in a plot to assassinate your father."

"Go on." Harrington's voice was clear and deliberate. Maybe that is what racing experience gave him, Martin thought.

"There are explosives in Karim's car and, we believe, in other undisclosed locations around the race track."

"Are you sure about this?"

"We're sure." Martin paused before conveying the most dreaded part of the briefing, "Mr. Harrington, I also need to inform you that Tygre Topolska has been cooperating with us, working undercover. Malik Youssaf discovered she was wired and has kidnapped her."

"Tygre? Did you say she's been kidnapped?"

"I'm afraid so," Martin said.

"Working under cover for the FBI?"

"Yes, that's correct."

"Jesus Christ!"

Martin could only imagine what it would be like to try and absorb such news while at the wheel of a speeding race car.

"Where is she?" Harrington's voice came, flat and demanding.

"We don't know where she is. We're working on it."

"You're working on it?" Martin could hear the whine of the engine climb as the car downshifted into a turn, the scream of tires following soon after. "What the hell was she doing working for the FBI?"

"Tygre knows Khalil Karim. She was in a unique position to gain information about the terrorist plot and assist us with our mission here at Le Mans."

"Tygre knows Karim?" Martin heard the disbelief in Harrington's voice. Brad's thoughts immediately flashed to his conversation with Tygre at the Harrington Ranch. *So that must be what she was trying to tell me.*

"Listen to me, you son of a bitch. Did Tygre break up with me because of all this?"

"That's part of it," Martin admitted. "Listen, Mr. Harrington, I'm afraid there's more bad news."

"How much worse can it get?" Brad's voice was strained.

"We believe that Youssaf is carrying at least three remote control devices and has the capability of detonating them at any time. We strongly suspect he is planning this to coincide with the end of the race. We've dispatched a team of snipers to take out Khalil Karim on one of the secluded turns and stop his car."

"You must be fucking dreaming!" Brad shouted. "There are less than 10 laps left in the race. Are these snipers in position?"

"They're on their way," Martin said.

"And so is Christmas," Brad snapped. "Listen, Agent Martin, I'll take care of Karim myself!"

"Mr. Harrington," Martin said firmly, "Don't try anything foolish. Leave it to the FBI!"

"Leave it to the FBI? I don't think so! From what you're just told me the FBI has fucked everything up to begin with!"

"Mr. Harrington, I implore you, let us handle this!" The radio went silent. "Mr. Harrington?" But there was nothing in return.

This is fucking great, a frustrated Martin thought staring gloomily out the window as the van skidded to a stop beside an unmarked car stationed at the airport perimeter. *I've got a kidnapped civilian with terrorist, bombs about to be detonated, and now the son of the President thinks I'm an incompetent jackass!*

Martin, the agents and the French Special Forces officers scrambled out of the van. Using the vehicle for cover, Martin pulled out a pair of binoculars to survey the cluster of aircraft and helicopters lined up on each side of the airfield.

In seconds he had spotted them: Youssaf and Tygre hurrying toward an American-made four-passenger Bell helicopter, its powerful turbine engine running, the blades furiously cutting through the air.

"Ben, Tygre and Youssaf are in sight!"

Martin turned to Pullet. "That man attempting to board the helicopter holding on to the blond woman…that's Youssaf and Tygre! That helicopter cannot go airborne."

—

At that same moment, Brad Harrington came out of a hairpin turn, clutching the wheel of his car, still trying to come to terms with what he had heard from Agent Martin. *Tygre has been risking her life for me and my father and I doubted her? I should have known something was wrong!*

Brad, determined to save the lives of those he loved, decelerated. *Where is that son of a bitch Karim?* Brad's eyes became slivers as he focused on his rearview mirrors. *Seven laps to go, he'll be pushing for all he is worth.*

—

Tygre, locked in Malik's grip, glanced over her shoulder to find Agent Martin and his men slowly advancing from the far side of the airfield. *Thank you, God!* she prayed silently. She tried to pull back but Malik dragged her on with iron force. They were now only a few yards away from the chopper.

"Don't do it, Malik. Give it up. Look, it's the FBI and the French police? You'll never get away."

"Watch me, bitch," he said. His face looked haggard and exhausted, but his resolve seemed unwavering. "I have you and the detonators, remember? I can blow up the chopper and all the other shit, at any time! The FBI will try to save you. They won't let you die. Americans value life too much, even, such an insignificant life as yours."

As Martin and the others cautiously advanced, darting from the cover of one aircraft to another, Malik grabbed Tygre's waist and slid up close behind her. He held his Glock against her temple for the benefit of Martin and the others. He jerked his arm from her waist and locked his elbow around Tygre's neck, holding one of the remotes in his hand for all to see.

Martin watched in frustration as Tygre was pulled backward toward the chopper. Her frightened eyes pleaded to him. Martin franticly tried to calculate his options. *Think!* Martin implored himself. *Think!*

Brad Harrington's hands were damp inside his gloves. He had slowed down enough for Khalil Karim to pass. Car No.7 was now a few yards ahead of him. He knew that Karim was beside himself with happiness. *Perfect,* thought Brad.

"What's wrong, Brad? What the hell is going on?" The voice of his race team manager blasted over the car radio.

"Don't worry," Brad said calmly. *"Everything's under control."* He was negotiating the tight corner of Virage Porsche leading up to Le Mans' notoriously treacherous Porsche Curves.

"Have you lost your fucking mind? Why did you give up the lead? What's going on?" The manager's voice was frantic but had no effect on Brad. He kept his focus on Karim's rear left tire with steadfast concentration. Seconds after the turn, Karim's car, aware of its lead, took advantage of the straight near the new Maison Blanche and hurtled forward with a roar.

Brad renegotiated the Virage D'Arnage and increased his own speed as they advanced onto the Curbe Du Buisson. *Here we go!*

"Take the lead! Do it! You're on his ass! You've got him!" The frenzied manager radioed as the New Deal team watched spellbound on the closed-circuit TV feed.

"You bet I do!" Brad responded. As the two cars approached the first turn of the Porsche Curves, he made a deft maneuver, which took a second, maybe two, expertly clipping the left rear end of Karim's car. As the cars touched, Brad instinctively hit the brakes, trying to veer away from the traffic now roaring upon him from behind. To his crew and to the many thousands of Le Mans spectators, it was a bonehead accident at a critical time of the race. But to Brad it was a victory of monumental proportions.

Brad's car was sliding out of control. As it turned broadside to the skid, its force sent them airborne, then rolling, over and over, until it eventually came to a smoldering stop, miraculously intact, while other cars screamed past him on either side, like a divided swarm of angry hornets.

The air reeked of burnt steel, fuel and smoke. The last thing Brad saw was the image of Karim's skidding car turning sideways, bouncing off the metal barrier, hurtling into a death spiral. With a metal fury, it careened to the other side of the race track, landing on its top and shattering into pieces.

Colored metal parts and glass gleamed momentarily with the spray from the ruptured fuel tanks until sparks ignited the mass into a glittering inferno. Seconds later, even that spectacle was topped by a series of thunderous explosions. To spectators in the distance, it seemed as if a bomb had gone off. Brad was the only one who knew that indeed, one had.

It's done. Thank God, It's over. Brad thought and then his eyes were closed.

Tygre felt the tarmac move as the explosion sent earthquake-like shock waves through the ground beneath her feet. Martin and the others instinctively dropped to the ground.

Youssaf seemed unfazed, however, using the diversion to his advantage. He quickly stepped aboard the chopper and forcefully jerked Tygre inside.

"What the hell was that?" the pilot asked. He was a slender man in his early thirties sporting a crew cut, and seemed unperturbed at the sight of Malik holding a pistol to Tygre's head.

The pilot is an American! Tygre thought as she heard the pilot's accent. *How did Malik get an American involved in this?*

"Get going!" Malik screamed in response. "Get this thing in the air! Now!"

He shoved Tygre aside and swiftly pulled out a cell phone to hit a number. "Adis!" he spoke into the phone. "If I don't make it to the party, you'll have to deliver the cake!" He snapped the phone shut and placed it back in his pocket.

Even over the noise of the helicopter blades, Tygre could hear the words of the radio commentator over the loudspeakers near the airport runway.

"Ladies and Gentleman, we have a report of an accident involving the New Deal's No.1 car and Karim Racing's No.7 car. An explosion has ensued. We will update you as soon as we learn more..."

—

"Doug, I'm going to check on Brad's condition," Sean Ives called to Martin as they crouched behind the cover of a Beechcraft, waiting for Youssaf's next move.

"You stay here," Martin said, without taking his eyes off the 'copter. "That's an order! Other field agents have already been dispatched by the command center."

"Brad Harrington is my responsibility!" Ives called back. "Who the fuck are you to tell me how to do my job?"

"If he tries to go anywhere, handcuff and detain him!" Martin signaled to two FBI agents who flanked them. "He's under my command, now. Medics and the recovery teams are on their way. They will handle the matter."

"He's *my* responsibility," Ives insisted.

"You are wasting time, Ives!" Martin shouted back. "We need to get Tygre out of that chopper…now! So shut the fuck up and do as I tell you!"

As the helicopter rose, Malik looked down at the huge plume of smoke that rose from one corner of the track below. He indicated the scene to Tygre with a triumphant smirk. "I pray they are both dead! I'll kill the rest of the infidels soon enough. Praise Allah!"

"You sick bastard!" Tygre cried out.

Youssaf flicked the barrel of the gun against her temple, silencing her abruptly. It felt as if a dull knife had penetrated her skull.

In the next instant, Malik's eyes came to life with frustration and anger as he glanced out the windows of the helicopter to find that–500 feet above ground–they were now flanked by an EC-130 attack helicopter and three French Air Force EC 725 helicopters.

"This is an order! Land your aircraft! You're completely surrounded! I repeat! Land your aircraft immediately." A stern voice bellowed on the external loudspeaker of one of the French Air Force helicopters.

"What the fuck have you gotten me into?" The pilot shook as he screamed at Malik. Streams of sweat ran down his face. "I did *not* sign up for this!"

With a swift movement of his gun in the pilot's direction, Malik dismissed his concerns. "Get back to the job I'm paying you for, or you'll die with the rest of them." Malik ordered. "Ignore them!"

The pilot gave him a look of frustration, then snatched up his microphone. "Attention, FAF. I hear your orders but I cannot comply. I'm being held at gunpoint here. Do you understand? At gunpoint!"

"That's enough," Youssaf called, waving the pistol at the pilot's head. Malik pointed below at the scant remains of Khalil's burning prototype and Brad Harrington's car, which had landed on its roof. Both were obscured by wafting clouds of smoke. "Harrington and

Khalil are dead," he said. "We've got to get to the Rolex Bridge. Move! Move!"

"You must immediately land your aircraft. If you fail to comply with this order you will be fired upon! I repeat! Land your aircraft now or you will be fired upon!"

"This was not part of the deal," the pilot pleaded. "I agreed to fly you out of here, period! What the fuck, Malik!"

"If you want to live, go where I tell you!" Malik pointed his Glock at the pilot's head. "I'd rather put a fucking bullet between your eyes than see you land."

Keeping the Rolex Bridge clearly in his sight line, the pilot turned back to the controls and continued their climb.

On the tarmac below, Doug Martin brought his binoculars to his eyes, focusing on Karim's helicopter as it continued past the plume of dark smoke billowing from the scene of the accident. He raised his wrist communicator and reopened the connection with Ben.

"I'm told we can take Khalil Karim officially off our subject list!"

"Good! What about Brad Harrington?"

"I haven't heard yet," Martin replied. "Keep your fingers crossed. The French Air Force has Youssaf's 'copter surrounded up there. We're hoping to force him down, but if it comes to it…"

"I understand," Ben said. "There are way too many lives at stake. If they have to, they'll blow Youssaf's 'copter out of the sky."

"Understood, sir."

"What about Adis, the one who's suspected of planting the explosives?"

"Still at large, sir."

"Get back to me the instant anything changes."

"Roger that."

Inside Karim's helicopter, battered now by the updrafts from the blaze below, Malik's eyes darted from the pilot to the helicopters flanking their craft on either side. It seemed to Tygre that he was ready to jump out of his skin.

"This is insane, Malik. Give it up, please."

He turned, fixing her with a look that suggested he'd forgotten she was there. "You know," he said mildly. "I really am sick and tired of your voice. No one is going to know whether you're dead or not." He let go of the back of the pilot's seat and advanced upon her with his pistol raised.

Tygre felt the bitter taste of copper filling her mouth. He was going to kill her now, she was sure of it.

"Say goodnight, you mindless slut…" Malik broke off as one of the French helicopters burst out of the smoke and their own pilot swerved desperately to avoid a collision.

The bottom seemed to drop out of their craft and Tygre clutched the seat support to avoid being flung toward the ceiling. She watched in astonishment as Malik shot straight upward as if he'd been propelled out of a cannon. His head met the ceiling of the helicopter with a thud, and the pistol flew from his hand.

I'm alive! Tygre thought as she watched Malik crumple back to the floor of the craft. He was stunned, groping for the Glock which slid around the bucking cabin like a boated fish.

"Land your aircraft now! You are surrounded! If you fail to comply with this order you will be fired upon! Land your aircraft immediately!"

The chopper veered again and the Glock ricocheted off a seat support, landing inches from Tygre's foot. She knew nothing of guns, but she also knew there was no other option. Malik lunged quickly toward the pistol, but Tygre, in survival mode, was quicker. She clutched the pistol in her shaking hands and raised it toward Malik, who stopped as if confronting a cobra.

Tygre felt her chest heaving and fought to keep from hyperventilating. If she fainted, she'd be dead. Malik's eyes held hers steadily now. His hand slid to his boot and in the next moment there was a gleaming blade between them. He moved it slowly back and forth as if expecting the bright steel to hypnotize her.

"Pointing a gun is one thing," he said, grinning. "It is quite another to shoot."

"Stay away," she told him, hating the weakness she heard in her own voice.

Malik laughed, then abruptly lunged at her with the blade. She pushed her foot hard against the seat support and slid back, the tip of the knife slicing cleanly through her jacket. There was no pain, but she felt a trickle of blood descend between her breasts. Another centimeter and he would have slit her throat, she realized.

"You useless bitch," he said. "I'm going to butcher you like a pig." He grabbed the seat support and threw himself toward her then, and, finally her finger responded to the clamor in her mind.

The explosion was deafening in the small cabin and the recoil of the pistol nearly snapped her wrist. When she opened her eyes, she found that, incredibly, Malik's leering face was still inches away, unmarked. He blinked, as if he too, could not believe she'd missed. With a blood-curdling scream, he raised his knife and flung himself toward her again.

The black pit of his gaping mouth seemed to Tygre like the entrance to Hell itself. If that was where she was going, she thought, she would enter with a bang.

Tygre pulled the trigger....again and again....and again. The weapon obeyed, emptying itself into the face of Malik Youssaf, shell casings cascading onto the cabin floor. The first three rounds blew away Malik's jaw, painting the cabin wall with bits of flesh, teeth and a shower of blood.

With each round she fired, Tygre felt a greater sense of relief. The noise was deafening but her mind was calm. *No more threats! No more insults, No more fear!* Her conscience was clear.

Malik's body slumped inches away from her. His face was obliterated: she saw one empty eye socket and what was once a nose turned into an irregular bloody hole. Bright blood dripped from the cabin ceiling and painted the walls and the seats.

"You've blown out one of the hydraulics," the pilot cried, and for the first time, she noticed the irregular lurching of the helicopter. "Buckle yourself into a seat. Now!"

Tygre, stared at him dumbly, then back at the body in front of her. She glanced down at herself, realizing she was covered with

Malik's blood. Suddenly she found herself vomiting violently. She paused to catch her breath, and a few seconds later, she vomited again.

"Oh my God!" She muttered. "Oh my God!"

"Get into a seat." The pilot screamed. "Right now!"

Tygre struggled up into the nearest seat and managed to buckle herself in. She waved a hand in front of her face, trying to get air so she wouldn't pass out. She did everything she could to keep from looking at Malik's body on the floor near her feet.

"You've got to land this thing!" she shouted to the pilot.

"Fuck that," the pilot said. "They won't shoot me down with you aboard. I'm getting out of here!"

"And where do you think you're going? Look around! We're surrounded!"

"I'll worry about that later," he said. "Shut up and stay seated."

He pulled on the wheel then, veering sharply to the south. Malik's body slid sideways and his lifeless hand flopped open, releasing one of the detonators, the black garage door opener that he had been carrying. Tygre stared at it for a moment, then reached carefully to retrieve it. *Dear God,* she thought, *what if it was the device that fired the explosives in the helicopter?*

She unbuckled herself from her seat and fell to her knees at Malik's body. The floor of the cabin was covered with a mixture of his blood and her vomit. But what was that compared to the horror that the devices could visit upon everyone below. She groped about his pockets until she found the second of the devices. But where was the third....

"What the hell are you doing?" The pilot yelled. "Get back in your seat! I'm having a hard time controlling this son of a bitch!"

Tygre ignored him. *What am I looking for? Oh, yes. The cell phone! Here!* Her fingers closed around the grey case of the cell phone, sliding it from Malik's blood-soaked shirt pocket.

"Lady, get back in your fucking seat!" The pilot ordered. Hardly had he spoken than a burst of machine gun fire erupted from the helicopter on their right. Tygre saw a rush of bright bullet tracings cut the air just inches in front of their helicopter's

Plexiglass windshield. The roar of the machine cannon was deafening.

"For God's sakes, they're going to shoot us down! Land this thing right now!"

"Did you hear me?" Tygre screamed. "Land it now or I'll blow your head off and I'll do the best I can!" She pointed the gun at the pilot, hoping he would not realize the chamber was empty.

"Go ahead and shoot," he said. "I'm fucked, anyway."

Tygre glanced at the pilot's hands, which were now shaking at the controls. "You're an American for God's sake! You're wearing a wedding band! Your wife must mean something to you?" The pilot was quiet, but she could see she was right.

"What's your name?" Tygre asked calmly.

"What?" The pilot repeated stunned.

"What is your name?"

"What difference does it make?"

"What is you name! Tell me! I want to know!"

"Eddie," he said, after a moment.

"Listen to me, Eddie." Tygre was inches away from his face as she spoke. "I'll tell the FBI you weren't part of this plot with Malik. I'll tell them that he had his gun on you all the time." For a brief second their eyes met.

"They won't believe I wasn't in on it!"

"It's the best chance you have, Eddie. Unless you bring us down they'll be certain you were involved, whatever happens. Come on. Bring it down! I'll vouch for you." She glanced over at the adjoining helicopter, where a sharpshooter had a rifle poised. "Eddie, I don't want to die, do you?"

He glanced at her. "Nobody's going to believe you, but I'll do it. You can put the gun away."

From the ground, Doug Martin and the rest of the FBI team and the French commandos watched as the helicopter reversed course and slowly began its descent. As the helicopter settled toward its landing space, Ben's distressed voice erupted in Martin's earpiece.

"Doug, switch over to channel B-8. I need to speak with you privately."

"Done!" Martin said, tapping his wrist communicator.

"Doug, we've just analyzed several wire transfers from Khalil Karim's Islamic Foundation. Now we know why Sean Ives didn't attempt to stop the wire transfers in the trailer. He received a pay-off from Youssaf. He's part of it, Doug. You've got to neutralize him before he escapes."

"Roger that," Martin told Ben calmly, his gaze shifting to Ives. *Traitor bastard,* he thought as he contemplated his next move.

"Watch your back, Doug," Ben warned. "I just briefed Russell and Harrington about Ives as well. Where is he now?"

"Right beside me," Martin said.

"Take him into custody after you tie all the loose ends," Ben ordered.

"Confirmed," Martin responded, keeping his eyes on Ives.

At the first sight of ambulances gathered near the Porsche Curves, Special Agent Lawrence Russell accelerated on the service road toward the scene. His heart pounded until he finally had a visual of Brad Harrington. The President's son had been removed from the car and was being examined by a team of medics. Russell brought his car to a halt at a roadblock just beyond a fence separating the race course from the road. He waved his FBI credentials at the attending French Special Forces officers and made his way quickly to where the medical team was gathered.

He found Brad Harrington physically jarred and still a bit dazed, but apparently uninjured. "I'm Special Agent Lawrence Russell, Mr. Harrington. I'm here to tell you Tygre Topolska is all right. I assume you'd like to see her."

Harrington pushed himself away from a medic who was dabbing at a scrape on his cheek. "You got that right, Agent Russell. Let's go."

As they approached the airport, Russell pointed toward Karim's chopper on the tarmac. Brad frantically scanned the scene, his heart aching to see Tygre safe. Several heavily armed agents and French Special Forces officers cautiously advanced toward the grounded helicopter. He caught sight of Youssaf's arm lifelessly dangling from the partially opened door. *But where is Tygre?*

The pilot emerged first, hands up in the air, followed by Tygre.

"Tygre!" Brad shouted. He began to move toward her but out of nowhere he saw Sean Ives sprinting toward the helicopter.

"Sean," Brad cried. "What the hell are you doing?"

"Brad, you need to let us handle this," Agent Russell insisted.

In one abrupt move, Ives had his arm around Tygre's neck and his pistol pointed at the pilot. "All of you back off or I'll kill the girl," he said. He swiveled his pistol toward the pilot.

"You, get the fuck back in the chopper. Now!"

"Tygre!" Brad called out.

Tygre stared back at him in desperation. *I thought I'd never see him again,* she thought. *But here he is, and now we're going to lose each other!*

Ives' face was grim. He dragged Tygre toward the other door of the chopper as Brad, Agent Martin and the others watched helplessly. "Stay the fuck away or I'll kill them both. I've got nothing to lose."

Ives swung his gaze at Doug Martin, who stood nearby, his hands flexing helplessly. "Don't test me Agent Martin! I swear I'll do it! Get the fuck back. You too, Russell! All of you get back!" Ives yelled.

"Ives, I won't let you do this!" Brad called out again, inching closer to the helicopter.

"Brad! Don't move! Do you hear me? Stay back!" Martin's commanding voice did little to calm him.

"There's nothing you can do about it," Ives said, his gaze still on Martin and Lawrence.

"Like hell," Brad said, and made his charge.

Ives swung his pistol toward Brad and in an instant, a shot rang out. Brad stopped in his tracks, his eyes wide.

Tygre screamed, then stumbled forward, crumpling to the ground.

"Tygre!" Brad shouted. "Oh God, no! Tygre!"

Ives was lurching backward like a man who had just learned how to walk. His mouth was open, his eyes blank. Blood was pumping from a black hole in the middle of his forehead. Agent

Martin stood with his smoking pistol in his hand until Ives toppled beneath the open chopper door.

"I wasn't involved with any of this!" The pilot desperately pleaded, "Ask her…ask her! Go ahead…ask her!"

He pointed at Tygre who'd been thrown to her knees when Ives recoiled from the shot that killed him.

"Get him to a secure location for questioning!" Pullet ordered his men.

Tygre struggled up as Brad rushed forward. "Are you okay? Are you okay?"

"Oh Brad," she said, throwing herself into his arms.

"I was so scared. I couldn't imagine life without you!" Brad said.

"You don't have to!" she said.

Abruptly, Tygre turned to Agent Martin. "There are explosives in the Rolex Clock," she began. "Malik has another man around somewhere. Adis someone…"

Martin held up a hand to stop her. "We caught him approaching the clock, disguised as a repairman. He's in custody and the explosives have been disabled."

Tygre felt a wave of relief wash over her. "Thank God," she handed Martin the three detonators which she retrieved from Malik.

"Thank YOU," Agent Martin replied.

At that moment, the voice on the runway loudspeakers erupted:

"Ladies and Gentlemen, Mesdames and Messieurs, this race is over! Brad Harrington's New Deal car No. 2, driven by American driver Chris Summers has won the 24 Hours of Le Mans!"

Escorted by the Secret Service, FBI Agents, the French Police and French Special Forces, Brad and Tygre were transported to the New Deal Team's trailer. Tygre quickly showered and changed. Even as she disposed of her blood-stained suit, the image of Malik's utterly grotesque bullet ridden face lingered until she heard a soft knock on the door.

Brad poked his head inside the dressing room. "Are you ready, darling?" he asked.

"I've never been more ready," she told him. "But there's something I need to tell you, Brad."

He heard the note in her voice and looked at her with concern. "It's about Khalil. I..."

"Agent Martin told me everything," he interrupted. "You've got nothing to be ashamed of. No one could have known how evil Khalil and Malik turned out to be. You have no reason to feel embarrassed about having known them, especially Khalil."

"But..."

"It's over," he assured her. "You and I are going to start with a clean canvas and paint our own picture."

Tygre came to embrace him. "We'll never forget what happened here. But, we will move forward."

Brad hugged her, then motioned toward the door. "Let's go and get our trophy!"

Moments later they were on the podium to join Chris Summers as he accepted the prized award. Thunderous applause echoed as Moet & Chandon champagne rained down on Chris, Brad and the other team members.

Chris turned to hand Brad, the team owner, the first-place trophy. Soaked in champagne, Brad turned toward Tygre and handed it off to her. "You deserve this one more than anybody," then he smiled. "Besides, I have three just like it."

Tygre took the trophy as Brad leaned in for a kiss. A hundred cameras clicked in unison as the Le Mans media and the paparazzi rushed in to get 'the money shot.'

"Promise me you'll never leave me again," Brad said as he embraced her tenderly.

"I promise!" Tygre said, waiting for another kiss.

"Speaking of promises," Brad said. "I'm ready to settle down. How about you?"

Tygre nodded, and without hesitation, Brad dropped to one knee. "Will you marry me, Tygre Topalska?"

"Yes! Yes, my darling!" As Tygre kissed him, the crowd erupted.

"Ladies and gentlemen I've just heard we have one more reason to celebrate! The announcer proclaimed. "*Mr. Le Mans, Brad*

Harrington, has proposed marriage to his girlfriend Tygre and she has accepted..."

The rest was lost in pandemonium, and Brad and Tygre seized the chance to duck away to the private boxes of the Automobile Club de L'Ouest where Brad's parents were waiting.

"We're very proud of you, Tygre," the President said while the First Lady looked on with admiration. "What an extraordinary act of courage."

"You're welcome, Mister President," Tygre said while holding on to Brad's hand.

"And, I guess congratulations are in order? We're so happy for you both," the President said, as Brad's mother rushed to kiss them.

At that point, the Secret Service detail chief motioned to the President. "They are ready to take you to the airport, sir."

"These next few days are going to be a circus," the President said.

"We'll see you soon," the First Lady waved as she followed her husband to the presidential limousine.

A bit later, as Brad and Tygre sat in the New Deal trailer, Brad noticed the pensive expression on Tygre's face.

"What's the matter, sweetheart?" Brad asked.

Tygre looked up at him with a wistful smile. "I'm...I just wish my father was here to see all this..."

"Me too, darling, I would have loved the opportunity to meet him. But we're going to do the next best thing."

The early morning flight to Poland, on a military jet arranged by the President, took less than two hours. The Bristol Hotel's manager was delighted to welcome Tygre back when she and Brad checked in along with a detail of Secret Service Agents.

"If it weren't for Brad by my side, I wouldn't have survived Daddy's funeral," Tygre confided to her mother two days later. They spent many hours in the Warsaw apartment catching up with each other while Brad was out sightseeing.

"Embracing your father's death by celebrating his life will help you overcome your loss, Theresa," her mother assured her. Tygre nodded in agreement. Helena's appearance finally matched her real age. Jash Zavojski, her lover, was long gone. Finding her mother looking older and somewhat vulnerable made her feel responsible for her well-being.

"Mother, I know we've had our differences…" Tygre began tentatively, "But you're all alone now. I want to make sure you're well taken care of." Tygre paused and extended her hand, "I brought you a present. I've meant to give it to you for quite some time."

"Oh! Tygre!" Helena cried at the sight of the pink emerald-cut solitaire in Tygre's palm. "Is it real?"

Tygre burst out laughing, "Oh, Mother! I would never dare to give *you* a fake! You taught me too well!

"Thank you dear Tygre!" Helena stole a peek in the living room mirror and frowned at the sight of her face. "Now," she said, turning her full attention back to Tygre, "tell me about Brad."

"He is everything I ever wanted Mother. I love him desperately and it would mean everything to me if you would come to our wedding."

"My dear, you have my blessing. Of course, I'll be there!" Helena hugged her daughter.

After a moment, her mother paused and stepped back. "Your father was a good man, Tygre. I'm sorry to admit that I allowed our adversities to come between us. Don't ever let this happen to you and Brad."

"We won't," Tygre put her arm around her mother. She would never forget all the disappointments of the past, but a better tomorrow beckoned.

Within weeks, Le Mans became ancient history. Tygre and Brad returned to the United States and, in a very private ceremony, they exchanged vows at the beach cottage on the Harrington Ranch. Except for Brad's parents and Tygre's mother, no one else was present.

"When you married Brad, you got us all!" The First Lady kissed Tygre tenderly as Helena and the President, looked on.

"We're a family now. Welcome home, Tygre!" her new father-in-law said. "You too, Mrs. Topolska." The President motioned for Helena to join them.

Family! Tygre thought. *Home!*

EPILOGUE

The morning sun crept through the open window of Brad and Tygre's bedroom at the Harrington Ranch. They heard small footsteps tentatively approaching the door. Eleanor, their blue-eyed four-year-old daughter, walked in.

"Mommy, Daddy, tell me the story. Tell me again how you met."

Eleanor climbed up on to their bed and snuggled between Brad and Tygre.

"Get comfortable, little Elly, there's lots to tell." Brad said as he pulled the comforter up under her chin. "But I'll let Mommy go first..."

ABOUT THE AUTHOR

Ava Roosevelt is a former columnist and feature writer for the Palm Beach Journal and also Cavallino Magazine, which specializes in financial and motor racing matters. She studied French literature at La Sorbonne, Paris, France and creative writing at Columbia University, New York. Ava is the widow of William Donner Roosevelt, FDR's grandson. She worked for an international intelligence company, The Fairfax Group, based in the Washington, D.C. area, headed by the internationally-recognized counter-terrorism expert, Michael J. Hershman. Ava currently divides her time between Palm Beach, Florida and Wilson Point, Connecticut. This is her first novel. Visit the author's website at www.theracingheart.com.

The Racing Heart, a romantic thriller, is a tale about a passion-filled, life-long quest to achieve emotional security which transforms its heroine, Tygre, from a timid, vulnerable and provincial teen into a glamorous supermodel, and ultimately involves her in a life or death drama of international intrigue.

In the whirlwind, Tygre is forced to adjust her skewed sense of values, displays intelligence and abundance of courage, and – against all odds – finds love. She emerges victorious, an honorable and passionate 24-year-old beauty.

Several of the characters are inspired by prominent U.S., European and Middle Eastern personalities and celebrities whom the author met on the international circuit.

For more details please visit

www.theracingheart.com

Made in the USA
Charleston, SC
13 April 2012